FLIGHT 19, PART II

GRANT FINNEGAN

ISBN: 978-0-6486522-0-5 (pbk.)

ALSO BY GRANT FINNEGAN

The Seventh List

Flight 19, Part 1

For Sharon,
my Yin

FLIGHT 19, PART II

Time.
Clocks move forward;
they never go backward.
Neither should we.

PROLOGUE

Again and again, my mind drifts back to the day our plane did the impossible for the second time.

I don't care anymore what hour of the day it was, what day of the month, or what month of what year.

Especially the year.

I don't even care how it happened.

Time travel, excuse the French, is bloody overrated.

You can take the DeLorean, Doc Brown, and shove it right up your ass. No offense to the Doc; I liked that movie.

Think I could pick the winning numbers in a lottery that had already been drawn in the future? It's a bit hard when you didn't write them down in the first place. Same goes for anything else you can make some financial windfall from. We were so busy trying to get our heads around losing five years of our lives that we didn't bother jotting down who won the Super Bowl, or anything else for that matter.

We traveled five years forward in time, then two and a half years back. Do the math—we still lost two and a half years of our lives. Worse, the only hindsights I could offer myself were the ones shrouded in misery and heartache.

But it all pales in comparison with finding the love of my

life, who I'd been waiting for since my eighteenth birthday, only to have him taken from me as if the universe or God himself had just been messing with me the whole time.

I can't think of any medicine that would soothe this feeling of loss. It's as if I woke up the other morning without a soul.

And no, Tinder can get stuffed. The guy is—or should I say *was*?—one of a kind.

You can only swipe up for guys like him.

The others tell me that in time, things will get easier.

They all have someone now. Most of them, anyway.

I just have to live with his vision in my mind. For how long is anyone's guess. At least a while.

I remember the exact look on his face when we all found out we'd gone back the two and a half years. It will haunt me for some time.

And now he's gone again.

God I miss him.

CHAPTER ONE

Ross and Tony shared the same look they had the last time this happened.

Confusion. Horror. Surprise. What the hell?

This time it was all amplified.

"ARTCC are asking us to call in, Roscoe." Tony, as always in times of crisis, appeared so relaxed he could close his eyes and have a catnap. Ross himself was by no means a panic merchant; the guy had been in the cockpit long enough to know the last thing you ever do is lose your shit in times of crisis. There had been many, but nothing like what happened six months ago, and now this. This was top-shelf shit.

Ross studied the date stamp on the transponder again, and this time tapped on it in the futile hope it would change, like people did when their petrol gauge was on empty and the car was starting to conk out.

It didn't change.

July 20th, 2021.

Ross could feel the heat rising from underneath his shirt. He looked over to Tony, and then over to Michael E. Darcy.

The three men sat there for a few seconds, which felt like much longer.

"Jesus Christ," Darcy said to the two pilots in a near whisper.

The ARTCC (the Oakland Air Route Traffic Control Center) was already going through the motions, as it had done six months earlier.

Ross knew the seconds were ticking.

He took a deep breath and glanced over to Tony. "Okay, we need to take this one step at a time," he said.

Then he glanced back over to Darcy. "Sit back and take a deep breath, my friend." Ross showed that signature grin that always made people around him feel he could take care of anything. "Let's deal with the ARTCC and then figure out what to do next."

What happened in the next couple of minutes made it feel as if they had gone back not two and a half years, but six months. Every step, every process, every panicked tone in the voice of the ATC (air traffic controller) and his superior was identical to what had happened the first time they had returned from their five-year hiatus.

But this time, Ross spoke in careful, measured tones. He didn't want to sound too at ease, but nor did he want to sound like he was currently manning the controls of the world's first legitimately verified 1.2 million pound time machine.

Fighter jets had been dispatched just as they had been when the A380 had reappeared out of nowhere the first time. But these were some time away, not minutes like before. This would come in handy, for the three men needed a couple of minutes to formulate what they would tell the people on-board with them about what had just happened.

"This was not what I'd hoped for," Michael said, closing the cockpit door. He didn't lock it behind him; that would send the wrong message if Melanie or Tammy decided to check in with the men and see how things were going. But he knew the clock was ticking, and they had agreed a second ago they wanted to get to the passengers before the expected fighter jets appeared in the cabin windows.

"You're not the Lone Ranger there," Tony said, then took a deep breath and turned to Ross for his words of wisdom.

He didn't have to wait long.

"We need to get the passengers together and give it to them straight," Ross said as he glanced over his main screens and checked that all the plane's vitals were as they should be.

He looked at the two other men before peering over to the cockpit door to ensure it was still closed.

"What we'll encounter out there is a repeat of what happened six months ago. Most of them will be completely gutted about this, and then some."

Tony thought of his wife, Tina. He'd have to go through the whole rigmarole with her, finding out (again) she was now a lesbian and in a relationship with his ex-sister-in-law. One of his heartstrings pinged for a second before he remembered that he now had Tammy.

Farck. One thought leads to another.

Tammy.

Her sister had tried to kill her only a couple of hours ago, according to their own sense of time, and was "now" dead.

But in this year, 2021, Annie was alive again.

For the first time in his life, the ice-cold blood running through Tony's veins warmed up somewhat.

He muttered to himself as reality washed over him like a 44-gallon drum full of motor oil.

Ross looked over to him. "What did you say, Tone?"

Tony wiped the motor oil from around his mouth and said, "We need to get out there and prepare all of them for this."

Dave Collins received the call from his brother as he had done in 2024. Hold on, as he *hadn't* done, because it was 2021. But this time, he wasn't in the tower. He was home on one of his rare days off.

His brother was on shift at the ARTCC in Fremont, California, and had called Dave on his cell phone.

Dave disliked vacuuming as much as ironing. But it had to be done, and he was halfway through it when Jeff called.

The vacuuming would not get finished today; Dave would have other issues to contend with.

"What the hell do you mean?" said Dave.

Jeff repeated the sentence a third time.

"The plane claims to be Pacific International Airlines Flight 19." This time, he added, "Brother, I am not shitting you."

"Transponder?" Dave said as he dropped the vacuum on the floor.

Jeff wasted no time in answering the question. "Same transponder number. Identical."

Dave's mind was spinning. He reached for the edge of the sofa, and when he found it, pulled himself over and sat down hastily.

"Where's it heading?" he asked.

Unlike when Dave would ask in 2024, his brother had no issue about discussing this over an open line.

"Vandenberg," he said.

Dave leaped from the arm of the couch like a soldier coming to attention.

His only daughter was on that flight.

He looked over to the picture of her and his heart skipped a couple of beats. She looked back at him through the glass with that killer smile of hers.

"I'm going there now," Dave said, his mind racing.

His brother was about to tell him not to bother, since the security would be off the charts by the time he got there, but Dave had already rung off and was racing for the front door.

CHAPTER TWO

MELANIE AND TAMMY LOOKED AT EACH OTHER AS ROSS let the words flow carefully from his lips. There wasn't much for him to say, really. The facts were pretty simple.

The five of them were huddled into the cockpit, Ross and Tony in their seats but with their legs sideways, with Michael, Melanie, and Tammy all standing behind them.

Out of instinct, hundreds of hours of training, and thousands of hours of flying, Ross and Tony kept checking screens and information in front of them every few seconds.

The gravity of the situation had not even begun to sink in for the two couples.

What lay ahead of them was a headache of biblical proportions.

As the mutters and profanities continued, it was Melanie who called the others to attention.

"Guys." She spoke quietly but with a sternness normally reserved for the board- or court-room. "God knows how long we have before the jets are upon us."

The three men nodded.

Tammy just stood there with a frightened, panicked look on her face.

Annie.

Alive.

She has my children.

She is married to my husband.

She tried to kill me.

This is not happening.

What the fuck was I thinking when I got on this plane?

This was a big mistake.

Darcy's words cut through the thick fog of her thoughts. "I'm responsible for this. I'll tell them what's happened."

ARTCC had instructed Flight 19 to turn around and head back to California, but Ross, Tony, and Michael had agreed not to do so until the passengers had been told what happened.

Melanie and Tammy went and asked all the passengers to come together in the main economy-class cabin.

Déjà vu was about to come at them in spades.

When everyone was seated as one large group, Darcy stood at the front and looked across the cabin and the sea of faces. They all waited for him to speak.

Time's up, he thought. Those pesky fighter jets would be on them at any moment, and he had to tell the passengers before they got to his plane.

"There's something I need to tell you all," Darcy said, raising his voice above the sound of the cabin air.

The mutters and coughs around the cabin ceased.

"Damn it. The fighter jets are here."

The sound of them arriving to encircle the A380 was loud and abrupt, and it almost sent Darcy into a full-blown panic.

Damn it, I should have done this minutes ago, he told himself in frustration.

Someone from the back shouted, "Oh, you've got to be kidding me!" His words got louder as each new one came out.

Darcy thought he knew what the guy was implying, but wasn't exactly on the money.

Passenger David Windebank rose from the seat next to his wife Christine, trying to catch a glimpse of the fighter jets in the opposite cabin windows, but the expression on his face was not one of shock or terror, but delight.

He thought they'd gone back the whole five years.

Now seeing the smile on David's face, Darcy realized the guy's wife had cottoned on to what her husband was saying and was smiling too. He felt as if someone had punched him in the throat.

"No, *no*." Darcy was nearly shouting, the strain in his voice making it clear this was not what he was about to say.

David, seeing the distraught expression on Darcy's face, slowly sank back to his chair and looked over to his wife.

Darcy took a deep breath and looked across the rest of the passengers, most of them now looking gravely concerned. Tony, standing right next to Darcy, said something to him.

The ex-billionaire knew the only thing to do was just get the hell on with it.

"It's happened, people; it's happened," he shouted, but there was no joy or celebration in his demeanor.

Before anyone had a chance to say anything, he pushed on: "We've gone back…" He closed his eyes and rubbed the pain in the middle of his forehead. "To … 20 … 21."

Tony went back to the flight deck and told Ross to turn the

plane around. Ross pretty much knew they'd have to do this now that the four US Air Force fighter jets were in a tight formation around the A380. Ross instigated a gracious 180-degree turn, ensuring none of the now gobsmacked passengers fell on top of each other. That would be the straw that broke the camel's back for many of them.

"Tell me," Ross said, looking over to Tony as he strapped himself back in his seat.

Tony looked out through the cockpit windows at the bright blue sky and wondered what he'd gotten himself into when he became a commercial airline pilot. He wasn't sure if this was part of the job description, but it certainly wasn't in the training simulator flights he and Ross regularly undertook.

"Fucking time machines are not meant to be this big," he said with his best effort at a dash of humor. "And you're supposed to be able to control them too, right?"

"I wish we could, buddy, " Ross said.

Tony shook his head. "Many of the passengers are understandably dumbfounded."

This was probably the last thing on earth most of them wanted. They'd have thought this was going to be some sort of joyride. They'd have thought it would give them the chance to move on.

"Well, they've left the past behind them," Tony said. "Or was it the bloody future? I don't know, but I do know that what we encounter when we arrive at Vandenberg is going to be vastly different…" He sighed in clear frustration. "…to what we did six months ago."

Ross shook his head. "How the hell are we going to explain to the authorities what happened?" He looked at the open doorway before turning back to Tony. "They'll think we're all certifiably crazy. They'll lock us up and ask us if we like the shade of the fabric on the padded walls. And how do we explain the fact that we have 120 passengers less than the original fli…"

"I've got it all covered," Darcy announced, appearing at the top of the access steps into the cockpit after overhearing Tony and Ross.

"Well, I guess you can explain it to us both, then," Tony said. He looked at Ross, who was also looking forward to hearing how Darcy was going to pull it off.

No words came from Darcy. Tony and Ross looked the guy up and down. "Well, go on—tell us," Ross said.

Darcy showed his teeth, but it was by no means convincing. He looked like a used-car salesman trying to palm off a Model T Ford for the price of a 2020 Mustang GT Coupe V8.

"I've convinced the passengers to make a pact," he said, as if he could solve the world's problems over afternoon tea.

Tony was the first to scoff. Ross didn't bother, since his best friend had beaten him to it.

"What sort of pact?" Ross said, though he pretty much knew what Darcy was implying.

"We've agreed to not tell them we've come back from 2024," he said forcefully.

At that moment, Melanie and Tammy had entered the cockpit and stood silently behind Darcy.

Melanie shared a look with Ross. Biting her bottom lip told Ross she thought the ex-billionaire's concept was as ludicrous as it was impractical, and more importantly —impossible.

Tammy bent sideways out from behind Darcy to look over to Tony. Once again, these two people who'd genuinely fallen for each other only had to meet each other's eyes to know they were both thinking the same thing.

He's goddamned crazy.

Out of his gourd.

CHAPTER THREE

OF ALL THE PASSENGERS WHO SAT IN STUNNED SILENCE during Michael E. Darcy's announcement and proposal, Tim Erwin most felt he was carrying the weight of the aircraft on his shoulders. All 1.2 million–plus pounds. He, like a few others, had returned to their original seats, where they would drown in their own thoughts of "what now?"

But Tim's thoughts were different. There wasn't a chance in hell anyone could be thinking what Tim was thinking— and thinking, and thinking—right now.

He reached down into his daypack and felt it again. Another passenger had caught Tim with the object in his hand before, and Tim had been relieved when the guy said, "Arthritis, huh?" As he watched Tim put the artifact back in his bag, the man had added, "Those things are great for rubbing the sore spots. My old Ma used to swear by them for helping her joints."

It was stone cold, and had remained so for a while now. But Tim had no doubt it was the object that had taken the plane back the two and a half or so years to 2021.

His mind raced, thoughts bouncing off each other like dodgem cars in a tight pen. With the time counting down to when they would descend into Vandenberg Air Force Base, amid the daze of a hundred thoughts all going on at once, he almost had to write down who was alive in 2021 and who was not, just to keep it all straight.

Tim reassured himself he'd done the right thing by telling Sean the whole story. But a part of him felt sick when he thought of Sarah sitting in front of the television in 2024, seeing the news the plane had disappeared again.

Sean would be all she had left now.

But then it dawned on him. They would be here in 2021.

None of what happened in 2024 had happened yet. There should be a night-school course on understanding time travel, Tim thought.

For now, he would sit in silence and rub his sore knee with the actual object that had caused him and the other eighty-nine people on-board to go back in time two and a half years.

He closed his eyes and thought of his best friend.

He'd missed her.

His heart longed for her little arms to be wrapped around him, her hair itching his nose when they stood and hugged each other.

He opened his eyes and looked out the plane window. The blue sky offered him no solace. And then he thought of the one person who'd be there to greet him when he was released from Vandenberg.

His daughter, Sarah.

She'd be all alone when he opened the DONR: the doors of no return.

No, Tim, she would not.

Ross felt déjà vu as he approached Vandenberg AFB.

He wondered how they'd begin to explain what had happened to the 120 passengers and crew who were originally on the flight.

This would be the tricky part.

Damn you, Darcy, Ross thought, what have you got all of us into?

Tony snapped him out of this deep musing.

"Are you ready for this?" Tony said, continuing to look straight out through his side of the cockpit window, watching the rugged Californian coast come into view.

There was no need for Ross to answer right away. He peered through his small side window and watched in fascination at the grace and ease with which the fighter pilot was flying his jet alongside them. Those guys knew how to fly. The guy was so close, Ross imagined himself passing morning tea to him through the window.

Déjà vu would have struck again if Ross had cared to look a little closer. He would have noticed the pilot's killer mutton-chop sideburns: it was the same man who'd sat alongside Ross and his A380 the first time he'd flown into Vandenberg.

"Never been more ready," Ross finally lied.

We landed the A380 as Tony and I had done probably over a thousand times before.

On a crystal-clear, sunny afternoon, with little to no onshore breeze, the landing was as routine as it was easy.

The main runway at Vandenberg was as expansive as the whole place was. Landing was a piece of cake, just like the last time.

As our plane slowed at the end of the runway, the vast array of military and emergency vehicles appeared.

The impossibly enormous aircraft hangar where this actual plane had lived for the last six-plus months came up to our right, and before the tower supervisor had even told me over the comms to head in its direction, I started to steer our plane there anyway.

"Pilot of the A380," the supervisor said, finally, "direct your plane into Hangar 1, to your right. Confirm request, over." It certainly wasn't the guy from six months ago, but he had the same serious tone with a don't-mess-me-around tilt to it.

"This is Captain Ross Moore." I gave Tony a smile as fake as the last Rolex I bought in Bali (as a gift for a friend obsessed with the brand). "Request received and confirmed."

As the front wheels rolled into the hangar, I hit the internal comms button and spoke to everyone on-board.

"Well, here we are, people; you know the drill," I said, slowing the A380 down as we came into the middle of the gigantic hangar.

Darcy had arrived back in the cockpit, having decided after his chat with the passengers that he'd stay with them and try to talk individually to as many as he could.

He felt it was the right thing to do.

"I've gotten around to most of them," he said, "and believe they're all on-board, pardon the pun."

I nodded. Tony just kept looking out the cockpit windows, watching as armed soldiers started to form a perimeter around our plane.

His eyes were open, though his vision was clouded by the things whirling through his mind like in a washing machine on spin cycle.

Tammy. Tina. Tammy. Tina. Six more months of this bullshit.

He wondered, as many on-board the A380 did in those

few moments, if just staying in 2024 would have been the wiser thing to do.

He had Tammy, he was in love, and things were starting to get better.

Now, he'd have to jump through another dozen hoops, most of them on fire, some dipped in cow shit, and maybe just one sprinkled nicely with salt or sugar like the rim of a cocktail glass, to get back to where he wanted his life to be.

"Captain Ross Moore, this is Colonel Ted Frances, the tower supervisor. Please commence procedure to power down your aircraft immediately."

I was about to confirm we were already doing this before he added, "Then proceed to the main cabin door, where you will open it and have your hands up and sticking out of the aircraft."

"Bloody hell," Tony said, turning to Darcy and me before removing the headset from his Ben-Stiller-alike noggin. "Are these fuckers in 2021 just that little bit more wound up than the ones back in 2024 or what?"

As I removed my headset before adjusting my tie, preparing to exit the cockpit and do as Colonel Bossy-Boots demanded, I could only shake my head and grunt in response to Tony's comment. He was definitely onto something.

I quickly refocused my thoughts on the mission at hand. It would be the second time in my life, and the second in six months, that I had to go through the quite uncomfortable process of sticking my hands up in the air while more than one person pointed an object at me that could end my life in an instant.

The process of surrender.

CHAPTER FOUR

IT TOOK MUCH LONGER THAN LAST TIME FOR THE personnel at Vandenberg to bring the mobile staircase to the aircraft. Ross stood in the open doorway and at one point shouted, "My arms are going to fall off if I have to hold them up any longer."

The soldiers below ignored him, though one did turn to see where in God's name the mobile staircase was. It appeared in the distance, and after some time finally arrived at the A380, where it was wheeled into position.

Just as they had six months earlier, the two soldiers came up the staircase with their guns trained on Ross the entire time. "Step out onto the staircase and turn around," one of them said matter-of-factly.

Okay, this is new, Ross thought. It hadn't happened last time. But he was in no position to tell them how this would go down.

The second soldier, obviously in no mood for pleasantries, searched Ross as best as he could with what looked like a high-powered submachine gun holstered across his chest.

The soldier then said, "Okay, Captain Moore, we will

now lead you down the staircase. Please proceed first." His words were stern, but not angry. I could live with that.

As the two soldiers led me to the same door I'd walked through before, quite some distance away, I looked back at the A380.

In many of its windows there was a face just staring back at me. Most had no discernible expressions.

And then there was Melanie. She waved to me, and with her million-watt smile, told me in her own way that every-thing would be okay.

Maybe.

I sat in that damned tiny office for over an hour. It felt like longer, but I'd been keeping an eye on the time. My Rolex kept good time. Okay, it was for me, jeez. Those Bali fakes look identical, at a fraction of the price.

The air in the room was stuffy, the window was shut, and so were the mouths of another set of guards standing outside the closed door. I stood a couple of times and did a few laps of the tiny office. Yep, these were the same chairs and table as last time.

Fifteen minutes later, the door swung open and the two soldiers entered and stood either side of the open doorway.

Two other men entered the room behind them, in civilian clothes, wearing red lanyards with identification cards so big you'd think they were volunteering for the next Olympic Games.

Bugger me dead, Ross quipped to himself on seeing one of them, it's the same schmuck from last time. Remember, he's never met you. Don't act as if you know him or you may end up breaking up rocks on the chain gang, if they still do that shit these days in prison. Be cool.

But the other guy was definitely someone different altogether.

The two men sat down across from Ross.

"Max E. Brown, NTSB," said Mr. Buzz Cut. With one of the strongest handshakes Ross had ever come across, the man reached over and nearly, or so it felt, broke all twenty-seven bones in his hand.

Buzz Cut sat back and looked to his left at his colleague, indicating it was his turn to introduce himself.

The guy reached over his outstretched hand and said, "Graeme Joyes, FAA."

Ross had lived close enough to the land of the long white cloud to detect a hint of Kiwi in the new guy's accent.

Ross grinned. "Newzilnd?" he asked.

The guy looked at Ross as if the pilot had just asked him how long his penis was in millimeters. His dark-colored eyes stared at Ross through rimless glasses for probably five seconds before a small, rather sarcastic grin exposed his eggshell-colored teeth.

"Born there, raised there, don't live there anymore, *mate*." He emphasized the last word as if the he was talking to Ross across the bar with a pint of Speight's beer in his left hand.

Excellent. Ross surmised that this time round he had two hard-asses to contend with, not just one as in this same meeting six months ago. Back then it had been Max E. Brown of the NTSB ripping shreds from him.

This time, Brown waited for the sarcasm and smart-ass remarks to evaporate into the stuffy air of the office before starting his questions.

"Well, son," he began. Jesus, Ross thought, he's going to repeat the same opening line as last time, word for word. "Ah was going to ask you one simple question. We'd like to know where you and your plane…"

But this time the question ended differently.

"…have been for the last two and a half years."

Ross sat forward, feeling dread at the prospect of a long afternoon stuck in this room.

"Fucking Disneyland!" he shouted at the top of his lungs, standing abruptly and sending his chair crashing to the floor as he pushed the table directly back into the now very angry-looking men.

Snapping out of his nanosecond-long daydream, Ross put his elbows carefully on the table and rested his chin on both hands.

"I am going to tell you the same thing as many times as I need to, gentlemen," Ross said, looking from one man to another before ending on Brown from the NTSB with a glare, "before you eventually realize I'm telling you the truth."

Joyes of the FAA didn't blink even once. Crikey, Ross thought, the guy was made of stone. Brown, sitting alongside him just stared at Ross as if he were from another planet.

The silence lasted nearly thirty seconds, in one of many Mexican standoffs that afternoon between a hard-ass American, a hard-ass ex-Kiwi, and a good-ass, lying son of a bitch Australian international pilot.

Ross finally ended it. "One second, we were in 2019, and a second later, we were in 2021." He sat back and shrugged his shoulders. "I have no idea what happened to us or our plane, or *how* it happened."

At least half of that was true.

Brown and Joyes sat back in their seats, Brown staring at Ross as if his eyes were trying to bore into his mind for the truth. Joyes rocked subtly in the cheap, military-issue office chair, his gaze darting between the pilot and the small window behind him and to his left. There was nothing to see outside other than acres of dry, near-barren land that stretched to the Pacific Ocean. Joyes came across as wanting to be out there instead.

Brown leaned forward and flicked open his notepad, reading something Ross couldn't see.

Ross had nowhere to go, and no pressing engagements, but he longed for the comfort of his bungalow at the Beverly Hills Hotel. He'd grown quite fond of the place and the person he had been sharing a bed there with.

It wouldn't be the last time that afternoon he'd long to be home with his girlfriend.

Not that she'd be his girlfriend much longer.

Ross requested a toilet break, and was escorted to a tired restroom that needed a clean.

When he returned, it was as if the two men had been on pause and somebody simply hit the play button.

"I guess the first thing we need to discuss with you, Captain Moore…" Brown trailed off, then picked up his pen and fiddled with it for a moment. He looked up from the table and straight into Ross's eyes.

"Where are the other 120 passengers and crew?" he said.

This would be the main reason that this time around, circumstances for the A380's passengers would be different.

The authorities would find it extremely implausible that the 120 missing passengers and crew had simply vanished mid-flight.

As though by comparison, reappearing five years later than scheduled was just run-of-the-mill unusual? It was manifestly ridiculous.

These thoughts cascaded through Ross's mind as the men questioned him endlessly.

Two hours later, Ross threw his hands in the air out of frustration.

"You can ask me a thousand questions. You can ask me the same question a hundred different ways. It's not going to change what I'm telling you," Ross barked.

After a few moments of silence, he went through it all over again.

- One minute he was flying the plane, and it was 2019.
- A second later, he received a message on the transponder from the ARTCC, asking him to identify himself or the plane.
- He did this, and a few minutes later realized his entire crew, and a large number of passengers from the flight, had disappeared without a trace.
- He then looked down to the transponder to see the date stamp was 2021: two and a half years later than it had been just moments before.

Joyes looked over to Brown, and thankfully for Ross, asked him one more question before the meeting ended.

Ross couldn't help but continue to hear the clear tones of a New Zealand accent throughout his long sentences and snide remarks.

"So the passengers and crew—poof!—vanish into thin air, right, Captain Moore?"

Ross was getting annoyed. How many times did they need to cover this off before the Kiwi got the mail?

Ross shot him a dirty look. If he called him Captain Moore one more time with that smart-ass grin, even in an accent Ross normally had a soft spot for, he might just jump over the table and head-butt his bald dome.

"The Lord works in mysterious ways—mate," Ross said.

Joyes looked over to Brown, and they both would later confirm in private what they were thinking at that very moment. One, they didn't like this Australian pilot, and two, something was way off about all this.

Hell, guys, you don't need Einstein to figure that out.

Dave Collins arrived at the gates of Vandenberg.

In 2024—not that this Dave knew anything about that —the place had been a circus of news crews, loved ones of the missing passengers, and anyone else who wanted to know what all the commotion was about.

But today, in 2021, Vandenberg was as quiet as a mouse, at least at the main front-gate complex.

The security guard in the entrance office refused Dave access after he'd pled his case. The guard had no idea what he was talking about. At that point, no one other than a handful of people had any idea the Pacific International Airlines A380 had come back from la-la land.

But that would change in less than 24 hours.

The news crews would come and so would the loved ones of the missing passengers and crew. Then, the guard would realize what Dave had been talking about the night before.

And at that point, things would become very, very interesting for Darcy and his flock of Flight Nineteeners.

Who once called fate a bitch?

It had nothing on déjà vu, Flight 19 style.

CHAPTER FIVE

Twenty-four hours later.

CUE THE CIRCUS. AND WE'RE NOT TALKING CIRQUE DU Soleil.

It was the security guard at the main gate who kicked it off, by going home and telling his wife about Dave Collins coming to Vandenberg out of the blue, asking about that Pacific Airlines flight that had vanished without a trace two and half years ago. The guard told his wife that this random guy claimed the "missing" plane had landed at Vandenberg that afternoon.

When the wife called a girlfriend of hers an hour or so later, as she did on a near-nightly basis when she'd couldn't find anything on cable to watch, she told her about the strange encounter her husband had with the random civilian earlier in the day.

Ten minutes after the wife hung up, her girlfriend posted on Facebook that she'd heard something strange a short time earlier.

And one of her 966 friends on Facebook was a friend of a friend of another friend who happened to be, you guessed it, a journalist. A reporter for the *San Francisco Examiner*. Wow —would this ever be her big break.

By midday the next day, the word was on the street.

And on the television screens.

And on Twitter, Facebook, Instagram, Reddit … have I left any out?

The press, online or offline—it was everywhere, and the momentum would be as feverish as it was the last time it… Well, it hadn't yet happened for the world, even if it had for Ross and his fellow passengers.

Dave had slept in his car in the visitor car park, only to have the security guys patrolling Vandenberg wake him up in the middle of the night and tell him to bugger off. He found a cheap motel at nearby Lompoc, and after the hot water refused to work, he took a cold shower, ate at the greasy take-out across the road, and headed back to the base.

Within a couple of hours, the number of news vans had grown from one or two to eight. By nightfall, the number would peak at fifteen.

Everyone was asking the same question, with Dave at the front of the line.

Was there a Pacific International Airlines A380 sitting on the grounds of Vandenberg Air Force Base, with the flight number PI019?

It would be another twenty-four excruciating hours for Dave before he and the rest of the world received official confirmation.

Phil Brady, second in command at the Department of Homeland Security, became the spokesman for a contingent of personnel from a large number of agencies brought together to work as one to investigate this deepening mystery. And just as they had in 2024, within the week a *New York Times* reporter nicknamed this group the American Fraternity of Acronyms, or AFOA.

Brady, not one to mince his words, made his first official announcement at the front gate of Vandenberg, choosing to remain behind the closed front gate. He did it partly to annoy the shit out of the press, but mostly because he didn't want to answer the thousand questions he knew would be thrown at him when he finished speaking.

The throng of reporters, cameras, and anyone else who wanted to join in the madness jostled on one side of the fence while Brady stood a good ten feet from his side of it.

"Ladies and gentlemen, I am here to confirm that we currently have in our possession a Boeing A380 that had ninety people on-board when it landed here…" He cleared his throat as the crowd on the other side went deathly silent, and continued. "…which is purporting to be the Pacific Airlines International PI019, Flight 19, that disappeared without a trace two and a half years ago between Hawaii and California."

Before anyone in the large crowd could say even one word, he barked, "That is all I have to say at this time." Brady turned and stepped into a waiting car. It sped off a second later.

The mass of news crews, reporters, and other people crowded on the other side of the fence stood in stunned silence for a few seconds before the words "what the hell?" exploded from many of them. They looked at each other as if it had been Medusa standing on the other side of the fence.

And in the middle of them all was the LAX air traffic control supervisor, Dave Collins, frozen where he stood.

He didn't know what to do next. He put his hand to his chest and felt his heart to ensure it hadn't stopped beating.

Ninety people.

When it had disappeared two and a half years ago, they said there had been 210 people on-board his daughter's flight.

Emily—was she one of the ninety, or one of the 120 who were no longer on the flight?

He knew it would only be a matter of time before they would announce the names of those who remained. Jesus, he thought, this is going to be torture.

The AFOAs organized comfortable accommodation for the passengers and crew, setting up large marquees within Hangar 1—soon to be known to the world as Hangar 19—with stretcher beds, tables, chairs, toilets, and showers. They also told the ninety people on-board they would all have to undergo medical and psychiatric tests as part of their investigations.

In their last few moments in the cockpit, Ross, Melanie, Tony, Tammy, and Darcy had a chat about something they'd nearly all forgotten about.

And it may have been an issue if they hadn't remembered this when they touched down. It may have made things just that little bit trickier for the two couples.

All of them but Ross and Darcy were supposed to be in other relationships, with other people, as they had been when the plane originally disappeared in 2019.

Tammy was married to Brandon.

Tony was married to Tina.

Melanie was married to Charles.

So, when the plane touched down inside the hangar, the two couples took turns going into a secluded place inside the A380 and saying their goodbyes, so to speak.

They knew once they left the plane, they had to act as if they didn't know each other.

"Are you going to be okay?" Ross said to Melanie in their last moment together for a while.

Melanie asked Ross if he could just hold her for a moment.

Like Tammy, she was worried.

Melanie was one mentally tough cookie. But when someone you know almost kills you, it can nearly break you.

In 2021, her husband Charles was very much alive.

And she would have to face him—again.

Her husband would have killed her on that day months ago if not for the chauffeur.

At that moment, while Ross held her tightly, she didn't know he was quite worried that Charles might try the same again here in 2021. But he didn't say a word. He just held her and told her everything would be okay.

Tony and Tammy kissed as if they were two teenagers on their first date, sitting in the back row at the movies.

Tammy didn't want to talk. She knew it would be some time before she could do this again.

But they knew their time was up when there was a tap on the door. They stood back from each other and looked long and hard into the other's eyes.

"We will be together once we get through all of this, right?" Tammy asked.

Tony kissed her again.

He stood back and held her hand in his. Tammy had dropped her gaze to the floor, so Tony reached over and lifted her chin so their eyes met.

"I promise you," he said with the passion of a man in love, "we'll get through this."

CHAPTER SIX

THE AFOA's SENIOR PERSONNEL MET THAT NIGHT AND discussed the situation at hand in detail. Although there were only eight agencies involved, close to forty senior staff talked well into the evening in a private room on the grounds of the Vandenberg base:

CAP: The Civil Air Patrol
CIA: The Central Intelligence Agency
DHS: The Department of Homeland Security
FAA: The Federal Aviation Authority
FBI: The Federal Bureau of Investigation
NTSB: The National Transportation Safety Board
TSA: The Transport Security Administration
USAF: The United States Air Force

Hangar 19, as it had now been dubbed by one of the reporters camping at the front gate, was under heavy guard.

Over a hundred armed security guards patrolled inside and outside the facility, and would continue to do so until further notice, twenty-four hours a day. The authorities would take no chances until they were satisfied they had thoroughly investigated the plane and the people on-board.

The AFOA meeting stretched well into the night. Phil Brady, from the Department of Homeland Security, suggested they all call it quits at 1am.

As he started to get his notes together to leave, he said matter-of-factly, "So—do you trust him?"

Brown looked Brady up and down with a small dose of disdain. He wasn't a big fan of pen-pushers who had risen through the ranks but had never stood firm on God's earth and fought for their country as he had done.

Before he could answer, the woman who had been sitting on the other side of Brady at the boardroom table chimed in with a question to both men.

"Forget about Captain Moore, no one in this room could say they trust him right now," said Senior Special Agent Dianne Scoffield, from the FBI's Los Angeles office.

Brown liked Scoffield. He knew she'd served in Iraq before retiring to the slightly less dangerous world of the FBI. And she didn't take shit from anyone, no matter how far up the tree they were.

Not like Brady, the pompous bastard.

Scoffield came forward. "I'm more interested in one of the passengers, a female," she told them both.

The two men wondered what she meant.

"When that plane took off two and a half years ago, she was twenty-eight weeks pregnant."

As she gathered up her belongings, she looked at the two men for the final time.

"So tell me—how is it that when she got off that plane two days ago, she's not pregnant anymore?"

Tammy, you've got some serious bullshitting to do.

36

Over the next two days, every passenger was interviewed by one of the AFOAs. The interviews started at 9am and were still going well into the night.

Amazingly, the pact held tight. They all told the same well-constructed and well-rehearsed story: one second they were flying along, and the next, people throughout the expansive airplane had simply vanished.

Retirees Bob and Judy Phillips, who after learning in 2024 that their entire multimillion-dollar fortune had been carved up between their very large family, who had all warred against each other for more, decided they had less than nothing to lose. They'd signed up for the Darcy flight, and were now two of the many people getting their asses chewed out by investigators. When they were able to speak in private, which was quite difficult in Hangar 1, they agreed with Darcy's proposal to keep the pact. It was well worth it to them.

They would walk away from this bizarre situation with more than they had had before they boarded the plane the second time around.

Bob and Judy had already agreed to live out their twilight years in one of their favorite places: Queenstown, New Zealand. And their determination to see that through led them to give one of the stand-out performances of Flight 19's early days in 2021. Darcy would later thank them for their stunning portrayal of a senior couple who had absolutely no idea what was going on, which would be one of the pivotal interviews in convincing the investigators the story of what happened to them was plausible.

Darcy realized later why they'd both been so convincing. The couple had spent the better part of their lives in front of the small screen and onstage in theaters from Broadway to the West End.

Coming back to 2021 would also give them the opportunity to right some wrongs. They were yet to realize it, but it would soon become clear that getting back on the A380 would be the best decision they had ever made.

Later that night, the press received the official statement from Phil Brady, spokesperson for the AFOA.

It was across all major news channels worldwide less than ten minutes later.

CNN was the first to make the announcement.

"This is Roberta Wright at the CNN desk in New York, interrupting this current service with breaking news from Vandenberg Air Force Base, Santa Barbara, California.

"We have an important update concerning the A380 that landed recently at Vandenberg AFB, with reports claiming it is the missing Pacific International Airlines flight which vanished without a trace over two years ago." Roberta checked her private monitor before looking straight back into the camera.

"Without further delay, we will cross to our reporter at Vandenberg. Laura Messer, are you there?"

The on-site reporter for CNN looked tired but excitable. Behind her, the darkness of the landscape was punctuated by the bright light being shone directly at her. In the background, a cyclone fence swayed with the wind, and the distant lights of the base twinkled at the camera. Millions of people across the globe were now glued to their screens.

"Yes, Roberta, I am here. Can you hear me okay?" Laura said, holding the microphone in her right hand while pushing an earpiece in with her left. The anchorwoman confirmed a second later, and Laura knew she was good to go.

"Roberta, they've released the names of the people who were on the A380 when it landed here a few days ago."

She looked to her notes on a clipboard and gave thanks that it had a bright strip of LEDs surrounding her documents.

Roberta chimed in from New York. She knew the answer to the question but asked it for the viewers. "Laura, do you have the names of the ninety people who were on-board the Boeing A380 currently behind you under tight security?"

Laura went along with the script.

"Yes, Roberta, I have the names of the ninety passengers here with me now," she said.

"And can you read these names out now?"

Laura took a deep breath, her eyes darting to the other reporters dotted along the fence for the next 100 meters. Her heart pounded, knowing she would be the first to read out the names. It would be the highlight of her career.

"Yes, Roberta," Laura gushed, "the names are as follows."

She started reading.

By now, most news services worldwide were covering the latest update.

Radio stations throughout America had interrupted whatever was currently being aired on their stations. They had cut directly to Laura Messer's live report from Vandenberg AFB.

KBIG, Los Angeles' top-rated radio station, was one of them. They crossed to Laura Messer's report.

By the time they patched in, Laura was about twenty names through the ninety.

And when she got to the fiftieth, fate struck like a bolt of lightning 150 miles away.

After a long shift, the driver needed just three things: a visit to the restroom, a hot coffee, and a donut. He switched off the car and looked over to the guy who'd sat next to him for the last eight hours.

His passenger was about to say something when they both realized what the person on the radio was talking about.

They looked at each other, and at the same moment both went for the volume control on the car radio.

The driver got there first, and turned it almost to full blast. He swallowed hard as the reality of what he was hearing began to sink in.

Twenty seconds later, Laura Messer read the name that made the guy freeze in his seat.

And then he looked out the window and had the strangest feeling he'd ever felt. He couldn't quite put his finger on it.

A group of rowdy kids were entering the 7-Eleven nearby. One of them looked to his car and shot him a dirty look. But in his profession, a punk giving him a dirty look was water off a duck's back.

That punk would want to pull his pants up, too. Jesus, his ass was nearly falling out of them.

The name of the driver's son had just been announced as one of the ninety on-board the A380 sitting at Vandenberg AFB.

He sat in his car for another ten minutes in stunned silence.

He felt like he'd seen a ghost in the reflection of the convenience store's window.

CHAPTER SEVEN

THE PASSENGERS AND CREW EACH CHOSE A BED IN THE large marquee. There they would sleep and spend most of their time until their release from the base. Small room dividers in their dozens, like those of the field hospitals of yesteryear, offered a little privacy, though not much. Couples took up adjacent beds, and as the night sky filled with darkness, would pull them just that little closer to each other.

Todd and Emily chose beds like this. That way, they could spend time together as they wanted to. When all the lights were out, they would reach for each other's hand and hold on until dawn.

Gerald Rusgrove Mills and Charles Boon, eat your heart out. That's romantic, huh?

But when the lights went out on this particular night, Todd lay on his back and stared at the white roof of the marquee with his hands intertwined behind his head. No holding hands yet, Em.

The idea of sleep was at the back of the line too. Other thoughts crowded his consciousness. He was yet to get his head around the whole time-travel thing.

Who was alive, now, and who was dead.

The vision of him pulling the trigger.

The look on his half-brother's lifeless face.

If he thought too long about the photo Jason had been trying to pull out to show him they shared a father, he'd shed a tear.

That photo, and what was written on the back.

Dad.

He breathed deep and hard.

Dad. You betrayed me and Mom.

A minute or so later, he felt a tap on the side of his bed.

Emily's hand.

He gladly took it, and held on tightly.

The AFOAs convened a meeting with the ninety passengers and crew. This time, Phil Brady would be doing the talking, not Ross.

Compared to what they'd experienced in 2024, the number of counselors, medical personnel, and security staff present had scaled down to match the number—ninety out of 210—who'd survived and chosen to come aboard. But the plan was identical, as if it had come from a manual on crisis management.

"Ladies and gentlemen." Brady scanned across the faces to see who was still chatting, like a headmaster at morning assembly. "May I have everyone's attention?"

He waited for everyone to quieten down.

"As most of you are aware, you have been through quite the mysterious event. All the government agencies represented here today have not only been trying to figure out what happened, but also to come up with a plan for you all as well."

He looked down to his notes and continued. "But while

this investigation continues in earnest, we need to take you all into the next phase of your rehabilitation."

After the grilling Ross had been through, he felt as if they were playing a game of cat and mouse with the investigators this time around. They could all feel it in the air—either it was mistrust, or they were just being a little paranoid. Truth be told, there was mistrust and paranoia on both sides.

The couples, Ross and Melanie and Tony and Tammy, knew they'd have much to deal with before they could become couples in the open again.

Darcy had things to contend with too. People who he thought were trusted friends had screwed him over big time.

Though not officially part of this little group, Todd Roberts and Emily Collins were in a similar situation, and would devise their own plan of attack post-Vandenberg.

"So we come to the part of this conversation…" Brady was saying. He now seemed to be in full swing. "…where I need to inform you what has actually happened to you all."

Here it comes, the ninety thought. This was one of the points Darcy had brought up on the plane just before it landed, and again while they waited to disembark.

Brady's pause to build suspense was overblown. Actually, the guy was shitting bricks—but his trepidation would turn to rage if he knew the truth.

"Whatever has happened to you all," Brady said, looking across the room and to the many AFOA representatives and counselors, "it has caused the last two and a half years of your lives to pass you by in a matter of moments."

Action, people.

At least a dozen of the passengers starting groaning. Bob and Judy Phillips flicked the switch and unleashed a melt-down worthy of a Golden Globe. Many others started crying, some even flailing their arms. That was probably a bit too much, though for anyone in the marquee who had not been on the plane, this was all completely new, so they had no idea what to expect.

Ross just tilted his head and rattled off a long list of profanities while offering Tony a comforting hand on his shoulder and watching as he wiped invisible tears from his eyes. Tammy and Melanie, sitting together, shook their heads while Tammy held on to her stomach as if her poor baby had been ripped from it a moment ago. Her raw emotions were easy to tap into; she felt as if it were only yesterday that her third child had been taken away from her.

Melanie eventually stood, reached over, and held her. She knew that as much as they were all putting on one hell of an act, for some, like Tammy, it wasn't all fake.

Like last time, the passengers were split into groups, this time nine groups of ten, with one lead counselor and two support counselors for each group. They had no idea what they were doing was a complete waste of time.

But the Flight Nineteeners didn't care. They had other things to contend with.

For many, though they had not received a detailed file of what had gone on in their friends and families' lives while they were in la-la land those five years to 2024, they'd been told some and taken in the information.

But there would be the odd surprise, and for some it was a matter of rolling the dice as to what they were going to find here in 2021. Every action has a consequence, and if you think you can change your past, you'd better beware. There's a reason time travel is so goddamned elusive—it's the universe's way of telling us that hindsight is a double-edged sword, and having the ability to act on it is just too dangerous.

The group counselors worked through the list of passengers and crew on their clipboard, talking to each one individually during the long day, confirming and discussing the details of their lives, and also the lay of the land outside Vandenberg.

For the counselors, it was a long and often arduous conversation to have. For the passengers, the only difficulty was pretending to be surprised at what they were being told and keeping up the smoke and mirrors. Crocodile tears flowed here and there, but Bob and Judy Phillips toned down their Oscar-winning performance from the start of the day, making it a more subtle pantomime of frowning faces and wrung hands. Bravo!

As the sun set over Hangar 19, the AFOAs had collected enough information to instigate part two of the operation.

They chose a building on the base where they could put three doors on a wall that sat between both sides. Passengers would then pass through one of these doors to meet whoever had come to Vandenberg to take them home.

At their nightly meeting away from Hangar 19, where they could talk in private, the AFOAs carefully laid out plans to get the ball rolling. The sooner they did this, the sooner they could focus on the other point high on their agenda: how they would monitor most of the ninety people who had been on the A380 when it landed a few days ago.

The people the passengers suggested should come to Vandenberg to bring them home would be contacted as early as 7am the next morning, and the AFOA representatives would help them get to Vandenberg as quickly as possible.

Pacific International Airways offered free flights for anyone who had to fly internationally to California and on to Vandenberg to be reunited with their loved ones from the flight.

Not surprisingly, most of the people offered the free

flight decided to pass on the offer and fly another commercial airline altogether, at their own expense.

Funny, that.

But one wouldn't fly on a commercial airline anyway.

He could afford to fly private.

Charles Lewinson.

CHAPTER EIGHT

AFOA Flight 19 Investigation File 109
Passenger number: F19109
Name: Emily Collins
Age: 26 (at time of disappearance, January 17th, 2019)
Occupation: University student, Redondo Beach, Los Angeles, California, USA

EMILY COLLINS WOULD BE THE FIRST PERSON TO BE processed at the DONR building the next day.

Emily and Todd spent their last few minutes together privately in the marquee at Hangar 19.

They struggled immensely with not being able to be in each other's arms. Emily felt as if she was getting on the Saturn 1 spaceship and heading for the moon. She felt that when she left the gates of Vandenberg, everything would be different. And she was just about right. Her only true concerns at this time were twofold: not to lose what she had with Todd, and for the secret they all now held to remain a secret.

Talking in hushed tones in those last few moments, the

two devised a plan to ensure they would be back in touch with each other in the next couple of days.

"This just feels so surreal," Emily said in a near whisper.

Todd ached to lean closer and plant one straight on her beautiful lips, but took a deep breath and resisted.

"We're going to be okay, I promise you," he leaned in and whispered in her ear. "I'm so glad I met you, Em."

Emily's eyes began to mist, though she took a breath as if she were about to dive into a pool a hundred meters deep. That helped.

An AFOA representative appeared and said gingerly, "Emily, it's time for you to come with me."

Emily looked up at her. "I'm coming; just give me one more second."

Emily waited for the woman to turn her back, and the second she did, planted a quick and very light kiss straight on Todd's lips. Before he knew what to do, she'd already backed away just a few inches. She thought there was nothing wrong with a woman who'd bonded with a man over the last few days to give him a peck on the smackers.

Emily then whispered in his ear, "I love you, Todd."

Todd gulped, the statement catching him by complete surprise. It was the first time she'd ever said it to him.

And he knew he felt the same.

"I love you too," he said.

Emily arrived at the DONR door and took long, drawn-out breaths. Her mind was a mess of feelings and thoughts, all jumbled up around each other and making her anxious.

She'd only seen her father a couple of days ago. Not two and a half years ago, as it would have been for him now.

The Dave Collins of 2021 had lived with the loss of his

daughter stoically, though standing on the other side of the DONR door he felt excited and nervous.

He knew this mystery must have had a profound effect on his daughter. Losing two and a half years of your life was no small thing.

Then how about five years, Dave?

The AFOA representative who had brought Emily over to the DONR building gave passenger F19109 her last pep talk.

"You'll be fine, Emily. Remember everything we spoke about on the way over."

Emily recalled the counselor talking about a myriad of things, most of it psychobabble. She'd zoned out, nodding for a few seconds as she pretended she was listening. All she could think about was Todd.

She was sincere; Emily would give her that. Emily headed for the door.

The AFOA representative held out her hand.

It was time.

Emily reached for the handle and opened the door.

When she saw her father standing there, the smile on his face was just as big as it had been the last time she'd done this. Not that he would ever know.

"DAD!" Emily cried, running toward him.

* * *

AFOA Flight 19 Investigation File 120
Passenger number: F19120
Name: Michael E. Darcy
Age: 57 (at time of disappearance, January 17th, 2019)
Occupation: CEO, Darcon Industries, Los Angeles, California, USA

Darcy strode into the DONR building as if he owned the

place. You've gotta give it to the guy, he oozed arrogance as if it were an aftershave peddled by a world-famous football player and sold in a bottle the shape of a large penis.

He went through the motions with his group counselor, who, truth be told, could not wait for the imbecile to walk through the damn DONR door. He hoped for his own sake it really was one of no return. He never wanted to lay eyes on Michael E. Darcy again. The guy just blew off any suggestion of further counseling and guidance from anyone.

But what the counselor thought was a man just being an arrogant pig, was Darcy acting out his previous self.

The truth was, Darcy felt anything but arrogant and pig-headed. He knew all the ins and outs of what had happened to his business empire in the two years after the plane had disappeared. And if anything, it had brought him crashing to earth as if he were a hot-air balloon made of lead.

And then there was the thing in Missouri.

When he'd told Ross about it that first night they shared a drink, it had brought all the pain back to the surface.

Michael E. Darcy, circa 2021, knew there would be one place he would visit soon.

Piedmont, Missouri.

But for now, the ex-billionaire stared at the green door and wondered what else he could do to keep up the asshole act.

He looked back to his lead counselor and said, "Does it open itself?"

The counselor wondered if all those years at university had been worth it, just to end up dealing with an idiot like this.

Nope. But he still had a job to do.

He looked Darcy up and down. "You have to open it, Michael." He ensured his condescending tone was kept just beneath the surface.

Darcy, satisfied by the look on the guy's face that he'd maintained his false persona, spun on his heel and walked to the door.

As he held the knob, he'd forgotten who was coming to take him back to Los Angeles.

The one thing Ross, Melanie, Tony, Tammy, and Darcy had agreed after the plane landed was that the Beverly Hills Hotel would be their meeting point.

Darcy would go back there tonight if possible, and hope the bungalow he'd called home for some time would be available.

He opened the door and walked through.

The room on the other side was a hive of activity, with all three doors being used to release the passengers. Each door opened into its own zone, cordoned off with ropes and ending with the people standing there waiting for their passenger to walk down and greet them.

Counselors, security guards, and other AFOA representatives milled around to ensure the operation went as smoothly as it could. Two medics stood to one side looking bored: nothing had happened yet that required their expertise.

Michael closed the door, looked down to the end of his zone, and grinned. Ah, yes, that's who was here to take me home, he thought.

Tom Clark was one of his senior men at Darcon in Los Angeles.

Darcy liked him. He wondered if he weren't the most Scottish man he'd ever met. If the guy didn't shit haggis, Darcy would run down Sunset Boulevard without any pants on.

When he reached him, Darcy outstretched his hand and reached for Tom's.

"Aha, if it isn't my favorite kilt-wearing Scot," Darcy said with genuine enthusiasm.

Tom shook his hand, though Darcy could instantly see he looked uncomfortable. He was sweating and his face was ashen.

It's okay, Tom, Darcy thought. I know what's happened to my empire.

Tom went to say something, but the words came out muffled and hard to understand, even for a Scot.

"What did you say, Tom?" Darcy said.

Tom seemed to hesitate.

Then he looked at Darcy and shook his head.

"It's Joanne. Something's… She's in hospital."

Darcy felt a chill pass over him.

Joanne Darcy.

His wife.

CHAPTER NINE

AFOA Flight 19 Investigation File 128
Passenger number: F19128
Name: Tammy Hourigan
Age: 31 (at time of disappearance, January 17th, 2019)
Occupation: Housewife, Chesterfield, St. Louis, Missouri, USA

Tammy struggled, the last night at Vandenberg. Tony had spent has much time as he could with her under the circumstances, but he knew she was getting more and more overcome with the stress of what she'd face back home in Missouri.

Or, more to the point, *who* she would face.

Annie. Teflon Fanny.

Putting on a brave face is an easier thing said than done, reader.

Imagine having to face the person who had tried to kill you only days ago.

And that the person is your own flesh and blood—your sibling.

And had started shagging your husband one week after you originally disappeared a couple of years ago.

For Tammy, the poor girl, it didn't even end there.

She would now have to go through the whole rigmarole with her ex-husband, her parents, and most heartbreakingly, her children, all—over—again.

Then there would be the whispers and the undercurrent of suspicion, for people the world over would not believe her story. That would be hard to escape on the streets of Chesterfield, Missouri.

One minute she was twenty-eight weeks pregnant, the next, she wasn't.

Try explaining that.

But in time, that mystery would be her savior. People would remain focused more on that than what had really happened to Tammy.

＿ ＿ ＿

Tammy looked Tony over one more time.

It was mid-morning, and time for her turn to be processed for release at the DONR building.

Tony fought the urge to step a foot closer, put his arms around her, and hold her as long as he could.

The two lovebirds knew that at any moment, their time together would come to an end for now. She'd have to go home to Missouri and try to figure what she'd do and how, if possible, Tony could fit into the picture.

But there would be a few hurdles to jump over first.

Tony seldom showed any hint of emotion, especially in public, but as Tammy got the final call to leave Hangar 19, his feelings were running hot.

He took a deep breath. As she drew closer to him and they hugged as best as "friends" could without giving too much away, he whispered words in her ear that she would never forget.

"You still owe me $10 for the hamburger we had at the Burger Lounge."

Tammy laughed. It was just what she needed at that moment. "Add it to my bill," she said.

As she made the trip over to the DONR building, she felt good about one thing.

When her lead counselor asked her who she'd like to come to take her home, Tammy had nominated her best friend, Lee Lather.

It would be one of a few times that Tammy, like the others, would come close to tripping up. When the counselor asked immediately why she wouldn't want her husband, Brandon, to come to Vandenberg to take her home, Tammy had nearly come out and said, "Because we both know he is not my husband anymore."

But she caught herself. Tammy explained she'd rather Brandon stay home with her children, as they were her main priority right now. The counselor bought it. Besides— although she didn't say this—Tammy thought it would be better to spend the trip home with someone she really wanted to see. Her best friend. They'd have plenty to talk about.

Again.

AFOA Flight 19 Investigation File 116
Passenger number: F19116
Name: Tim Erwin
Age: 67 (at time of disappearance, Jan 17th, 2019)
Occupation: Scientist, NASA, retired, Alameda, California

Despite appearances, Tim was lonely most of the time at Hangar 19.

He talked and mingled with other passengers to the point where he felt as if he'd inherited some brand-new friends. David and Christine Windebank were kind to him, but it felt unusual forging new friendships without Sandra involved. Most of his friends had been *their* friends, not his alone. The retiree from Alameda was in uncharted waters, but he held it all together and rode out the days with relative ease.

He still thought of Sandra constantly; she'd been a part of his life for over four decades, and he missed her deeply.

Part of him wished she could, somehow, be at home waiting for him.

But the reality was as black as it was white.

His wife had died in 2024.

They were now back in 2021, where she'd disappeared two and a half years ago.

He'd just have to figure out the impossible.

How to control the artifact.

He'd rubbed his knee with it so often, he wondered if it would wear a hole in his pants. But he did this on purpose. He wanted everyone to think it was just another one of those inventions made to try and stave off the onset of arthritis.

Tim was starting to get itchy feet, stuck at Vandenberg. He looked forward to returning home and at least being back in more familiar surroundings, especially the workshop.

There, he'd try and figure things out.

How had the device enabled the plane to travel five years into the future, and then two and half years back?

And had his son, Ben, been mixed up in something to do with it before he and his family disappeared, possibly murdered?

Tim naturally nominated his daughter, Sarah, to come to Vandenberg to take him home.

What surprised Tim was that the AFOAs hadn't asked him about Sandra at all. When he disembarked from the A380, his mind was in a whirl about how he could keep all he knew from spewing out over the table to the investigators.

He decided, in his mildly panicked state, to only answer questions asked and not discuss anything else.

Fortunately, the AFOA investigator who questioned him seemed distracted by his phone for the whole duration of the interview, and asked his questions between tending to whatever the hell was going on with him.

What Tim didn't know was that the file in the hands of this distracted investigator wasn't his true file.

It was an altered copy.

But for now, Tim had a small bus to catch to get over to the DONR building. He had his daughter to meet, and then the four-plus-hour drive home back to his home in Alameda, San Francisco.

He wondered how the conversation would go with Sarah, and how bloody confusing it would be for him to organize all his thoughts into separate files for 2019, 2024, and now 2021. Geez Louise, Tim thought, he'd have to work hard on ensuring all the notes in his sixty-seven-year-old head were kept in order.

"This is it, Tim." His group counselor led him to DONR door number one, on the left. Tim took the last brief from the guy before he shook his hand, grabbed his daypack, and thanked him for all he'd done. And Tim was being genuine: the guy had been friendly and enthusiastic. Tim also felt a stab of regret that he couldn't have been more open with him; there was much more to this than the counselor may ever know.

As Tim arrived at the green door, he wondered what he'd do if he opened it and, by some miracle of God, the universe, or Doc Brown from *Back to the Future*, his wife Sandra was standing there waiting for him.

He grabbed the handle and then opened the door.

As he stepped through, he felt his heart in his throat.

Jesus Christ, it can't be.

Sarah. No.

It was Sean. Sarah's husband.

Oh no, Tim thought, now this is going to be tricky.

As Tim looked at his son-in-law, it quickly dawned on him that the Sean of 2021 knew jack shit about absolutely anything. Tim had talked to the 2024 version of Sean the day he boarded the plane, a few days ago now, but not this Sean.

As he reached Sean and put out his hand, he came up with an idea that would help him on the drive home.

"Tim, my God it is good to see you," Sean said.

Tim shook his hand and the two men stood awkwardly for a moment.

Tim looked around at all the people appearing to watch him, and knew he'd better get this show on the road pronto.

"Sean—very happy to see you too." He motioned for the man to head for the exit door. "No Sarah?"

Sean followed Tim out through the door and as it closed behind him, he said, "She wasn't feeling well, so she stayed home and will see you when we get there."

Tim shook his head before starting his plan of attack for the long drive home. "Okay, then. I'm feeling quite tired, you know," he said to Sean as they continued to walk toward his car. "I think I may have a snooze on the way home, if that's okay."

"No problem at all. I'm sure you've been through a lot. All good," Sean said.

As the two men reached the car about five minutes later, from the other side of the SUV, Tim asked, "So, what's wrong with Sarah?"

Sean answered, but Tim didn't hear him clearly.

He thought he'd said, "Don't know; they've both come down with something."

CHAPTER TEN

AFOA Flight 19 Investigation File 170
Passenger number: F19170
Name: Todd Roberts
Age: 27 (at time of disappearance, January 17th, 2019)
Occupation: Officer, California Highway Patrol, Los Angeles, California, USA

TODD SPENT THE LAST NIGHT AT VANDENBERG ALONE.

He already missed Em, and the words she'd said to him just before she left were running on an infinite loop in his head.

I love you.

Saying those three beautiful words to her in return was one of the most enjoyable things he'd ever done.

He'd never said that to anyone before.

And as he lay staring up at the ceiling, there was someone else he also couldn't stop thinking about.

When the counselor had asked him who he'd like to come to Vandenberg to pick him up, it was a no-brainer.

Kylie Roberts, his mother.

He'd not mentioned his father at all to the counselor. It all felt too surreal, too hard to comprehend. By all accounts, his father had been murdered by his half-brother a day or so ago.

He didn't look forward to going through all of this again. Especially with the kaleidoscope of thoughts dancing in his mind.

He longed for a good night's sleep, though he knew the chances of it were less than those of Elvis emerging from his secret bunker with a burger in his hand.

But he closed his eyes and, sometime later, sleep came to him with open arms.

Todd sipped on his lukewarm coffee. He'd passed on breakfast; he wasn't hungry.

As they took the few minutes' drive over to the DONR building, his counselor simply said, "How you feeling, Todd? All okay?"

Todd rustled up a half smile and lied: "Feeling good. Looking forward to getting out of here."

Well, the second part was true.

As he reached the building, he could feel the apprehension rising, and knew he'd have to work hard to keep it all together. But any time in the last twenty-four hours when he'd felt as if things were getting the better of him, he just thought about her, Emily Collins, and that made it better.

Todd's counselor led him through to the Hangar 19 side of the DONR room.

Like every other passenger who passed through the building over those few days, Todd felt a wave of déjà vu wash over him.

He wondered what was on the other side of the green door.

"Todd, you're now clear to walk to the door and go through," his counselor said.

"Thanks for everything," Todd said.

When Todd stepped through, he looked to the other side of the room and found his mother's familiar face.

Her smile and enthusiasm was like nothing he'd ever seen before. Receiving the crown for Miss Santa Monica High School 1981 on her prom night would have been close, though Todd had only heard about this in his father's stories.

He was glad to see her.

One obvious thing he could see, as he walked toward her, made his emotions roll as if on a spin cycle.

She was alone.

Jesus Christ. Todd gulped as he reached her.

His father was dead.

It had happened.

He didn't know how to feel.

"My darling." Kylie reached out for him and wrapped her arms around his waist, because he was too tall for her to put them around his shoulders. He was used to hugging his mother like this. It felt good regardless.

She was the one person apart from Emily he really wanted to see.

They stood there for a few moments and just held each other.

Todd knew that as far as his mom was concerned, this was the first time they'd seen each other in two and a half years.

He didn't want to say anything, other than that he'd missed her and was happy to see her. He didn't want to ask her about his father, even though he knew what he'd be told.

He knew he'd just have to wait patiently for the process to begin.

Counselors would materialize from nowhere and lead them into the small office in the corner of the room, where he would then be told.

Your father is dead, murdered in cold blood.

Todd closed his eyes and held onto his mother just a little bit longer. She felt quite at home just standing there hugging him.

As he was about to open his eyes, he felt a hand on his shoulder.

Right, he thought, a counselor ready to lead him into the corner office. His heart sank, though he knew it was time to get on with it.

"You're going to give him a complex if you don't let go of him," someone said. The voice was calm, measured, and hauntingly familiar.

The hairs on the back of Todd's neck sent a pulse of electricity almost down to his feet.

The counselor looked at him weirdly.

It took Todd a full second for his mind to register the unusual and extremely alarming fact that it wasn't a counselor standing there having just spoken to his mom.

It was Andrew Roberts, his dad.

AFOA Flight 19 Investigation File 136
Passenger number: F19136
Name: Melanie Lewinson
Age: 45 (at time of disappearance, January 17th, 2019)
Occupation: Lawyer, Johnson, Neville, and Tolls, Sydney, Australia.

Melanie and Ross had spent most of their time together at Hangar 19 with Tony and Tammy. Their conversations were always in hushed tones, and they didn't discuss 2024 or anything related to it. Before they left the A380, they'd agreed this would be the way it worked during their time at Vandenberg.

Besides, they all had their fair share of the other life they'd have to deal with before they could return to the one they wanted to actually lead.

Melanie, like Tammy, had a life-and-death situation to process.

For her, it was being nearly strangled by her husband in 2024 before the chauffeur stepped in and shot him. Melanie had no need to wonder why in the wedding ceremony there was the line, "till death do us part." Till I kill you do us part, was what Melanie thought it should have been changed to in their vows.

So when Melanie's counselor interviewed her and asked if it were her husband who she'd like to come and take her home, her thoughts were tearing themselves apart.

Her initial plan was to go home to Sydney, see her family, and tell them she was leaving Charles. The main reason would be his rampant infidelity, which she'd known about before boarding the flight back in 2019.

Now, after going through the painful experience of being lost for two and half years, she'd say she could not see her marriage continuing, knowing Charles had probably spent the thirty months rooting his way through his own grief. Which was true, of course.

Her family would rejoice and not even care about her reasons. They'd open a bottle of champagne and toast not only her return, but the end of her marriage to Charles Lewinson.

But at Vandenberg, she didn't want to show that

anything was out of the ordinary for her. Particularly, she didn't want her relationship with Ross to come out—yet. It was a confusing situation, and one she wanted to carefully work through to ensure she'd make it through intact to her desired endgame.

She was wealthy in her own right, but knew she could take Charles for half his fortune, especially given there was a hole in his will the size of the Sydney Harbour Bridge. He'd probably be as vulnerable when it came to divorcing him. She didn't even want half, anyway. Melanie would ask for a nominal amount, less than a quarter of his accrued wealth. That would be enough for her to plan what she wanted to do in the future.

So when the counselor pressed her for an answer—do you want your husband to come to Vandenberg to come and get you?—she answered yes.

Ross was beside himself when she told him this was her decision. She told him to focus on the big picture, that this was what she was doing, and not to worry about her safety.

Ross wasn't at all worried about her safety. He was shit-scared about her safety, period.

He told her there had to be another way. Surely she could just tell Charles at the DONR building that she wanted a divorce right there and then.

Melanie simply showed her million-watt smile, her jade-green eyes glowing as she did so, and told Ross she'd have everything under control.

She wouldn't.

Melanie looked at Ross one final time in the marquee at Hangar 19. He felt the fear rising up within him; it was hard to control. This would be the first time in a while that they would be apart. He did his best to hold himself together.

Ross was scheduled to leave Vandenberg in a couple of hours with Tony. They would both be transported by representatives of Pacific International Airways back to Los Angeles, where they would board a flight home to Sydney early the next morning.

Melanie found herself staring at Ross in those final moments.

She was not one for emotional farewells, but could feel the weight of the moment, and wondered how she was supposed to say goodbye without kissing him the way she wanted to.

"Are you going to be okay, you large hunk of spunk?" she said.

Ross stared at her green eyes just for a moment.

"Better when all this is over, my friend." Ross stepped forward and put his arms around her. He knew he had to make it look like they were nothing more than friends, so he kept it light and stepped back a moment later.

"Take care of yourself, huh?" he said.

"I will if you do," she replied with a nervous smile.

Like every other passenger who stepped onto the small bus from Hangar 19 in those few days, Melanie could feel her nervousness rise a notch the second it started to move. Deep in her body, she felt a weird sensation of loss, as if she and Ross were magnetically connected on some level. The further she traveled away from him, the weaker the connection became.

When she arrived at the DONR building, she started to feel lightheaded. She could not escape the vision of Charles on top of her with his hands around her throat, the warmth of the pavement rising up through her body, her lungs screaming in pain, and the darkness engulfing her vision. She tried her best to shake it off with a deep breath and a drink of water.

After saying her goodbyes to her counselor, Melanie looked at the green door. She felt as if it were a portal to another dimension. It pretty much was—the dimension called 2021. What lay beyond this door was the great unknown. Her last thought before she turned the handle was —should we have all boarded the A380 again?

It was too late now for regrets. Her time was up.

Melanie opened the door.

As she moved through, closing it behind her, she spotted him.

He stood bolt upright with a look on his face she could not decipher from the current distance.

Her feet didn't want to move. Neither did her legs.

But she knew she had to get through this. It had to begin to end.

She longed for Ross to be by her side, knowing that if he had his way, he'd knock Charles out without a moment's notice. But for now, she was alone.

The counselor standing behind Charles motioned for Melanie to come forward.

After what felt like a few seconds, Melanie knew she had to.

She took about three strides forward.

When she was halfway between the door and her husband, she could clearly see the look on his face.

Charles was not smiling. Nothing on his face registered happiness. His expression was—nothing.

As she took another step toward him, her heart felt as if it were taking a lunch break. She could feel her shortened breaths taking hold of her.

At this point, something finally registered on his rather unattractive face.

His lips curled into a snarl.

Seeing this, Melanie stopped, and for a split second, she wanted to make a 180-degree turn, run back through the DONR door, down the road, and straight into Ross's arms.

Instead, she fainted.

CHAPTER ELEVEN

Tammy and Lee smiled at each other as they raised their glasses and brought them together with a subtle chink.

After her first sip, Tammy hoped their flight back to St. Louis would be delayed a few hours. She'd be happy to sit at this bar with her best friend and drink this wine indefinitely.

Lee also ordered the Chianti-braised chicken tacos, which went down a treat with the glass of Pinot Grigio.

"So, what happened to you?" Lee spoke quietly, looking around to ensure their conversation was not being broadcast over the LAX public address system.

Tammy had thought long and hard about what she would tell Lee. She'd run it past Tony, who told her she was completely mad. Tony told her that if she spilled everything, it could bite her, them, and all the Flight Nineteeners on the ass. But Tony didn't know Lee like Tammy did. The two women had shared a long list of secrets way back to their early teenage years, when they had generally involved boys and cigarettes.

Lee sat patiently, sipping her wine and taking a bite of

her taco. She wiped her mouth and looked Tammy straight in the eye.

"There's much to tell you," Tammy whispered, "but for now, all I can tell you here…" She indicated she was talking about the airport. "…is that we have no idea how we disappeared for that amount of time."

This was actually true, for now.

Lee seemed to digest the words; she sat back and Tammy could tell she was deep in thought.

"And your pregnancy?" Lee looked down to Tammy's midsection before looking back into her eyes.

Tammy could tell Lee was unsure how to take all this in. She wanted to tell her everything there and then, but knew she couldn't risk it. She'd take Lee to her favorite park back home, the one with acres upon acres of open fields, where she'd know they were alone, with no one around them. Forest Park.

"I'll say more when we get home," Tammy said. "For now, all I want is to see Beth and Noah."

Lee swallowed her glass of wine awkwardly, putting it down a moment later and wiping her mouth. She avoided Tammy's gaze for a few seconds before eventually meeting her eyes.

"I've got a lot to tell you, too, Tam," Lee said, "especially involving the kids."

Tammy reached for Lee's hand. When she found it, she said simply, "Annie?"

Lee recoiled on her stool so hard that Tammy had to grab her to stop her from falling off.

Tammy stood and put her hand on Lee's shoulder.

She gave her a kiss on the head and put her arm around her before whispering in her ear, "I know about her and Brandon."

Lee looked up to her and with a puzzled look responded, "How?"

Tammy sat back and shook her head, smiling as she finished the last of her wine.

"I got my hands on some crystal balls," she said, smiling.

Tammy's flight to St. Louis was the sort every passenger wishes for. Smooth as a bowling ball. Everything went as it should, and the flight even had the obligatory crying baby. If not completely perfect, it was at least perfectly complete.

Hearing the sound of those little lungs crying out pulled hard on her heartstrings. She thought of her lost daughter, and wished Tony was nearby. The guy made her feel good.

When they arrived at Lee's car at the airport, Tammy could feel her nervousness rising. She had told Lee during the flight home that she wanted to go directly to her parents' place when they landed in St. Louis. Lee was against the idea, though Tammy said she wanted to get it over and done with as quickly as possible. Lee had already invited Tammy to stay with her, and she had accepted in a heartbeat.

The drive from Lambert International Airport to Tammy's parents' home in Chesterfield was filled with awkward silence.

All Tammy could think about was her two children and Tony. For most of the trip, she imagined a home she would share with him, with her two kids playing in the front yard. This image filled her heart with a warmth she desperately needed to quash the feeling of apprehension pushing its way through.

As Lee turned her car into Tammy's parents' place, Tammy could feel her head getting light and woozy.

Lee looked sideways at Tammy as the house came into view. "Are you ready for this?" she said.

Tammy swallowed hard. "Yep, let's do this."

Lee gave her a puzzled look. "You want me to come inside?" she said.

Through gritted teeth, Tammy said, "If you don't, you may need to call the police."

At the front door, with Lee a step or two behind, Tammy knocked and stood back.

She could hear footsteps coming down the hallway. "Phew, this is it," she said. Lee stood closer and put her hand on her shoulder.

The front door handle spun slowly, then opened slower than the main safe door at Fort Knox.

Bloody hell, how long does it take to open a door? Tammy thought. It was excruciating.

Then she realized why.

It was a little person who'd opened the door.

Beth.

When she finally got the door open all the way and saw Tammy, the look on her face was like she'd just been let into Disneyland, knowing she had the place all to herself.

Tammy's knees nearly buckled; she almost fell to them just over the threshold as she reached for her daughter and wrapped her arms around her. Beth started to cry before she said, "Mommy, I missed you," her sobs getting bigger by the second.

Tammy closed her eyes. She never wanted to let go of her daughter. After a few moments, she felt Lee tap her on her shoulder, but she ignored it.

Lee came closer and said, "Tammy, um…"

Tammy opened her eyes, her vision foggy for a second before it cleared. She looked to the end of the hallway, and her heart froze.

Tammy's sister stood looking back down the hallway at her, as if she'd seen a ghost.

Annie.

Teflon Fanny.

CHAPTER TWELVE

TIM DOZED IN AND OUT OF SLEEP FOR MOST OF THE trip back to San Francisco. When he was awake, avoided talking to Sean. He was afraid of making a mistake in his story or letting anything slip about where they'd come from. It was damned confusing to have come back to 2021.

Tim felt uneasy with how things had panned out. When he opened his eyes, all he could see was the last few moments with Sarah before he said his goodbyes. Sandra was a constant presence in his mind as well; he'd return home to an empty house and an empty heart. At least a half a dozen times during the trip home that day, he wished he'd never boarded the flight back in 2019, and they'd taken the boat back to San Francisco instead.

Opening his eyes, Tim realized he'd properly drifted off for a little while. He didn't mind; it killed the time. He sat up and saw the Oracle Arena, right next to the Nimitz Freeway in Oakland, only about fifteen minutes from home.

He looked at Sean and said genuinely, "Thanks for this; I really appreciate it."

Sean patted him on the shoulder. "No problem. I don't mind a bit of a country drive from time to time."

Tim ran his hands over his face. It was time to wake up and get it together, he thought. He looked over to Sean and patted him back. "I owe you one," Tim said.

A few minutes later, Sean's car arrived at the High Street Bridge, and as he drove it across, Tim could feel the sense of being home. Coming over this drawbridge felt like driving down his own driveway. Once he crossed it, he was on the island he'd called home for many decades. He loved Alameda nearly as much as he'd loved his wife and children.

The silence in the car for those last few moments was fine with Tim. At home, he could rest, catch up with his daughter, and start to dig deeper into what was going on with what he had in his backpack.

As Sean drove into the driveway, Tim felt the intoxicating feeling of déjà vu run through his body. The place was as neat as a pin; everything was in better condition than when he'd left back in 2024. Especially after the house had been trashed. He wondered if the children had spent the first few years of their original disappearance tending to its upkeep, and maybe as the years rolled on they had become more complacent. He wasn't sure, and frankly, he wondered why the hell these thoughts were running through his head just now.

As Sean's car came to a stop, Tim could have sworn he saw the curtain in the living room move a little. He turned to Sean. "Thank you again for coming to get me," he said.

Sean nodded. A second later, his phone beeped.

"You go ahead; let me just check this message, okay?" Sean said.

As Tim walked the steps up to his front door, he wondered why so many lights were on inside, if Sarah was unwell and in bed. He pushed the thought aside.

On the front porch, he looked to see if Sean was coming,

though his son-in-law was still in the car, deep in whatever was happening on his phone.

Sean saw Tim looking down to him, and a second later was out of his car, saying, "Sorry, I was just sending Sarah a message."

Tim was confused. Why would he send Sarah a message if she was inside resting?

As he watched Sean close the door of his car, he felt something really odd. Then, a rush of air, followed by the uncomfortable sense of someone standing behind him.

He turned around to see who it was.

The front door was wide open.

There she stood.

Tim wondered if he was still asleep, still somewhere on the trip home from Vandenberg, and this was one hell of a realistic dream.

But he was very much awake.

And Sandra, his wife, stood there looking at him. Her tears came a second later.

Dave held a crying Emily for what seemed like an eternity. It had been a long and often painful thirty months for the LAX tower supervisor.

At the two-year mark from the disappearance of Flight 19, Dave started to come to terms with the loss of his only daughter. It was a cruel blow. First his wife and son killed years ago, then this.

But he kept her picture stuck to the fridge, and every day would say good morning to her when he got up and had breakfast.

And every day, he wondered where the plane was.

Then his brother had called and told him the news that the plane had reappeared.

But like many others around the globe, the news that more than half the passengers were missing came as an even bigger shock.

The wait to find out if Emily was on the list had been harrowing.

The counselor told Dave his daughter would probably be suffering from stress and anxiety after what she'd been through, and to expect her to take some time to return to being the bright, bubbly, and well-adjusted young lady she was known to be back in 2019.

The conversation after leaving Vandenberg was sparse and frivolous. They'd spoken of nothing of importance—yet.

As Dave drove, he tweaked the volume on his car audio system in the hope some classic Foo Fighters might rouse Emily from her somber mood.

By the end of "Learn to Fly," it had seemed to break the ice just a little.

"This is so fucked," Emily said.

"You've been through something not many people have, honey."

As the highway twisted around the Refugio State Beach to the right, Emily said, "Can we stop for a break? How about the El Capitán beach?"

Dave wondered why his daughter wanted to stop only forty-five minutes into the trip home.

But who was he to argue? It was only another five minutes down the road. There was a general store there, and they could grab something to drink and eat.

Ten minutes later, Dave and Emily sat in the car overlooking the beach. It was quiet for this time of year. The waves folded and disintegrated into the sand, with the odd seagull darting around the place looking for morning tea.

Dave swigged from his bottle of America's favorite—Coca Cola—while Emily sipped her bottle of iced tea. Dave could have sworn the donut he'd just taken a bite out of was as old as José Francisco Ortega, whom the beach had been named after more than 200 years ago. After the second bite, he knew for sure, and decided the rest would go in the trash.

Emily kept sipping her drink and said little.

Dave was starting to get a bit curious as to why she'd wanted to stop so soon. There had to be a reason.

"What's going on in that beautiful head of yours, darlin'?" He doused the sentence with his best attempt at a Southern drawl. That normally got a smile from Emily.

Not today.

Wait, there it was—a smirk. Something, at least.

A second later, it was gone.

Emily turned to Dave, putting her bottle in the center console. She seemed to gather her thoughts, and as she drew in a deep breath of the warm sea air from outside the car, she avoided Dave's concerned gaze.

When she looked back to him, her eyes were watery.

"What is it, honey?"

Emily eventually met her father's eyes, and a second later Dave could see her bottom lip quivering just a little. Whatever was going on was really serious to her.

It took a few seconds more before she finally spoke.

"I … there's … so much … I want to tell you, but I…"

Dave was perplexed.

He reached over and put a fatherly hand on her shoulder.

Her tears came a few moments later.

"Oh, my," Dave said. He reached over and gave her a hug—awkwardly, since they were both in the front seats.

"We have plenty of time, babe." He sat back and studied her.

Emily wiped her eyes and took a deep breath.

"I'm not supposed to say anything." She knew she'd already put herself in harm's way even by saying this much.

Dave put his seatbelt on and started the car.

But now he was *really* curious. With another two hours in the car, he could take his time trying to get her to talk.

He was already concerned about what she'd been through and what it would mean for her. Something seemed wrong about the situation.

As his car drove out of the El Capitán beach car park, Emily would have to decide fairly quickly how much she actually trusted her father.

If he knew the whole truth, it could spell serious problems for every one of the ninety passengers on-board Darcy's flight of fancy.

Especially Darcy.

Be careful, Emily.

Once you say it, you can't take it back.

Todd's life may even depend on it.

And his half-brother's.

CHAPTER THIRTEEN

When the town car left Vandenberg's front gate, Michael E. Darcy was already on Tom's cell to his oldest son, Andrew.

They dispensed with the pleasantries and the "what the hell happened to you and the plane" conversation. Darcy wasn't interested.

Nor was Andrew, Darcy's oldest son—the only one of his children who still had a smidgen of respect for the ex-billionaire. The other three had practically disowned him.

Darcy hadn't spoken to his other son or two daughters for as long as he could remember. Probably a year, in reality, closer to two. And that was before 2019.

They'd count him as stone-cold dead now, two and a half years on. His reappearance would do nothing to thaw the ice in their feelings for him. They'd never understood their father and probably never would. In time, they'd eventually realize no one is perfect—and their father was a good ten tons short of perfect—but that Darcy had a heart, even if few people ever saw it beating.

Andrew, on the other hand, had always kept in touch

with his father and didn't care that their relationship had put him offside with his siblings.

Andrew was a multimillionaire in his own right, though his start had come thanks to his father. But Darcy never lorded it over him, or even reminded him of it. He was just happy Andrew had made his own way, even with a loan that to this day he'd never asked him to pay back. What's a billionaire going to do with a million dollars, anyway?

"What happened to her, son?" Darcy's tone was genuine.

The few seconds' delay between two continents allowed him to take a quick glance at the outside world. The dry Californian surrounds of Santa Barbara offered little in return.

"Mum had a stroke, a really bad one." Andrew sounded like he was on the helm on the *Steve Irwin*, the Sea Shepherd ship, fighting Japanese whalers in Antarctic waters.

"Hold on, Drew." Darcy held the phone away from his mouth and looked over to Tom in the back seat of the SUV. "Get me on the next flight to Australia. I don't care where I'm bloody sitting; just do it."

Tom reached forward to grab the cell phone the driver was already handing back to him.

"Sorry, Drew," Darcy said.

Having heard what he'd just said, Andrew had no need to ask when his father could get there. "That's fine, Dad. As I said, she's had a stroke. A hemorrhagic stroke, the doctors said. It's good that you're coming; she's not looking good."

What in God's name is happening here? thought Darcy.

He closed his eyes, curling his left hand in a fist and tapping his forehead with it.

This had not happened when we reappeared in 2024.

This had not happened when we reappeared in 2024.

The thought was stuck in a loop at the front of his mind.

Jesus: *this had not happened when we reappeared in 2024.*

Why now?

He'd never stopped loving his wife, Joanne.

Their relationship was so bad even Dr. Phil wouldn't be able to help. They lived separate lives on separate continents. Shit. Marriage experts the world over would ask—what was the bloody point? Michael? Joanne?

Because neither one of them wanted to pull the pin.

And living those completely separate lives ensured they somehow kept the fossilized remains of their once-happy marriage on barely functioning life support.

In 2024, Darcy had been beyond angry with his wife for what she'd done to his business empire, but realized soon after it was pure revenge. He'd somehow forgiven her for this; he'd come full circle and wanted to do good. And the first thing he needed to do, he knew, was lose some emotional baggage. Forgiving her for destroying his fortune had been the first step.

Now, there's a man with a fresh perspective on life—a billionaire stripped of his wealth who still forgives the person who orchestrated it. Wow.

At that moment, he was completely lost in his thoughts.

He could hear Tom booking a flight. Good.

Andrew was saying plenty, but sounded like he'd moved from the helm of the *Steve Irwin* to the front of a train hurtling through the frozen landscape of Siberia.

Something caught Darcy's attention in what his son had just said.

"What did you just say? Sorry, mate, this line is crap." Darcy was nearly shouting.

A couple of seconds later, Andrew repeated his last line.

It sent Darcy's blood nearly as cold as that Siberian landscape it sounded like Andrew was calling from.

"I said Mum had the stroke…" Hell, Darcy thought, this

line is terrible; I can barely hear him. "…seconds after hearing the news."

Darcy peered at the phone screen as if it would give him the answer he wanted. It did not. He put the phone back to his ear.

"Hearing what news?" As the words came from his mouth, he understood and felt ill.

The news—his plane had reappeared.

"I'm on my way, Drew." Tom gave him the thumbs up. The flight was booked. He held up four fingers.

"I'm on a flight in four hours," Darcy clarified.

"Hurry, Dad," Andrew shouted. "She's on borrowed time."

"Sir," the head nurse said again, this time more vigorously, "I need you to calm down. This is not helping."

The man looked down at her sitting behind the counter as if he wanted to squash her like a bug.

That might prove a little difficult, considering she was probably double his weight.

"But you don't get it, err…" He peered through squinted eyes at her name tag, and it took a couple of seconds for him to read it properly. "…Lizzy. I have to be somewhere else, thousands of miles away."

Lizzy, the head nurse at the Lompoc Valley Medical Center, took a deep breath. She'd dealt with her fair share of unhappy "customers," as management had brainwashed all hospital staff into calling them years ago, but this one was currently vying to make it into the top ten assholes of all time.

As she went to say something, he slammed his fist on the counter and shouted, "Who is in goddamned charge here?"

Lizzy turned to the hospital security guard standing at the entrance area and telepathically asked for his help.

He was already walking toward her and the "customer."

When the guard arrived, he sized the guy up and wondered how easy it would be to give him a Tombstone Piledriver. Big Jim was a huge WWE fan, and his favorite wrestler, the Undertaker, would dispose of opponents with this move to finish them off for good.

Big Jim was also Lizzy's little brother. Probably not a good idea for a "customer" to upset her. If Lizzy was double his weight, Jim was triple. And most of it was muscle.

When the customer saw Big Jim giving him the once over, he recoiled a little, though he'd lost none of his venom.

"Do you know who I am?"

Lord, not that line.

Charles, you're not in Australia anymore. You're in regional California, tens of thousands of miles from where pulling out your overinflated ego might occasionally get results.

Not here.

Big Jim glanced to Lizzy and they shared a "you've gotta to be kidding" look. Jim was moving forward to ask the guy to step away from the counter when a doctor about ten feet away said quietly, "It's okay. Jim, Liz." She walked to the counter and looked Charles Lewinson up and down. Phew, the Aussies sure know how to choose awful aftershave, she thought.

"Charles … Lewinson, right?"

The Australian millionaire looked at the doctor without losing any of his attitude.

"Mila Stibrova." She offered her hand even though she didn't really want to. "I'm your wife's doctor, and I'm tending to her at present."

Charles ignored her hand. This did not go unnoticed.

Through gritted teeth, in a condescending tone and without any preamble, he told Dr. Stibrova, "I'm going to say this one more time. I. Need. To. Be. Back. In. Australia. Now."

Mila looked to Big Jim, too. He knew what she was thinking: stay on this guy's ass until he's out our front door.

The doctor gathered her thoughts as she checked out the guy's shoes.

If my husband came home wearing those, she thought, I'd divorce him in five seconds flat. They were like women's shoes.

"Charles, your wife passed out only a few hours ago. She is exhausted, out of sorts, and feels quite ill at present."

Before Charles could say a word, she raised her hand swiftly and said, "And to be honest, I do not feel comfortable with her leaving right now because you have a prior engagement."

Charles was about to launch into a tirade that could have resulted in Big Jim knocking him out, but thought the better of it. He stepped back and raised his hand.

"Okay, I get it, she needs to stay here." He looked at all three staff and wondered how much it would cost to buy the hospital so he could fire them all. "But I can't. I need to go," he said.

No one said anything. Eventually, after about five uncomfortable seconds, Dr. Stibrova said, "As you wish. If you call in, we can keep you posted as to her progress."

Charles was about to walk off, much to their delight, but stopped and asked the doctor, "Can I see her one more time before I leave?"

"Okay, though she may be asleep at the moment," Dr. Stibrova said. "I'm not sure."

Charles nodded before watching the doctor turn on her heel and walk off down the hallway toward Melanie's room.

He followed a few steps behind.

Big Jim motioned to his sister that he should go and keep an eye on things. Lizzy shook her head. "We'll know soon enough if you're needed," she told the man mountain.

Charles arrived at Melanie's room a few moments later, and could see immediately that she was sound asleep.

He wanted to slap her, and may have, if that smart-ass doctor hadn't been in the room with him. He'd come all this way to get her on his private jet, only for her to pass out and, as he put it, "fuck me around to no end."

Dr. Stibrova studied Charles carefully as she stood on the other side of Melanie's bed. She wondered what in God's name this gorgeous woman saw in such an asshole of a man. She let the thought drift away as Charles stared at his unconscious wife and seemed to get angrier by the second. His face reddened and he seemed to be sweating.

He wondered what the doctor would be like in bed. He had a thing for uniforms, and would ask his regular escort back home to put on a hospital doctor's uniform next time he employed her services.

"Well, I guess there's nothing I can say to her right now, huh?"

Dr. Stibrova took pleasure in saying, "I guess not, Mr. Lewinson. I'll make sure I inform your wife of your departure when she wakes up."

Charles grunted, and before he was halfway out the door, he muttered, "You do that."

In his head, he finished the sentence with, "You dumb-ass bitch."

Dr. Stibrova waited about thirty seconds before she glanced at her watch.

Then she walked to the door and stuck her head into the hallway. Big Jim saw her and gave her the nod. He grinned a moment later.

Charles had left the hospital through the main entrance. His town car was out the front, and he got in the back seat before it sped off.

Dr. Stibrova went back into Melanie's room.

She tapped her patient's toe lightly through the sheet.

Melanie opened her eyes.

The doctor said, "He's gone. I've double-checked. All clear."

Melanie took a deep breath and wiped her forehead.

Dr. Stibrova could see the wave of relief wash over her.

"The things you do to get out of a flight," Melanie said.

Todd had felt as if he were experiencing death. He felt outside his body, looking down at himself.

His father had his arms around him, and Todd was doing his best to find joy in seeing him.

It was difficult, to say the least.

In 2024, his mother had spent a couple of years mourning the loss of her beloved husband, then met someone else.

Todd felt as if things were starting to fall into place.

For him, it was Emily. For Kylie, it was Dave.

Then there was his little half-brother.

Todd had blasted his brains onto the wall of an underpass, a second before he'd tried to pull out a picture of the man who now had his arms around Todd.

As he pulled back from his dad and looked to his mother, it dawned on him.

In 2021, his half-brother would still be alive.

"Let's get this big guy home," Andrew said to his wife.

On the drive to Santa Monica, the conversation was constant, though awkward most of the time. Kylie seemed to want to talk Todd's head off, though Todd felt like looking out the window and just getting his thoughts in order. "Darling, let Todd just get used to his surroundings," Andrew said. "We need to give him time."

Todd studied the back of his dad's head and thought.

Time.

What a pain in the ass it is.

Especially when you mess with it.

And we've messed with it twice now.

He let out a chuckle and mustered his strength to say, "It's all good; I'm just getting my head around everything."

The rest of the two-and-a-half-hour drive home was uneventful for Todd Roberts. He drifted in and out of sleep for most of the second half, and from time to time could hear his parents talking in hushed tones. He tried to make out what they were saying, but he struggled over the noise of his dad's Ford F250 and the busy Highway 101 outside.

When they eventually pulled into the driveway of his parents' Santa Monica home, Todd had his turn at feeling déjà vu. Most of the Flight 19 ninety knew it well by now.

As they all got out of the pickup, Todd walked to the end of the driveway and stood there looking around. His mother was already at the front door, with her husband a few feet behind, when they realized Todd was not with them.

"You go in," Andrew told Kylie. "I'll go and talk to him." Kylie squeezed Andrew's hand and ventured inside. She had a big meal to prepare for her son's homecoming.

From the corner of his eye, Todd saw his father stepping off the patio and heading down the path.

Good.

He hoped by walking to the end of the driveway, he'd lure his old man to come investigate what he was doing. Todd expected his mom would be more focused on making a special dinner for him. He was right on both counts.

As Andrew came within a few meters, Todd looked over to him. The first thing his father noticed was the blank expression on Todd's face. Or was it something else?

Todd turned away from him and took in a long, panoramic view of the street, the sky, and anywhere else he could look and not see his father.

Andrew stood and wondered what Todd was up to before he took another stride closer and said quietly, "Everything alright, son?"

Todd looked down at the cracks in the sidewalk directly in front of his parents' driveway. He remembered them from his childhood. One of the cracks would always cause him havoc when he skateboarded down the driveway hoping to build up enough momentum to fly onto the road and down the street. The thought made his mind segue instantly into another one, about someone else's childhood.

He looked at his father.

Todd's expression was no longer empty; he was angry.

The son shifted his feet, as if whatever was going on his head was causing him to unbalance.

That it was.

Andrew could feel apprehension rising in his own body. Something was not right with his son.

The two men stood on the driveway and just stared at each other.

Andrew, starting to get concerned, said, "Are you okay? What is it?"

Todd stepped a foot closer.

From nowhere, he threw the mother of all punches.

Andrew went flying to the ground, and a second later, Todd heard his mom's screams coming from the living-room window.

Todd cleared the vision from his mind.

The two men continued to look at each other.

Andrew was about to repeat his question, but Todd then actually did step a foot closer.

No fists were raised. Todd needed only quiet words to knock his father out.

"I know—about Jason."

CHAPTER FOURTEEN

Tim's heart froze.

He stared at his wife as if she were an alien from another planet.

His brain had completely shut down.

Nothing was making sense.

Sean came up from the car and hit an invisible wall at the top of the patio.

He wondered what was going on and then realized it had been two and a half years since husband and wife had seen each other.

Incorrect, Sean. That was true for one of them, but the other had buried Sandra six months or so ago.

"Honey?"

Tim could see his wife's lips move just for a second, though his felt like they had changed into cast iron, as had his legs.

Sandra stepped forward and her emotions overcame her. She wept and shook, her whole body convulsing from head to toe.

Don't worry, Tim, she's not having a heart attack.

He broke down like he'd never done before. The first and

until now only time had been at her funeral. Until then, Tim had never shown raw emotion like that to anyone.

He lifted his arms, and as he did so, she almost ran into him and wrapped her little arms around his body.

They cried for a long while.

Tim didn't want to let go.

When her eyes met his, he said, "You'll never know what it means to me to see you right now."

Sandra said, "ditto."

They eventually parted and ventured off inside, much to the relief of Sean, who'd wondered if he'd be standing there forever.

As they walked down the hallway toward the kitchen, Tim surveyed his surroundings. His emotions had bamboozled him, but another part of his mind was on high alert.

He took in every square inch of his home. It appeared pristine, as it had before they'd left for Hawaii all those years ago.

There was no evidence of the carnage from when they'd come home from Vandenberg in 2024.

When they got to the kitchen, Tim couldn't help but stare at Sandra.

His wife. Alive and well.

What. The. Hell.

"Cuppa, honey?"

Tim sat on a stool and felt the purest joy overcome him. It started at his toes and ended up at the tips of every hair on his head.

He pinched himself a moment later.

Nope—this was not a dream.

Maybe this was his idea of heaven and he was dead?

Sandra stared at him.

"Was that a yes?"

Tim laughed and said, "That would be lovely, darling."

The small talk between Sean, Sandra, and Tim went on for what seemed like an hour.

They talked about everything and anything, none of it serious, mostly about other people, world events, and things Tim didn't really care about, but the others thought he'd be sorry to have missed.

Sean eventually pulled up stumps and told Tim and Sandra it was time for him to go home and tend to Sarah.

"It's good to see you home," Sean said as he stood up and reached over to shake his father-in-law's hand.

Tim pulled himself up, and in a rare show of affection, embraced his son-in-law. "Thank you, Sean," Tim said, leaving the sentence open to imply "for everything."

When Sandra closed the front door, Tim took her into their living room, where they sat together on the main sofa.

Tim reached out for Sandra's hand, which she gladly handed over. The couple sat in silence for a few moments as the shock of their reunion slowly dissipated for them both.

"I thought I'd never see you again." Sandra did her best to hold back her tears, to no avail.

Tim handed her a tissue. "Darling, you'll never know how true that was for me too." He pictured her coffin being lowered into the ground only six months ago.

The disappearance of Ben and his family in late 2020, only seven months earlier, had been brought up soon after Sandra handed Tim his cup of tea in the kitchen a little while ago.

Sean filled in most of the details, as Sandra couldn't talk about it without crying uncontrollably. She sat there and cried through the whole story.

Tim knew exactly what had happened to Ben and his family, because he'd been told about it before in 2024. But he knew he had to act surprised, for as far as his wife and son-in-law were concerned, this should have been the first time he'd heard about it. Tim pulled the act off well, and believed they would suspect nothing.

Tim's mind was like the front wheel of a Formula One car on the first lap of a race.

To say it was spinning hard was an understatement.

He was trying to figure out the one thing you probably are right now, reader.

How.

Is.

She.

Here?

Tim took a deep breath before standing up and heading for the drinks buffet. He opened the little door and reached in for his bourbon. Maybe this would help slow his spinning mind so he could figure it out.

He didn't want to say anything to his beloved wife that would give anything away.

"Darling, you died six months ago after we'd traveled five years into the future, but then I traveled two and a half years back and you're alive again."

Certainly not that.

As Tim's bourbon passed through his lips, he welcomed the slight burn of the alcohol in his throat as it washed through his senses and relaxed him.

He knew tonight, this bottle might end up in the trash, empty. And he'd be right, for what Sandra was about to tell him would make him want to down the whole thing on the spot. Right now, it was half full.

He offered his wife a drink, and she asked for a nip of her favorite—Christian Brothers Cream Sherry. He poured her a generous glass, and after handing it to her, sat back down on the couch with his bourbon.

After about ten minutes of chitter-chatter, Tim could feel the bourbon working its way through his mind. It was a welcome feeling, as it stopped the wheel spinning almost completely, giving him the opportunity to think.

As Sandra finished her sherry and put it on the side table, Tim finally started to figure out a way to ask the question that had been burning him way more than the bourbon had his throat.

They'd talked about many, many things over the course of the evening.

But the one thing Tim still could not figure out was how Sandra had come to be alive when he returned to 2021.

None of it made sense.

She'd been on the plane with him when it landed in 2024, and had died there.

How had she magically come back from the dead?

He couldn't go to bed without the answer.

Then the penny dropped.

Why had it taken him all night to finally realize it?

He cursed himself for not thinking of it sooner.

"Imagine if you'd been on the plane with me," he said to Sandra.

She seemed to think about what he'd said for a moment.

"I know, darling. I would have been, if I weren't being such a doting mother." She smiled before moving over and putting her head in Tim's lap. "You can thank your son and his love of tequila and Mexican food."

He thought about what she'd just said. Nothing was adding up.

"With everything we've talked about tonight, I'm not sure what you mean."

Sandra tilted her head backwards. Now she was looking up at him, and could see the slightly confused, very alarmed look on his face.

"You okay?" she said.

Tim's gaze was a thousand miles away.

Actually, it was about 2,300 miles away.

In Hawaii.

Where they were before they boarded the flight.

"After the couple of bourbons I've just had, I'm a little confused."

Sandra rolled her eyes, taking a deep breath before reaching up and stroking the side of Tim's face. It felt good.

"Oh, my poor man," she said. "It's getting late; we'd better be off to bed."

Tim sat there. He didn't want to move until he knew what he wanted to know.

"Someone wasn't feeling well in Hawaii?" he eventually said.

Sandra closed her eyes, and Tim could see her demeanor change within a few seconds.

She wiped a tear from her left eye a moment later, though her eyes remained closed.

Without opening them, she finally brought up the courage to move beyond the heart-crushing emotion and say his name. She missed him dearly.

"Ben," she whispered.

Tim looked down at her and repeated his name.

Sandra then opened her eyes, and realized Tim had completely forgotten the whole event. It must have been everything he'd been through since being missing.

"Darling, Ben was ill."

Tim still had the blankest of looks on his face.

What Sandra said next made her husband once again want to down the rest of the bottle of bourbon in one go.

"He begged me to stay in Hawaii until the next day and help him recover. "So I did."

"I never get sick of business class," said Tony.

"I do," said Ross.

The two Pacific International Airways pilots sat in their individual pods in business class, but with the little divider open between them so they could talk.

"Why?" Tony asked.

"Because there is such a thing as first class."

"Sorry, Borry." Tony gave Ross his signature Zoolander look. Being Ben Stiller's doppelganger, Tony pulled the perfect pout. Even Stiller himself would be impressed for sure. "I forgot you have a silver spoon stuck permanently up your…"

"Drinks, you two?" The flight attendant appeared from nowhere, startling the men. Both looked up to her at the same moment, and all three Pacific International Airways employees said variations of "Well, I'll be," all at once.

"Mandy Clarke! What a small world," Ross said, grinning at the flight attendant. "It's been forever."

Tony turned to Ross and then to Mandy. "You're looking the goods, Mands." Being the closest to her, he reached up and shook her hand lightly. "How's the world's number one bluenose going?"

Tony, Ross, and Mandy had known each other for many years. They'd worked in the same crew, zigzagging the world over dozens of times. Tony knew Mandy was one of Birmingham City Football Club's biggest fans, hence the bluenose label.

"Well, haven't you two been on quite the journey?" Mandy said in her sharp English accent.

"All in a day's work, huh?" Ross said.

Mandy checked around the cabin before peering back down at them. "I'm amazed how well you're both holding up." She heard a familiar ding nearby, signaling she'd have to go and see what a passenger wanted.

Shrugging her shoulders, she said, "You look like you've been through this all before. I'll be back shortly with your first round."

Ross and Tony waited for Mandy to walk off before looking at each other with a knowing smile. "Been through it all before, eh? You could say that," Ross said.

Ross spent most of the flight dozing in and out of sleep. As they neared Australia, he felt he'd rested enough to avoid the gift long-haul flights had bestowed on human beings —jet lag.

He couldn't stop thinking about Melanie, or worrying about her. He longed for her to make contact and tell him she was safe.

He'd be relieved to know part one was done and dusted, gone off without a hitch, unless you counted Charles throwing a hissy fit at a regional hospital before storming out.

But Melanie had been expecting that, and would have been more surprised if it hadn't happened.

So all in all, part one had gone okay.

Melanie decided only a few moments before they parted at Vandenberg to tell Ross what she intended to do at the DONR building. She didn't want him to worry, which was why she didn't want him to know, but when she saw the look on his face, she knew it would give him a little hope and put his mind at ease.

She had no intention of boarding her husband's private jet.

No way in hell.

She hadn't even made it to the tarmac last time, so why would she risk fifteen-plus hours alone with him on a private plane?

Of course, there were the pilots and a flight attendant, but they wouldn't be with her every minute of the flight home.

So she faked passing out.

That had gone okay, too, save for crashing to the floor just a little harder than she'd rehearsed in her head.

It was hard to pretend to be passed out when your left hip was throbbing from throwing yourself to the ground.

She kept her eyes closed and flailed a bit when she was finally put onto a stretcher. All the time, she heard not one word from her husband. Not once did he ask if she would be okay, ask a medic if it were serious, or offer any word of support. Husband of the year, Charles—not.

When she arrived at the Lompoc Medical Center, she was feeling quite off, which was good, for it made the con just that little bit easier.

When she opened her eyes at one point, she realized she was alone in her room with Dr. Stibrova.

She asked if she could have a private word with her, and if she could ensure her husband would not walk in at any moment.

When Dr. Stibrova told Melanie her husband had grumbled off to get a sandwich and coffee, Melanie knew she had a couple of valuable minutes in which to enlist the doctor's help.

Melanie told her Charles was a violent sociopath with a history of verbal, mental, and very physical abuse toward her. She told her straight up what she had wanted to do: fake it so she didn't have to get on his private jet. Melanie told her she genuinely feared for her life. And as we know, she had the clear-cut hindsight to back that up.

Dr. Stibrova took only a few seconds to decide, thank God, that Melanie was telling the truth, and agreed to help.

Ross would find out within forty-eight hours that

Melanie was alive and well, and safe in California. He knew she would head back to Sydney as soon as she could, to get part two of her plan rolling.

Ross looked over to Tony. He was watching an old movie, with headphones, chuckling occasionally but keeping his eyes glued to the screen.

For a moment, Ross wondered what the movie was. Then he recognized it. Ah, *Mrs. Doubtfire*, Ross thought, a Robin Williams classic. Whenever Ross saw that one, it took him home quicker than the Concorde on steroids. His mum was the spitting image of Mrs. Doubtfire, and he wondered if the character had actually been based on her.

Memories of her came flooding back to him. In this current time, 2021, his mother had died only six months ago. Why couldn't Darcy's flight have come back three years earlier, not two and a half?

Ross knew if he'd been there, his mother wouldn't have killed herself. He would have stopped it from happening. He wouldn't have been able to save his apartment or most of the things in it, but at least he could have saved her life.

But in time travel, circumstances and timelines get thrown into chaos.

Six months ago, in 2024, Ross had cursed his mum's two brothers, who hadn't given a rat's ass about her while she was dealing with her son's disappearance.

Eddie and Charlie were the names of Ross's two uncles. Eddie was the oldest, and the one he'd spoken to six months earlier. Both were assholes.

Eddie had come up with plenty of creative excuses about why neither of them had been there for his mother.

Ross thought they were the lamest excuses he'd ever heard in his life.

The bottom line was, they didn't give a shit about their sister.

But they did give a shit about money. Funny that. Enough to drive the twenty-four hours from Townsville to Sydney to grab anything of value from her flat, some of which was his.

Then, Ross had an epiphany.

It had taken the two brothers nearly six months to get around to the trip down to Sydney.

Six months.

Tammy could have kept her arms around Beth forever. She had no intention of moving, though she knew Annie was still staring at her from the other end of the hall.

When Tammy had closed her eyes and opened them again, her heart nearly stopped.

Noah, her son, was standing there next to the sister who had pointed a gun at her.

Tammy would never know that she was two and a half seconds away from death that day. That's how long she would have had if the security guard at Vandenberg hadn't pulled his trigger and killed Teflon Fanny in 2024.

The guy's old man had owned and operated a firing range; he'd practically grown up there.

He could shoot a bee's dick off from 500 meters away.

So a woman standing less than 25 meters away with a head slightly larger than a bee's appendage was no problem.

He'd saved Tammy's life.

But now, Annie was alive again.

Tammy called out to her son, ignoring her mole of a sister for a moment.

"Noah, honey, come to me," she said, with tears welling in her eyes.

Noah didn't budge.

Annie said something Tammy and Lee couldn't hear.

Noah slipped behind her and darted back into the kitchen of his grandparents' house.

Tammy and Lee shared a puzzled look.

Then Tammy rose to her feet. Beth stayed glued to her.

The two women stared at Annie.

"Hello, Annie," Tammy finally said a few seconds later.

"Tammy," Annie said quietly, and with every ounce of sarcasm she could find, "you've had quite the trip."

Tammy took a long, deep breath through her nose.

Lee was about to mutter something to her, but Tammy said, "And you've been quite the slut, Annie."

Ouch. Score one for team Tammy.

"And where is your lovely husband?" Tammy added.

As she asked the question, her parents appeared from the dining area, just near Annie.

"He's not here. He's home doing stuff," Annie said coolly.

"Tammy, come in," her mother said, stepping into the hallway and walking toward her.

When she reached her at the front door, she gave her an awkward hug. Her mom then turned to Lee and said, "Nice to see you; thank you for bringing Tammy back."

Lee had never liked Patricia Sanders, for the same reasons as Tammy. But she could feel the sincerity in her tone, and thought it was a nice thing.

"It's the least I could do," she said, her voice giving some kindness in return.

Tammy's father stepped into the hallway.

"We never thought we'd see you again, Tammy." Her father sounded disappointed she'd returned.

Lee picked up on the innuendo. She wasn't surprised; she knew Tammy's parents had never been the type to show an ounce of emotional intelligence.

They said what they thought.

And most of the time, not in a good way.

Lee could see why Tammy had always wanted to leave as soon as she was old enough. The stories she'd heard from her while they were growing up made her skin crawl. The Sanders weren't violent or nasty people; they just had a life-long focus on a guy who lived over two thousand years ago, and his father. Lee wondered why they hadn't just moved into their church and lived there full-time. That's where their hearts were, not with their children.

Bartholomew Sanders ushered everyone into the living room.

If you Google-imaged the word *awkward*, the first result would surely be of Lee, Annie, Tammy, and her parents sitting in the living room of the Sanders' Chesterfield home.

If a pin had dropped at that moment, it would have sounded like a car backfiring.

Tammy could hear the sound of a video game in the distance. She guessed the kids probably spent most of their time in front of the television these days.

Bartholomew and Patricia Sanders sat staring at Tammy as if she were the devil herself.

Or a ghost. Take your pick.

Tammy returned their stare, but couldn't help her eyes being drawn back to her sister.

Tammy decided to try and make conversation with anyone in the room who cared. "So, what's been happening while I've been away?"

Patricia Sanders shifted uncomfortably in her chair, picked at a piece of fluff on her woolly jumper, and said, "We've been praying for your return."

"And what about you, Dad," Tammy said. "What have you been up to?"

Lee wondered what planet she'd just landed on.

Bloody hell, she thought, could this get any more

uncomfortable?

Bartholomew Sanders sat forward, his arms still crossed against his chest.

"It's been quite the hard time," he said to Tammy quietly.

"It's been very difficult for us all since you've been gone." Then he ventured a look to Annie, this time raising a piss-weak smile. "It's been hard on Brandon too."

Tammy's glance at Lee said, "What are we doing here?" Then she turned and shot Annie a look that could kill.

"Yep, I know one thing that's been hard for Brandon," she said.

Lee stifled a laugh, but couldn't help but let out a little grin. She put her hand to her mouth and hid it from view.

Tammy had always been the queen of the one-liners.

If she could bottle her wit, she could make a fortune selling it online.

Annie would never be as quick-witted as her sister. The quip went straight over her head before it disappeared into the dark-paneled walls of the Sanders home.

Patricia straightened up and gave Tammy a disapproving glare. She didn't really get what Tammy had just said, but knew it was disrespectful.

"Brandon was distraught when you were gone," she said with an air of authority. "Thankfully, your sister was there to take care of him during his darkest hour."

Tammy rolled her eyes and wondered if her mother would ever wake up and smell the roses. They'd have to be wedged into the pages of her Bible, she thought.

Although she knew the answer to her next question, she still needed to ask to imply she knew nothing of the subject.

"What about all my belongings?" she asked her mother.

Bart Sanders showed the skerrick of chivalry he possessed by stepping in and sticking up for his wife.

"You had a lot of stuff, you know," he said, sitting

forward and showing more attitude than before.

Here we go, Tammy thought, the lies are now flowing freely. She instantly looked forward to being back at Lee's apartment with a glass of chilled Pinot Grigio in her hand. She just wished she could take Beth and Noah with her.

Before her father could say any more, Tammy spat back, "So it's all gone, I guess?"

Annie scoffed. Lee took her turn at giving her a dirty look. As it happened, things *could* get more awkward. Tammy turned to her twin sister as well, and snarled, "You got something to say, Teflon?"

Score two for Tammy.

But she'd pay for it.

Annie had heard the nickname years before. She knew most kids in college called her this behind her back. She hated it with a passion. And she knew Tammy knew it.

The room was silent for the ten seconds it took Annie to formulate a good enough response.

"Well, at least I got to keep the one thing you really want." Annie's tone was soaked in venom. She looked in the direction of the sound of the video game coming from the spare room.

Tammy jumped from her chair and stood bolt upright.

Oh hell, Lee thought, it's going to be on.

Lee, to her credit, sprang from her seat and stepped in front of Tammy, who was ready to jump the six feet or so to where her bitch of a sister was, and probably grab her by the throat.

Now it was Patricia's turn to get off her ass and join the melee going on right in the middle of her living room.

"That's enough, young lady," she barked at Tammy.

Lee wondered why she'd singled Tammy out and not included Annie, who sat back in her chair and gave her sister a look that said, "Come on, then."

Now Patricia and Lee stood between the sisters.

Her father hadn't moved an inch. Gutless, Lee thought.

Tammy cooled slightly and locked eyes with Lee. "I think it's time for us to leave."

Lee agreed. She couldn't wait to be back in her car, driving the hell out of Chesterfield.

As her mother stood out of Tammy's way to let her leave, Tammy said, "Just let me say goodbye to them."

Annie turned to her mom, and with the coldest expression possible, simply shook her head from left to right.

No.

Lee put her hand on Tammy's shoulder, and rather nervously said, "It's okay, Tam. Let's just get out of here. We can work it out later."

Tammy wondered how she could possibly be her twin.

It was as if Dr. Jekyll and Mrs. Hyde had shared the same womb. The two sisters were polar opposites of each other in every sense of the word.

As Tammy and Lee walked off down the hallway, Tammy could hear Beth and Noah continuing to play their video game.

She just wanted to say goodbye to them.

She regretted how this visit had gone, and felt as if she'd put her foot in it big time.

As she walked through the front door, she stole one more glance down the end of the hallway.

Her two children now stood peeking around the corner.

Beth's expression was one of sadness.

She missed her mom.

Noah stared at Tammy as if she were a stranger.

Tammy waved and hoped that one day, they'd all be together again.

Thanks to the most unlikely of allies, her wish would be granted.

CHAPTER FIFTEEN

Tony patted Ross firmly on the shoulder. They'd just cleared customs at Sydney International Airport, and this was where they parted ways.

Ross looked incredulously at Tony's hand. "What the hell is that?"

Behind the joke, Ross meant that in moments like this, a bit of man-hugging was quite acceptable. The two men hugged it out right there amid the hundreds of people trying to find their luggage.

"You going to be okay?" Ross said, serious for a moment. Tony managed a brave smile.

"It's not me I'm worried about, my friend," he said.

"I think we share the same feelings for two very special women," Ross said. Tammy and Melanie.

Tony looked around the busy room and wondered why no one ever stood behind the yellow line at the baggage carousel. If you ever met Tony and asked him for one of his first-world pet hates, it would be this.

Ross caught Tony looking over his shoulder and turned to check out what had caught his attention.

He laughed. "One day, you're going to have to deal with

it, Tone. People just love to ignore any semblance of common sense."

Tony said, "Yep, I guess so."

They knew this was it for now. Tony would fly onto Brisbane in ninety minutes, while Ross would check into a city hotel and get his bearings. He only had one reason to return to his hometown: Melanie.

After the last six months, Ross had been starting to feel more at home in Los Angeles. He'd fallen in love with the Beverly Hills Hotel. Ross had grown fond of his little bungalow and the beautiful woman who had stayed with him there.

Melanie was relieved Ross would be back in Sydney, even though she would only be able to see him under a cloak of secrecy for now. Just knowing he would be there among the other five million Sydneysiders was good enough for her. She knew if push came to shove, her knight in shining armor would be there at the drop of a hat.

She worried about how her husband would take the news of her decision to leave the marriage. From 2024, she knew all too well how he'd reacted to her fling with a co-worker, and now there was the fact he'd flown to California to bring her home only to be told she wouldn't be coming with him.

The guy would be pissed.

If he found out about Ross, it could blow the man's top.

Tony's flight to Brisbane was much like the other four thousand or so flights he'd taken in his life. His beer could have been a little colder, though that concern only distracted him for a few seconds.

Tammy had agreed they'd contact each other as often as they could. She'd given him Lee's phone number, and Lee was on-board with being the conduit between the two of them in the short term.

After he dealt with what he needed to in Brisbane, he would call her straight away and check in with her. He didn't intend to spend too much time in Brisbane, or Australia, for that matter.

Like his best friend, he wanted to be back in California.

The taxi driver talked too much, and Tony tried his best to ignore him. Fortunately, the drive from Brisbane Airport to his home in Paddington at this time of the afternoon was no more than twenty to twenty-five minutes. The guy was sincere, but Tony just couldn't muster the mental strength to discuss the current state of football and new freeways.

"So I guess there is no other way to tell you this," Tina said rather unemotionally. "I have…"

"You're with Suzanna."

Tony's wife's expression was as if he'd just slapped her.

She stumbled over her words as she tried to formulate a credible response.

Tony looked bored and disinterested.

He was.

"You knew?" she said.

Tony rolled his eyes and wished he could tell her honestly *how* he knew, though he realized he could never do this. Tina had a mouth the size of Hangar 19's doors at Vandenberg. It would be world news within an hour.

Tony checked out Tina's right wrist. The tattoo was there already. The one that matched another on Suzanna's left wrist.

How romantic, Tony thought. Maybe he should do the same thing with Tammy.

The ensuing silence in the kitchen of his home was palpable.

There was nothing more to say to his now ex-wife.

He would visit his parents and have the awkward afternoon with them. Their reaction would be similar to that of Tammy's parents, though not as intense or blindly Bible-driven.

Tony stood up, and realized it would be the last time he ever set foot in this house. Ironically for Tony, only seven months ago he'd thought this would be his forever house, where he'd live for the rest of his life.

With the woman who now loved another woman.

His heart felt a tiny pinprick of nostalgia before he said, "I hope you have a long and happy life. I wish you and Suzanna all the best."

Tina burst into tears. She literally fell to Tony's feet, and between sobs said, "Maybe I've made a grave mistake."

Tony pulled her up to her feet, placing her back on the nearby stool and putting his hand lightly on her shoulder.

At that moment, he felt genuinely sorry for her.

It wasn't her fault his plane had disappeared.

She'd been left all alone.

He didn't blame her or have any harsh feelings toward her.

Let's face it; he'd already dealt with this before. He was crushed back then, but thanks to Tammy he'd gotten over it okay.

Surprising himself, he put his arms around Tina and held her tight.

She cried for what seemed like minutes before Tony slowly took his arms from around her.

He leaned forward and kissed her.

On the forehead.

"I'll always love you, Tina," he said stoically, "though I believe everything happens for a reason."

Tina wiped her eyes and looked at the tattoo on her wrist.

Seeing this, Tony picked her right hand up and kissed it gently.

"Send my love to Suzanna," he said, before putting her hand down and walking out of the kitchen and the house.

Darcy looked around the cabin and wondered how long it had been since he'd flown on a commercial jet. Save for the ill-fated flight from Hawaii to Los Angeles in 2019, it must have been at least thirty years, he surmised.

He pondered what his life would have been now, in 2021, if he'd never boarded that flight. He blamed the private jet company for the fault in his plane that put him on the ground in Hawaii at the time.

If it hadn't happened, Darcy would not have endured what he had in the last six months.

But would he take that flight again?

As he saw his reflection in the blank screen embedded in the back of the seat in front of him, he knew fairly quickly the answer to that question.

Yes.

Life now had a new meaning to him.

His obsession with making more money, on top of the mountain of money he already had, had been replaced with the deep-seated desire to care about people and give back.

Watching many of his fellow passengers accept their predicament had made Darcy see he wasn't better than them in any way. He might have made a fortune, but these people had shown him the kind of strength no amount of money could buy.

Emotional intelligence was never measured by a figure in a bank account.

And now, to complicate things, his wife had a major stroke when she'd heard his flight had reappeared—two and a half years earlier than it had when he'd first traveled in time.

Darcy could think of only one explanation.

When their plane had reappeared five years later, Joanne had completely moved on.

She'd had an extra two and a half years to get over Darcy's disappearance, and to move on from having put a large stick of dynamite under his business empire and reducing it to a pile of rubble.

The drive from Melbourne Airport to the Alfred Hospital was a blur. He was dog-tired from the flight. The only seat available for Darcy on the way back had been in premium economy.

The cabin was full of people coughing, chatting, and tending to at least two continuously crying babies. Sleep would not be an option under these circumstances.

Andrew had met him at the airport, and Darcy hugged him harder than he'd ever done before.

Andrew had given his father the latest news on Joanne as they drove the forty-five minutes from the airport to the hospital.

The report was grim.

Andrew told him he was thankful Tom back in LA had been able to get him on the flight back home so soon. It was a good thing, under the precarious circumstances.

As Andrew's Audi turned into Commercial Road, the enormous Alfred Hospital complex coming into immediate view on the right, his words sent a cold chill down the back of his father's spine.

"Mum's been a bit out of it the whole time. One minute she's awake and the next she's out. But every time she opens her eyes, she looks at me and says, 'I must speak to him before I go'."

His oldest child was clearly struggling with the turn of events. His eyes were misty and Darcy could see the pain in his tired face.

First, his father had disappeared for two plus years, and the moment he came back from wherever the plane had been, his mother had a life-threatening stroke.

As Andrew reverse parked into a spot across the road from the entrance, Darcy's heart felt as though the weight of the car itself were on it. Somehow, he felt responsible.

And then there were his three other children to contend with.

"Are they all up there?" Darcy asked, though his tone indicated he probably didn't want to know the answer.

Andrew stepped out of the car and the two men met each other's eyes across the top of it.

"Probably," was all Andrew said. He knew this would be hard for his father, though he had his own emotions to deal with first.

After the two men arrived at the intensive-care unit of the hospital and checked in with the head nurse behind the counter, Darcy walked the few meters down the hall and realized he'd come straight into the waiting area of the ward.

All three of his other children were sitting there, deep in conversation. As if he'd cracked a twig underfoot, when Andrew arrived next to his father's side, the three other siblings all looked up at the same time.

For a few brief seconds, it felt like the air had been completely sucked out of the waiting room. The five family members stared at each other as if they were strangers on their first Tinder dates. Worse, their expressions were blank and without emotion, not warm or welcoming.

Darcy could feel the particles in the air firing toward him from his three children like radiation. He wished he could turn back the clock and have been a far better and more involved father.

Ben, his second oldest, looked down to the floor. Darcy knew he'd held a grudge against him for as long as his derrière had been pointing south. But it still punched him hard in the chest, especially under the circumstances.

Ethan, his youngest son, reached for his phone and started looking at something. Nice, Andrew thought, how's that for a way to greet your father? Andrew had always had differences with his youngest sibling since becoming successful in his own right.

Samantha, Darcy's only daughter, looked long and hard at her father. She'd generally lived with disdain for him since she was old enough to call herself an adult.

But Darcy could see the tears welling in her eyes. She wiped them with a tissue, rose out of her chair, and surprised him by coming over and reaching out for him.

Darcy put his arms around her and could feel a tsunami of emotions bursting to come out.

For the first time in their entire lives, the four Darcy children saw their father crying. As he wept on his daughter's shoulder, his body convulsed with decades of pent-up emotions pouring out.

At this moment, the head doctor of the intensive-care unit walked around the corner, and when he saw what has happening, hesitated for a moment to venture any closer to the family.

"Andrew," the doctor said quietly, nearly in a whisper, "can we speak for a moment?"

Darcy let go of his daughter and kissed her on the forehead.

Everyone but Andrew sat or stood as if superglued to the spot. The oldest son nodded stoically before walking forward and speaking to the doctor up at the ward nurse's station.

Darcy and his other three children watched the two men deep in conversation. None of them moved an inch, or appeared to even be breathing.

After they'd talked for about a minute, Andrew thanked the doctor. Darcy could tell his son was struggling with what they'd just spoken about. His son walked back to his brothers, sister, and father, and didn't waste any time on his words.

"Mum's health is deteriorating. She wants to see us kids first, then Dad on his own."

Samantha sobbed. Ben and Ethan were already on their feet. Neither man had made any attempt to greet their father in any way. They moved past him as if he were a stranger. As he sort of was, and had been for a long, long time. Darcy was the architect of this, and knew if he wanted to see who was to blame for his children's current behavior toward him, he need only look in the nearest mirror.

Right now, he only felt for one person. Joanne.

Soon, it would be his turn to see her.

CHAPTER SIXTEEN

Darcy had been sitting in the waiting room chair close to ten minutes when he heard footsteps and hushed conversation from the other end of the hall.

Samantha, Ethan, and Ben were coming toward him, though Andrew was nowhere in sight.

Darcy could see the strain in their anguished faces. Ethan appeared to have been crying; Ben looked as if a shadow had come over his face. Samantha's cheeks and eyes were beetroot red, and her nostrils looked like they'd been wiped with sandpaper. She walked awkwardly, as if she were drunk on the most painful of emotions: saying goodbye to someone you love.

Darcy could feel tears in his eyes. He brushed them away, though he knew they would be back in no time.

Samantha reached her father. "You need to go and see her now," she said.

Darcy gave his daughter another hug before he walked the twenty meters up to his wife's room. It felt like twenty miles. When he arrived at the door, he could see Andrew standing at the end of the bed.

His wife was in terrible shape. She was as white as a

ghost, her hair disheveled and unkempt. There were tubes everywhere, one tucked in the side of her mouth, others zigzagging across her body. Monitors nearby flickered and let off constant beeps and other noises.

They met each other's gaze.

Darcy could see a range of emotions firmly in Joanne's normally beautiful and mesmerizing eyes. He could see confidence in her attempt to be on top of things, coupled with absolute fear of what was coming for her.

Andrew stepped to the side of his mother's bed and kissed her on the cheek. He held her hand and said, "I'll be just outside the door, okay?"

As he was about to step away from her, she said, "Remember my wishes, my darling son."

Andrew patted Darcy on the shoulder as he silently left the room.

Darcy moved next to Joanne's bed and put his hand out to pull a chair closer.

His wife grunted and patted the side of the bed, trying to move a little sideways to give him room to sit on the edge instead.

Darcy carefully sat down, and reached for both of Joanne's hands.

He wished above all that he could fix this. As his eyes filled with tears, he found it hard to speak.

"I'm so sorry," he whispered.

Joanne shook her head and said, "It wasn't your fault what happened to you."

Darcy shook his head vigorously, dismissing what his dying wife had just said.

She stared at him strangely before he said, "No, I'm sorry for all the years of heartache and hurt I caused you."

Joanne closed her eyes and said, "It was quite the ride we both had, huh?"

Darcy was amazed by his wife's stoicism. She'd always been quite well grounded, but this was beyond that.

As one of her monitors made a couple of unusual sounds, Joanne coughed and was breathing heavily. Darcy wanted to do something, though he knew there was nothing for him to do.

Joanne squeezed his hands much harder, and as her eyes flickered, she said, "I'm sorry for what I did to your companies. And I've asked Ben, Ethan, and Sarah to forgive you too."

Darcy knew there was no time to explain anything. He also dispensed with looking surprised right now. His wife wouldn't notice, nor would she care.

Darcy moved closer, and with one hand stroked the side of her face. It was stone cold.

He was closer to his wife now than he'd been in a long time.

Darcy could tell the life in her body was starting to slowly evaporate.

He tried for a grin and said, "Well, I guess that makes us even."

Tears were in her eyes, and a second later Darcy held her in his arms.

He was just happy to be there at that very place, at that very moment.

As Joanne sat back against her pillow, she reached for both Darcy's hands again. When he had them in hers, she said, "I'm sorry for what I did to the businesses you loved."

Darcy went to shake his head, dismissing the need for a second apology, but she said, "So I instructed Andrew to change my will."

Darcy looked at her perplexed.

"I've given Darcon back to you," she said.

Darcon was Darcy's baby, and by far his biggest company.

None of the others ever really mattered to him. Darcon was the one. It had a yearly turnover of over a billion dollars.

Then she flicked her hand to ask for something he wished, at that moment, he'd done 500,000 times more in the last forty-plus years.

She wanted to kiss him. Darcy sat forward and met his wife's lips. She held him there for a long time.

When he finally sat back, he could see she'd been crying.

And with one last breath, she broke his heart.

"Please. Forgive me."

Ross felt a stab of excitement as the phone in his hotel room began to bellow out its rather dull and dated ring tone. His legs couldn't get him from the bathroom to his bedside table quick enough.

"Ross speaking." He wondered why he still continued the weird habit of always answering the phone this way rather than just with a plain "Hello?"

The pause on the line was as nerve-racking as it was exciting, until it was finally put to rest.

"Is that my favorite international pilot?" Melanie's words —or more her velvet-ensconced tone, better suited to a radio commercial plugging something luxurious and expensive— were as good as her standing there with her arms around him.

"That it is." Ross could feel the days of apprehension evaporate around him in an instant.

"How's my man going, huh?" she said. Ross could hear she was relaxed and in good spirits. This only made him feel better.

"Much, much better now," he said. She could almost feel

his wide, beaming smile radiating over the thousands of miles of telephone lines.

"You and me both, my darling," she said after the usual time delay.

Ross sat down and looked out his hotel-room window.

It was another beautiful day in his hometown, and the sun shone brightly across the blue sky. He loved the weather here. When it was good, it was great.

"How did everything go with…" Ross seemed to stumble as many in his shoes would. Verbalizing the name of his girl-friend's ex—in his mind they were long split up—made him feel slightly awkward.

By the time his words reached Melanie in California, she was already answering him. "It went as well as expected. He's no different than he ever was, or probably will be in the future."

Ross took a long and welcome deep breath. So far so good. But he knew if there was any time the proverbial shit would hit the fan, it would be in Sydney.

"So he bought it?" he said.

Ten seconds later, Melanie laughed. "Well, he had to. The security guard at the hospital was like the Rock's twin brother. Charles may have ended up in hospital in the next room if he really said what he wanted to." She laughed some more. "My doctor, bless her—she was my savior."

After what was close to thirty minutes of healthy conver-sation, there was only one more thing Ross dearly wanted to know.

"Tell me…" he said. He could feel nervousness pooling in his stomach, though he couldn't understand why.

Before he could ask her the rest of the question, she finished it herself. She seemed to do that a lot lately, as if she knew exactly what he was thinking.

"…will I be there?" Ross could almost see the grin on her face from the other side of the world.

"Well, the good news is, my dear," Melanie said with excitement, "I'm on the first flight out of here tomorrow."

Ross wanted to lie on his bed and relax; it was the only news he really wanted to hear. The sooner she got there, the sooner they could be on the fast train to a happy life together. Toot toot.

There's only one thing, Roscoe.

There would be a boulder the size of the Sydney Opera House sitting right in the middle of the tracks, just a couple of miles up the road.

And the boulder had two names.

Charles.

Lewinson.

Tim couldn't remember the last time he'd slept so soundly. It would have been years ago, he thought, maybe even decades. He slept as close as he could to Sandra, who seemed to welcome his presence right next to her in bed.

When Tim woke to the sounds of the outside world, rousing him as dawn appeared on the horizon, for a split second he had to register the amazing revelation that Sandra was sleeping soundly right next to him, very much alive and well.

He wondered if, from this point on, he'd ever take that simple thing for granted ever again.

Breakfast tasted like he'd never eaten breakfast before. Sandra made pancakes, his favorite and she knew it. The coffee flowed as freely as the conversation, and Tim wondered for the hundredth time if he was in some sort of

Lost-style television paradigm, not in his own version of heaven.

After they washed up and Tim was about to head to the shower, Sandra said, "So, what are you going to do now?" For the rest of the day, she meant.

Tim smiled at her for a moment as if he were thinking about it, but it was an act. He'd known precisely what he wanted to do long before she asked—go to his workshop and start working through the long list of things pinging around his head about artifacts and planes traveling five years into the future and then two and a half years back. About wives who one minute were being put into the ground, only to be found alive again elsewhere—or else*when*. If he wanted a whiteboard to map it all out, hell, he'd need one the size of a IMAX movie screen.

"I'd love to just tinker around the workshop for a while." He walked to her and gave her a hug. "If that's alright with you, my love," he said in her ear. Then he kissed her on the cheek.

"Of course you can, honey," she said.

Half an hour later, shaved, showered, and feeling refreshed and ready to tackle the day, Tim opened the doors to his favorite place in his home.

Once the doors were open, he stole a glance down his long driveway. It would be a habit that never left him, just what he would now always do. Without anything or anyone in sight, he returned his attention to the inside of the workshop.

Like a time capsule, everything was in order, neat as a pin. His son had once said, "OCD" under his breath one day in the workshop, just loud enough for his old man to hear. And Tim had responded, "When you get to my age, you can be as OCD as you want, boy."

So he liked things to be in order, Tim thought to himself,

recalling the exchange many years ago. If that's OCD, to hell with it—call me guilty as charged.

There was a fine layer of dust over everything. Tim ran his index finger across the workbench. He knew by morning tea, every surface would be so clean, you could eat a burrito straight off them, followed by a shot of tequila.

As Tim worked his way from one end of the workshop to the other, removing every speck of dust from every inch of the space, he came across Ben's box, in which he'd discovered some unusual things six months or so ago.

Instinctively, and with curiosity the driving force, Tim pulled the box out and onto the floor.

He assumed that when he opened the lid, he'd see exactly what he saw six months ago.

And sure enough, the small box of coffee-machine pods was in the same place as last time.

The blank piece of dirty paper was sitting underneath, bound to the box with an elastic band. He pulled it out and took it over to his workbench.

"You and your unique inventions," Tim said to himself, smiling as he lay the piece of paper out on the now-clean workbench.

He knew there was no point getting out the motor oil and wiping the paper with it. He already knew what it would say.

But then he had another thought, about what Sandra had said last night.

Hawaii.

Ben had made her stay.

His eyes found the shelf nearby.

The small bottle of motor oil sat there looking at him.

Tim could feel his heart beating a little faster.

He poured the motor oil out onto the paper, just as he had done six months earlier.

Then he carefully wiped it over the entire page, and let it seep in for a moment.

He took a deep breath and picked up the now-soaked piece of paper.

As he held it there, up in the air, the words started to appear.

Three seconds later, his heart froze solid in his chest.

He read the words again, and thought back to what the message had said six months ago.

The message was completely different.

"Meet me at Shirley. ASAP."

CHAPTER SEVENTEEN

MELANIE'S FLIGHT WAS DUE TO TOUCH DOWN IN SYDNEY late the following evening, and Ross was counting down the hours to her arrival.

After a long shower and some breakfast, he decided one thing he could get out of the way while he was waiting was his desire to go to his mother's dingy little flat for the final time. It would be his way of saying goodbye.

"Make sure I'm not buried in the ground," she'd told him a few times over the years. She preferred to be cremated and have her ashes spread out at one of the coastal beaches Sydney was famous for. She didn't care which one, she told Ross, just as long as her ashes were washed into the ocean. That was her wish. She told Ross she didn't want him to ever have the obligation of visiting a tombstone—it wasn't her cup of tea. All she asked for instead was that for the first five years after her passing, he light a candle on her birthday and sing aloud her favorite song of all time, "Mull of Kintyre," by Paul McCartney and Wings. Ross loved it as much as his mother did, and would ensure he followed her wishes.

To avoid the crippling peak-hour traffic that choked

Sydney most mornings, Ross decided to go to the hotel gym and work out until at least 10am.

By the time he stepped out of the hotel doors, it was closer to 10.30. He welcomed another sunny day in the harbor city.

The taxi ride to Crows Nest was okay. Ross hadn't been over the Harbour Bridge for what felt like years, though in reality it was closer to seven months. Not that he could tell the cab driver; the guy's English was as bad as his body odor.

As the cab drew closer to his mother's flat, Ross could feel himself starting to get anxious.

He assumed he wouldn't be able to go inside. Her flat would have been sold. And even if he could, he wasn't sure he wanted to.

When he stepped out of the cab, he welcomed the outside air, hoping the next one he took was driven by someone who'd showered recently.

Ross turned his gaze to the block of flats and nearly fell over.

Looking at his mother's allocated car space—not that she had owned a car for many years—his heart skipped a beat. A moment later, the feeling went from shock to anger.

In the car spot sat a large Ford pickup: an F250. It was weather-beaten and seriously unroadworthy.

But it was the pickup's number plates that had Ross balling his hands into fists without even knowing he was doing it.

The number plates were from Queensland.

Far.

North.

Queensland.

Todd didn't move an inch.

He could feel the tension coursing through his body. His breaths were short and difficult, as though his throat were the width of a drinking straw.

There.

He'd said the words he'd been dying to fling in his father's face ever since he walked through the DONR doors and Andrew had appeared out of thin air.

Andrew was a strong, fit man, and quite intimidating when he wanted to be. His police career was largely built on his physique, bravado, and testicles the size of well-grown avocados. He was known for his toughness and lack of fear at times when other "tough" guys would be running in the opposite direction.

Todd was ready to punch on with his father if required. The anger had pent up since finding the photo in his dead half-brother's hand. After ending his life for killing his trophy father, it had ignited the pilot light under a fury Todd had never experienced in his life.

His gut burned with insane rage, all directed at the very guy standing directly in front of him.

Andrew stood looking at Todd, devoid of any expression.

The guy knew how to negotiate AK-47s out of trigger-happy, high-as-a-kite thugs. It was all about the expression, to start with.

But none of them had been his son—the guy who knew Andrew Roberts better than anyone else did.

Todd had seen this expression plenty of times before, so it went straight over his head.

Andrew turned back to his home. He did it slowly, deliberately, as if Todd had just cut him open and revealed the guy's biggest secret to all four judges on *America's Got Talent*.

He inched forward just a little, and in a sharp, cold tone said to Todd, finally, "Who?"

Todd didn't flinch. He narrowed his eyes, and without any delay, said in a whisper, "Your illegitimate son, Dad."

Andrew bit his lower lip hard, as if trying to hold back the monster within, before taking a long, deep breath.

"This conversation will continue later." Andrew stole another surreptitious glance back to the house. He wanted to ensure Kylie hadn't come out to ask what the two men were talking about.

He continued to stand there, giving his son the coldest look he'd ever given him.

Todd didn't budge. He'd been through enough in the last week or so to not be perturbed.

As Andrew slowly headed back to the front door, Todd threw one last grenade at his long-revered old man.

"I'm going to find him, you know."

If he'd heard what Andrew had said under his breath, with his back to Todd, he probably would have regretted his last comment.

"Not if I find him first."

＊　　＊　　＊

Ross had never before gone to the arrivals area of an airport to greet someone arriving. It felt a little strange to enter for this reason and in plain clothes, not in his crisp, dry-cleaned pilot's uniform.

But he had dressed up just a little. Greeting the woman you were head over heels for in public, especially at the airport, called for a little bit of style.

His mustard-colored chinos complimented a crisp white shirt and navy-blue suit jacket, and he wore his Berluti shoes more as a joke than out of a desire to look like a male model at a Paris fashion show. It was the same pair he'd worn when he met Melanie for the first time at the Beverly Hills Hotel, and he remembered how much she seemed to love them.

He dawdled around the exit of the customs area after seeing Melanie's plane had landed.

A few other drivers waiting looked at him twice before turning away and choosing not to look again. Ross knew the reason, and was more embarrassed than anything else. He hoped Melanie wouldn't freak out when she walked through the doors. He wished he were the type to be able to put foundation on to hide the, err, blemish.

Ross knew that before too long, she'd be walking through the doors, and ideally she'd be able to run straight into his arms. But they had discussed all this, and knew it would be too risky under the circumstances.

Ross pulled out a piece of paper neatly folded in the side pocket of his jacket, and as he unfolded it, couldn't help but grin from ear to ear.

The idea was as simple as it was cunning.

As the doors opened, he moved closer to the others standing there.

He adjusted his sunglasses on his head, seeing how the other guys wore theirs. He was getting in on the disguise of sorts, and wanted to look like the rest of the dozen or so drivers standing there waiting to pick up their paying passengers.

His piece of paper had the words "MELANIE LEWINSON" written neatly in block letters.

A large number of passengers started to filter out through the custom doors, most with trolleys full of suitcases, others with just the one on four wheels, keen to be on their way.

Then there were a small handful who only had carry-on luggage, small bags they carried with ease.

Melanie Lewinson was one of them.

When she saw Ross, her eyes lit up. He started to walk alongside her with the large barrier separating them.

A few meters later, the barrier ended. Ross held up his piece of paper and said loudly, but without shouting, "Melanie Lewinson?"

Melanie almost laughed hysterically, though she kept it all in check.

Then she came within a couple of feet of him, and saw something which made her laughter stop immediately.

She was horrified, though she knew she couldn't look too surprised until they were in private.

"My God," she whispered as they walked to Ross's waiting car, "what happened to you?"

Ross continued to walk, but spoke without looking sideways at her. If he had, he would have seen the look of concern etched on her attractive face.

"It's a long story." He touched the side of his face, which still hurt considerably. "But I'll give you the short version when we get outside."

Fifty meters of busy international terminal later, they walked through the exit doors and headed to the town car that was waiting for him and Melanie.

Ross folded his piece of paper and put it back in his pocket.

As they walked across the zebra crossing, he finally spoke.

"I bumped into one of my uncles at Mum's flat when I went to visit today."

Melanie walked on, though she wanted to know more. "And?"

Ross smiled, though it hurt to do so.

"Well, the good news is I got my record collection back."

As they neared the town car, Melanie studied his face, this time seeing the true extent of the souvenir from his chance meeting with his uncle. His black eye looked like he'd been in the ring with Rocky and Rocky had gotten the upper hand.

"You mean *the* record collection?" she said, sounding surprised.

"Yes, the one and only," Ross said.

Ross's vintage record collection had been valued in late 2019 at close to fifty thousand dollars.

And it wasn't his mother who had found it after Ross disappeared originally, as he'd thought. It had been his uncle, who found it at his mother's flat and had stupidly tried to act as though it was just another bunch of records to give to the Salvation Army as a donation. Actually, he'd planned to try and pawn them off, though thanks to Ross, he wouldn't get the chance.

As they sat in the back seat of the car, Melanie reached over and grabbed Ross's hand.

"Are you going to be okay?"

Ross winked. Ooh, it still hurt, but he didn't care. He'd had a great day, and now Melanie was with him. Even better.

"Let's just say one thing, babe," Ross said. "Uncle Eddie may have got a lucky one in after I bumped into him at the top of the stairs, right outside Mum's flat…" He held up his fists as if he were about to return to the ring. "…but it was only a light punch."

Melanie had no idea what he was talking about. Ross continued. "Now, when I retaliated and threw with my left— I broke the guy's nose and put him on the canvas. He was out cold."

Melanie had never understood the attraction of boxing, and wasn't a huge fan of violence. But after her husband had nearly killed her, she'd started to believe some people deserved a punch in the face. And she knew from the stories

Ross had told her about his uncle that the guy also deserved nothing less.

As the car started to drive out of the car park, Melanie asked Ross, "So he then just handed over the record collection?"

Ross shook his head. This time, his smile was broad. "When I thought it might be a good idea to hightail out of there, I walked past his ute on the way out. Sitting there in the back was all this junk, probably Mum's stuff." Ross nodded with sheer satisfaction. "And right there in the middle was my box of dear old records. Two minutes later, my record collection and I were in a cab heading out of Crows Nest as quickly as we could."

Melanie shook her head and laughed. "Well, if you're happy," she said, smiling over to him with her drop-dead-gorgeous jade eyes, "I'm happy too."

Melanie may have retracted those words if she'd known what had just happened in the same car park less than thirty feet away.

A private investigator sat surreptitiously in his car. He knew the art of staying hidden from view very well. Years of practice had him doing it with ease now.

And as they drove off, the guy had sent his current client a rather clipped and concise message.

It didn't need to be long.

The PI loved working for the big-knobs, the "squillion-aires," as he called them to his PI mates. People with millions exceeding a hundred, that was.

They paid hideously well, more for their anonymity than his services. The PI had worked for this client before, a few times at least.

Personally, he didn't like him, though he knew he wasn't the Lone Ranger there. The word around the traps was nobody did.

Confirmed.
Just arrived.
As suspected.
The pilot.

CHAPTER EIGHTEEN

"Where?" Sandra asked.

Her eyes were as they'd generally always been: genuine and sincere. He knew she'd trusted him his whole life. And Tim was trustworthy.

The things he hadn't told her, over the decades, well, he wasn't allowed to.

That was how things worked, where he worked.

Tim knew there were hundreds of thousands, hell, maybe millions of people just like him. Husbands and wives who had to massage the truth when talking with their partners, mostly when they first got home from work.

Okay—they had to lie through their teeth.

"How was your day at work, dear?" a spouse might ask.

Lie: "Had a good day. I snared that new client I've been trying for months to win over. The boss is ecstatic!"

Truth: "I had no choice. The guy wouldn't talk. Spies can be such a moody lot. We dissolved him. He died instantly and without any pain."

Or…

Lie: "Great. I made the quarterly sales target. The boss is over the moon!"

141

Truth: "I don't know how the hell we got it to work. But we did. Aliens know how to build the coolest things. Bloody pains in the ass, they are. They could have given us a goddamned instruction manual!"

So when Tim had told his wife where he needed to go for a couple of days, the lie came easily. It always did when it concerned work. In this case, he'd long been retired, though he still classed what he had to do as work. It was work-related, he believed, in a roundabout kind of way.

"Reno."

Sandra stepped a few feet back. Like this, she could see him clearer, without having to strain her neck.

"But you just got back home, darling."

Tim agreed, though he wanted to be on the road just as soon as he could. He planned to head out at dawn tomorrow morning. "Honey, the investigators of the flight want to question me more about what happened," he said.

Sandra, not one to take no for an answer, said, "But why can't they just come here?"

Tim was already a step ahead. He'd known she'd say this.

"They've set up a workshop there, I don't know why, but I really can't say no. I want to get this done and be back home in my own workshop, with you overhead baking my cheesecakes." Tim stepped forward and gave her a kiss on the cheek. He knew how to soften her with compliments. And the truth was, she should have run the Cheesecake Factory company. She made the most amazing cheesecakes. Best in Alameda. Best in America, even.

Tim—focus on the job at hand, not your wife's cheesecakes.

Sandra stood looking at him for a few more moments. Tim knew he could just walk out and drive off, but didn't really want to. Not without his wife's approval or at least acknowledgement. It was better this way.

Sandra studied the world outside her window for a moment before meeting Tim's eyes.

"Be careful." She came back to him and gave him a hug. "Get it done and come home to me." He could see instantly she was getting emotional. "I've only just got you back, my love," she said. Oh no, Tim thought, here come the tears.

Little did he know he'd eventually be gone again.

For much longer.

Tim left on schedule the next morning, at 7am on the dot.

The sun rose gracefully over Alameda, bathing the island in a soft, warm glow. Tim loved being up at this time of the day. Normally, it was to fish, though Tim surmised he was sort of going fishing.

Fishing for answers.

The streets were as they should be this time of morning, quiet and devoid of much human activity. By the time this changed, he'd be well out of the city and heading for a lovely little town.

Reno, Nevada.

Fast forward two and half hours or so, and Tim found himself singing at the top of his lungs to his favorite Rolling Stones album, *Exile on Main St*. He'd always had a soft spot for the Rolling Stones, Queen, and The Who, and had albums from all of them on hand in the glove box.

As Tim passed over the Sacramento River, he decided to let Mick Jagger do the singing, so he could do the thinking.

About the message.

Etched on paper in lemon, or whatever the hell his son had concocted.

Motor oil unlocked the words. The boy had always been fascinated by Tesla, Einstein, the pioneers.

And the visitor.

But the visitor was an enigma, a legend in folklore. Most

believed he didn't exist. An urban myth, but not in circles where urban was involved. Especially not Keith. Only in the places where Tim and Ben had worked over the years. It was a name they'd never even said outside the workplace. Doing so could cause premature death.

Was Ben dead?

Had someone else written the revised message to look like it had come from Ben? And they wanted to get him to Shirley? Was it a trap? His gut told him no, though his gut had also been thinking about cheesecakes on and off for the last two hours.

Tim's favorite song on *Exile on Main St*, "Loving Cup," started playing. He loved the way Mick Jagger sang in it; it snapped him out of the many thoughts swirling around his head.

He only had another thirty to forty-five minutes before he'd arrive. Then he'd check into the hotel, call Sandra, and decide when he would go.

To Shirley.

—　　—　　—

Kylie could sense something was amiss between the two men dearest to her heart.

She knew the signs of Andrew being off. His jovial, affable demeanor would disappear and be replaced with silence and awkward movements. He'd seem unable to sit still, he'd fidget, and normally he'd go outside and find something to sweep up or the like.

Asking him what was wrong would have been like asking Donald Trump if he'd ever heard of a thing called a wig. Not a good idea. He'd get more withdrawn and start sweeping the street, for Pete's sake.

Todd was nothing like his father under strain. He'd talk

more, ramp up the nervous laughter, and on the odd occasion seem to scratch at something on his right elbow that was never there.

With the two of them acting like this, she was close to asking them to stand on either side of her at the fireplace, reaching up and grabbing each one by the nearest ear, and then pulling their collective heads together to smack some sense into them.

Her father used to do it to her and her sister, and it seemed to have the desired effect.

As Andrew cut the beef Wellington into slices and Todd poured the wine, Kylie's anger began to rise. She thanked Andrew for the two slices of beef, and Todd for the generously poured glass of white.

"So…" She took a long sip from her wine. "Which one of you is going to tell me what the hell is going on here?"

Neither of them made eye contact with the other. Only after all their plates were full did Andrew finally look over to Todd.

Phew. The look in his face said it all. Todd had never seen his father this angry.

Kylie took another sip of her wine—actually, more of a giant mouthful. She felt the effect of the alcohol immediately, and it gave her the Dutch courage she needed to launch.

"That's it," she shouted. Father and son realized they'd unleashed the beast.

"Whatever the fuck is going on between you two, get it on this table," Kylie barked, slamming her hand down next to her glass. Andrew's eyebrows flew upwards. His wife almost never swore, unless she was really pissed off.

Both men squirmed in their seats. Todd took a long drink from his glass of red. Andrew, on the other side of the table, sipped his beer and carefully put it back on the placemat a moment later. He wiped his mouth with his left hand and turned to his wife. He was about to tell her to pull her head in, but Todd interrupted the thought gloriously.

"I'll tell you what's going on," he said.

Andrew's chest expanded with a long, measured breath. His eyes narrowed so far they were almost closed.

Andrew shifted his gaze to Kylie.

She was staring straight at Todd as if in a trance.

If she found out what Todd knew, it would not be good, Andrew pondered.

For the first time, an awful thought passed through his mind. He wondered if it would have been better if Todd's name were not on the list.

But Andrew, let's give you the heads up.

If Todd's name hadn't been on the list, you'd be dead.

You only stayed in the car at the 7-Eleven because you heard his name called out.

Kylie stared at her son, taking another drink but not taking her eyes off him.

"Todd, if you have something to say," Kylie said sharply, "can you just get it over and done with?"

Todd stared over at his father one final time.

He had his old man right where he wanted him: a deer in the crosshairs. Maybe more of a grizzly bear.

But this didn't involve his mother. Not yet, anyway.

One day it would.

"I want to return to the police force," he said, "but Dad doesn't want me to."

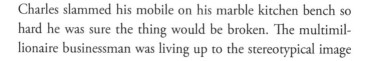

Charles slammed his mobile on his marble kitchen bench so hard he was sure the thing would be broken. The multimillionaire businessman was living up to the stereotypical image

146

of an extremely wealthy middle-aged man who thought money bought him the right to super-sized tantrums.

He stomped up and down his kitchen area looking for something to throw across the room. Finding nothing, he opened a cupboard and took out a cup. He spun on his heel and threw it across the kitchen-dining area, and it flew through the air before hitting the far wall just millimeters from an enormous mirror, smashing into many pieces.

He felt slightly better, but not by much.

He grunted and walked back over to his mobile. Miraculously, he'd only cracked the screen down one side.

Charles wondered if the whole episode at Vandenberg, and then later at that country hospital full of dumb hicks, was all an elaborate setup.

He was starting to think it was. Melanie obviously hadn't wanted to fly back with him.

She'd probably wanted to meet up with the pilot, and that would have been the main reason why she'd put on the too-sick-to-fly act. Charles's temper rose quickly at the thought of that son of a bitch putting his hands all over his wife.

Not that he considered putting his hands over more than a dozen prostitutes while his wife was "away" a sin.

The guy's level of hypocrisy nearly matched his bank balance.

Charles then started to wonder if she'd been seeing him before she boarded the Pacific International Airways flight two and a half years ago.

As his anger continued to grow, he decided to do one thing: get back on the blower to that imbecile of a private detective.

Charles would tell the guy he wanted his slut of a wife, and the dumb-ass pilot, followed around the clock, effective immediately. Tomorrow night, the guy would tell Charles where they were.

He'd pay the lovebirds a little visit. And he wouldn't care what his anger would make him do.

The smell of musty air greeted Tim when he opened the door to his hotel room. He'd stayed in his fair share of dives, but the Vagabond Inn, Reno, was not one of them. It was clean, and neat as a pin. The bedspreads were a bit 1980s, but he wasn't Martha Stewart, so he didn't care. Tim sat on the bed and called Sandra. He checked his watch as the phone dialed. Just after 11am. He was satisfied with his day so far: the journey up had felt long, but the roads were light and the weather was perfect for a country drive, with not a cloud in the sky.

After a short, pleasant conversation with Sandra, Tim told her he had to ring off so he could prepare for his meeting with the investigators, which was scheduled for 1pm. He told her he wanted to get a decent lunch in first. Of course, only the latter statement was true. As he hung up, he knew he couldn't have lunch this early, but decided the sooner he ate, the sooner he could be on his way to his intended destination.

Shirley.

Tim decided he'd have lunch at 11.45, and would make it a quick one. He wanted to be on the road by noon.

After resting on one of the two double beds in the room, marveling at the two identically matching bedspreads, which reminded him of the film clip for David Bowie's "Starman," he checked his watch and could feel a rush of adrenaline pass through him. It was 11.40am.

He'd driven only 400 feet down the road when he

spotted a Wendy's on the next corner. His stomach growled at him.

Tim treated himself to a peppercorn mushroom melt burger, fries, and a Coke.

After disposing of the wrappings and wiping his face and hands, he checked his watch. A wave of nervous anticipation passed through him before colliding with the burger and fries. It was one minute past noon.

This was it.

Time to head for Shirley.

CHAPTER NINETEEN

Tony arrived back in Sydney having cut the trip to Brisbane short. He'd allowed a week to do all the things he thought he'd need to do, but after the final meeting with Tina and then a painful evening with his parents, who couldn't accept his marriage to her was over, Tony had decided about 1.30 the next morning to get his ass back to the harbor city pronto.

The Ben Stiller lookalike felt there was nothing left for him in Brisbane. He felt like he belonged somewhere else.

Ross and Tony had spoken about where Ross would be staying. The original plan had been to meet up in a week's time, or thereabouts, depending on how things went for them in Australia. Ross was surprised to see Tony so soon.

"It's been a while," Ross said, opening his hotel-room door all the way so Tony could enter.

"I missed you too," Tony quipped. The two men shared smirks.

"I guess you got everything done quickly," Ross continued, ribbing his friend as he took a seat on a chair in the corner of Ross's room.

Tony shook his head. "I got the important things done." He shrugged his shoulders. "So I'm all good."

Ross sat on the edge of his bed and stared out through the hotel-room window. Still a good view. Nothing had changed there. "You want to get out of here?" he said. Meaning not just Sydney, but Australia too.

Tony stood and dug his hands into his pockets. Without turning to Ross, he said, "More than you know."

Ross studied his friend of more than twenty-five years. He looked agitated and out of sorts. He swayed slightly from foot to foot, and Ross could tell the guy had some heavy stuff on his mind.

"Have you heard from her?" Ross asked.

Tony stopped swaying instantly, as if Ross had put him in a trance. He shook his head. "Not yet," he said. He spent the next few seconds figuring out what time it would be in St. Louis. He wanted to call Tammy, though he didn't want to wake her in the middle of the night. He'd have to wait a couple of hours.

"I'll call her soon," he said. "What's happening in your neck of the woods?"

Ross sat further back on his bed, resting a hand on either side of himself.

"Not much. Melanie stayed at her mum's house last night. I think she plans to stay there tonight, and then tomorrow, she'll tell her husband she wants out."

Tony raised his eyebrows at the news and said, "Alright, then. And where are you going to be when this happens?"

"I hope to be in a car very close by," Ross said, though the look on his face did not share the confidence of his words.

The afternoon dragged on somewhat for the two pilots.

At 4.30, they binned their earlier thoughts of eating at the hotel for dinner. Ross told Tony he wouldn't mind dropping into one of his old haunts, Otto, at Finger Wharf in Woolloomooloo.

He needed some air, he told Tony, and hadn't been to Otto for what seemed like five years.

After ordering their dinner and accompanying wines, the two friends agreed that getting out of their hotel had been a great idea.

As they chinked their glasses, Ross's pre-paid mobile phone let off the ubiquitous sound indicating he'd received a message. As only Melanie currently knew his number, he made the safe assumption the message was from her.

He checked his phone as Tony took a gulp of his wine. "I guess you don't need to be Einstein to know who the message is from?" Tony said.

He put the phone down. "It seems she's feeling like some fresh air too," he said. He stared out over the water to the Sydney Tower as a number of thoughts passed through his mind. He really wanted to see her, but something made him wonder if it were a good idea to do so tonight. She'd only arrived in Sydney yesterday, and was yet to see her husband and tell him what she was thinking about their marriage.

For a moment, his head fought with his heart. The logical part of him told him to tell her it wasn't a good idea, but his heart told him he really wanted to see her.

And as is often the case, the heart ruled out over the head.

But as is also often the case, the head was right.

Ross replied to her a minute later, telling her where they were, and asking if she wanted to meet him and Tony at one of his favorite bars, Finnegans at the Rocks. It was a Sydney institution, one of the oldest Irish bars in the city, and the rooftop deck gave you breathtaking nighttime views of the Harbour Bridge and the Opera House.

It didn't take her long to reply.

One of my old haunts. See you there on the rooftop at nine?

She threw in a smiley face with a love heart on the side of its cheek. Nice. Ross sent her one back with, "It's a date."

Charles's private detective worked hard for his money that night. Keeping up with Melanie's sister's Jeep was hard work. He wondered if she were a NASCAR driver or the like. She sped through the streets of Sydney as if her car would evaporate into thin air if she didn't make it to her destination on time. Fortunately for him, many people drove like this in Sydney. Tailing her wouldn't look or seem unusual to her or anyone else on the roads.

When he watched them wander in the front doors of the Irish pub, he was already calling Charles Lewinson.

"She's just walked into Finnegans at the Rocks," the guy said. He could hear Charles fuming before he barked, "Pilot?"

The PI shook his head and was about to say no when out of the corner of his eye he saw a taxi pull up directly outside. He waited a second to see who got out of the car. The answer would be much to the chagrin of his current customer.

"Well?" Charles barked.

The PI waited another second before seeing the two men get out of the rear doors. When Ross stood up straight, the guy immediately recognized him from the night before at the airport.

"He's here, just got here," he said.

"Get in there and wait for me. I want your eyes on them the whole time, right?" Charles shouted before ending the call.

Geez, the detective thought, Lewinson was one wound-up asshole.

He grabbed his phone and his jacket, and got out of his car.

Finnegans was busy, though not as packed as it got on the weekends. Ross and Tony didn't mind; they weren't ones for overcrowded bars where you'd line up at the bar for hours just to get a drink. Less than half an hour later, you'd be back in the throng lining up for another. No thanks.

Finnegans had been in the news a few years ago, Ross recalled, when they'd let too many people in one Friday night during a football World Cup semifinal match. England versus another European country or something like that; Ross couldn't remember. The bar had been so packed that a poor sod who'd probably drunk way too much and was squeezed against the railing lost his balance and fell three stories to his premature death on the road below. Finnegans was fined heavily for breaching their maximum occupancy, and also criticized for the low height of the railing on the deck. But they were yet to raise the railing height.

Ross inhaled the beautiful view. The lights of the Harbour Bridge shimmered, as did the thousands more dotted over buildings, apartments, streetlights, city skyscrapers, and the Opera House.

He looked around the bar and then to the corner of the terrace, where he spotted Melanie and her sister standing at a table, chatting and sipping drinks.

"I've found them," he said. Tony returned the nod and headed for the bar to get both men drinks, leaving Ross to go straight to his lady.

Melanie had told Ross the night before that she wouldn't even tell her family members about him. So as Ross started to make his way to them, he stopped and went back to Tony at the bar.

"Just a reminder, Tone," Ross said in his ear, "Melanie's sister doesn't know about us, okay."

"Roger that," Tony said.

As the two women continued to chat, Melanie caught sight of Ross in the corner of her eye. She swallowed her excitement along with a mouthful of her Aperol Spritz, and put her drink down a second later. She turned to her sister and said, "My God, what a small world!"

When he was close enough, Ross said with pure surprise, "Melanie?" and with a smile, "Wow, what are the odds?"

When he pecked her on the cheek, Melanie turned to her sister and introduced him. Susie offered her hand. "It's nice to meet you, Ross," she said.

Tony was only ten seconds behind, and as he arrived, Melanie did it all over again. "Well, what a coincidence, Tony. I guess wherever Ross is, you are."

Tony laughed, and within five minutes the four of them were chatting like old friends.

Ross did his best not to stare at Melanie, though he found it difficult.

Melanie had the same problem, but found she could look around the bar and the view and then back at Ross, so it didn't look so obvious.

Speaking of staring, it was something Melanie had long ago gotten used to. In bars, especially, she would often find a guy staring at her for extended periods. For a beautiful woman, it came with the territory, and most of the time she took no notice.

But tonight, a particular guy was going hardcore.

When she studied the view as an excuse to look at Ross on the way back, Melanie would also now swing her eyes back by this man and look straight at him, staring at her. When he got busted, he'd quickly avert his gaze.

She brushed it off as something she had lived with for a long time. Nothing new.

But when Melanie looked across to another part of the bar on another round trip, her heart froze.

Jesus, she thought. Of all the bars, in a city populated by millions of people, what would be the odds of this particular guy being at this very bar tonight. He was no more than twenty feet away.

He was part of a large group, all dressed in corporate attire, and was chatting with a woman, one on one.

Now it was Melanie's turn to stare. She stared at him for so long, more out of shock than anything, that the woman he was talking to noticed and stared back at her.

She met Melanie's eyes, much to her surprise, and then went to say something to the guy she was with. When he looked over to Melanie, the shock on his face was nearly as startling as hers.

At that moment, Melanie heard what she thought was the bark of a small dog, and wondered what sort of idiot would bring a pooch to a rooftop bar.

The guy now smiling at her, and the woman who he'd been chatting to, heard the strange sound as well.

When she saw where it had come from, Melanie's hands began to shake. She stumbled and dropped her glass on the bar table.

The sound was no small dog.

It was her husband, Charles.

He was standing near the entrance to the bar.

He'd called out something to her, though she hadn't heard what he said through all the noise.

Then he started to make his way toward her.

Charles's detective kept his distance from his client, standing near the rear wall of the rooftop bar and wondering exactly what the guy was going to do in a crowded bar with dozens of witnesses.

Melanie's short breaths and panicked demeanor had caught the attention of Ross, Tony, and her sister. They all realized why a moment later.

And the guy with the woman in the larger group, who'd smiled at Melanie, nearly peed his pants when he caught sight of Charles.

"Well, well, well," Charles hissed, "what do we have here, then?"

Melanie held up her hand. "Charles, I arrived last night. I just needed a night alone before…"

"Shut up," he screamed at the top of his lungs, not caring what sort of scene he was already making in front of many people, "you goddamned slut."

Ross and Tony looked at each other. They knew whatever went down in the next few moments, they'd protect Melanie without question.

"Calm down, Charles." Melanie spoke with a confident but not overbearing tone. She knew the best thing was to try and defuse the situation. She, more than anyone, knew Charles had a short fuse and under the wrong circumstances was capable of extreme violence. But she also knew that this time around, thank God, Ross was by her side.

He stepped closer. "So, this is the guy you're fucking

behind my back," he snarled, nearly spitting in Ross's direction.

Bloody hell, Ross thought, the guy's pretty confronting, even though he's not well built. Sometimes that could be misleading; they could still pull out a knife, or worse still, a gun.

Melanie turned to Ross, and by chance to the stranger who was only ten feet away. She felt almost sick the moment their eyes met, and wondered how long it would be before Charles realized who he actually was. She hoped, somehow, he would be so angry that he wouldn't take any notice of him. That would be better. And if she could read this stranger's mind, she'd know he wished he were in any other bar in Sydney right now.

"Well, are you going to answer my question, you slut of a woman?"

Even now, the PI was starting to feel a twitch of unease. His gut told him this didn't feel right. He started to regret even working for the guy. He instantly made a wise decision, for no other reason than self-preservation.

He slipped his hand into his pocket, pulled out his mobile, and started to film the scene without anyone noticing.

Charles's temper was about to explode. He stomped his feet, drawing whispers from around the terrace. Realizing he was acting like a deranged lunatic in front of all these people, he shot a dirty look at many of them and spat, "Why don't you all mind your own fucking business?" As his eyes darted around to the strangers, his gaze stopped at the two people standing ten feet across from Melanie and the others.

Suddenly, his eyes started to bulge and his fists curled up into tight balls. He'd finally realized who the guy standing there with the woman was.

"You!" he thundered, shuffling his feet and looking about to explode.

He spun around, searching for anything within grabbing distance, and saw an empty pint glass not three feet away. In one swift motion, he stepped over to it, picked it up, and like a baseball pitcher throwing for the World Series, threw it with might and laser accuracy at the poor guy standing watching the madness unfold before him.

Instinctively, the guy ducked his head, a super-quick reaction that avoided the projectile hitting him in the noggin.

But what was lucky for him was very unlucky for the woman standing behind him.

The glass struck her so hard in her head, it smashed into several large pieces, with a sound like the millionaire had thrown it against a brick wall.

The thud was sickening. A second later, she was out cold on the floor.

Blood began pouring from a big gash on the side of her head.

And then it was on.

The guy she was with had never been in a fistfight before.

For the next few minutes, though, all he would breathe was rage. The guy almost jumped the ten or so feet between the two of them and started throwing punches he'd never thrown before. As the mayhem started to unfold in the next few moments, people, chairs, and tables were scattered in every direction. Charles screamed words Ross couldn't understand, clawing and kicking at the guy.

The other guy got the upper hand a moment later, just as bouncers appeared from the entrance doorway. When the two big men saw the scene in front of them, one said to the other, "Cops and ambos *now*."

The guy Charles had been punching on with broke free

from him and pushed him back toward the railing of the terrace.

He looked down to his girlfriend and could see the pool of blood. He wondered if she were still alive. He spun back to Charles, and as he did, someone let out a high-pitched scream.

When the police questioned the poor guy two hours later at the hospital, where he would be at his girlfriend's side, they would ask him many times over what had happened.

The guy could only remember the evening until the point when he'd heard a woman's scream. The rest was a blank.

But it didn't matter. The private detective was more than forthcoming in handing over the footage on his phone to the police.

After throwing the glass at the woman, Charles Lewinson had pulled a small handgun from his belt.

But before he had a chance to do anything with it, the guy whose girlfriend was on the floor in a pool of her own blood had charged at him with a level of anger he'd never felt before.

When they both hit the railing and were falling over the edge a second later, Ross sprang from where he stood and grabbed the guy's belt from behind.

Ross's quick thinking had saved the guy's life.

But not that of Melanie's husband.

He was now on the road below, his gun still in his right hand. When Ross peered over the edge, he could see Charles staring back up at him.

Ross wondered, if Charles's mind was still working, what the moron would be thinking right now.

If Charles, who was now 100% dead, could have been thinking anything at that moment, it would have been this.

What are the odds?

Two men at the same bar who'd slept with his wife.

One he'd suspected of doing so was international pilot Ross Moore.

The other, he knew, most certainly had.

Kevin Brewster, lawyer at Johnston, Neville, and Tolls, Sydney.

CHAPTER TWENTY

TIM WATCHED THE CD DISAPPEAR INTO THE SLOT OF his car audio system. A moment or so later, Freddie Mercury started to remind Tim why he liked Queen so much. Tim loved the guy's voice and the way he sang the many hits the band was famous for.

He drank in the sunny skies as he drove closer to his destination. Without a solitary cloud in the sky, the blue was as intoxicating as the day was bright. The air was cool and still, perfect for a drive out to this beautiful part of the world.

After passing through the small town of Lovelock, Tim knew the chances of seeing anyone else on 7 Troughs Road would be slim to nil. The road wound its way through the sparse landscape like a giant python, turning and twisting around hills and valleys. The land was devoid of tall trees now, a desert of billions of tons of sand, rock, and the odd shrub, with mountains dominating the horizon. It was tranquil—a nice place when you wanted to be alone.

Tim's heart was starting to beat faster with every mile closer he got to Shirley. Part of it was anxiety that he might have been tricked into coming all the way out here by someone he didn't know, someone who wanted to ask him about what he knew—not Ben. But as curiosity had long overtaken his reason, Tim knew he was now so close, turning around was not an option.

He drove on and tried to ignore the rising apprehension, now a constant companion in the front passenger seat of his car.

An hour or so after passing through the last small town, Tim came up the fork in the road that meant he was very close to his destination. He took a long drink from his bottle of water, and for a second felt as if he were being watched. He looked up into the distant mountains, and the feeling remained, only to depart when he shook it off with a shrug and a small, nervous laugh.

When the road became dirt, Tim drove on. He couldn't take his eyes off the taller hills and mountains almost surrounding him. The sun was high in the sky, and he knew somewhere out there, someone was—possibly—waiting for him to arrive.

When he arrived at the destination, he pulled up and stepped out of his car.

Tim held his hands up over his glasses, shielding his eyes from the bright sun overhead.

It had been decades since he was last here. Tim had forgotten how desolate and lonely the place was.

Vernon wasn't famous for its cafes, nightlife, or any tourist attractions you could post on Instagram or Facebook.

It had been abandoned over a century ago. Any sign of human life had gone with the people.

Tim walked away from his car for a bit.

In the distance, he heard an eagle or some sort of large bird squawk, high in the sky. Other than this, he could neither see nor hear any sign of life.

He started to wonder if coming all the way out here had been a good idea, and to hope there wasn't a highly skilled marksman sitting on top of a hill a few hundred feet away, with his scope trained on the middle of the back of Tim's head. He knew this was a thing that happened from time to time, and hoped it wasn't his turn yet.

After a couple more minutes, he felt the uneasy urge to get back in his car and just sit it out. He decided to turn the car around so he could see the landscape he had come from, hoping that if someone was coming, he'd see the dust trail on the dirt road from some distance away.

An hour later, Tim wondered what the hell he was doing there. He'd seen no one coming up from the road from Lovelock, the only way in and out of Vernon, as far as he knew.

He was busting for a visit to the toilet too.

Knowing he was probably the only person around for twenty or so miles, he ventured out of his car and, strangely, went to the rear bumper bar and had a quick pee on the dirt nearby. He wasn't sure why he chose there, but he did.

As he was about to get back into his car and curse the whole stupid idea of coming all the way here, the hairs on the back of his head stood on end. That feeling of being watched came from nowhere, but he couldn't shake it.

He turned up to his left. In the distance, he knew there was another abandoned town over that way, some ten minutes up the dirt road. It was known as Tunnel Camp.

He was about to turn away and open his car door when his eyes latched onto something in that direction.

It was the sun catching itself on something bright, like a mirror. It sort of flashed at Tim, and it made his heart skip a beat.

There was only one thing to do: get up there and take a look.

Ten minutes later, he drove into Tunnel Camp.

Unlike Vernon, there were the remnants of around six to ten buildings of different sizes and shapes, shacks, assorted sizes of machinery, and cars, probably a little too old for restoration. The Powerhouse, as it was known, was the largest building among the scattering of abandoned dwellings. Tim decided to look there first. He was instantly disappointed.

No mirror. No one.

He found the same in the shacks and smaller outbuildings.

The wind picked up from time to time, and only added to his frustration by serving him an entrée of fine sand and warmer air.

He was starting to feel like a real idiot, like this was just a stupid goose chase and someone was taking him for a ride.

Tim ventured back to his car, cursing louder to himself as the afternoon sun continued to crawl across the pale blue sky.

He took his bottle of water out of the car and decided to rest in the shade of the Powerhouse, where the large red brick walls would take some of the heat from the air. Once he felt he was rested enough, he'd consider driving back home to Alameda directly from here. A night at the Vagabond Inn, under David Bowie's personally designed bed cover, was not something he was now feeling really up to, thanks to this blowout of an afternoon.

"You stupid old fool," Tim said, sitting dejected on a pile of rubble inside the Powerhouse. He stared outside through the empty window frame and added, "What were you goddamned thinking?"

Tim took a long drink of water from his bottle.

A second later, Tim nearly shat his pants and sent water from the bottle all over his face and clothes as he lurched with fright.

"You've never been a stupid fool," the voice said calmly from the darkest corner of the ruined building.

"Tammy!" Lee, sitting glued to her TV, shouted to her best friend, who was in her room doing chores.

Tammy dropped what she was doing and came straight away.

Before Lee could say another word, Tammy was sitting on the armrest on the couch right next to her.

Both women watched the screen.

"And in other news," the anchorman said directly into his nearest camera, "we have new developments in the ongoing saga of Pacific Airlines Flight 19."

Tammy and Lee met each other's eyes for a second before turning their gazes back to the large screen.

An image of the Pacific Airlines A380 appeared behind the newsreader with the words "Flight 19 Mystery" added artistically below.

"Charles Lewinson, husband of Flight 19 survivor Melanie Lewinson, died suddenly last night in his hometown of Sydney, Australia."

Tammy managed a muted "Oh, my god."

"Reports from local sources at the scene have spoken of an altercation with another man shortly before Mr. Lewinson fell to his death from the balcony of a famous Irish bar in Sydney's Rocks district."

Tammy's heart sank. She immediately thought of Tony. She'd spoken to him only the day before, and knew he was back in Sydney with Ross. She put her hand up to her mouth, and a second later could feel a wave of emotion overcome her.

Lee turned to her friend and said, "Oh, Tammy. Come, sit."

Tammy fell off the armchair and rolled to a stop next to Lee.

Before either of them could say anything, the anchorman had more.

"And it doesn't end there. We have received reports earlier this afternoon that the wife of billionaire Flight 19 passenger Michael E. Darcy passed away from complications arising from a sudden stroke in another Australian city…" He checked his notes and knew no matter how many times he'd rehearsed the city's name before the broadcast, he'd still get it wrong.

"Mell-born." He cursed himself. It didn't sound right, but he had no choice to move on.

"Some are calling it…" He took a breath, the producer upstairs cursing his name aloud for the one-second delay. "…the curse of Flight 19. Or in short, the Flight 19 effect."

Tammy sat forward and put her head in her hands.

Everything was going to shit. None of this had happened when they'd landed in 2024.

What her heart really ached for was Tony. She wanted him by her side right here, right now.

Then Tammy thought of Darcy. She hadn't gotten to know him that well, but Melanie had spoken highly of him. She wondered how he was going and what he was having to deal with himself.

Lee rose from the couch and silently moved into the kitchen. Tammy could hear her open the fridge, and a moment later the chink of a couple of wine glasses held in one hand.

Lee sat down next to her and poured her a wine. Tammy quietly thanked her as the news cut to an ad break. Lee reached for the remote and switched off the TV.

"Tony will be fine," Lee said, putting her hand on Tammy's shoulder. "I'm sure of it." Tammy sat back on the couch and wiped tears from her eyes.

"The curse of Flight 19," she said out loud, taking a drink of her wine. "I wish I was never on that damn flight."

Lee stared out the window of her apartment in inner-city St. Louis. She wondered what it would have been like to be a passenger on the Pacific Airlines flight.

Tammy muttered something, though Lee thought for a second that she was hearing things.

She peered over to Tammy and said, "What did you just say?"

Tammy almost froze in surprise, a look of shock appearing on her face a second later.

"Ah, no—thing," Tammy said in a near whisper.

Lee put her glass down on the nearby coffee table and sat upright. She stared intently at Tammy.

"What did you just say?" she repeated.

Like the universe was trying to help Tammy out, Lee's mobile rang not a second later. Lee reached for it and could tell it was from an overseas number. She knew it had to be Tony. She handed the still-ringing phone over to Tammy, who gladly took it, jumping up to answer as if doing so would let her off the hook with Lee.

"Hello?" Tammy said excitedly.

It was Tony.

Lee watched Tammy talking on her phone. Her friend was clearly over the moon to hear from him.

But Lee could not stop thinking about what Tammy had just said a few moments ago. The sentence continued to replay in her head.

"This didn't happen when we landed in 2024."

Lee wondered what that meant.

She wouldn't let Tammy off the hook until she found out.

Emily struggled to rein in her excitement.

She'd hadn't been to the Venice Whaler for years. It was one of her favorite places on Venice Beach to have a couple of drinks and a bite to eat, especially on a day like today, with the late morning sun melting over the beach, a slight sea breeze coming in off the Pacific Ocean, and the place buzzing with a chilled vibe. The decision to meet Todd there for lunch was the best she'd made all week.

She was close to fifteen minutes early, so—what the hell —she ordered her favorite cocktail, the Whaler's Famous Margarita, along with chowder fries. She'd die of thirst if she had to wait, and a drink would calm her nerves. Those two reasons alone were good enough for her.

"Ah ha," Todd said, striding up to the bar table all smiles, "I see someone was thirsty." He planted a kiss on her cheek, making her blush. Then he whispered in her ear, "The next one will be on your lips."

He waltzed off to the bar and minutes later came back with a pint of beer. He sat down and checked out his surroundings. "I love this place. I used to drink here most weekends."

"You have no idea how much I have missed you, babe." She could feel the rush of her emotions coming to a boil.

Todd reached over and placed his hand on hers. "I've counted down the hours, honey. I barely slept last night with excitement."

For two further rounds of drinks, they sat together and talked about anything that didn't involve time travel or the years 2019 or 2024. They kept it light and very fluffy, their conversation straight-out cotton candy. If anyone nearby cared to listen, they'd have soon grown bored of the mindless banter.

Not long after Todd arrived, he had typed out a message on his phone—to Emily.

And rather than sending it, letting it end up in the telecommunications cloud for someone to access later, he just handed his phone to her. She read it and then deleted it. Simple, really.

"We'll talk about the serious stuff later when we go for a walk on the beach," the message said. "I don't want to do it here. By the way, you look smoking hot today. I love you xx."

Eventually, after polishing off a fourth round of drinks, the couple agreed a walk on the famous Venice Beach would be a good idea to stretch the legs and work off the alcohol and food.

When they reached an area of sand where no one else was in earshot, Todd held Emily's hand just that little bit tighter.

"I told Dad I know about Jason," he said without preamble.

"Jesus Christ." She seemed shocked by the revelation. "You wasted no time." She stopped walking and said, "Do you think it was wise to do it so soon?"

Todd's face twisted with anger, though he ensured she knew it wasn't directed at her. "I just can't play happy families anymore," he said.

"Dad seemed really angry about it when I told him."

He met Emily's worried eyes before once again checking no one was walking too close to them.

"I've got to find him, Em," he whispered.

Emily was clearly surprised by this, but even more so by what he said next.

"You haven't told your dad anything, right?"

Emily felt like Todd had slapped her in the face. She stepped back and took her hand away from his.

Todd realized what he'd just done. He stepped closer to

her and said, "Sorry, babe, I didn't mean to offend you. I just wanted to check."

Emily looked to her left, then her right, and started to walk slowly off along the water line. Todd followed her, and when he caught up, said, "Em, I'm sorry; I was just curious."

She stopped walking, clearly upset with his call on her trust.

"Coming from the guy that came straight out and told his father he knows about his illegitimate son?" She shot him a filthy look. "Really?"

Emily walked another three or four feet before spinning around and speaking through near-gritted teeth. "And you want to know if I've told Dad anything?" She stepped closer to him again. "No. I haven't told him anything. Just tell me you're not going to look for Jason anytime soon. I've got a bad feeling about all of this."

Todd seemed lost in his thoughts for a second, then snapped out of it and said with confidence, "I won't."

If Dr. Phil had been watching the goings on between the two of them from the comfort of his studio armchair, he'd be shaking his beautiful bald head from side to side.

They'd both just lied through their teeth to each other.

CHAPTER TWENTY-ONE

Tim stumbled to his feet.

His water bottle flew out of his hands, and half the water went with it. The sixty-seven-year-old slipped awkwardly on the sandy floor and nearly fell flat on his backside.

Ben slipped out of the shadows and took a few steps forward.

Tim was trying to speak, though the words were stuck in his mouth.

"B—en?" eventually spluttered out, though by the time the name left his lips, the three letters were a mere whisper.

His only son slowly walked over to him. Dressed in designer jeans, a white polo t-shirt and smart-looking casual shoes, he looked like he'd just left a photo shoot for a men's lifestyle magazine.

"You have no idea how good it is to see you, old man," Ben said.

Tim reached for him and the two men embraced.

But only for a second. Tim pushed him back and said rather bluntly, "What in God's name is going on?"

Ben glanced at his watch. He'd allowed ample time to talk to his old man before being picked up.

He stepped away from Tim and ventured back to where he'd been hiding.

He pulled some items from the corner before turning to Tim and smiling. "Come on, then, give me a hand with this stuff."

Tim walked to the corner of the building and realized Ben had brought, strangely, a couple of fold-up chairs, along with a medium-sized cooler box. Wow, Tim thought, the guy had come prepared, alright.

"Follow me," Ben said.

Tim took possession of the chairs, while Ben carried the cooler box. Ben seemed to know where he was heading, and Tim knew his son had always been this way. From the earliest time, he'd seemed to know what to do next. Today was no different.

Ben walked outside and to a shaded area nearby, motioning for his old man to hurry up and bring the chairs already.

When Tim unfolded his, he sat back and took a moment to enjoy the breathtaking view of mountain ranges to both sides, with a wide valley between them stretching as far as the horizon many miles away. The midday sun heated the air, but it was still cool enough to be comfortable in the shade.

Both Erwins had spent their fair share of time in Nevada. And for a time, both of them had actually lived in the state, though never permanently. The tourist mecca there had always been the bright lights of Las Vegas, and would certainly remain that way. But for father and son, now sitting within the ruins of Tunnel Camp, the desert wilderness of the Nevada high country was what they'd always preferred. It was peaceful, tranquil, and, in a few places, private.

Ben reached into the cooler box, and pulled out two chilled Budweisers.

He handed one to Tim before twisting off the lid of his own and looking into the vast openness.

Tim had been watching him the whole time.

"I guess I owe you one hell of an explanation," Ben said.

Tim took a deep breath and shook his head.

"That's the understatement of the year, my boy."

The corners of Ben's lips curled.

"I guess you need to figure out which year, Dad," he said.

Andrew Roberts carried the weight of his conscience squarely on his broad shoulders. He sat at his desk, lost in his own world of thoughts, staring at a photo of Todd and Kylie from a family get-together a few years ago. Todd towered over his wife just like he did, and she couldn't have looked any prouder of their son. And the problem for Andrew was—he'd always been immensely proud of his son on multiple levels. The first time Todd rode out of the California Highway Patrol depot on his maiden patrol, Andrew nearly wept. Todd following in his footsteps was something he'd carried with enormous pride.

But that was before Flight 19.

First, he lost Todd for nearly two and a half years. Andrew was shattered when the plane disappeared. It took him close to twelve months before he could bring himself to clear out Todd's locker at the depot. No one pushed him to do it. His co-workers could see the pain etched in his face every day when he came to work. He decided to start a small support group for other parents in Los Angeles who had lost children from the disappearance. It had helped him, and he felt it had helped many of the other parents too. They met the first Wednesday of every month. He wondered if they would meet next month. Even if the meeting was going ahead, he wasn't sure if he felt like attending. Things had changed. And the fact was simple—his son was back.

This was the second thing he was trying to come to terms with.

Todd.

Back in the flesh.

Andrew had mourned his passing, and with Kylie by his side, suffered through the pitch-black haze of loss.

So to have him just turn up, as if he'd been on some remote and secret island the whole time, was a tricky pill to swallow.

But the third problem trumped the other two tenfold.

How he'd found out about Jason, Andrew would struggle to figure out. For now, anyway. There was no logical explanation.

What made it all the worse was what Todd had said to him the first night they arrived home from Vandenberg.

Andrew had no idea why Todd would want to seek Jason out. They had nothing to do with each other. They were worlds apart, if his illegitimate son was even still alive, or still in the state of California, for that matter.

His other son was an ugly blemish on what had been a glittering career in the police force, and for the most part, in his mind, a glittering career as a husband and a father. He'd made a big mistake. And he'd thought it was all in the past. The thought of Jason alive and well and living in Los Angeles made Andrew feel angry and frustrated. Todd suggesting he was going to look for him only exacerbated his feelings.

Todd had no right to stick his nose where it didn't belong. It was none of his goddamned business.

He could feel his teeth clenching at the thought of another person standing in the photo alongside Kylie and Todd. The whole notion of Kylie ever meeting Jason made Andrew feel nauseous.

It was not going to happen, as far as he was concerned. He had to do something. He had to put a stop to this stupidity.

He stared at Todd's eyes through the very thin pane of glass in the photo frame, and knew the first thing he would have to contemplate was, to him, unthinkable. He would need to have Todd followed, or get a tracking device put on his motorcycle.

Or both.

~ ~ ~

"It means a lot to me that the three of you came today," Darcy said to Ross, Melanie, and Tony. The wake was three hundred people strong. Darcy had known there would be this many mourners.

Joanne Darcy was a popular Melbourne socialite. It was fitting for her wake to be held in the Grand Ballroom at the Windsor Hotel, in Melbourne's city center. Her children knew without question that this would have been her first choice. Although their marriage had gone a little weird, it was where their parents had celebrated their wedding, and it always held a special place in their hearts.

"How are you holding up, old fella?" Ross said to Darcy before resting his hand softly on his friend's shoulder.

Darcy stifled a sniff before he met the eyes of Melanie, Tony, and then Ross. "I feel somehow responsible for this," he said painfully.

Melanie stepped a little closer and put her arm around him.

"You weren't to know this was ever going to happen," she said.

Darcy studied the patterns in the plush carpet for a few seconds before looking up to Melanie.

"But she would still be alive if we hadn't come back," he whispered.

The four of them fell into a too-long, awkward silence.

Darcy noticed his oldest son waving him over from across the room. Andrew was talking to the premier of Victoria and a couple of other high-profile politicians. Darcy waved back and motioned he would be there in a moment.

Ross and Tony shuffled uncomfortably in their shoes, and Melanie felt as awkward as they did.

They had considered not attending Darcy's wife's funeral, and now wondered how long they would stay.

People were staring at them, and not with expressions of approval. They were beginning to feel distinctly out of place.

In the end, they'd be on a flight back to Sydney in less than three hours' time.

Before Darcy walked off, he turned to the three of them and said, "I just want to go home." When they gave him the same surprised expression, he added, "You all know where I am talking about, right?"

"I think we're all on the same page there," Ross said. "Are you guys in a hurry to spend any more time in Australia?"

Tony shook his head vigorously. Melanie did the same, but added, "I just need a couple of extra days back in Sydney to sort out all the legal stuff with the estate."

Darcy stepped toward the three of them and surprised Ross by shaking his hand and putting his other arm around his back. He did the same to Tony, but gave Melanie a warm embrace.

"Then I'll see you all back at the Beverly Hills Hotel in a week or two, I hope."

Pacific International Airlines welcomed the much-needed

boost in public confidence that Ross, Tony, and Melanie decided to give it by booking their return flights to Los Angeles with the struggling carrier. It just felt like the right thing to do. Ross and Tony had always felt they'd been taken care of as employees, and both were personal friends of Carl Kelly, the company's longest-serving CEO.

When Carl heard of the trio booking a flight from Sydney to Los Angeles, he made a phone call to upgrade their business-class tickets to first class at no extra charge as his way of saying thanks.

And then something else quite positive happened for Ross and Tony. When they touched down in Sydney that night, they both received a phone call at the hotel. Representatives from the American television network CBS had called, asking if they'd be interested in doing an interview on the American current-affairs show *60 Minutes*. Before Ross and Tony could even begin to consider the invitation, they were told something hard to believe: they would be offered two million dollars each for the interview. It didn't take them long to say yes.

Melanie would be informed the day before their flight back to LA that her husband's estate would be signed over to her without any significant issues. Her late husband's estranged sister publicly announced she would be fighting for a significant portion of it, but in subsequent negotiations would settle for a paltry $900,000. At the time of his sudden and quite shocking death, the schmuck's personal wealth had sat at around $269 million. Melanie, after legal costs and the like, would eventually receive a wire transfer of close to $263 million.

And on the day of her departure from the city she once called home, there was one other small piece of business she needed to attend to.

Ross accompanied her to the drive out to one of North Sydney's nicer harborside suburbs, Mosman.

When they arrived at their destination, they were met by two people, one still bearing the scars of the tumultuous night only a week or so ago. The other, Ross could tell, was still visibly shaken by the events he'd been directly involved in.

As Ross watched Melanie talking, he wondered if he'd ever met someone as grounded. Probably not. And she was generous, too.

"Both of you have been to hell and back," Melanie said.

She looked beyond them to the house. When no positive memories came to her, she knew the decision she had made was the right one.

She walked a few steps closer before pulling a bunch of keys from her handbag. She held them up in front of the two of them.

"You have had a profound effect on my life, and this is my way of saying thank you. Now, this is yours," she said.

They were speechless.

Melanie had just given them the keys to Charles Lewinson's $10 million Mosman mansion.

After some awkward but heartfelt hugs, Melanie said her goodbyes before getting into the back of the town car.

As it pulled away from the curb, Ross patted Melanie on the hand.

"Kevin Brewster and his girl are two happy people right now," he said.

Melanie kissed Ross passionately before whispering in his ear, "That makes three of us, darling."

CHAPTER TWENTY-TWO

"How did they end up calling this place Shirley, anyway?" Ben asked.

He checked out his old man before taking a sip of beer.

"A TV show back in the seventies—Laverne and Shirley," Tim said. He stared out into the landscape before turning back to Ben. "Someone, when I was at Homey, decided to come up with a creative code name for this place."

"Got it. It makes sense, reminds me of the movie *Airplane!* You know, 'And don't call me Shirley'?" Ben said.

Tim smiled but no laughter followed.

"I guess you don't want to talk about code names anymore, huh," Ben said.

Tim stared into the distance.

"Have you been at the shop this whole time?" he asked his son.

Ben sat back and, though Tim was not looking in his direction, shook his head before finally answering.

"Dad," he said, waiting for Tim to turn. When Tim eventually met Ben's eyes, he said, "No, I haven't."

He was about to say more, but caught himself.

Ben then realized he was only here today because of his

father's connection to the puzzle. He was under clear instructions. He'd been authorized to speak to Tim Erwin about the whole shebang, and it was the only reason the two men were currently sitting there, out in the middle of nowhere.

"I've been there on and off, but not the whole time."

Tim went to say something, but Ben waved him off suddenly.

"Sorry, Dad," Ben said, "just let me unpack this the way I rehearsed it a hundred times before today."

Tim took a deep breath. He knew he had to be patient. There'd be more than just two beers in the cooler. He had no idea how Ben got here, but he suspected it was by helicopter. This meant there was no hurry to push the subject.

"I've…" Ben sat forward. "We've—been somewhere I doubt you know even exists," he said.

Tim studied his son. Jesus. He recalled the phrase "when the student becomes the master." He'd always had a sneaking suspicion Ben would go much further up the pecking order than he had.

Ben had Tim's advanced mechanical aeronautics DNA coursing through his veins. Tim had seen it when Ben was barely a teenager. It came to him as if it were second nature.

But his son had taken that knowledge and combined it with his own specialty: advanced computer science.

"You, Jenny, and the kids?"

Ben stared at Tim before dipping his head as if in shame. He said, "Yes. All of us."

Tim looked like he'd just been told we were all living on the island of *Lost*. He was lost for words himself.

"Dad, we were forced to fake our disappearances." Ben looked genuinely upset. "It wasn't what I wanted."

Tim picked up his beer, and could feel the despair rising within him.

Ben ignored his father's cold stare and pushed on.

"I need to show you something," he said.

Tim stared out into the desert again. For some reason, he was starting to care less about finding out how Ben was involved, and more about going home to his wife.

"I know what the artifacts look like, Ben," Tim said dismissively.

Ben could tell his father was getting annoyed. He had expected this much. But he had to stay focused on the plan. Tim was going to be a part of the plan. He just hoped his dad would cooperate.

"I'm not talking about them," Ben said, finishing his beer and motioning for his dad to pass him another.

"Then what is it you want to show me?" Tim asked.

Ben stared at his old man for a moment.

"How about—where the artifacts came from? Or should I say—come from."

Tim lost his balance in his chair and a second later dropped his beer right between his legs. After retrieving his beer, he turned to his son incredulously and said, "You've seen it? That's why you had to 'disappear'?"

Ben was not surprised by his reaction.

He checked his watch and decided to send the signal to the chopper, knowing it would take at least fifteen minutes to come and get him.

He could tell Tim was hanging on his every word.

"No. That's not the reason."

Tim went to say something, but Ben decided enough was enough. It was time to drop the big one.

"It was because," Ben said, sitting up straight and grinning, "I've figured out how to make it work."

At Todd's own request, his return to work was devoid of any

fanfare and publicity, externally and internally. Unlike his father, he shunned the limelight. His old man seemed to revel in it. He loved being onstage, receiving yet another accolade for being a top cop.

But Todd always stood at the back of the crowd, even if his mom were waving him onto a stage or to the front of the mass of people clapping and cheering. It just wasn't him.

Now, his desire to fly underneath the radar was as strong as it had ever been. He just wanted to return to work and get on with his life. He wanted to put all of the Flight 19 bull-shit behind him. As far as he was concerned, it was done and dusted. The only two things on top of his to-do list at present were:

1. Continue his relationship with Emily.
2. Find Jason.

His first shift back on his motorcycle was busy. He dished out three fines for the same violation: talking on your mobile phone while driving. Will people ever stop doing this? Todd wondered.

It was his first shift with his new partner. The guy was a surprisingly able rider for a rookie, and came across as a good guy.

His new partner also made the right move by not asking Todd about the Flight 19 thing.

He was known at the depot as "Johnny the Mac," and Todd now realized where the nickname had come from.

He was obsessed with eating Big Macs.

At the end of the shift, Johnny made Todd's day with his suggestion. Actually, it was more about where the Mac wanted to eat a Big Mac.

There were, at last count, well over eleven hundred McDonald's restaurants in the state of California.

But Johnny the Mac's favorite was one familiar to Todd. McDonald's Westmont.

Johnny the Mac said he'd grown up in Westmont, and the restaurant was part of his upbringing. He had good memories there, and would often end a shift nearby so he could go there for a bite to eat.

Shit, Todd thought, the place brought back anything but good memories.

But that was then.

And this was now.

Todd felt as if his coffee was laced with a heavy dose of déjà vu. Sitting in the restaurant with a view to the car park, he felt like he had been there only yesterday. He watched his partner eye off the three Big Macs on his tray as if they were the last he'd ever eat.

Add to the burgers a large fries and a black coffee, and Todd wondered how in God's name Johnny wasn't the size of a house.

Todd recalled the night he'd nearly put a bullet in the wrong man less than thirty meters from where he was sitting right now. The guy falling on his ass in his own puddle of piss up at the back of the lot. But with that vision came the next one: Jason's lifeless eyes staring at Todd, and Jason's brain now splattered over the concrete wall behind him.

Todd took a deep breath and decided he'd lost his appetite.

Half an hour later, after the Mac's meal and most of the conversation were done, Todd told Johnny he may as well leave without him. Todd said he needed to visit the restroom and might be a while. It was no use waiting, he said.

The Mac looked beat, so he headed off.

Todd wasn't lying when he said he needed to visit the toilet. He just took a couple of minutes longer than he needed to ensure his partner was long gone. He ventured out of the restroom slowly, and breathed a sigh of relief when he saw his partner's bike was no longer sitting in the lot.

Todd rode out of the McDonald's car park, but pulled up at the entrance before looking up and down Imperial Highway for any signs of the Mac.

He was nowhere to be seen.

Todd rode the short distance to the intersection with S. Figueroa Street and turned right. Less than a hundred feet later, he pulled a sharp left and rode into the empty car park at the Jack in the Box restaurant. The car park was empty save for a car that looked like it had been there since the moon landing in 1969.

Todd rode up to a row of empty spaces alongside the rear fence line. A cold shiver ran down his spine as he recalled being there before. He pushed the feeling aside and dismounted. He knew time was of the essence and that he'd have to get back to the depot soon so as not to arouse suspicion. Before long, his partner would wonder why he was taking so long.

He stepped up to the fence before stealing a glance from side to side, ensuring there was no one around to question what he was up to. Below, the exit ramp rumbled every few moments, the cars and trucks passing fast enough that their drivers wouldn't even think of looking up.

He took a deep breath.

He was armed, though the last thing he wanted was to arouse anyone's attention.

He cleared the fence and stumbled a little on the steep embankment. Todd checked out what was in front of him.

His homeless half-brother's hideout.

As he reached the bottom of the embankment, the area underneath the overpass came into full view.

Todd caught his breath.

There was a mountain of junk under there.

When he took another step forward, movement from the middle of the junk heap made him freeze suddenly.

On the other side of the embankment, in a car park about two hundred feet away, there was also movement—which Todd was completely unaware of.

The lone figure took the binoculars away from his eyes and spoke into his mobile phone, which was glued to his ear.

"Yes, Andrew. The underpass right next to the Jack in the Box in Westmont." Then he went on to say something else he probably shouldn't have.

"We're even now. Todd's done nothing to me."

Johnny the Mac rang off and slipped his phone back into his jacket pocket. Andrew Roberts had done him a favor only six months ago, getting him out of a sticky situation one night involving broads and blow. He knew he'd have been finished as a cop if it weren't for the revered policeman. And when Andrew called for the favor to be returned, he knew he had no choice.

But Johnny the Mac knew his tough words about being even with Andrew Roberts were wishful thinking.

There'd be more to come.

Much more.

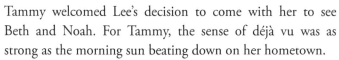

Tammy welcomed Lee's decision to come with her to see Beth and Noah. For Tammy, the sense of déjà vu was as strong as the morning sun beating down on her hometown.

She'd organized for Brandon to drop Beth and Noah at a

familiar spot: the steps of the St. Louis Art Museum in Forest Park.

But she was the only person who knew it was familiar.

Lee had driven, and after finding a car park in the lot a couple of hundred feet away, the two friends set out on foot to the steps of the museum.

"How you feeling, babe?" Lee said as they walked along the tree-lined path.

Tammy walked for another ten or so feet before she turned, trying to muster a confident smile for her best friend.

"I'm getting there," she said. "This is all just a bit surreal to me."

Lee dipped her head and studied Tammy over the rim of her sunglasses. Then she walked on. Lee was starting to grow suspicious, but knew she'd have wait for the right moment to ask Tammy what the hell was going on.

The two women eventually came up to the majestic statue of the Apotheosis of St. Louis. Tammy felt dread, thinking about the last time she'd been there. She looked down and across Art Hill, where the Grand Basin Lake sat in the distance. Down there, she had heard the harsh words her sister had spat at her: "Brandon was fucking me well before you got on that plane." A stab of anger poked her heart as she replayed the scene with Annie in her mind.

Tammy hadn't realized she'd stopped walking. Lee pulled on her arm and said, "Come on, we need to get across the road."

Tammy shook off the memory, and a moment later walked across Fine Arts Drive. The steps of the museum were empty—no Brandon, no Beth, no Noah.

Tammy's watch told her it was 11am sharp. She decided there was no point in getting annoyed. If Beth and Noah were a few minutes late, it would probably not be their fault.

Fifteen minutes later, Tammy could feel the deep-seated anger she harbored for her twin sister and ex-husband.

After the first ten minutes Lee had suggested they walk down to the bottom of the steps and sit on one of the two seats on either side. Tammy had attempted to call Brandon at the fifteen-minute mark, and it had gone straight to his voicemail. She left a terse message asking where he was.

Lee found the conversation with Tammy increasingly sparse. Both women had checked their mobiles a number of times and found nothing of interest.

Lee rose to her feet, deciding a stretch would be good for her legs. Checking her watch, she caught her breath, realizing the time was getting close to 11.30. Now she was getting really pissed with Brandon. The guy was an asshole. With no communication at all, he'd made Tammy wait this whole time. But she also wondered if Annie had something to do with it.

She walked over to stand in front of Lee, who could see tears forming in her eyes.

"I'm sorry about this," Tammy said.

"It's okay, honey. It's not your fault you're dealing with a bunch of assholes like those two."

Tammy wiped her face and produced a weak smile.

"Well, I owe you one," Tammy said. "Tell me anything I can do for you, and I'll do it."

Lee looked across the road to the statue of the Apotheosis of St. Louis as the most random of thoughts came to her.

She came forward and said into Tammy's ear, "Promise me you won't get upset if I ask you a question."

The two friends stared at each other for a moment.

"Okay," she said.

Lee swallowed before gathering the courage to come out with it.

"A few nights ago, at home, I overheard you saying something."

Tammy realized she wasn't even breathing.

Lee watched her friend carefully as she went on. "You've been here before, haven't you?"

Tammy never played cards; her poker face was terrible.

Her mind whirled. The idea of Lee knowing what had actually happened to them all was at first scary.

They'd made a pact.

No one off-plane was to know.

But a part of Tammy wanted to tell one of her oldest friends all about it. Keeping a secret of that magnitude had weighed heavily on her.

Tammy checked her watch. It was pushing 11.40. The arranged meeting was a complete blowout.

The anger she felt pushed her thoughts toward rebellion. It shouldn't have been the reason to tell, but she was over the day already.

Tammy took a deep breath, wondering if she'd end up regretting what she was about to say.

"You must promise me, on your life, that you will never, ever, repeat what I'm about to tell you," she said.

"I promise."

Tammy looked directly into Lee's eyes. Here it comes.

"I was here…" She hesitated, but knew it was time to let go of the burden. "…three years from now."

Lee blinked. The shock of what her best friend had just said was nowhere near starting to sink in.

"You've come back from the future?" Lee stammered.

Something in Tammy's vision made her nearly jump ten feet. She sat back and looked behind Lee, who hadn't taken her eyes off Tammy for a second.

"What the hell?" Tammy said, nodding for Lee to look behind her.

Beth was running toward her, only about twenty feet away from them. Behind her was Noah, walking slowly and in no hurry to reach his mother.

Walking alongside him was the Antichrist.

To Tammy, at least.

Teflon Fanny.

CHAPTER TWENTY-THREE

THE HELICOPTER LIFTED OFF FROM THE RUINS OF Tunnel Camp, and as it rose, Tim watched the desert landscape peel away from his line of vision.

His son had surprised him beyond words.

If someone had told him, first thing that morning, that by afternoon he'd be in a chopper flying toward Homey with his son by his side, he'd have laughed in their face.

But here they were.

Ben looked over to the security officer sitting in the back of the chopper across from Tim and himself.

Ben and the guy both knew what had to come next.

It was company policy. It didn't matter who it was: Ben's father, the President of the United States, the Queen of England. The guy grabbed the object from a compartment behind him before shaking it out and resting it on his lap for a moment.

Failure to do this would make his next paycheck his very last. The bosses of the shop didn't muck around. They'd written the book on stealth. There had never been, and never would be, second chances when it came to this policy.

Tim wasn't surprised when he saw it. He'd just been away for long enough to forget about the thing.

Tim slipped off his headphones and took the black pouch from the man. He slipped it over his head and put his headphones back on. When they arrived at their destination, the headphones would come off, but the bag would stay where it was. It would only come off when they, not he, felt it was time for Tim to see what they wanted him to see. If he attempted to remove the pouch, now securely though comfortably fastened around his neck, thanks to the security guy, his day would turn out vastly different.

He knew how that scenario went.

He'd wake up sitting upright in his car, nursing what would feel like the mother of all hangovers. He would have absolutely no recollection of the last twenty-four or probably forty-eight hours. And his first thought would be: what the hell am I doing sitting out here in the middle of the Nevada desert?

Forty-five minutes later, Tim felt the chopper commencing its descent.

In the darkness of the hood, he could feel a distant echo of déjà vu. They were entering a place he once called home.

Funny thing—what a coincidence, Tim thought.

The official name of the place.

Homey Airport.

Tammy looked down at her watch before looking pointedly at Lee.

Before she could say anything, Annie, who had continued to walk toward her, shouted, "Car trouble."

The tone was quintessentially Teflon. It meant, "So I'm more than half an hour late—get over it."

Tammy did her best to shut her sister out. She stared directly over to Beth and Noah.

"Hi, guys," she said with a heartfelt smile. "How you both doin', huh?"

Beth wasted no time walking to her mother. She almost crashed into Tammy as she awkwardly flung her little arms around her. It warmed Tammy from top to bottom, making up for the coldness she could feel emanating from her sister.

Tammy turned to Noah.

He stood close to Annie, and was not moving any time soon.

"Hey, little man." Tammy did her best to fight a sinking feeling. "Are you ready to come and spend some time with us?"

Noah shook his head. He stared at Tammy as if she were a complete stranger.

Lee could see just the slightest smile on Annie's face, and thought how nice it would be to take the ten steps over to her and smack that smart-ass expression right off.

Teflon, not taking her eyes from Tammy the whole time, leaned down and whispered in Noah's ear. He put his arm around her leg and a second later shook his head vigorously.

He then said, loud enough for Tammy to hear, "I just don't want to go with her, mommy."

Tammy nearly flipped. She crossed her arms instantly, and before she could begin to think of what to say to Annie, her sister barked, "Noah does not want to do this."

Tammy was about to plead with Noah to spend some time with her and his sister, but Annie plainly had other ideas.

"You can't just walk back into their lives and expect them to go on like nothing happened!" Annie said.

Tammy looked down to Beth. Thankfully, she did not

share Teflon's views. She could see the pain in Tammy's face, and wrapped her arms around her again.

Now it was Lee's turn to call a spade a spade.

"It wasn't Tammy's fault, Teflon," she said harshly. "Why don't you look at this from her point of view?"

Aside from Tammy's recent meeting with their parents, Annie hadn't been called her most despised nickname for as long as she could remember. That made it cut all the more deeply.

But she had the upper hand, and she damn well knew it.

"Listen here, Lezzy Lee," Annie snarled though through a broad grin, obviously enjoying herself, "when the day comes that you can actually hold onto a man, you can ask me stupid questions about points of view."

Lee had sported a short, Peter-Pan hairstyle for as long as she could remember, and on that account, some people made the mistake of thinking she was a lesbian. It didn't bother her at all. She was quite comfortable with how she looked and her current marital status. Coming from someone like Annie, "Lezzy Lee" meant nothing.

"Sure thing, Teflon Fanny." Lee indicated by her tone that she'd already forgotten what Annie had actually said. "Cutting your sister's lunch makes you God's authority on relationships, I guess?"

Annie blushed, but her expression then went dark.

She shot Beth a dirty look. "I'll be back here in an hour and a half to pick up Beth," she said.

"But I was supposed to have them for two hours," Tammy snapped.

Her sister began to walk off with Noah. She'd taken a few strides before she said, "Well, since I was late, it's now an hour and a half. Get it?"

Tammy could feel her emotions beginning to boil over.

She didn't want Annie to see this, so she turned in the other direction and stifled a sob as the tears came.

Lee stepped closer to comfort her.

As they walked off, Lee took one last look behind her at Teflon Fanny.

Wow, she thought, the woman was a complete bitch.

Teflon Fanny had obviously seen Lee looking back in her direction, and just for the sake of it, was now holding up her middle finger as she walked off with Noah in tow.

"We need to put a stop to that—bitch," Lee said. She whispered the last word, as she didn't want Beth to hear.

"In another lifetime, it actually happened," Tammy said.

Lee couldn't contain her shock. "You've gotta be kidding me. How?"

Tammy, still reeling from what cut her more than anything—Noah calling Annie "Mommy"—could feel the overwhelming desire to tell Lee everything grow stronger.

As she wiped tears from her eyes and held tight to her daughter's hand, Tammy knew it might make things better if she did.

As the chopper touched down, Tim felt Ben pat him on the arm. "You remember how this works, old man?"

He sure as hell did. And he didn't speak, because that was one of the many rules you were expected to follow as a visitor.

Ben opened the back door of the chopper and stepped out and onto the ground. He slipped his sunglasses on and welcomed the afternoon breeze. Today was already feeling like a good day. He'd been over the moon when he got confirmation from the surveillance people that his dad's car was heading in the direction of Vernon. A tracking device had been placed on it before he'd arrived back in Alameda. Ben had been on standby when he knew his father had gotten home, hoping that soon he would find his secret note telling him to go to Vernon.

Ben watched the security officer escort Tim off the chopper. He knew the guy would take good care of his old man. Tim was quite the special guest today. Being the father of one of the most senior people at the shop, and an ex-employee himself, Tim would be treated very well.

The SUV Tim was riding in wound its way across the expansive military base. If he'd been allowed to look, he'd have seen it had changed little since he was last there. Near-identical buildings were perfectly aligned in a small grid of roads. Functional but bland. Bases as highly classified as this one weren't designed to look pretty.

If there was anything attractive about Homey, you wouldn't see it on a conspiracy theorist's website, Google Earth, or the six o'clock news. This was for a good reason: the better-looking parts of the base were where all the secrets lived. If they'd spent the same amount of money on the visible parts of the base as they had on the top-secret ones, it would look like Kensington Palace Gardens on steroids.

After doing what the insiders called the "lap of strangers," where any car with a guest who had just arrived undertook five laps of the base in different directions, the SUV arrived at its destination.

Most now deemed the lap of strangers a silly old tradition, but the idea behind it, back when it was first conceived of, was to throw off any sense of direction the visitor may still have had, so they wouldn't have any clue where they were on the base, or be able to retrace their steps if they somehow returned uninvited.

The SUV pulled up at the nondescript single-story structure. It was one of the oldest and plainest-looking on the base, with three separate single-car roller doors to the left of the building, and just one entrance door for pedestrians. If you passed the building driving through an old town, you'd forget about it as soon as your eyes found the next uninteresting thing to look at.

The middle roller door rose without any fanfare, and the SUV rolled carefully through to reveal a garage containing two other identical SUVs parked directly in front of the other two roller doors. The rear of the garage looked like any other you'd see, with racks full of car parts and the like. Very authentic.

To the right of the room, a small office sat idle. Seen through a large window, a desk, computer, phone, and just for added authenticity, a fake plant, all gave the appearance of a functioning office.

There were two additional doors at the end of the garage office block, one with the letter *M* stamped on it, the other an *F*.

The security officer hopped out and opened the SUV's rear door. He indicated for Ben to jump out before speaking to Tim. "Please exit the transport, sir."

Ben walked to the door with the *M* on it, and the security officer and Tim went to the *F* door.

Ben switched on the light before walking to the bathroom vanity. He stared at himself in the mirror and kept his head still.

"Ben Erwin. Security clearance six-zero-thirteen-eight-sixty-nine," he said to his reflection.

He counted ten seconds in his head before adding, "I love the way your lips feel first thing in the morning."

A moment later, he heard the familiar sound. It was always a barely audible click.

Behind the two-way mirror, a state-of-the-art facial and voice-recognition program had identified Ben. If he messed this up, or hadn't been in the Majestic VA6 staff database, an odorless gas would have been released into the room thirty seconds after he hit the light switch. His heart would have ceased beating within another twenty.

He walked over to one of the two cubicles and opened the door.

The toilet itself had moved backwards and into the rear wall.

Ben stepped into the cubicle and closed the door.

Another few seconds passed, and Ben knew the sophisticated security program was now checking his weight through sensors in the floor.

All MVA6 staff were weighed on a weekly basis, and the security program recorded the precise measurement down to the gram. In addition, their clothing and shoes contained microchips that registered their weight.

A few moments later, the floor started to move downwards, the cream-colored walls of the toilet cubicle disappearing before being replaced by walls of gray, polished concrete.

When the lift came to a stop, Ben opened the door and stepped into the room.

The low-hung ceiling matched the walls of black mirrored glass. Multiple cameras were behind every one of them.

Ben looked over to the other door, next to the one he'd just come out of. When it opened a moment later, he watched the security officer escort his father out of the lift to where Ben was standing.

All three men stood and waited. A few moments later, the wall to Ben's left slid sideways to reveal an adjacent room, which appeared identical to the one they were currently in. All three men walked into this new section.

The wall moved back, plunging them into complete

darkness. A thin strip of lights then cut through the darkness on both sides of an elevator door, which opened automatically.

There were no buttons, or elevator music, or little screens telling you to have a nice day.

The lift dropped into the earth with a mere whisper. There was no vibration, no shudders, nor any indication they were actually in a lift.

When the lift stopped, the door opened and all three men stepped out into the main entrance hall of the facility.

Ben turned to the security officer and said, "Thank you."

The security guy gave a faint nod before walking off into a hidden door nearby.

Ben stepped over to his father and, after loosening the tie around the bottom, slipped the hood off his old man's head.

Tim wiped his face, and as his eyes registered his son, he took a deep breath.

Ben stood next to him and, as if on cue, the wall in front of them parted in the middle to reveal an astonishing sight.

"You've gotta be kidding me," Tim said.

Ben continued to look straight ahead, but said, "You are currently twenty-five stories below the Homey Airport softball pitch."

He let the words sink in before turning to Tim and adding, "Welcome to where I work."

CHAPTER TWENTY-FOUR

Ross, Melanie, and Tony arrived back in LA.

Luck was on their side; when they arrived at the Beverly Hills Hotel, the bungalow they'd all shared was available.

Actually, there wasn't any luck about it—Ross realized when they called the hotel before leaving Sydney that Michael E. Darcy had reserved his and Ross's bungalows weeks earlier.

Darcy had been paying the rent almost since they'd reappeared back in 2021.

He must have known they'd all end up there. He was on the money, that was for sure.

And now that he had Darcon back, the guy was once again a fully fledged billionaire. So money was very much not an issue for him. There'd be no problem of an unpaid bar tab for the Flight Nineteeners residing back at the Beverly Hills Hotel. Between them, they had more than enough cash to cover bar tabs until the end of time.

"Shall we make breakfast 10am tomorrow?" said Melanie, casting an eye over Ross and Tony as they stood at the entrance to their bungalow.

Tony nodded. Melanie could tell he was tired, and see

the longing look in his eyes for Tammy, who was due to visit in a couple of days' time. "Done," Ross said, confirming he was good for ten.

When Ross and Melanie crawled into bed twenty minutes later, Melanie said, "Can you believe Michael had reserved our bungalow this whole time?"

"The guy is one of a kind," Ross said.

Melanie kissed him, and after she switched off the bedside light, said, "The guy is full of surprises. You never know what he'll have up his sleeve."

"Whoa, man, whatta you want?"

Todd stepped closer to the underpass, his heart in his mouth. His gun was holstered to his left thigh with the safety on. He didn't want to have it drawn; he wanted to tone it down a little this time around.

"What is your name?" Todd said, slowly putting his left hand down and onto his pistol.

Todd stepped closer again. By now, the top of his head was touching the concrete of the underpass, and his vision began to adjust to the darkness underneath.

As the guy sat up and the blanket and cardboard lying over him fell away, Todd's gut told him it wasn't Jason.

Time was ticking. He knew he had only a couple more moments before he had to leave. Johnny the Mac would now be seriously wondering where he'd got to. Little did he know Johnny knew exactly where he was, and had headed up to the depot only thirty seconds ago.

"I said," Todd was getting impatient, "what is your…"

The street kid sat up all the way this time.

Todd was now sure it wasn't who he was looking for.

"I didn't do nothin', cop. Whatta you want from me?"

Todd snarled. "Just answer my question. What is your name?"

The kid knew he didn't really have a choice. God knows why he hadn't just told Todd already.

"Franco," he said.

Todd turned to his left and right, checking out the entire area underneath the underpass. There were no additional hiding spots for another street kid to be hiding out.

"Well, Franco," Todd said, kneeling down before continuing, "I'm looking for a kid just like you. His name is Jason."

Todd watched the guy closely after saying his half-brother's name. It took about five seconds before Todd could see a flicker in Franco's eyes.

"I don't know anyone by that name, doh."

Todd's instincts said he was lying. He pulled his gun from his holster. The guy sat up and stiffened.

Todd knew the safety was on. He just wanted to get an answer, not kill him.

He held up his pistol, and slowly brought it up so it was pointing at the guy's head.

"Let's try that again, doh," Todd said sharply.

Franco seemed to contemplate the situation.

"Oh, Jazzman," he said.

Todd now was out of time and patience.

He flicked the safety off, ensuring the punk saw him do it.

"Okay, okay—I know him, man, don't shoot me, huh? I'm too young to die. I know him, I know him, ye."

Todd put the safety on, but didn't put his gun down.

"Do you know where he is?"

Franco nodded, swallowing a big gulp of air.

"I know, I think. If I tell you, will you leave me alone?"

Todd put his gun back in his holster and pulled out his notepad.

"I'm listening, Franco."

"Talk to me, girlfriend."

Lee turned to Tammy, who was watching Beth on the playground as if she were in a trance. Her mind was so full of thoughts, she'd talk for an hour if Lee asked her to run through them.

"What did you say?" Tammy said.

Lee nearly rolled her eyes, but thought better of it. She could see Tammy had been shaken up by her sister's late arrival and flippant attitude. And that it had been Brandon who was supposed to drop the kids off, not bitch-face.

"I have a feeling you want to tell me something," Lee said.

Tammy studied her, though a second later her eyes drifted away to a point over Lee's right shoulder. It was as if someone was there, walking toward her. A flicker of excitement came over Tammy's eyes, but the vision of Tony walking across the park toward her was only her imagination. It came as soon as it went.

A shriek on the playground broke Tammy out of the fog in her mind. She recoiled at the sound, but knew it wasn't her child.

Tammy watched Beth running around the large playground with another girl. Good, Tammy thought, she'd hopefully play for a little while so she and Lee would have some time to talk.

Tammy sat sideways on the bench seat.

"If you repeat what I'm about to tell you," she said, leaning forward and nearly whispering, "things will go really bad for me."

Lee started to give her an easy reassurance, but Tammy

sat closer and grabbed her friend's wrist, squeezing it surprisingly hard. "I don't think you understand how serious I am, Lee Lather," she said.

"Jesus." Lee looked down to her wrist before looking at Tammy again. "Babe, you can trust me with your life."

Tammy let go of her wrist and said, "We *are* talking life or death here, and not just for me."

Lee began to wonder if it were a good idea to actually know. But for most people in such a situation, curiosity comes before consequence. Gossip is fifty-five percent of the spoken word for good reason. We all love to do it. Men, women, young or old, it doesn't matter. It sells magazines, keeps social media afloat, and gives most people something to talk about.

But this wasn't gossip.

Lee took a deep breath. "You don't have to tell me anything, honey. I will still love you, no matter what."

With the word *love* came the tears.

"Where do I start?" Tammy said through sobs.

Lee sat closer and put her arm around her friend.

"Anywhere you want, honey," she whispered.

Tammy came straight out and said it.

"My newborn daughter. She died in 2024."

Before Lee could even register what Tammy had said, her friend said more.

"So did Annie. She tried to kill me. But she was shot dead."

Lee sat back and waited for Tammy to make eye contact with her. When she finally did, she stared at Tammy for close to ten seconds before repeating what she thought Tammy had just said to her.

"You. Were. In. 2024? But now you're back in 2021? Annie was killed in 2024? Your third child made it to 2024 but died?"

"I know this is impossible to believe, Lee…" Tammy started to regain her composure, though pangs of regret were starting to make her question if this was at all a good idea. "…but I'm telling you the truth. Our plane originally came back in the year 2024. And then we got on again, only half of us, and it disappeared again but came back to this time, 2021."

Lee had gone pale. Her lips were moving, but her words appeared to be coming out somewhere else.

Both Lee and Tammy could see Beth making her way toward them, so Tammy added quickly, "I know what Annie is capable of. I'm scared out of my wits."

"If you think I am going to stand by and watch that bitch do anything to my best friend," Lee said, "you obviously don't know me that well."

When Beth reached Tammy, she said, "Why can't you and Daddy just get back together?"

The question surprised them both.

Tammy tried to figure out what to say.

"I'm not sure if it's possible, Beth," Lee said. "Your father is married to Annie now."

Beth looked blankly at Lee and said, "Daddy told me the other night. He told me to keep it a big secret."

Lee and Tammy shared a puzzled look.

Beth shrugged her shoulders, wondering what the big deal was.

"Daddy said he doesn't like Annie anymore. He wants to get back with Mommy."

CHAPTER TWENTY-FIVE

Tim Erwin had worked between Homey Airport and Edwards Air Force Base for nearly eighteen years. Close to eight of those saw him at Homey almost full-time. Tim knew the projects he worked on were top secret and directly connected to matters of national security. He enjoyed what he did, and had no desire to get involved in the "black" projects.

Employees at Tim's clearance level knew other projects went on at Homey. Having a top-secret clearance meant little in certain parts of the facility. That's just how it was. It was like working at a large university campus and you were only ever allowed to enter the one building you worked in.

Most of us can walk up to the high fences of the White House or Buckingham Palace and accept the fact we will never be given permission to enter them, or be invited in.

And likewise, Tim had never yearned to enter the off-limits hangars at Homey. He'd rather have been at home in his workshop.

But Ben, unlike his father, wanted more.

When he made it into the top-secret level of space aeronautics, Ben knew he wanted to go all the way.

Father and son worked on projects together here and there, but as Tim headed for retirement, Ben went on to others. Both father and son knew Ben had moved into the black projects, though they never said those words to each other. It kept them both in good stead with their employer.

It had taken Ben ten years to reach the security clearance he was now on. Part of the reason it was a decade-long process was that the vetting process actually took that long. There was no higher clearance than this. It was known as Majestic-VA6. It stood for Majestic, Vernon, Area 51. Five and one makes six, in case you were wondering.

But due to recent developments, management of the shop had made an executive decision. Tim would not have to wait ten years to get the same clearance as his son. Time was of the essence.

"Well, I'll be damned," Tim said, though his words seemed to barely make it out of his lips.

Ben was enjoying the moment. He'd always dreamed of showing his old man the facility, though until recently he thought it would always be just that—a dream.

Then things happened.

And now, here he was.

Tim stared through the large glass doors into a vast open space. It was the most pristine hangar he'd ever seen, about twenty meters high and, Tim estimated, about an acre in size.

The entire facility was lit by giant LED downlights. The walls were the same as those of the entrance rooms, all black glass, and impossibly clean, as was the polished floor of dark-gray concrete.

Tim could see the total area was divided into various glassed-off sections, which he had no doubt could all be reconfigured if needed.

Another security officer appeared from nowhere and

handed Ben an ID badge. A moment later, he was gone. Ben handed his father the badge and said, "It's time to see something only a dozen people in history have ever seen. That includes yours truly.

Ben walked to the edge of the glass doors before turning to Tim. "Follow me," he said.

Ten minutes later, father and son left yet another side room next to the subterranean hangar. They both donned dark-gray jumpsuits and special shoes. For a moment, Tim felt like Tom Cruise in *Top Gun*, though when he saw his reflection in the black glass wall, he thought maybe he was more like Maverick's grandfather.

The few who worked down there nicknamed the facility "the soft pit," because of its location beneath the softball pitch on the base, or just "the pit."

Somewhere along the line, another nickname had come into being: "the shop." The general theory was that this came from the countless myths about everyday inventions coming from alien technology: the microwave oven, aluminum foil, and—you've gotta be kidding—even the condom. All of them—not from here, apparently.

But down there was the only place they ever mentioned these nicknames. Back on the surface, loose lips sunk ships. And to the people involved in Majestic-VA6, their ship was the biggest of them all.

As Tim followed Ben through the hangar, staying close and not asking questions or making any comments, as per his many instructions, he found a vast array of different-sized flying machines zoned off in their own "pods," as Ben called them.

Ben would later tell Tim that most of these looked alien,

but they were not. They had been designed by humans over the decades to replicate what MVA6 believed were alien craft. Some of them had even worked, but only for a short time. Dozens of pilot deaths came with the ill-fated maiden flights.

Ben continued to walk at a steady pace, occasionally looking behind himself to make sure Tim was close.

About halfway across the hangar, Tim noticed that in the far corner there was a large, cordoned-off area. Tim could see big LED lights beaming down into the area, but nothing inside it.

Tim then realized something that made his heart skip a beat.

His son was leading him there.

$$\rightsquigarrow \quad \rightsquigarrow \quad \rightsquigarrow$$

The chink of glasses was loud enough for other people at the poolside bar to take notice.

Ross studied the others there with him: Melanie, Tony, Tammy, and Darcy.

"It's good to have you here, Tammy," he said.

Ross turned to the billionaire. "Michael, we are all happy to have you back. And we'd all like to offer you our sincerest condolences for your loss."

Darcy patted Ross on the shoulder. The two had grown close in the last six months. Ross now counted Darcy as a close friend, and Darcy did the same. They'd been through quite the journey together, and it wasn't over yet.

Darcy put his Old Fashioned down on the table and turned to the other four people. He then cast his eyes down to his lap for a moment before he said, "Joanne and I had a really unusual marriage. But on some level…" He then made eye contact with them all. "I will always believe we loved each other."

Darcy took a drink from his cocktail, and as he placed it back on the table, added, "I still can't believe she gave Darcon back to me. It doesn't make sense."

"Us coming back in this time obviously had a dramatic effect on her," Ross said. "I'm sorry it all happened this way." He was the only one who had the courage to say what they were all thinking. Darcy was beginning to make his peace with it—it was the truth.

After a few moments of silence, Melanie decided it was time to try and lighten the mood. "So, what happens now, team Flight 19?" she said.

Darcy sat back on his barstool and stared out across the gleaming pool. It was late afternoon and the air was warm with a subtle breeze. A couple frolicking at the far end of the pool sent the odd ripple across the surface.

He said, "Well, the one thing I'm going to do is visit a place I wish I had a long time ago."

Ross and Tony shrugged at each other as the foursome wondered where Michael was referring to.

"Piedmont, Missouri," he said. "I need to go and make peace with something that happened there a few years ago."

Darcy then waved to the barman. Another round of drinks, please.

He then thought he'd try and give them a little lift. With his best attempt at a chuckle, he said, "Oh, and on the way back, I need to go drop in on my old mate Bert Sargeant. Apparently, he's launching his third space flight."

Albert Sargeant was an old friend of Darcy's, an English billionaire famous for his business prowess, balls the size of watermelons, and his old-school British humor.

Bert also loved anything that could fly, and owned airlines across the globe. He'd flown in hot-air balloons, helicopters, and even with a jetpack strapped to his back. Any machine that enabled a human to leave terra firma and venture into the blue sky above—he'd been on it.

In the last few years, one of his passions had been getting people into space. His company Sargin had been a major benefactor to a consortium whose sole purpose was to get paying customers outside the world's atmosphere. To date, they'd done it twice.

"I'm surprised he hasn't invited you on one of the flights yet," said Tony, who Darcy had one day given the long version of his history with Sargeant.

Darcy sipped his cocktail and said, "Matter of fact, Tone, he actually has.'

Melanie smiled, "Are you going into space, Michael E. Darcy?"

Darcy gave her a cheeky wink. "The final frontier," he said. He seemed reflective for a second, but snapped out of it quickly. "Well, after where we've been, where else is left to go?"

CHAPTER TWENTY-SIX

"What do you call this?" Annie snarled as Brandon put the plate down in front of her.

Beth and Noah sat stiff as boards at the dining table. In a situation like this, they knew never to make eye contact with their stepmother. It made her even angrier. And when she got angry, bad things happened.

Beth once told her grandmother that Annie had hit her —slapped her so hard across the back of the head she had a headache for the rest of the day. And what broke Beth's heart even more than what Annie had done was her grandmother's dismissive attitude.

Patricia Sanders was really good at a couple of things. One: believing the Bible was society's go-to manual on everything, and two: living in a bubble where Adam and Eve still ate only apples, a fantasy land where nothing ever went wrong.

On some level, she'd known Annie was broken, so to speak.

Patricia never thought the minor accident when she dropped Annie as an infant was her fault or a big deal. And as the years progressed and the complaints at school and church about Annie's antisocial behavior started to add up, the bubble wouldn't allow looking back to find a cause.

"Pork steak simmered with barbecue sauce," Brandon said, lightly putting the other two plates in front of his children. He nervously sat down and followed the same rule Beth and Noah lived by most of the time now: he looked anywhere but in the direction of his wife. She was the modern-day Medusa, except her gaze wouldn't turn you to stone—she'd just throw stones at you.

Annie continued to stare at him until she eventually turned her attention to her plate.

In Brandon's defense, cooking was one not one of his strong points. He couldn't even cook a frozen pizza without cremating it.

But he had to try, because Annie hated to cook. She actually hated to do anything except whine, curse, and moan about everything and everyone. So this was the only way he could get a decent meal.

Annie ate a piece of the pork. So, it was a little over-cooked, Brandon could concede. The tension in the room became thicker than the pork steak on their plates, and probably harder to cut.

As she swallowed the leathery meat, she realized she had bitten off more than she could chew.

Beginning to gag, she slammed her fist on the table and burbled, "Brandon, I'm ch-o-k-i-n-g."

For a split second, he had the dark thought that he should let her choke.

Annie pushed her chair back in a rage and stood up. Brandon snapped out of his daydream and in a second was standing behind her. He put his arms around her waist and began the Heimlich maneuver. On the third go, the piece of pork came flying out of Annie's mouth, and knocked over a pepper shaker before landing unceremoniously in the middle of the table.

The smile on Beth's face was too big to hide. She couldn't help herself.

Annie was the first to notice.

"You think this is funny?" she shrieked, and flung her plate across the table. The entire contents flew in every direction.

Worse, the plate kept moving in Beth's direction, and hit her hard enough to send her and her chair flying backwards. Her screams came a second later.

As Beth's chair crashed to the floor, Noah cried out in the middle of the mayhem and went to her aid.

"Don't touch her!" Annie shouted.

Brandon couldn't believe what he'd just witnessed.

The guy knew how to spell the word *brave*, he just didn't know how to be it.

But something inside his head clicked. As Beth lay on the floor crying, with Noah now crouched on the floor next to her, Brandon grabbed Annie by the arm and said, "Why did you do that?" As she stared at him, he wasn't finished. "Are you out of your bloody mind?"

If you thought Beth's smile was enough to send Annie "out of her gourd," nothing compared it to what Brandon had just said to her. For most of her life, people had asked her this same question, and when she'd been asked it about the thousandth time, it started to begin sending her anger to dangerous levels.

Annie's fuse blew at that moment. She shook his hand off her left arm, spun around and brought up her right fist. By the time her body had performed a 180-degree turn, her right arm was up and her fist heading straight for Brandon's face. The tip of his nose would be ground zero.

When he eventually made it to hospital, his tail stapled

firmly between his legs, the doctor would wonder if his excuse of walking into a door by accident was true. By then, Brandon would be sporting two black eyes.

"I wish I'd never married you," he snarled. As he made the mistake of touching his nose, he said, "I'd be better off getting back with Tammy."

As he tried to get to the other side of the table to see how Beth was doing, Annie grabbed him by the throat and hissed chilling words right to his face.

"If you ever say that again," she said, the rage in her eyes like nothing Brandon had ever seen, "I will kill you."

"That must have been one hell of a dump," Johnny the Mac said.

Todd had just bumped into his partner in the locker rooms at the patrol depot after getting back from Westmont.

It took Todd a second to register what he was talking about.

"You could say that." Todd patted the Mac on the shoulder. "I got a little sidetracked on the way back."

Johnny the Mac studied Todd, wondering how he'd react if he knew his old man had blackmailed him into keeping tabs on him.

All Todd wanted to do was get changed and be on his way to see Emily and update her on what had happened this morning. She'd be the only person he could talk to about this for now.

Johnny the Mac took his time getting changed from his police uniform into his clothes. Out of the corner of his eye, he watched Todd doing the same, and hoped Todd would decide to have a shower at the depot after his shift. Many of his co-workers only did this at the peak of summer.

"Need to get rid of some of this grime," Todd said a few moments later. His partner let out a small sigh of relief.

To be honest, the Mac felt slimy about what he had to do. But if he didn't, Andrew Roberts could easily get him taken off the force. He had enough dirt on him to bury him. Roberts senior had considerable pull in the department, and the Mac and Andrew both knew it.

"No problem, bud," the Mac said. "I'm gonna go to the gym on the way home, so I'll have a shower after that." A lie.

Todd nodded, and as he walked off with his towel, said, "Sure thing. See you next shift."

The Mac waited about thirty seconds before he tiptoed to each end of the lockers to check no one else was around. He was in luck. It was a rare moment, having the change room all to himself. But he didn't want to tempt fate. He'd just do what he needed to, right now.

He opened Todd's locker and in a few seconds had his partner's mobile phone in his hand, sweaty with fear for his job and guilt at betraying his partner.

"Nice photo," he said to himself quietly as an image of Todd and Emily appeared on the screen.

He prayed Todd didn't have a passcode for his phone, and his prayers were answered. The Mac was in. The home screen of Todd's phone now stared back at him.

A second later, the Mac froze.

Someone was standing behind the open locker door. He hadn't seen him walk around the corner.

"What the hell?" they said.

⌐ ⌐ ⌐

"How many drinks have you had?" Ross asked.

Darcy shook his head and stifled a laugh.

"Not enough to not know what I'm saying," he said, and

took another sip of his Old Fashioned. But the guy was well on his way to another considerable hangover.

Michael E. Darcy could hold his liquor as well as he could make money. But everyone had a tipping point; his just hadn't arrived yet.

Tony turned to Tammy, and they seemed to nod together in agreement.

The same two-word sentence was forming in both their minds. Tammy was the one to say it.

"Why not?" she told Darcy. "The $300,000 per ticket is certainly going to put a big hole in my savings, though.'"

Darcy, flush with the sort of cash most people would never see, allowed his tenth Old Fashioned to make the next decision.

"Well, you needn't worry about that—any of you," Darcy said, surprising his four friends.

Ross laughed as he turned to Melanie, who confirmed she was in with the slightest shrug of her shoulders followed by a subtle smile.

Through the million-watt grin he was famous for, Ross said, "You not only want us all to come into space with you —but you're now prepared to shout us all the tickets?"

When you're worth over three billion dollars, 1.2 million is only loose change. He'd spent more on a car. Whether to drop that amount on tickets to get his four newfound friends into space was an easy decision. Especially when he was near drunk.

Darcy raised his glass to Ross, who was starting to feel the effects of his tenth bourbon. He *wanted* to feel it. It numbed his mind enough that he could cope with the things trapped there, even if it was just for a few hours.

Darcy sat back and watched Ross, Melanie, Tony, and Tammy all study each other one final time as they considered his offer. He relished the welcome feeling of their company.

They had become family to him, and he liked the idea. He'd spent most of his life shunning family, and the family he'd shunned would probably never have him back.

"Well, I guess we're in too," Melanie said, smiling at Ross.

"You beauty!" Darcy put down his drink to fist-pump the air with both hands.

"We're off to where only a few have ventured before," he decreed, with a level of happiness he'd not felt for a while.

It would be short-lived.

Only four out of the five of them would make it on-board.

Johnny the Mac's heart had surely stopped beating.

Shit. Todd?

How the hell am I going to explain this? the Mac wondered.

He came out from behind the locker door.

The other Roberts stood there looking at him.

"Where is he?" Andrew said without any preamble.

The Mac flicked his head over toward the showers.

Andrew stepped forward and said, "Go keep watch. Tell me when he finishes. Go."

He walked the couple of steps to where the Mac was standing with Todd's mobile. Andrew snatched it out of his hand.

The Mac went to the corner of the locker room and kept watch.

All but one of the six showers were in use. Somewhere in his mind, Johnny still felt like this was all crap. Andrew was becoming more of an asshole as each day passed. And on the flip side, his son was doing the opposite.

He could hear the odd murmur from the lockers. Andrew was now, obviously, going through his son's phone at full tilt.

"Aha," Andrew said. A second later, Todd was done.

"He's done," the Mac said under his breath.

Andrew put Todd's phone back in his locker.

"Get out of here," Andrew said as he walked past the Mac. "I've got what I was looking for."

As he was about to turn the corner, Andrew spun back to Johnny.

"Keep your phone on," he snarled. "This isn't over yet."

CHAPTER TWENTY-SEVEN

BEN ARRIVED AT THE CORDONED-OFF AREA. Two security guards stood on either side of the entrance, both with submachine guns hanging across their chests and serious-sized handguns holstered either side of their hips.

One of them pulled what looked like a large mobile phone from a compartment, and held it toward Ben, who pulled the ID badge on his lapel out on a cord and placed it on the screen of the device.

A second later, a little green light lit up on the screen. The same thing happened for Tim's pass.

The machine took a few seconds longer than it had for Ben, but the light went green all the same. The security guard gave a subtle nod and reached across to pull the curtain back. As he did, Tim realized there was yet another access door directly behind. The guard pressed something on his device and Tim heard an audible click in the door itself.

Ben entered, and Tim followed closely.

Tim looked around the pod. It took about a second before his vision fell on the object sitting right in the middle.

"Oh, my God," he said when Ben hit the controls of a

pulley system to lift a large black curtain off the outside of the object.

Tim had always pictured what an alien spacecraft would look like. The internet was filled with thousands of photos of what people purported to be the real thing. Then there were the ones that people had created from their imagination. Hollywood and the film and TV industry had also done a pretty good job at making some fairly believable looking crafts.

If this one had been dropped right in the middle of a comic convention, the geeks wouldn't have batted an eyelid. They'd dismiss it as another special-effects marvel.

What surprised Tim was the size.

It was surprisingly small in the scheme of things: no bigger than a large SUV wagon.

The outer shell of the craft was black. Its surface was so shiny, Tim thought it looked like it were made from porcelain. It had a weird shape, like a tear drop but without the tip. Its edges were rounded. Whoever designed it had aerodynamics nailed big time. About three-quarters of the way up, a small change in the surface indicated there was a foot-high window surrounding the craft, blacked out.

Tim lowered his stance to take a look underneath the craft. Three legs protruded from its underside, wafer-thin in comparison to the craft itself. At the end of each of these legs was a flat circular disk about the size of a small plate.

Ben stood and watched his dad. Tim was in a trance; he couldn't take his eyes off what was one of the most beautiful things he had ever seen.

"You're allowed to speak in here, Pop." Ben stepped closer to Tim. "It's just you and me in here."

"I'm lost for words, son." Tim shook his head as the thought of pinching himself crossed his mind.

"You think it looks pretty cool?" Ben said proudly.

A few moments later, Tim turned to Ben and said, "So this is it, huh? This is what brought the devices here to earth?"

Ben looked at him for a long time before a tiny smirk appeared on his face.

"No, Dad," he said.

Tim raised his eyebrows and instinctively crossed his arms. For a second, he felt cheated, but the feeling passed a second later and was replaced by confusion.

"I don't get it. What do you mean?"

Ben put his arm around his old man's shoulder.

"This is the one *we made*," Ben said.

Now Tim was really confused.

"This is man-made?" he asked.

Ben took a deep breath and said, "This is a working replica of the real thing."

Tim couldn't believe what he was hearing.

"So I guess my question to you now is this. Do you want to see the real thing?"

"You bet," Tim said.

Ben backed away from his father, watching him, then walked toward one of the walls in the corner of the cordoned-off pod area.

He took one last look back at his father, who hadn't moved an inch. Ben then walked up to the wall on the right side of the corner, and after checking his distance from the corner, stepped up so he stood only inches from the wall. He raised both his hands and placed them carefully against the glass, and counted to ten before placing his nose an inch away from the wall. Then he counted another ten seconds.

In this time, one of the world's most advanced security

systems was authenticating Ben's identity. Fingerprints, retinas, face, and even breathing were checked against what the system had on file for Ben Erwin. When he saw the tiniest red dot appear in his left eye from behind the glass, he undertook the final part of the process. "Ben Erwin, security clearance MVA6-5161516151," he said quietly.

Ben remained completely still. Nothing would happen if he moved.

Twenty seconds later, the opposing side of the corner wall began to move backwards, revealing another subsection of the facility.

"Okay, Dad. What you're about to see is beyond classified. Come, let me show you."

Tim let out an audible gasp as he walked the few steps to where Ben was.

"Jesus Christ," he swore.

The craft was identical to the one sitting in the main area, but severely damaged. Its front and right sides looked like they'd hit a brick wall at subsonic speed, and the roof section like it had nearly been ripped in two. Half the "window" on the left and rear was missing. And then Tim noticed something else unusual.

Something you'd never guess.

The smell.

He inhaled audibly and said, "What is that?"

Ben was long used to the odor. He'd spent so much time with the craft he barely noticed it anymore.

"That is the smell of what we believe is death, Dad."

Tim walked closer to the craft, and noticed only one of the legs underneath was intact.

"They died when it crashed at Vernon?"

Ben stared at Tim for some time before answering.

"Yes—they died when it crash-landed at Vernon." Ben

watched his father still staring at the craft. "All but one," he said a few moments later.

Tim felt like someone had slapped him in the face.

Ben studied the craft before turning back to Tim and giving him an even bigger slap.

"And he wants to meet you," he said.

CHAPTER TWENTY-EIGHT

"I HAVE A BAD FEELING ABOUT THIS," EMILY SAID.

Todd shook his head. "I can't explain it, babe." He placed his hand on hers. "He's my half-brother, and I killed him. Now he's alive. I need to make amends. I need to try and help him."

Emily turned her gaze to the living-room window.

A picture of her father came to mind. She wanted to talk to him about this. He'd give her sage advice. But obviously, that would mean telling him the whole story. Specifically, the part about Flight 19 actually coming back from 2024, not forward from 2019 as the world had been told.

"Okay, you know I support you on this," she lied, but then switched back to the truth.

"I want to tell Dad everything, and for us both to talk to him about this," she said warily. But Todd's reaction would surprise her. The reality was, this was weighing heavily on him.

"We've made a pact with Darcy and the others," Todd said.

Emily said, "I know." She contemplated something for a

moment. "I firmly believe, with all my heart, Dad can be trusted. He won't betray us."

Todd gave her a peck on the lips.

"And I trust you more than anyone," Todd said.

He just hoped he could also trust Dave Collins.

Ross and Tony sat in what was now almost their permanent booth in the corner of the Cabana Cafe. Of the four places they could eat or drink at the Beverly Hills Hotel, this was their favorite. It was just on 8.30 in the morning, and breakfast was solely on their radar. Melanie and Tammy had left early, Rodeo Drive beckoned, and they were both in the mood to buy an entire wardrobe of clothing and shoes.

"Good morning, gentlemen," their usual waitress, Veronika, said as she handed them a menu.

Both men waved the menus away. They knew the entire breakfast menu off by heart now.

Ross ordered his favorite: eggs Benedict with Canadian bacon. He was feeling particularly peckish, so he decided to add the truffle sauce. Veronika didn't bother asking him if he wanted a tea or coffee; Ross always had a large flat white.

Tony ordered a breakfast burrito and the avocado toast.

"You worked up an appetite, old boy?" Ross ribbed Tony as Veronica sauntered toward the kitchen with their orders.

Tony dipped his newspaper just enough to just make eye contact with Ross.

"What can I say," Tony said, grinning, "other than—do you blame her?"

Ross laughed. Tony had always traded on the whole playboy thing.

After their coffees arrived, something in the newspaper

caught Tony's attention. He slapped Ross with his signature Zoolander pout. "Mm," he said, "now that is interesting."

"Talk to me, stud-muffin," said Ross. "What have you got?"

"Hey—only Tammy calls me that, please."

Ross grinned. "The walls in the bungalow aren't as sound-proof as you think, baby."

He was kidding, of course.

"I've just found us something to do," Tony said. "Unless you want to return to the cockpit." He took another look at the page that had caught his interest.

Ross and Tony had decided recently that they would both retire as commercial pilots. They hadn't told the girls yet, but would soon enough. This meant they would now have to decide what to do with their time.

"I told you once before," Ross snarled, "I don't like flowers. I don't want to be a florist."

Amid the laughter, Veronika arrived with their meals.

As Ross tucked into his delicious breakfast, he told Tony, "Okay, so if we're not going to be strippers, I guess I don't have to worry about going to the gym."

Tony laughed between bites. "There's a flying school up at Monterey for sale."

Ross motioned to Tony to pass him the newspaper.

He read the blurb on the flying school, and had a really positive feeling about it.

"What are you thinking?" Ross asked.

Tony took a sip of coffee before saying, "We become joint owners. We can teach people how to fly, and work nine to five. Imagine that."

"You're talking about settling there, right?" Ross said.

"I've always heard good things about the place," Tony said. "Some say it's one of the best things about California."

Ross agreed. For all the cities he'd been to in the Golden

State, Monterey was one of the nicest. "I like it, brother." His heart warmed from the vision of a life at Monterey. "But I'll want Melanie to be part of my future there," he added.

"Sounds like a good idea. Don't ever let that one go, huh," Tony said.

Ross acknowledged Tony's words. He planned to do something that would make the depth of his feelings for Melanie known.

"What about Tam?" Ross said.

Tony pondered Ross's question for a moment.

"I think I'm going to want her around all the time too," he said.

Ross patted him on the back. "I say go for it, my friend. You never know what's around the corner," he said.

Ross would curse those very words.

"One of them is still alive?" Tim's words struggled to come out.

Ben walked to the edge of the secret room, and studied his pride and joy. To himself, he called it "the kettle." For some reason, it reminded him of one. All it needed was a large silver handle and an extension for the nozzle.

"Yes. There was a sole survivor," he said.

Tim scratched his head before a big frown appeared on his face.

"That would make him very, very old, right?"

Ben shook his head.

"You're thinking of time as we see it on earth," Ben said. He walked over to look closely at the older kettle before turning back to his father.

"Where he comes from, he's probably about middle-aged now."

Tim's head was beginning to spin. Not in his wildest imagination would he ever have believed he'd see and hear what he had today.

"Okay." Tim took long, deep breaths, and decided there was no time to waste. He checked every corner of the room for sign of another secret hidden compartment within the one he was standing in. Maybe that would be where "he" lived.

Ben was two steps ahead.

"He's not here," he said, checking his watch.

Tim looked confused, and before he could ask another question, Ben waved his hand and said, "Dad, in a few moments you will be flown back to Vernon. I want you to go back to Reno, or home. The choice is yours."

He motioned for Tim to follow him back out into the main cordoned-off area.

When he got back near the kettle, he turned to Tim and this time, just out of habit, spoke more quietly.

"In forty-eight hours' time, you will be picked up from your house. Tell Mom you're assisting the AFOAs with the continuing investigation of Flight 19. Tell her what you are assisting them with is classified, and she is not to tell anyone this. This is not negotiable, Dad," Ben said.

Tim went to say something, but Ben softened somewhat. "Sorry. I've worked here so long I've forgotten how to be personable."

"I'm sure she'll be okay." Tim smiled faintly and added, "And she'll be fine with me going off for a night or two."

Ben shook his head. "Where we will need to go to meet him will take more than a few days."

"How long are you talking, son?" Tim said.

Ben took one last look at his pride and joy before answering, "About forty-eight hours each way," he said.

"It takes that long to see him? He's not somewhere here at Homey?" Tim said.

Ben walked up to whisper in his father's ear, "He's not even on this continent, Pop."

As Ben went to head toward the door, Tim grabbed his arm. "Where is he?" he said.

Ben shook his head. "I can take you there. But I can't tell you where it is." He walked a couple of steps before turning back to Tim.

"Let's just say the place makes a mockery of the word *remote*."

CHAPTER TWENTY-NINE

Tony watched Tammy hop back into bed. Whenever they made eye contact, he couldn't help but smile at her in some way.

The guy was head over heels.

But tonight would be their last together for two weeks.

The time apart was only getting more difficult, especially for Tony. He was worried sick about Tammy. Understandably so, since Tammy's twin sister was a sandwich short of a picnic, and that's putting it kindly.

Tammy snuggled up to him, letting out the sort of sigh that generally meant only one thing. She didn't want to leave.

"You okay?" Tony stroked the back of her neck.

Tammy looked up to him. "It's getting harder when I leave."

They lay in silence for a few moments, just holding onto to each other.

Tony then made a wise decision to try and make the vibe a little more upbeat.

"Ross and I are thinking about buying a pilot-training school, up at Monterey. We don't want to fly commercially anymore."

"Sounds like a good idea, honey," she said, but her heart felt hollow.

Tony guessed something wasn't right.

"Well, here's the thing, babe." Tony kissed her. When he sat back, he said, "We're going to need someone to man the office when we're both flying kids around." Tammy's eyes lit up at the suggestion.

"If you're interested?" Tony said.

Tammy kissed him passionately. He'd just made her year.

"I'd love to." Happy tears crept from the corner of her eyes, and her mind started to wander to the possibilities.

Would Annie ever let her children come and live with her? No.

Would Brandon decide the children would be better off with her? Yes.

Would he find the courage to let it happen?

At the Beverly Hills Hotel that night, there must have been something in the air. Well, in bungalow 19A, anyway.

In the main bedroom, not far from Tony and Tammy's, Ross and Melanie sat in bed and discussed the future as well.

"Pilot school, huh?" Melanie rolled the idea around in her head. "Monterey. Central Coast, California," she then said aloud.

Ross hoped she would warm to the idea.

"Cute place, Monterey," she said. She turned to him and could see the hope in his eyes.

The truth was, the pilot-training school could have been on the tallest mountain in Tibet. It didn't matter where. She would want to be wherever he was. She was quietly relieved, though—she loved Monterey. It was her favorite part of California, along with San Francisco.

"Well, I'd hope that." Ross wondered how the hell he was going to do this, so he decided to improvise. "Excuse me for a moment." He hopped out of bed and headed for the en suite, closing the door as he went in.

Melanie lay back and wondered what he might have been about to say.

And a minute later, she wondered if he'd been sucked into the toilet. She was about to ask, "Are you right in there?" but just as she had nearly opened her mouth, he appeared at the open doorway.

The light was too dim for her to notice the sheepish grin etched on his face.

As Ross stepped into the bedroom, he suddenly tripped on something and fell on the floor.

"Jesus," Ross said.

"Are you alright?" Now Melanie sprang out of bed. As she raced around to the other side, Ross rose slightly and held his left knee in his hands. His right knee was supporting him, firmly on the floor.

"You're such a clumsy good-looking man. Are you okay?" she said as she reached him. She leaned down and grabbed his head with both hands. She kissed him softly on the forehead.

When she stepped back and met his eyes, she nearly fainted.

Ross had slipped something from his dressing gown. No, not that. Something from his pocket.

And now the little box was open. Inside, a ring sat nestled there, glistening in the candlelight.

Melanie then realized the whole falling down thing was a setup. The best one of them all.

Ross swallowed awkwardly and said, "I love you, Melanie. Would you make me the happiest man in the world tonight?"

Melanie was lost for words.

But eventually, she said the one we all hoped.

It was three letters long.

Love was in the air.

"Don't fuck with me, Shell."

"No need for that language, Todd. Ever heard of the Queen's English?"

Todd smirked at Michelle. "Not when I'm an American, living in America."

Todd and Michelle went way back. They'd stayed friends long after going to the police academy together eons ago. Todd had gone into the highway patrol, following in his father's footsteps, and Michelle had ended up at the San Bernardino Police Department.

"You'd know if I was pulling your leg, Todd." Michelle looked serious for a moment. "Are either of them hurting right now?"

Todd shook his head. The answer was certainly no.

"Johnny the Mac. Jesus." Todd felt wounded. "And your contact knows this for sure?"

Michelle ignored all the distractions at her desk: her phone ringing, her mobile pinging, email notifications.

She leaned forward and signaled for Todd to do the same.

"He was on his ass, Todd. Gone for sure. But And—, I mean, your dad, got him off with nothing but a slap on the wrist," she whispered.

"Shit, this can't be good." Todd went pale.

Michelle gave him a quizzical look. "What's with you? Why is that such a big deal?"

Todd rocked from side to side, and wondered what he should do next. Could he trust Michelle enough to tell her he was about to knock on his half-brother's door? He couldn't help but remember that in 2024, it had been Michelle who helped him find Jason. But of course, she had no memory of this in 2021.

Todd stepped around to the other side of Michelle's desk and pulled a chair from the nearby cubicle. He sat down and pulled the chair closer.

"What I'm about to tell you must remain between you and me."

Michelle agreed.

Todd took a moment before making eye contact with her.

"Dad has an illegitimate child. His name is Jason. I only found out about it…" Todd nearly stumbled on the biggest secret of all, but swerved just in time. "…recently."

Michelle let out a quiet "phew" before Todd continued.

"I think I messed up, Shell. I confronted Dad and told him I knew about—him, when I came home from Vandenberg. To make matters even worse, I told Dad I wanted to find him."

Michelle now took a deep breath before putting her hand on his right shoulder.

"If Andrew knows you're looking for him, you'd better think there's a chance he's asked the Mac to keep tabs on you," she said.

Todd cursed himself as he pushed the chair back, stood up, and said, "I was planning on knocking on his door tonight."

Michelle sat back in her chair and shook her head. "Alone?"

Todd nodded.

"Where is he?" she whispered.

"Someone told me he frequents a friend's apartment, spending most nights on the sofa." He swallowed hard. "Avalon Gardens."

Michelle's eyes went wide. Avalon Gardens was one part of South Central Los Angeles you'd never go near unless you were unlucky enough to live there, or your life depended on it.

She was about to say something but Todd cut her off. "But he's known to spend time somewhere else. I have this address as well as the Avalon Gardens one."

Michelle was already going to tell Todd going to Avalon Gardens was the king of bad ideas, but he then left her utterly speechless.

"The Star Apartments," he said.

Michelle waved her hand at him immediately.

She rose to her feet. "Not *the* Star Apartments," she said.

When he nodded silently, she shook her head. "You are out of your freaking mind, Todd. When was the last time you entered Skid Row?"

Todd could see the whites of his friend's eyes on high beam.

"It's been a few years, I will admit," he said.

Michelle grabbed the front of Todd's shirt and pulled him closer. "I can't believe I'm about to say this." She was clearly annoyed but pushed on. "I'll come with you. You are not going to those places alone."

Todd started to tell her this was not going to happen.

But he'd had enough of arguing with her. She was no shrinking violet; she could hold her own. And that was before you put a weapon in her hand.

"Okay," he said. "You can come with me. I'll call you later and confirm what time I'll pick you up."

As Todd walked off, she said, "Psst."

Todd spun around. She whispered inaudibly, but he could read her lips.

"Make. Sure. It's. Fully. Loaded."

CHAPTER THIRTY

Lee entered the foyer of her apartment block and said hello to the security guard, who was able to peel himself away from his smartphone long enough to grunt back at her.

At least he didn't have his feet on the desk behind the counter, and was making a little effort to look mildly interested in doing his job.

"Lee."

The voice from the corner of the foyer sounded like it was speaking from the other side of St. Louis. Lee had barely heard it, and for a second wondered if it was solely in her imagination.

When she saw who it was, she nearly dropped all her bags of shopping.

It wasn't about who it was, but how he looked.

"Jesus, Brandon." She stopped dead in her tracks and stared at him, startled. "You scared me to half to death."

He walked slowly toward her, as if he feared she'd drop her shopping for real and start throwing punches at him.

A large swath of gauze covered most of his nose.

Lee had never admired Brandon, and had barely warmed to him. At the outset, he'd been just a harmless, average-looking guy, who she'd always thought was batting a bit above his average. She'd never come out and said it to her best friend's face, but had thought about it in the early days.

She thought Tammy could have done better.

Maybe someone like the pilot type.

Watch this space, Lee.

"What happened to you?" She couldn't help but cut straight to the chase.

Brandon walked toward her until he was about three feet away.

"I walked straight into a door in the middle of the night." He'd said it a couple of times now, and it was starting to feel like the truth.

Lee studied his face for a few moments longer, and was only half convinced.

"What are you doing here?" she asked.

Brandon turned to the security guard, and seeing the guy's face couldn't be any closer to his phone, he said, "I was hoping you could just tell me something."

Lee stared at him blankly. She knew it would have something to do with Tammy. This was a sure thing.

She could feel the shopping bags cutting into her hands, so she said, "Clock's ticking, Bran. Can we cut to the chase?"

"Do you think there'd ever be a chance Tammy would be interested in getting back with me?" he said.

Lee put her shopping bags on the floor, two on each side of herself. Ah, that was better; her hands stopped hurting for a moment. She rubbed them together before focusing on Brandon again.

What a schmuck, she thought. He'd hooked up with Annie only weeks after Tammy's plane had disappeared, presumed crashed. And now Tammy was somehow back, he wanted to leave Annie and go crawling back to his ex-wife?

If she didn't still feel sorry for him, she'd have told him what she really thought of his ridiculous question.

"I will give you my honest opinion," she said, but as she took a breath, he interjected.

"But…"

He looked over to the security guard once again. He *really* didn't want him to hear what he was about to say next. Still, like half the world's population these days, he had his head bent permanently forward, looking straight at a miniature screen.

Brandon stared at Lee in such a way she now felt genuine pity. She could see his sunken eyes starting to mist over.

"You want to know," he whispered, leaning in closer, "if she did this to me."

Lee thought, if he's one step ahead of me, who am I to stop him?

She wanted to get upstairs and start dinner. A glass of Sauvignon Blanc was also on the radar, and would be especially welcome now.

"Did she?" Lee asked, without making any attempt to speak quietly.

Brandon felt affronted by her lack of discretion.

"*Yes*," he hissed, causing Lee to step back and instinctively reach down for her shopping bags.

"Sorry," he said. "Can you just tell me what my chances are, huh?"

Lee shook her head before looking toward the lift and thinking how she couldn't wait to be standing in it alone, hopefully in mere moments.

"There's more chance of Donald Trump pulling off a mask and revealing he's actually Elvis Presley in disguise."

She held Brandon's eyes for a moment before heading for the lift.

"Goodbye, Brandon," Lee said, not even in his direction.

When she got about ten feet away, Brandon nearly shouted, "I still love her, you know!"

Lee stopped on the spot before turning around to face Brandon and not mincing her words in the slightest.

"Well, you really showed her how much." She shook her head and laughed sarcastically. "Jesus, Brandon, when are you going to stop being such a certifiable dickhead?"

As she headed for the lift, Brandon bit his bottom lip and said, "I'd die for Tammy, you know that, Lee?"

Lee heard what Brandon said, but ignored him.

Fate certainly wouldn't.

"Tim Erwin," he said, giving his name to the security officer.

"Sir, allow me to take your bag."

Tim was escorted into a small, neat office. There, he was directed to sit on the couch against the far wall, which afforded him a rather bland view of the section of Oakland Airport he'd come to.

After fifteen or so minutes of sitting there alone, Tim heard the distant sound of a helicopter in the air. Being an airport, this was quite the common sound, though it was the first he'd heard today.

When he heard it directly above him, he knew it was his ride.

As the helicopter began to descend, Tim sat forward and waited until it dropped into view through the office windows. It landed with complete finesse, and Tim could not help but be in awe of how easy the pilot made it look. It was also a sleek-looking chopper, jet-black, with matching windows Tim couldn't see into. When Tim saw the rear door of the chopper open and a man jump out and onto the ground, he knew it was his son.

Ben was dressed in black from head to toe. He ignored his hair flinging around his face as he slipped the glasses in his left hand over his eyes.

He ducked instinctively until he was clear of the chopper, and came heading straight for the office.

"Here he is," Ben said, closing the door and grinning at his old man.

Tim stood up, and when Ben walked over to him, they gave each other the mandatory man-hug.

"You ready for this?" Ben couldn't have appeared more relaxed than he did at that moment.

"Never more ready, my boy. Let's do it," Tim said.

Ben slipped his glasses over his eyes with a smile.

"Follow me," he said.

Tim pulled the seat belt tight as the adrenaline coursing through his body started to come under control. Ben had strapped in next to him, but the security officer sat in the front of the chopper with the pilot.

Tim looked out through the heavily tinted windows as he felt the helicopter blades change position before the chopper lightly lifted off the ground.

When the chopper rose to about five hundred feet, Ben turned to his dad and said, "There's not much I can tell you right now other than we're on our way. But can I ask how you went with Mom?"

It pained Tim greatly he couldn't tell Sandra that Ben was alive. He hoped one day the enormous veil of secrecy Ben now lived behind could come down, and he could be reunited with her.

Ben could tell Tim was forming a response, and guessed correctly what was going through his old man's thoughts.

Lying to his wife wasn't something he was proud of.

"She bought it. Lock, stock, and barrel," Tim said.

Ben started to feel a little awkward.

Tim seemed to shake off his guilt, and as the chopper continued on, he said, "I spent many days and sometimes months away from home, as you may or may not recall." He rubbed the back of his neck. "So I guess she didn't really make an issue of it, which was a relief. If she hadn't wanted me to go, that would have made it very difficult indeed."

"I'm relieved to hear it went okay with her," Ben said.

Tim sat there for a moment and without any warning, the words just came straight out of his mouth.

"Do you miss her, son?"

For a moment, Ben's eyes shifted elsewhere.

"I've always missed everyone," he said eventually. A moment later, his demeanor changed from reflective to serious. "But I'm part of something pretty incredible here."

Tim wasn't sure how to take Ben's last words. He was trying to figure out if he should be a little offended, or understanding. Ben had pursued a dream, but at what cost?

Tim sat forward. "And do you think it is all worth it?" he said.

Ben nodded confidently, but Tim decided he'd ask him one more question. "Will you ever be able to return? You know, to life as you knew it? Do you think your mother will ever see you again?"

The thought had crossed Ben's mind from time to time.

"It's not on my radar right now." Ben checked his watch. "But one day, who knows."

Ben shifted in his seat before pulling out his tablet and turning it on. "Get some rest, Pop," he said. "We've got a bit of a journey ahead."

Ross woke to his fiancée's subtle movements. When he opened his eyes, he saw Melanie was sitting up in bed, looking with keen interest at her iPad.

He realized she was looking at pictures of a house, and presumed it was for sale on a real-estate website.

"Morning to you, future wifey." Ross kissed her.

"Soon-to-be-hub," she whispered, "how did you sleep?"

Ross put his hands behind his head and said, "Like a man who asked the woman of his dreams to marry him last night."

Melanie ignored his words before saying, "Whoa, this is nice."

Ross was about to ask her what she was referring to, but was interrupted by the sudden ringing of the phone on his bedside table.

He shared a curious look with Melanie before picking up the handset.

"Hello?"

Melanie continued to flick through the photos of the amazing beachfront property she'd just found in Monterey.

"Yes, this is Ross Moore."

She wondered who it was, but knew Ross would tell her.

Ross sat up. Whoever was on the other end of the phone was talking.

"You've gotta be kidding me." Ross peered over to Melanie before adding, "Ellen Degeneres wants to interview me on her show?"

Melanie could tell he was getting excited. The grin on his face was enormous.

"Uh-huh, yes. I'll call you back later today to discuss arrangements." A few seconds later he said, "You too. Have a great day."

Ross put the phone down.

"I've been invited to go on the Ellen Degeneres show to be interviewed."

"I could tell." Melanie put her iPad down on her lap. "That sounds pretty cool, babe." But a thought came from nowhere and straight out of her lips. "Do you think it's a good idea, though? You'll need to be really careful what you say."

Ross shook his head. "Agree, but for $750K for a half-hour interview, I think I'll be okay with all that."

Melanie whistled. "Wow, they're going to pay you that much? That's crazy. But money isn't something we need to worry about, honey."

Ross agreed, but he still felt he had to make his own way even though his wife was worth a quarter of a billion dollars.

"I know, babe, but I still need to contribute." Ross said before kissing her. "You know what I mean, right?"

It was one thing Melanie loved about Ross. Unlike Charles, Ross acted like a real man. If he wanted to work and feel like he was doing the right thing, who was she to argue with him?

"Well, in that case," Melanie said, picking up her iPad and shuffling closer to him, "you may want to see this."

Melanie showed him photos of the house she'd just seen, a gorgeous seaside place on Scenic Road at Carmel Point, Monterey. It overlooked Carmel Bay, and Ross immediately liked what he saw.

Melanie continued to flick through the photos, which only made Ross more interested in visiting.

When they studied the very last photo, Ross saw the open-for-inspection hours in a box on the screen.

"Well, I'll be damned," Ross said. "It's open this afternoon at three."

Melanie saw the time—8.46am. "We'd better get going, then," she said. "It's a five-hour drive to Monterey."

Ross pulled himself out of bed. As he thought about what he wanted for breakfast, he stared down at Melanie.

"What's going through that head of yours?" she said.

"No one is driving to Monterey today, baby."

As he slipped on his dressing gown, she raised her hands in the air and said, "Then how do we get there?"

Ross walked to the bed, "Darcy told me the other night that we have full use of his company helicopter if need be."

Melanie put her iPad down and motioned for Ross to jump back into bed.

"Well that gives us just a little more time, then. Get back in here, future hubby," she whispered, "I have something I want to show you."

CHAPTER THIRTY-ONE

Eighteen hours later.

TIM HAD DRIFTED IN AND OUT OF SLEEP FOR MOST OF the trip.

He'd had the hood on a number of times, and had grown so accustomed to it he wondered if he may as well have left it on the whole trip.

He knew the chopper had landed at an airstrip originally, and wondered if it were Homey. He could feel the wind and heat greet him when they landed and then eventually boarded an airplane.

When the plane leveled out, Ben took the hood off, and Tim could see that the windows were blacked out.

Ben told him the next leg of the journey would be over twelve hours long. He told his old man to get some sleep, which Tim did eventually after he'd had a meal and something to drink.

Tim woke with a fright as the rear wheels of the plane bounced on the tarmac. He opened his eyes to find Ben looking over at him.

"How you doing, Pop?" he said.

"Traveling is in my blood," Tim said as sarcastically as he could.

"Trust me—when we get there, it will be all worth it."

Tim wiped his face with his bare hands. He was still trying to clear the sleep-fog from his head. "How long do we have to go?" he mumbled.

Ben checked his smartphone before meeting his father's eyes. "We stay here overnight. At dawn, we take the final leg of the journey."

"And I'll have no idea where we are right now and where I'll sleep tonight," Tim said.

Ben said, "You've done this all before, haven't you?"

Tim tried to figure out where on God's earth he was right now, but he couldn't. If he wasn't in his hood, he was in a room with no windows, exit points, or ways to figure out where the hell he was. After more sleep, a meal, and a luke-warm shower, Tim was escorted from the room by his son once more.

The hood was back on, and to be honest, by now he was growing tired of it.

When the helicopter lifted off, he could tell it was much bigger and far more powerful than the last one. Tim then put two and two together. He was in the back of a V-22 Osprey. The craft was a hybrid: half helicopter, half plane. In layman's terms, it could land and take off like a chopper, but then fly like an airplane.

Now, Tim started to really wonder where the hell they were and where they were heading.

After about half an hour, Tim could feel himself dozing off. Without being able to see anything, he'd closed his eyes and, surprisingly, fallen asleep.

Tim was woken by the tap on his arm. "Dad, are you awake?"

Ben waited for an answer, and when one eventually came, he said, "You can take the hood off now if you wish."

Tim welcomed the freedom of being able to look around. The hood had been stuffy. Breathing wasn't difficult, but it sure was much easier without the darn thing pulled over his head.

He looked to Ben, and then beyond and through the windows.

They weren't blacked out, and no attempt had been made to cover them.

Tim could see they were flying at a considerable height and speed, over water. When he saw the rotors on the wings through the windows, he could confirm they were in fact traveling inside a V-22 Osprey.

"Are we getting close?"

Ben nodded. "In about an hour," he said, looking down at the hood with an expression almost of shame, "we will arrive at our final destination. You'll just have to put your friendly hoodie back on one more time. I'm sorry."

Tim smiled. Knowing they were this close, one more hour and another session of hood time didn't bother him in the slightest.

"Roger that," Tim said.

The V-22 went into helicopter mode.

That could mean only one thing.

They'd arrived.

After a bumpy descent, Tim felt relief as the wheels touched the ground.

Through his hood, he could hear his son speaking. A few

moments later, he was escorted off the V-22 and into a sheltered space off the landing pad.

Tim could feel the temperature and sound of the outside world disappear.

He heard the lift doors open, and a second later the sensation of descending.

When the lift stopped, Ben stepped over to Tim and said, "I'm now going to take the hood off, okay?"

"I've been looking forward to it, son," Tim replied.

A second later, Tim welcomed the relief of not having the damned thing stuck over his head.

He then turned to Ben, who'd been watching him the whole time.

His son looked quite pleased with himself. "Welcome, father," he said in a near whisper, "to the world's most advanced top-secret facility."

"Jesus Christ. I must be dreaming," Tim said.

CHAPTER THIRTY-TWO

Todd tried to muster something resembling a smile for Michelle.

Eventually, she said, "Are you really sure you want to find this guy?"

Todd drove on for a few moments before nodding. Looking straight ahead at the road, he said, "Yes. All I want to do is meet him and see if I can help."

The two police officers had gone to the address at Avalon Gardens a few days earlier.

They'd entered the housing estate in the late afternoon, and had no desire to be there after sunset.

But Jason was not at the address.

That meant they had to go to Star Apartments, in the heart of Skid Row.

The first issue they had was that they didn't want other cops to see them in the area. So they went in plain clothes.

As Todd drove down S. Alameda Street, knowing they were only minutes from entering Skid Row, he told Michelle, "If we don't find him today, maybe it's fate's way of telling me not to bother trying."

Michelle thought fate was a complete load of bull. But

she wouldn't argue with Todd if it resulted in him giving up on this. "Alright, it's a deal," she said.

Half an hour later, they parked a few blocks from the Star Apartments. The walk was a safer option than driving this far into Skid Row.

When they reached the top floor of the apartment block, Todd found the door he was looking for.

He took one last look at Michelle. She reciprocated before turning and continuing to watch the other end of the hallway.

Todd tapped on the door.

He couldn't hear any sign of activity inside the flat.

As he was about to tap once more, suddenly he heard something, perhaps movement behind the door.

Todd stood back and instinctively slipped his handgun out of the holster, but then thought the better of it and decided to take the mother of all risks.

The door opened.

Todd felt like he was looking at a ghost.

"Who are you, man?" Jason said, after looking Todd up and down.

Todd then snapped out of his daydream.

Now it was his turn to look Jason over. His clothes were shabby, but nowhere near as bad as they were when he last saw him. He didn't come across as drunk or high.

His demeanor was non-threatening, if not particularly friendly.

Todd put his hand up and said, "I mean you no harm. First, I just need to ask you—is your name Jason?"

His half-brother stared at him for a moment, almost curious.

"That's my name. What's it to you?"

A tsunami of relief washed over Todd.

He'd found him.

But just as Todd was about to speak, a gunshot punctured the air.

Ross and Melanie hopped into the rear of the helicopter. But they weren't alone; they had a guest.

"Are you guys sure you're okay with me coming along for the ride?" Darcy said.

Ross and Melanie shared a glance before turning back to him. Ross said, "When it's your helicopter, my friend, of course you can come along for a look."

The ninety-minute flight was full of light conversation about everything and anything. But with the pilot able to listen in at any time to the conversations of his three passengers, there were certain things they didn't discuss. They could do that in private.

"Are you still planning on going to Missouri?" Ross asked at one point.

"Yes. Funny you ask," the billionaire said. But every time he thought of Missouri, he felt his blood run cold.

He stared out the window for a moment, hoping the feeling of nausea would pass.

"I was hoping to tie it into our trip to the Mojave Desert for our little excursion with Berty, but I think the flight to the heavens has been delayed again. So I may end up going there at the end of this week."

Ross put on a smile for his friend.

"Well, I look forward to hearing how it goes out there," he said.

Darcy gazed out through the helicopter windows before looking back to Ross.

"You'll be the first to know, Roscoe," he said.

"Wow."

"Wow."

"Wow."

They all had the same reaction.

Melanie turned to Darcy. "So you like the look of the place?"

Ross thought it was beautiful. He'd always dreamed of living in a house with ocean views. And there were ocean views from just about every room in this Tuscan-style home Melanie had found online.

Ross walked out onto the front deck and instantly fell in love with what he saw.

Sitting to one side was a two-seater swing seat.

A six-burner barbecue with a hood and side burner, all built into a reclaimed wooden bench, sat nearby.

It was enough for him to turn to Melanie and say, "I love it."

Melanie stared into his blue eyes. "I think we've just found our home, future hub," she said.

"Can you two withhold the gushy stuff for five seconds?" Darcy roared at his own humor before walking to the edge of the deck, having noticed something going on in the house next door.

"Well, I'll be damned," he said.

As the three Flight Nineteeners stood there watching, a woman was hammering a sign into the front lawn of the house next door.

After she was confident it was secure, she noticed three strangers watching her.

"Beautiful day to be in Monterey," the real-estate agent said, before adding, "Are any of you in the market for a new home?"

Melanie shook her head, but said with sincerity, "I think we've just found it. Thanks anyway."

"You know what," the woman said. "Maybe you should just come over and have a quick look. You never know. Julia Reichstein, at your service."

Darcy, Ross, and Melanie looked at each other and thought, why not?

They had ample time. The helicopter would be waiting for them at Monterey Regional Airport no matter how long they took.

"Okay, then," Melanie said. "Let's see what you have over there, Julia."

Only when she entered the driveway of the house next door to her dream home did a thought enter her mind.

CHAPTER THIRTY-THREE

THE FACILITY WAS LIKE THE ONE BENEATH HOMEY Airport but more impressive. It was easily five times bigger.

But what made this facility so much more incredible was that half of it looked like it wasn't a top-secret facility at all, but a movie set, built to look like a small, picturesque township. Tim could see a main street lined with shops and buildings. At the other end of the town was a luscious oasis of trees. On a second look, Tim realized that it could have been a small lake or something similar, sitting in the middle of the area.

Tim followed Ben along a glassed-in corridor that gave him a much better vantage point of the facility.

He could see the other half of it now. It was a cutting-edge aerospace hangar.

A vast array of equipment divided into pods identical to the one at the shop sat on the other side of the hangar, opposite the aerospace area. In each of these pods were more examples of test craft that they'd obviously been experimenting on over the years.

"Amazing, huh?" Ben said in a near whisper as he motioned for Tim to keep up.

When Tim caught up to Ben, he said, "What's the point of the place below Homey Airport, if this one exists?"

Ben walked on for a few feet before he said, "It's a long story. We'll cover that off later."

Ben studied both sides of the facility. Every time he walked up there, he was still in awe of the place, even though it was familiar to him.

The two Erwins walked another twenty feet or so. At the end of the catwalk, Tim could see a staircase that would lead them down to the floor of the facility.

Ben said, "We will brief you in a few minutes, with the intention of then getting you to meet someone very special to us."

"The lone survivor," Tim said.

"He said what?"

Lee repeated the words. "He asked if you'd consider taking him back."

All Tammy could picture was Tony: the boyish good looks, the hair, the grin, the ears. She loved all of him. The last thing on earth she would ever do was get back with Brandon now. And Brandon was an A-grade cheater, with none other than Tammy's own sister. Even without Tony around, hell would freeze over before she went back to him. With relationships, she always held onto the belief that if it ends—you never go back.

Tammy eventually met Lee's gaze and said, "Has the man lost the plot? What would possess him to think that would be a good idea? And that I would ever consider it?"

Lee had waited for Tammy to get back to her apartment before she poured herself a wine.

She held up her finger, signaling that Tammy should hold on one second, before heading over to the kitchen cupboard and pulling out two wine glasses. Once she'd poured herself and Tammy a glass, she handed Tammy's to her and said, "Bottoms up."

As soon as she'd had a sip, she said, "There's something else you need to know."

Tammy sat a little more upright. "I'm listening."

Lee came and sat next to her on one of the kitchen barstools.

She studied her glass of wine for a moment as the vision of Brandon's busted-up face came to mind.

"Annie. Um, she…" Lee seemed to hesitate, so Tammy took another drink. That helped.

Tammy shook her head and said, "Annie did what?"

"Broke his nose. You've never seen two black eyes like it." Lee shook her head. "It was like she used a baseball bat."

Tammy went pale.

It was happening again.

Annie was losing her shit. She was going off-reserve.

The last time Annie lost it, she'd tried to kill Tammy. And out of nothing but pure luck, Tammy's life had been spared.

In an instant, her thoughts instinctively switched to worry for her two children. Her own safety would come a distant second.

Her gut told her something bad was on the horizon. All she wanted to do was take Beth and Noah back to California that very night. She felt much safer there.

"Shit," Tammy said.

"What are you going to do?" Lee put her hand on her best friend's shoulder.

"I need to get out of here," Tammy said.

Lee knew she was talking about St. Louis.

"But what about Beth and Noah?" Lee said.

Tammy studied the clear liquid swilling around in her glass.

"I think I'm just going to have to take them with me," she said resolutely.

Lee said, "Do you mean you're just going to take them without anyone's consent?"

Tammy silently nodded. Tears were starting to well up in her eyes.

"What choice do I have? Annie's a complete wack job. I'm worried sick she'll do something to harm them."

Lee scoffed. "Surely she'd never harm those two defenseless children?"

Tammy shook her head. "What better way to get back at me? And if she knew Brandon wanted to come crawling back, what better way to get back at him too? It would be a double whammy."

⸺   ⸺   ⸺

Todd locked the car doors the split second Michelle's passenger-side door closed. He started the car immediately and pulled out from the curb. Fortunately, at that moment there were no cars driving down his side of the road.

He turned to Michelle and said, "Thank you will never be able to cover it."

"If I had to work Skid Row," she said, "I'd have to consider wearing diapers."

They both broke into nervous laughter.

When they'd driven another block or so, Todd said, "Jesus. The gunshot sounded like it was right next to us."

Michelle wiped her forehead and shook her head. "I don't think I've ever jumped that high."

But as Jason had explained to Todd, living in Skid Row was like living next to an airport. Whether it was planes or gunshots—you ended up zoning out once you'd heard enough of them.

"So it went well, huh? You happy?" Michelle said.

Todd drove on, believing things had gone well.

"He was a bit standoffish at the beginning, but once he let me explain who I was and why I was there, he seemed to warm to me," he said.

"So what happens now, my man?" Michelle inquired.

Todd tapped on the dashboard with the hand that had been sitting across the top of the steering wheel. "He agreed to meet me again in a week or so," he said. "I'm just going to buy him a coffee and a sandwich."

When he'd given her a quick look to confirm she'd heard what he said, he added, "I'm going to take it slow. I just want to see if I can get to know him."

Michelle thought it seemed a reasonable idea.

She'd always known Todd had a heart of gold, and could see he was trying to do the right thing.

"Do you think you can help him?" she said.

"He was more articulate than I thought he would be. To be honest, I was expecting him to be a thug. Maybe I caught him on a good day, but he came across as just a normal kid, doing it hard. I think there's hope for him."

Michelle looked out her passenger window as the streets of Clement Junction flew past. The one thing that came to her mind was what concerned her the most.

Todd might think everything would be peachy-keen with this attempt to establish a relationship with his half-brother. But someone else, with considerable pull in this town, might have other ideas.

Andrew Roberts.

Michelle wasn't intimidated by Todd's father. But her superior officer? The guy she answered to?

That was a different story altogether.

And when the Mac reported to Andrew who he'd seen Todd with, things would unravel for Todd's friend Michelle.

CHAPTER THIRTY-FOUR

BEN LED TIM INTO A LARGE ROOM, WHICH AT SECOND glance Tim realized was a boardroom. The impossibly large table was surrounded by high-backed leather chairs.

The main wall was dominated by four enormous screens. To the left of the room, Tim could see the township, and to his right, in stark contrast, was the aerospace facility.

Tim knew the amount of money spent on "black-ops" projects was significant.

But looking around this facility, which Ben had called "Joe," Tim wondered if this was where a big portion of all black-ops money had gone. He wasn't far from the truth.

Ben offered Tim a water before telling him he'd be back shortly. He disappeared through the door, which shut silently behind him.

Ben was gone for about ten minutes.

Tim wasn't fussed. He'd spent most of his time toggling his fascination from one side of the facility to the other. He still considered pinching himself a couple of times, to ensure he wasn't in bed lying next to Sandra and dreaming it all.

"Sorry I took so long," Ben said as he entered the room. But he was not alone.

A tall, serious-looking man came in right behind Ben.

Tim could tell by his demeanor the guy was top dog at Joe.

"Dad," Ben said, watching the man walk to Tim, "I'd like you to meet our boss here."

"Steve King." The guy shook Tim's hand with vigor.

"I like a man with a strong handshake," Steve said. He turned to Ben. "I wouldn't expect any less from Ben's father."

Tim took the compliment comfortably, and as he withdrew his hand, said, "It's an honor to meet you, sir. You have one hell of a facility here."

Steve and Ben sat down in chairs next to Tim.

"This was originally built by the British in World War II. It was much smaller then, and was one of their most secret submarine facilities in the world," Steve said. "When the war ended in 1945, they basically abandoned the place. The Brits decided it was too remote for any future purpose."

He studied the black screens on the far wall before continuing. "When the CIA found about it almost by accident, they offered to take it off the Brits' hands for a tidy sum. When the British government agreed, the agency made just one stipulation for the deal."

"A man of your experience may probably guess what that is, Tim Bernard Erwin," Steve said.

Tim didn't freak out that the guy knew his middle name. Hell, he probably knew the last time I took a whiz, Tim thought.

"The facility was, as far as anyone knew, blown up?"

"Spot on. The CIA acquired the place for one sole purpose," Steve said.

Tim put two and two together.

"A place to hide him," he whispered.

Steve grinned. "There's a company man. He'll always whisper no matter where he is. I can assure you, you don't need to worry about that here."

Okay, Tim thought, I'll try the hell to relax.

Steve turned back to Ben, indicating it was time to get things moving.

"Dad, there's someone we want you to meet."

Ben reached for the phone sitting on the boardroom table.

"Bring him in," he said to someone on the other end of the line.

Jesus, I'm about to meet someone from another planet, Tim thought.

Steve could tell Tim was clearly more nervous than a pimple-faced sixteen-year-old boy on prom night about to try and kiss a girl for the first time.

"Relax, Tim," Steve said, looking at him with a grin. "No need to fret."

A moment later, the door opened and two guards entered.

As they parted, Steve and Ben rose to their feet.

Tim decided to do the same.

Tim turned to the person between them and three words came to mind immediately.

What.

The.

Hell.

If this is what an alien looks like, there must be billions of them on planet earth.

He looked like a normal, everyday man.

He was about six feet tall, and moderately built. He had short hair, a snub nose, and friendly eyes. His complexion was fair. For a split second, Tim felt as if he was looking at someone he knew.

He wore civilian clothes: mustard-colored corduroy pants, and a shirt Tim thought a little old-fashioned, tucked into the pants and finished off with a big belt and brown shoes.

Tim watched as the man walked up to him.

He stared at Tim for a second without any hint of expression.

Tim could feel the butterflies in his stomach going crazy.

Ben was about to say something, but then the stranger spoke.

"I understand I have you to thank," he said as a small grin appeared on his face.

Tim looked to Ben before turning back to the man and saying, "Thank me for what? I don't understand what's happening here."

Steve stepped to Tim's side and patted him on the shoulder.

"I think what he's trying to say," Steve said, "is he's here thanks to you, Tim Erwin."

The guy reached out his hand.

Tim shook it, still feeling like he was the only guy in the room who had no idea what was going on.

"Allow me to introduce myself," the guy said as he held onto Tim's hand. "Lieutenant William Portwood Erwin."

For a second, Tim felt like he was starring in an episode of one of his favorite shows—*The Twilight Zone*.

"Sweet Jesus," Tim said, realizing who this guy was.

"The pilot of the Dallas Spirit," said Ben.

Michael E. Darcy took the three-and-a-half-hour flight

from LA to St. Louis in the early hours of Thursday morning, keeping to himself for the entire flight. He was in a somber mood. It was too early to have a drink, and truth be told, he would have passed on the offer. It was the last thing he felt like. The coffee on the flight was surprisingly good, but the breakfast reminded him why he should have flown private.

The Chevrolet Tahoe was, he surmised after an hour of driving on the freeway toward Piedmont, a good choice of car to hire.

He was doing his best to think of anything but his destination.

The township was like many in middle America: quiet, almost a ghost town, but with signs of life here and there. Houses and the odd business were spread so far and wide he wondered why they hadn't been built a bit closer together. But he felt how serene and beautiful it was. It was pristine, the fresh air was intoxicating, and it was a million miles away from the megacities like Los Angeles.

When he spotted the Zephyr Cafe, he decided it was as good a place as any to drop in and grab a bite to eat.

"Hiya. What can I get y'all?" the friendly waitress asked Darcy as he planted himself at the counter. She reminded the billionaire of his daughter.

Darcy peered at the menu and said, "What would you recommend to a weary traveler?"

She wasted no time in replying enthusiastically, "My favorite is the almond berry chicken salad sandwich. We serve fries on the side. Whatta ya think?"

Darcy loved anyone whose enthusiasm for their job was this strong.

"Order me one of those…" Darcy studied her name tag. "…Carley-Jane."

"You want coffee or a Coke with that, sir?" she said.

Darcy laughed. It had been a while since anyone had called him sir. "A coffee would be wonderful," he said. "Thank you for your attentive service."

Darcy realized he was being watched, ordering his lunch. An older woman behind the counter walked up to him.

"Most folk from out of town aren't nearly as nice to my staff as you," she said.

Darcy looked over at the young girl now pouring another customer a coffee. "Carley-Jane will get a generous tip when I finish my lunch. She's very good at her job."

The cafe-owner turned to Carley-Jane. "That's my best worker by far," she said.

Darcy could feel his body warming from the simple interaction. The woman was friendly and quite attractive, with beautiful, almond-shaped hazel eyes. And although she showed the signs of middle age, her skin was still pale and smooth. Her smile made Darcy want to stay forever. He could look at that smile until the end of time.

"Her parents would be proud, that's for sure," Darcy said.

"That I am." The owner thought it was the nicest thing she'd heard about her daughter in a long time.

She put her hand out. "Janice Webb." Darcy gently shook it. "Owner and operator of this wonderful cafe."

The billionaire was clearly a fish out of water. He could feel his nerves; the merest physical connection with a lovely woman was messing with his mind.

"Michael Darcy." His name stumbled out of his mouth.

As Janice took her hand away, she said, "Excuse me a moment, Michael. I'll just tend to these lovely folks and be right back."

Darcy ate his almond berry chicken salad sandwich and

couldn't remember the last time he'd enjoyed a sandwich so much.

As he checked his watch and wondered how he was going to find the place he was looking for, Janice appeared from nowhere and stood directly in front of him.

"How was your sandwich, Michael?" she said. Hearing his name from her lips made him quiver. Her voice could melt polar ice caps.

"Nearly as good as the friendly service," he said.

"And what brings such a polite man to these parts?" she asked.

Darcy felt as if she'd just shot him with a taser.

Darcy took a deep breath. He was now the only person sitting at the counter. A family of four was in a booth by the window, and a couple in the one behind them. Otherwise, the place was empty.

Darcy swallowed hard and wondered if he should just come straight out and tell her exactly why he'd come all the way to Piedmont. He had nothing to lose, but felt awkward all the same.

When the passage of time after her question had nearly become awkward, Darcy knew he just had to be honest with her.

"A few years ago, I worked for a company that bought an agricultural business here in town," he said. Darcy felt the emotion rising up his throat, but knew he had to go on. "Well, after it was purchased, there was a guy who worked for the company, and, err, his fam…"

Janice's face went pale. Her bottom lip started to quiver, so slightly you wouldn't have noticed from a distance.

Although her smile had slipped away, she still looked at Darcy with sincerity.

"I remember that incident." She checked the other customers and knew they were far enough away not to hear.

"It was one of the most tragic things ever to happen here." She took a handkerchief from her apron pocket and wiped her eyes.

Darcy could feel the weight of the event coming down on him. He was starting to feel sick again.

Janice smiled at Darcy. "So you've come here for … ?"

Darcy looked down to the counter as he failed in the struggle to control the tears welling up in his eyes.

He said, "I just feel that our company was responsible for it. I wanted to go to where the house stood and pay my respects."

Janice turned to the far wall, where a large clock rested.

"I knock off in twenty minutes," she said. "If you're happy to wait, you can follow me in your car and I'll lead you there."

Darcy wondered if fate or something else had led him to the cafe. He told Janice he'd be waiting out the front.

Right on cue, Janice left the front door of the cafe twenty minutes later. She waved to Darcy, indicating her car was parked at the back.

A few moments later, she pulled out from behind the building and tooted her horn. Darcy pulled his SUV out and came up behind her.

He left a safe distance between them and followed Janice as she drove down the main street of Piedmont.

Darcy could feel the emotions coursing through his body only getting stronger.

He followed her through the town and then out into farmland. When the road eventually became dirt, she drove on for another ten minutes. After passing through a crossroads, she made a sharp right only a few hundred meters further on. She pulled up in front of a set of rusting gates.

They were here.

Janice stepped out of her car door, and watched Darcy exit his SUV and walk over.

"This is it." Janice waved over to a large vacant block about three hundred feet away.

When Darcy saw the charred remains of the homestead's foundations, he wondered if he would throw up. Sitting not far behind the ruins was the large stump of what would have been one hell of a tree.

Darcy took a deep breath and put two and two together.

This was *the* tree. The one the man had hung himself on after setting fire to his house with his family trapped inside.

"If you want to go and have a look, you can, but I'll wait here," Janice said.

Darcy stepped over the dilapidated fence to one side of the rusting gate, and walked up slowly to the burned-out foundations of the home. As he approached them, he turned to the tree stump and wondered what life was truly all about. He pictured the little sets of eyes looking down at him from the burning treehouse in one of his many nightmares, and realized that for most of his life, he'd had it all wrong.

Life wasn't about making loads of money.

It was about loving the ones around you, first and foremost, and doing everything you could to make sure they knew they were the most important people in the world to you.

Darcy's emotions boiled over. He cried like he never had before. His chest heaved, and all he wanted was for the earth to open up and swallow him.

"Hey … hey." Janice had appeared from nowhere and started patting Darcy on the back.

"What's the matter?"

He turned to her and said, "I haven't been honest with you."

Janice wondered what he meant.

She shrugged her shoulders. "What do you mean?"

Darcy studied the tree stump before turning back to her.

"I owned the company. The one that bought out this business in Piedmont. The one this guy worked for."

Janice stared at Darcy for a moment, before turning and looking at the stump herself. She walked a few paces before turning and meeting his eyes.

"I don't think I've been completely honest with you, either, Michael."

It was Darcy's turn to be dumbfounded.

Janice walked up close to Darcy. "The guy who died on that tree over there?" Darcy could see tears forming in her eyes.

"He was my baby brother."

Darcy went into shock. Without even thinking of the consequences, he reached out and embraced her.

She cried a few moments, and Darcy did the same.

Janice said, "My late husband, God rest his soul, took down the tree for me after it happened."

Darcy shook his head from side to side.

"I'll never be able to come to terms with the repercussions of my decision, which resulted in your brother's death, Janice."

She stood back. But something in the way she looked at him made him feel a little bit concerned.

She seemed lost in thought, but then suddenly said, "My God, I just realized what's going on here."

Darcy shrugged, and was about to ask what she was talking about when she waved her hand and said, "The press reported that my brother killed his wife and girls before taking his own life." He stepped back. "And that it was my fault because he lost his job when I bought the business he worked for."

Janice shook her head. She felt sorry for this friendly stranger.

"Michael, the reports were completely false." Darcy stared at the ruins of the house and the remains of the huge tree. Janice looked over to the tree, and as she did, lifted her hand and made the sign of the cross across her face and chest. She turned back to Darcy and said, "Billy didn't kill his family."

Darcy couldn't believe it.

He was about to open his mouth, but she waved it shut. "His wife was a drug addict."

Janice walked closer to Darcy and stood beside him. They stared at the ruins for a few moments.

"The local police at first believed what you did—what was reported to the press. But rumors have come out only recently, which I believe are true. We believe my sister-in-law owed a local drug dealer a lot of money. A story has emerged of threats made to her if she didn't pay up. We believe the fire was started because she couldn't come up with the money."

Janice turned to what was left of the house and could feel her emotions coming on again. Those poor kids.

"This drug dealer claimed he didn't know the children were in the house. The problem is, he died not long after admitting what he had done."

Darcy took a deep breath before putting his hand lightly on Janice's shoulder. "I'm so sorry for your loss, Janice."

The cafe-owner wiped her eyes with a handkerchief.

"When Billy got home that night, the same day he lost his job, we believe the house was so engulfed in flames, he wouldn't have been able to get in to save them."

She walked a few steps forward. It was the closest she'd been to the ruins of her brother's home since the tragedy.

Janice could feel the loss of her beloved family as her eyes rested on what was left of the tree.

She turned to Darcy.

"Your actions didn't take Billy away from us. He loved those girls more than anything. It was losing them and his wife that made him want to take his own life. It wasn't your fault."

CHAPTER THIRTY-FIVE

"Dallas Spirit?" Tim said, confused.

Ben stepped forward, ushering William Erwin to sit down on a nearby chair. He obliged without a word.

Steve turned to Ben, and Ben took his cue.

"The Dallas Spirit disappeared without a trace over the Pacific Ocean in 1927. William is my great-grandfather." Ben looked over to the latest addition to the meeting before turning back to Tim. "William is your grandfather."

Tim shook his head. He had an inkling of what was happening, but wanted to hear it all the same.

"Ben, take it right back to the start," Steve said.

Ben rose to his feet and decided he'd feel more comfortable standing at the head of the boardroom table. He'd spent many hours standing there and presenting to many, many people over the years at Joe.

"Dad, William here was the one who first discovered the crashed craft at Vernon. He was the first human being to come into direct contact with a being from another planet.

"Being a decorated pilot from World War I, he'd met men from all levels in the air force, government, and so on."

Ben looked over to William and smiled, though the pilot did not reciprocate the friendly gesture. He just sat there and stared blankly at Ben.

"It was Bill here who removed the craft from the site at Vernon and hid it in a remote mountain range known as the Black Rock Desert. In later years, it was moved to Edwards Air Force Base, before Homey Airport came into existence."

Ben looked out into the aerospace facility, then back to Bill, then Steve. Then he met his own father's eyes.

"He also buried the travelers who died as result of the crash. The whereabouts of their burial site are only known to a select few, out of respect."

Ben then took a deep breath and said, "Bill also took care of the lone survivor of the crash. He's actually credited with saving his life."

Tim studied Bill. "Does your friend from afar have a name?"

Ben answered for him. "His name is Vernon. But when William here disappeared in 1927, Vern, as we call him, went into some sort of a coma. When this happened, Bill's friends notified someone at Edwards. By then, the air force had created a secret department that would later fall under the joint jurisdiction of the CIA and the upper echelons of the air force hierarchy.

"Vern was at this point taken into their care. After the first major expansion of this base in the late 1960s, he was transferred here."

"Okay, then," said Tim. "I'm sort of getting it so far, but why did William disappear in 1927, and is now sitting here in 2021 looking not a day older than his early to mid-thirties?"

"Good question," said Steve. "Ben?"

Ben took a well-deserved deep breath.

"William discovered the small hand-sized disks in the craft," he said. "The ones I know you're familiar with, Dad."

Tim nodded. Yep, he knew *exactly* what they were.

"William, why did you eventually take it on-board with you when you took off in the Dallas Spirit?" Ben asked.

Tim's grandfather turned to Ben. "When our plane had mechanical trouble and we went back to Oakland, we found out two planes were missing. I had left the object in my bag in my locker. I was fascinated by the darn thing. There were many of them in the crashed craft. But I took one and left the rest with Vernon." He looked at all the men before resting his sad eyes on Tim. "To be honest, I just treated it like my good-luck charm. So when we decided to fix the Spirit and go looking for the lost planes, I remembered I had it in my duffle bag. I grabbed it in the hope it would bring us good luck and we could find the planes."

Steve had heard the story a few times now, but it still fascinated him. William Erwin had traveled ninety-seven years into the future. Steve wondered what that would feel like. He hoped that soon, he would be one of the first to do what millions of people had always wondered was possible— travel in time. The dream was already possible, thanks to Ben.

"But one minute we're flying in the air," said William, "looking down at the ocean for the two lost planes, and the next minute, these fast-moving, ludicrous-looking things are circling us."

Ben turned to his old man and said, "This is the part you're not aware of."

Ben looked over to William. "Dad, when your plane disappeared again in 2024," he said, "the Dallas Spirit came out of the time wormhole. You went in, they came out."

Tim shook his head, dumbfounded. He was about to ask

Ben if there was a whiteboard nearby, so he could start mapping this out in some way.

"But then, how did William Erwin get from 2024 to where we are, in 2021?"

Ben raised his eyebrows and suppressed a grin. "Because I was there, in 2024," he said. "I was the one who brought them back to 2021."

Tim studied Ben when suddenly another thought came crashing into his mind.

"Are you responsible for the Pacific International Airlines flight originally disappearing back in 2019?" he asked. Tim could feel his anger rising.

Ben met Steve's eyes for a moment. Steve gave him a subtle wink, which the other two Erwins didn't notice.

"Someone else put it on the plane by accident," Ben lied.

Later, he hoped, he would be able to explain to his old man what exactly had happened, but for now he couldn't afford to.

"You know how many people died as a result of that flight?"

Steve waved his hand in the air. "Tim, we can cover that off later. We're best to continue from where we are now," he said.

"So you were there in 2024, then." Tim stared at Ben and for a moment wondered if he could truly trust him.

"I spoke to Sarah and Sean. I went to their house at nearly the exact moment your plane disappeared from 2024," Ben said.

"What were you doing there?" Tim said curiously.

Ben could feel the glare of his father's gaze boring through him as if his eyes were lasers, but reminded himself where he was currently standing and why.

He took a breath and said, "I needed to get back the disk that Sean had."

Tim stared at his son with what could best be described as controlled disdain. "What did you tell them?"

Ben looked over to Steve before turning back to his father. "I told them I'd had to fake my own disappearance, as I was involved in something top secret. I also told them that in no uncertain terms should they ever mention me being there to anyone. He handed over the disk."

Tim took a long drink of water.

"Okay, I get it all so far," he said before looking to the other men in the room. "So, at what point do you make me understand why I am here?"

"I'm getting to it." Ben was feeling exhausted from the long explanation, but battled on. "But before we get to that, there's one more thing to explain."

Tim sat forward and said, "I'm all ears, son. I don't think I'm going anywhere in a hurry."

Ben could feel himself getting slightly annoyed by his father's attitude.

"Vern has been in a coma since William disappeared. For ninety-seven years. He has only regained consciousness momentarily half a dozen times before slipping back. When William arrived at Joe, we decided to let him see Vernon."

Ben turned to William and couldn't help but smile.

"When we took William to Vern's side, it was as if the greatest of miracles occurred."

Tim just stared at his son. Where was this heading?

Ben said, "Vern woke up. He's been conscious for the last two weeks, and has given us insights into the universe and worlds far outside our own. It's beyond our wildest dreams."

Wow, Tim thought, now we're getting to the true crux of the issue here.

"And?" Tim said.

Ben shook his head. "He told William he was aware of what I had done. He told him the disks were not created for this. The system was created to travel vast distances in seconds, not to travel in time. He believes it is the earth's atmosphere, possibly connected to its magnetic field, which has made them travel through time instead."

"So, in a nutshell, what have you achieved, son?"

Steve decided it was his time to speak.

He stared long and hard into Tim's eyes and said: "We've figured out how to do what is now truly possible.

"Time travel—controlled time travel."

Tim was taken to another wing of the immense facility he, too, now called Joe. There, he was shown what would be his private room for the time he was there. For a top-secret facility, the rooms were nice—almost as nice as the odd five-star hotel Tim had stayed in over the years, he thought.

After a welcome shower and some rest, security personnel led him into another section of the accommodation wing, where he was able to get something to eat.

The place looked like a modern restaurant and bar. If Tim tried hard enough, he could have pretended he was in some Las Vegas Hotel, right on the Strip.

"Here he is." Ben seemed to materialize out of nowhere, and Tim nearly threw his coffee cup straight up in the air.

After he regained his composure, Tim turned to Ben, but his smile was weak.

Ben could tell his old man was not happy with him.

Hang in there, Ben told himself, just ignore it. You're a part of something that's going to change the course of human history forever.

"Are you ready?" Ben said, with as much enthusiasm as he could find.

Tim studied Ben for a second. Now it was his turn to talk to himself.

You won't achieve anything by being pissed off with him, he thought. Find out more before making any judgments now, old fella.

"Never more ready," Tim said.

"Follow me, then."

Ben led Tim back into the main facility.

The trip through another section was long. Tim lost count of how many sealed doors and hallways he'd followed Ben through. Whoever had designed the place, they wanted to make sure their number one guest was hidden somewhere deep within.

The last set of doors appeared to be made from solid concrete, and they took two minutes to open far enough for Tim and his son to pass through. As Tim watched them closing, he realized they had reached their destination: what looked like a hospital reception counter.

Ben greeted both of the men sitting behind it. They were dressed in the same uniform he wore. Tim could see the glow of a vast array of screens and monitors, hidden within the counter, beaming toward the men.

"How is he?" Ben asked.

Both men looked quite happy. "He seems to be in a great mood, especially when Lieutenant Erwin comes to see him," one said.

"I have a feeling he'll be pleased to see you and your guest," said the other.

Ben turned to Tim. "Are you ready for this?" he asked.

Tim felt as if he'd just walked the length of Fifth Avenue and was hoping there was a far quicker way back, but said, "I'm ready."

Ben walked to the left of the counter and entered another set of double doors, once again automatic.

When they closed, he told his dad, "Those doors over there are the very last ones. Vern will be on the other side. I know this may be difficult for you, but just don't freak out when you first lay eyes on him. Take it nice and slow, okay?"

Tim could feel those darn butterflies rear up in his stomach yet again, but told them all to get back in their enclosure already.

Ben patted Tim on the back, and said, "Follow me."

As the doors opened a second later, Ben walked through and into the room. Tim shuffled behind him like a child sneaking into a candy factory behind a worker.

As the doors closed, he heard Ben say, "Vern, I have someone here I'd like you to meet. I have told you much about him."

Tim held his breath as he, nervous as hell, stepped out from behind Ben.

Tony, Ross, and Melanie raised their glasses of champagne, at where else but the pool bar of the Beverly Hills Hotel, a stone's throw from the bungalows they currently called home.

When the familiar chink was heard, Melanie said, "Congratulations, gentlemen. How does it feel to be the proud owners of a Californian pilot school?"

"Apart from asking you to marry me, I think this feels like one of the best things I have ever done," said Ross.

"And what better partner to have in crime than the smoothest operator in the air?" Tony said.

Ross laughed. "I'd ask Ben Stiller if he wanted to come to open our school, but…" He winked at Melanie. "Who needs him when we have our own, sleeker version?"

Tony laughed too. He'd gotten so used to being mistaken for one of his favorite actors that a couple of times he'd signed autographs on his behalf just to get rid of someone.

Ross turned to Melanie, and for the thousandth time, studied her as if he'd only laid eyes on her for the very first time. She made him quiver all over again.

"Well, since we're celebrating, maybe you can let my new business partner in on the other exciting news of the day."

Melanie squeezed Ross's hand. She wanted to squeeze something else, but quickly disposed of the naughty thought. This isn't that kind of novel, either.

"Well," Melanie said, smiling at Ross before turning her mesmerizing jade eyes to Tony, "it just so happens we went up to Monterey today. And to cut a very nice story short, we found the most beautiful house right on the beach."

Tony reached over to clink glasses with her and Ross again.

"That's wonderful news. Are you going to put in an offer?"

Melanie turned to Ross and felt the buzz of excitement go from her toes right to the top of her head.

"No need," she said.

Tony looked perplexed. "Why not, if you liked it?"

"We already did, and they accepted on the spot," Melanie said sheepishly.

Tony shook his head. "Look at you two. That's wonderful news."

He raised his glass and added, "I think at some point I'll need to do the…"

Tony's words were interrupted by the sound of a mobile phone ringing, just a little too loud for where they were.

"Shit, sorry," Tony said as he pulled his phone out of his pocket and fumbled with the volume.

He peered at the screen and said, "Sorry, guys. It's the boss on the phone."

He spun his screen around to show them who he meant, but they could already guess who it was.

Tammy.

"I'll be back in a bit," Tony said before slipping off to the rear of the bar, toward the poolside area.

Ross turned to Melanie. "At what point are you going to tell them?" he said.

She glanced at Tony, now twenty-five meters away, talking with as much animation as she'd ever seen.

She took a sip of her champagne. "When the time is right," she said.

Tony looked back at Ross and Melanie sitting at the bar, chatting and looking pretty happy with themselves.

"Yeah, babe," he said, shifting his gaze to the shimmering water of the pool, "they've bought a house in Monterey today."

Just under 1,900 miles away, Tammy felt genuinely happy for Melanie and Ross.

"Such wonderful news," she said, though Tony could hear strain in her voice. She was also talking rather quietly.

"Where are you, babe?" Tony said.

"I'm at Mom and Dad's," Tammy said. Tony could hear her taking careful breaths. "We're all here. For dinner."

Tony decided to take a seat. He walked over to the edge and sat down.

"You and the kids?" he said.

Tammy took a couple of seconds to answer.

"They're here, but so are Brandon and Annie."

Tony could feel the warmth of the champagne drain away.

"God," Tony said, and then regretted it. He didn't want to make her feel any more stressed than she sounded. He lightened his tone a notch. "I didn't think you'd want to play happy families with Brandon and Annie."

"Hold on," Tammy said quickly, as she decided to close the door of what had originally been her bedroom at her parents' house, now a guest room.

When the door was closed, Tammy spoke a little louder, and seemed less strained.

"The last place on earth I want to be is having dinner with my Bible-obsessed parents, my idiot ex-husband, and my evil slut of a sister."

When those words filtered through the 1,900 miles of airways connecting Tony's phone to Tammy's, they also traveled about fifteen feet in the actual air.

Air vents built in old homes in America must have originally been designed by the FBI.

If it was quiet enough, someone in another room, even a few rooms away, could get close enough to the vents and hear what was being said.

Annie stared directly into her mother's eyes and said, "See. You've heard it for yourself, mother. Tammy thinks she's above us all."

Patricia Sanders looked at the vents before eventually turning back to Annie.

Tammy's mother had never had a grasp on reality; her life had always been dictated by a book written as early as 3,400 years ago, and the result of her lifelong love affair with JC was an inability to judge the truth of matters for herself.

What she'd heard was damning, but it wasn't as though Tammy didn't have her reasons.

"You're right, Annie," her mother told her, hissing. "That girl is a bad seed. I don't know what we are…"

Annie, being Annie, had slapped her mother on the shoulder with such force that it gave her a considerable fright.

"Listen!" Annie snarled.

"I know, honey," they heard. Tammy could feel the pressure of wanting to get the hell out of Missouri growing heavier by the day. "But before I do that, I need to deal with Brandon."

Annie and Patricia stared at each other, as if their movements had been filmed by a slow-motion camera. They continued to hear the words filtering through the vents.

"He told Lee he wants to get back with me," Tammy said.

Annie screamed, but slapped her hand over her mouth.

Her mother stifled a gasp before biting her lips shut to avoid any threat of them being caught out by Tammy.

Annie could feel the deepest and darkest anger rising in her.

But Tammy wasn't done. If she'd only thought about it, she might have talked to Tony outside. Maybe in a soundproof Winnebago. Maybe one parked ten miles away.

"I wouldn't touch him for all the cotton candy in Disneyland, babe, especially after he's been with my slag of a sister. So that will be easy to deal with."

Annie could feel her hands curl into fists, so tightly her knuckles went white within seconds.

But then Tammy said the words that would set the wheels of heartache firmly in motion.

"No, Tony, that's not going to happen. I'll probably have

to kidnap the kids and bring them back to California with me on the sly."

Patricia met Annie's eyes one final time as they finished eavesdropping.

The look on her daughter's face was disturbing.

CHAPTER THIRTY-SIX

Tim could see someone behind a set of head-height partitions across the other side of the room, doing something that required subtle movement.

Tim scanned the room. Opulently decorated with ultra-modern furniture, it felt like a futuristic movie set, or the main office of a modern-day billionaire like that guy from *Iron Man*; Tim couldn't recall his name.

Ben took a deep breath before clearing his throat, and without delay said, "Hello, Vernon." He cast his eyes over to the partitions. "I have someone you can finally meet."

A few moments later, Tim heard the distant voice.

"Ah, finally. You have done as promised, Ben. Well done."

Tim listened carefully to the voice. If the guy wasn't already one of the narrators of those television documentaries he and Sandra loved to watch, he should have been. If his voice were a material, it would be velvet. It was as smooth as a bowling ball.

When Vernon stepped out from behind his little partition, Tim took a slight breath, and in an instant the realization of the moment fell over him like a bucket of ice.

He was looking directly at someone from another planet.

As Vernon strode toward him and Ben, Tim checked him out from head to toe.

Vernon was no taller than five feet. Sandra was just over five foot one, so Tim had a fair standard to measure by.

He had a friendly face, rounded and devoid of any eyebrows, or of any facial hair whatsoever.

His eyes were oversized, and almond-shaped, but a mesmerizing light blue in color. He had a small, Michael Jackson nose, and an even smaller chin.

His complexion was straight out of the hundreds of descriptions, online and in history, of visitors from another planet. Light gray, almost shiny, like the skin of a dolphin.

When he smiled, he revealed tiny, almost childlike teeth, which were impossibly white and very straight.

But then there were the other, more unusual things.

Vernon was dressed in what was best described as human clothing: smart blue jeans with a tight green skivvy, and small, tan-colored slip-on shoes.

Vernon looked like he was about to adorn the cover of *GQ* magazine. Maybe he should one day.

There was just one other thing, which made Tim think— what the hell? He tried not to stare at it, but it was almost physically impossible not to.

And with Vernon's head being larger than a human's in proportion to his body, it was damn near impossible *not* to notice it.

Tim wondered if one day he'd have one stuck to his own melon, but after today, he'd decide maybe it would never happen.

Vernon—had a toupee.

Tim blinked, and suppressed the urge to stare at the thing.

"I have heard much about you, Tim," Vernon said, motioning for the men to come and sit with him nearby.

"It is an honor to meet you, Vernon," Tim said as he sat on the couch across from him.

"You must have many questions for me," said the guy this whole facility was built for, looking over to Tim before giving Ben a weak smile.

Ben sat forward and said to Vernon, "Maybe we should tell Dad why he's here first, Vern." He cast a quick look over to his old man before turning back. "And later, Dad can ask questions."

Vernon stared at Ben. For a moment, Tim thought his son had offended him, but then Vernon spoke.

"If this is your wish, Ben, we can discuss this first."

A moment later, Ben turned to Vernon before taking in some much-needed air.

"I think you're safe to tell him, my friend," Ben said.

Then he stood to his feet, without taking his eyes off the sixty-seven-year-old Erwin.

Tim could have sworn he saw a slight smile appear on the left side of Vernon's mouth.

"Ben has brought you here, Tim—to help me," he said.

Tim looked to Ben for a clue, but he just continued to look at Vernon.

Without any hints from his son, Tim had to ask, "Help you, Vernon?"

The toupee-wearing GQ model from outer space said it so quietly Tim could barely hear.

"Go home."

Tim looked over to Ben, dumbfounded.

Ben stared directly at Vernon, with a smile of his own now.

Eventually, Ben said, "I guess you now have a few extra questions to add to your list, Pop."

"Do you mind if someone explained a few things to me?" Tim asked Vernon.

Ben and Vernon met each other's gaze. Vernon slowly reclined to his couch. A moment later, he said to Tim, "I would be happy to answer your questions now."

Tim sat back further on his couch, lost in thought.

"Where are you from?"

"At some point soon," Ben interjected, "we'll be able to spend more time with Vern. So maybe we should just talk about the big-ticket items today, Dad, if that's okay?"

Tim felt slightly offended by Ben's dismissive tone, but Vernon raised his hand and said. "Ben, let me just answer the question before we move on."

Vernon stared at Tim, and this time the smile on his little chinless face was unmistakable.

"I come from a distant galaxy known to astronomers here on earth as the Andromeda Galaxy. Among the many solar systems of Andromeda is one where you will find the three planets our people inhabit. I would tell you their names, but in my language, you would not understand, nor probably even hear me speak them."

Ben adjusted his seating position slightly and said, "Vernon's species speaks on a different frequency to us. It's so high-pitched you wouldn't hear it."

The visitor from another planet stared at Tim, and all Tim could look at was his toupee. But he pressed on.

"Can someone explain to me why the objects from your craft have made airplanes disappear? And to add to that— why did William's plane come back ninety-seven years later?

And why did our plane go back two and a half years the second time round?"

Ben took a drink of water from a glass nearby before looking to Vernon. "Ben, tell him," Vernon said.

"The disks are part of the craft's system to allow it to travel vast distances in very little time," he said. "It took Vernon only ten hours in earth time to get from his planet to ours.

"But the earth's gravitation, coupled with the magnetic force of both poles, altered their behavior completely. Instead of functioning as they were designed to do, traveling vast distances, here on earth they did something else entirely. They traveled through time instead."

Tim scratched his head, but it sort of made sense.

"So, on earth they became time-travel devices, but in space they will go back to being what they were designed for?"

Vernon simply said, "This is correct."

Tim took a long, deep breath, and said, "So, tell me why William's plane was gone for ninety-seven years, and our plane only five. Oh, and then ours went backwards in time. Has this ever happened before?"

Ben stared at the other side of the room, not at Vernon but somewhere else. He paused for a moment. "When your plane went on its second flight six months after landing in 2024," Ben said, "you believed you had the same disk."

Tim shook his head. "They're not all the same?"

"No. The one you had the second time was one of a kind. It was a different disk."

Vernon shook his head as best he could with what seemed like little or no movement in his neck.

Vernon turned back to Tim, "Eight disks are required to be installed in certain positions of our ship. I think that's what you call them here on earth. But we then have an extra two, which are positioned right in front of the two people who operate the ship. These two are what we call the directional, or operating disks."

Ben sat forward and said to Tim, "I discovered, once you had vanished in 2024 and reappeared in 2021, you had one of these two operating disks in your possession."

Tim was struggling to keep up, but was only a couple of steps behind.

"And who had the other one of these operating disks?"

"William," Ben said.

The older Erwin sat back and took his time digesting the information. Eventually, after a few moments it came to him.

"So is this why he reappeared, but I went back in time?" Ben nodded, but Tim then said, "Why did we not go back ninety-seven years? Why was it only two and a half?"

This time, Ben's expression was a little blank.

"Although I've figured out most things, the one thing I don't get is that one little detail. I'm still working on it."

Tim pressed on. "But you've figured out how to use the system to travel back and forth in time," he said. "Is that what you're going to tell me?" Ben shifted in his seat, but felt proud of his achievement. On some levels, his father didn't share his view.

"I have done it a couple of times, and think I have it all worked out," Ben said. "But there's always the risk that something will go wrong. So the answer is yes, but there are still risks."

"You went back and saved your mom's life. You made sure she didn't board the plane in 2019."

Ben studied the ground and a few moments later said, "I risked my own life going back to do that. It was the first time. I shouldn't have, but I had to. I felt like it was my fault she died in 2024, so I took the risk."

Tim softened a little. In the end, he would go home and

his wife would be there waiting for him. He now knew who to thank for this.

When the memory crossed Tim's mind of that fateful night when they'd first got home in 2024 and Sandra had another heart attack, he recalled her grasping the photo of Ben, Jenny, and their children in her hand.

"Where are Jenny and the children?"

"They're here at Joe," Ben said.

Tim shook his head and shifted in his seat. "Why did you fake your disappearance?"

Ben didn't look too happy about having to answer that one.

"Jenny is one of the scientists involved in this project," he said. "She always has been. We didn't meet at the scuba-diving club. Sorry, that was all made up. We met on the job."

When there was nothing but silence, Tim said, "So, it's about time you guys told me where I fit into all this."

Vernon turned to Ben and said, "Yes, I think it's time."

Ben nodded to Vernon before standing and stretching his legs. He walked a few feet away before coming back and sitting next to his father again.

"We need a fourth person to operate Vernon's ship. Along with Vernon, we need another three people to get it out of the earth's atmosphere."

Tim looked surprised. "You're going to help Vernon leave?"

"Yes. We also need to get all the disks off this planet." Ben rose to his feet and stood away from Tim and his friend from another galaxy.

"And who are the other people who make up the four?" Tim asked.

This time, Vernon answered. "I thought William would help, but he is too scared to get in my ship."

"Jenny has agreed to do it," Ben said.

Now it was Tim's turn to rise to his feet. "And what happens to your children if something goes wrong?" he said indignantly.

Ben shook his head. With authority, he said, "They'll be fine. Nothing is going to happen to us. All we need to do is get him out of the gravitational pull, and once that happens, we'll return to earth and Vernon will be gone, along with the disks."

Tim shrugged his shoulders. "What, is he just going to walk home?"

Ben shook his head, dismissing his old man's silly comment.

"He will be transferred to another ship. One will be there waiting for him."

Tim waved his hand toward the ceiling. "Why don't they just come down here and get him?"

Now Vernon stood too. "Same reason. The magnetic force of this planet will mess with their craft. It will malfunction and possibly crash."

Tim's head was now spinning in all directions.

"You and Jenny are going to help Vernon leave earth? Do you think the people you work for are just going to let you do that? I'm sure they'll have something to say about it."

"Jenny and I were always company people, Dad," Ben said with a hint of frustration. "We lived and breathed this project for years. But when your plane disappeared and we had no control over it, it made us rethink what was really important." Ben studied Vernon before turning back to Tim. "And if we want to be with our family, why shouldn't Vernon be able to do the same?"

This time, Tim felt sorry for the being. He was millions of miles away from his home, and Tim was sure without Ben and Jenny's help, he'd probably never see it again.

"You want to go home, Vernon?" Tim said matter-of-factly.

Vernon walked over to him, which took a few moments, before saying, "How soon do you want to see your wife, Tim?"

Tim looked down to him. He had a point. "Alright," he said, looking at Ben. "I guess you're going to tell me I'm here because there's no one else you can trust."

Ben met his father's eyes. Tim had hit the nail on the head.

"So, now you can tell me how you're going to pull off the impossible and get one of the most guarded people on the planet—off this planet."

Ben waved to the couch. "Sit down. I'll take you through the plan."

Tim sat and Ben indicated Vernon should do the same.

"First things first. We need to get Vernon back to Homey. Let me explain how we're going to do this, Pop."

CHAPTER THIRTY-SEVEN

"Wish me luck," Ross said to Melanie as he adjusted his belt after getting dressed, ready for his big day.

Melanie stood back and ran her eyes over her fiancé. He still made her heart flutter when he got dressed up.

"Luck is something you don't need, honey." She stepped up to him and planted her lips on his. "You're going to be a hit."

The day had finally come.

Ross would travel to Burbank and do something he had never done before. He would be interviewed on TV. And by none other than one of the world's most famous talk-show hosts, Ellen DeGeneres.

"Are you sure you're okay with me heading off to the arts thing afterwards?" Ross said.

Melanie adjusted his shirt to sit just that little bit better before looking up to him and smiling.

"Of course, babe. If you're invited to a charity event in the Arts District, I'm totally fine with that."

"Well, you're more than welcome to come," he said, but he knew what the answer would be.

Melanie had told him days earlier she'd opt out of coming with him to the interview and the charity event afterwards.

She'd decided to stay back and make the final arrangements for their move to Monterey in a couple of days' time. The preparations seemed to be taking up every spare moment of her time. Ross loved how excited she was.

"Okay, then, I'm off." He kissed her firmly on the lips, then put his arms around her and said, "I'll see you when I get back."

Melanie hugged him for a few moments before stepping away and watching him walk to the door. As he picked up the car keys on the bench, she said, "You take care of our baby, won't you?"

"Given what our new mode of transport cost, I'll be extra careful, trust me," he said.

Ross walked through the front door of the bungalow. When he closed the door, he looked down to the car key. Melanie said she'd always dreamed of owning a Jaguar, but when she told him she'd bought an SUV with a Jaguar badge on the bonnet, he shook his head in amazement. The thing was, she'd bought not one, but two. She said with the move to Monterey, they could both use wheels of their own.

Who was Ross to argue?

As he walked off, Ross turned back to the bungalow, which in two days' time would no longer be his home.

He had the strangest feeling as he stared at it, and wondered if he'd grown emotionally attached to the place. Maybe that's why he felt a little weird.

But in fact, that was not the reason.

It was because it would be the last time he would ever lay eyes on the place.

"Emily, I think we need to have a conversation."

Dave Collins had arrived home a little earlier than usual from his shift at LAX. Emily was waiting for Todd to come over. They were planning on a dinner out somewhere, though he was running late.

Dave sat down next to his daughter on the couch. He could tell she was wondering what he wanted to talk to her about. The look on her face told him she was slightly nervous.

"What do you want to talk about, Dad?"

Dave stared out through the living-room windows for a moment.

"I've told you once before that I had gotten to know Andrew Roberts a little. I guess you could probably call us just acquaintances, not much more than that."

Emily put her phone down on the coffee table.

She still didn't know where this was heading.

Dave took a deep breath. "He called me today," he said, "and told me he wanted to talk to me about something."

Emily's heart sank. Now she was feeling really nervous. She went to ask what Andrew had called about, but Dave went first.

"He told me he's really worried about Todd. Apparently, Todd has been behaving really strange of late. Andrew told me he has been spending time with some street kid. He claims Todd has made up some story this kid is Andrew's other son."

Dave moved closer to Emily and said, "And he thinks you may be in some sort of danger because of all of this."

Emily's feelings of nervousness quickly changed to anger.

She shook her head, and in that moment started to wonder what the real story was with Todd's father.

Now he was making up false statements and, what's worse, had gone to her own father and pulled him into the lie.

She swallowed hard before biting her bottom lip.

Emily knew Todd would be arriving soon, but she couldn't wait for him. She needed to speak right now.

"Dad, I think it's time you knew some things. Todd is on his way, but I can't wait for him."

Dave's concern was etched on his face.

"First things first," she said. "Andrew Roberts is not the man you think he is."

She met her father's eyes.

"I can't believe it," she said. "What he told you today was a complete lie. This street kid, his name is Jason. He actually is Andrew Robert's biological son. It was the result of an affair with a barmaid fifteen or so years ago. My God, this is getting out of control."

"Sweet Jesus," said Dave. "I'm guessing he doesn't want Todd and his other son to have a relationship, then. It'll ruin his reputation. And then there's Andrew's wife. What will she think of all this?"

Emily stared long and hard at her father. She wondered how he'd react if she told him that Andrew's wife, in another time and place, became his partner.

"Dad, there's way more to this than meets the eye. Remember on the way home from Vandenberg I was really upset, and said there would be a day I wanted to tell you things I knew I shouldn't?"

"I remember, darling. You seemed very preoccupied, but I understood that after what you'd been through, being missing for two and a half years, you would be."

Emily had no intention of just coming out and saying it.

But something tripped in her mind and connected to her lips. It just fell straight out of her mouth.

"That's the thing, Dad. We were missing for five years first."

Darcy arrived back at the Beverly Hills Hotel.

He'd only admit it to himself, but he couldn't stop thinking about the beautiful cafe-owner from Piedmont, not even for an hour. He was tempted to tell the gang back at the Beverly Hills Hotel about her, but decided for now it would remain his little romantic secret.

"Here he is," Melanie said, opening the door and reaching out for the billionaire. Darcy had grown very fond of her in recent times, and felt as if she was the sort of daughter he'd never had.

When he stood back, Darcy said, "Where's the boys? We should all get together tonight for dinner, whatta ya say?"

Melanie shook her head, though the smile remained. "I'm afraid it would be just you and me in that case, Mick. Ross is doing his *Ellen* interview this afternoon, and then he's going on to a charity function. He shouldn't be too late, but will probably miss dinner."

Darcy didn't look too fazed. "And his co-pilot? Where is he?"

"He's catching up with some airline friends today, so I don't know what time he'll be back."

Melanie then realized taking a break from organizing her new home wouldn't be a bad idea.

"You know what?" she said. "You and me for dinner, but can we make it about seven?"

Darcy winked. "Sounds like a plan. I'll see you at the usual place, then."

And with that, Darcy spun on his heel and made his way back to his own bungalow.

Dinner was a little quiet without Ross and Tony. Melanie realized it was the very first time she'd had dinner with Darcy alone. But they had all become good friends in the last few months; she had gotten to know him and knew at his core he was a good man.

After dinner was served and the thought of dessert had come and gone, Melanie leaned closer to Darcy, to whisper.

"So the big hush-bill will be coming up soon. Are you still going to go through with it?" she said.

Darcy studied his drink for a moment.

"I'm a man of my word, my friend," he said. "And a promise is a promise. I still think, for what it's worth, it was the only way to keep it in-house."

Melanie turned and studied the dusk sky enveloping the city of angels. She couldn't believe it had worked, but then again, it was one hell of an incentive to all those people.

"It adds up to a lot of money, Michael. Are you sure you're good for it?"

Darcy thought Melanie had a heart of gold.

"I haven't told anyone yet, and keep it between you and me for now, but I think I'm going to sell Darcon very soon."

Melanie's eyes went wide, but then she saw the tiredness on his face. The guy had been through one hell of a roller-coaster, and somehow had come out of it relatively okay.

"So, offering each passenger two million dollars won't be difficult to cover when I sell the company."

Melanie shook her head. "But we are talking around $180 million, Darce. That's a lot of coin."

Darcy raised his drink toward her until she met it with her own.

Studying the now-empty glass, he said, "Someone made

me an offer for Darcon only last week. I think I'll have enough change left over after I deduct $180 million from three billion dollars, young lady."

Melanie let out an audible "phew" before saying, "Well, there are many beautiful houses up in Carmel by the Sea. You may just have to snap one up so you own a home near your friends."

After ordering another drink, he turned to Melanie and said, "That's one of the nicest things anyone has ever said to me." Melanie could see his eyes getting misty. "I may just have to do…"

When Darcy realized Melanie had gone silent, he thought it was because of his reaction.

Then he felt the presence of someone standing behind him. For a second, Darcy thought it was the barman with his drink.

But when he went to say thank you, he was suddenly lost for words.

Two policemen stood behind him.

"Melanie Lewinson?" the taller policeman said.

Melanie swallowed hard, and the one word struggled to break through her lips.

"Y-e-s?"

Both policemen studied Darcy before one of them said to her, "Is there somewhere where we can talk?"

Melanie could feel something terrible was coming, but pushed on.

"Michael here is a close friend of mine. What is it you want to speak about?"

The policemen met each other's gaze and said, "Would you mind if we talked somewhere more private?"

Melanie rose to her feet, though her legs felt weak.

"Okay. Michael, can you come, please?"

Darcy was already on his feet, and as he reached her side of the table to escort her back to the bungalow, Melanie asked the policemen, "Is something wrong?"

The two men shared a worried glance before one of them said, "It's about your fiancé."

CHAPTER THIRTY-EIGHT

BEN HAD CONVENED A MEETING WITH HIS BOSS, WHO was on his way. Tim and Ben sat in the boardroom overlooking the facility, waiting for him to arrive. He always ran late.

"I've been meaning to ask you…" Tim said.

"I doubt if the questions will ever stop, Pop," Ben said.

"Why was a town built down here?"

Ben looked up from his tablet toward his father.

"It was built for them," Ben said. "Visitors like Vernon. The idea was to give them a taste of life on earth, but in a controlled environment."

Tim shook his head. "But you're keeping him a prisoner here, aren't you?"

Ben shook his head.

"It's for his own good. If he strode down the main street of Alameda, I doubt it would be good for him or the locals," he said.

The two men sat in an awkward silence for a few moments.

Tim eventually said, "Ben, where are we?"

Ben went to say something but was cut short.

The boardroom door opened before Ben's boss came striding in like he owned the place.

"Gentlemen," Steve said. He stood at the end of the table and stared straight at Ben. "What do you need to talk to me about?"

Ben sat up straight. "I need to run something past you," he said.

"You've got five minutes. I have a conference call with the powers that be in ten. Talk to me."

Ben took a deep breath and thought there was no other way to start but to come straight out with it.

"I want to take him to Homey."

Steve roared with laughter, but Tim could instantly tell it was drenched in sarcasm.

"You've got to be joking. He's been here for nearly sixty years, and for good reason. It'll never happen."

Steve checked his watch and turned to Ben. "Unless you have something else to discuss, I have other meetings to attend."

Ben shook his head. One thing the Erwin men possessed was tenacity. And truth be told, Ben had it way more than his father and his great-grandfather William.

"What if I were to tell you," Ben said, sitting forward and speaking seriously, "that he's agreed to show me?"

Steve waved his hand dismissively. "Ben, you told me you've figured out how to make the disks work. At some point, I've been instructed to give the brass a practical demonstration."

Ben decided he had nothing to lose.

"Forget about the time-travel thing, Steve." Ben rose to his feet.

"Vernon has agreed to show me what the disks are actually designed to do."

Steve shook his head, "I'm listening."

Ben took a deep breath and said, "Long-distance space travel. The sort that will make the speed of light look like dial-up."

"Jesus Christ." Steve looked lost for words.

"Imagine what this will do for us," Ben said. "Imagine where we'll be able to go."

Steve stared out into the aerospace facility. What Ben was talking about was the very thing they'd always wanted. This was big.

"Okay. I see what you mean. Let me think about it. I'll have to run it past the hierarchy. This changes everything."

⁂

"Hi, babe." Todd greeted Emily at her front door as he always did, with a kiss on the lips followed by a warm embrace.

But when she stepped away from him, he could instantly tell something was wrong.

"Are you okay?" he said quietly.

"I think you need to come with me," Emily whispered.

When they arrived in the living room, Todd felt like he'd walked straight into a brick wall.

"Hi, Todd," Dave said, rising to his feet. When the two shook hands, Todd could tell something had been going before he arrived.

"Sit." Dave took a deep breath. "I know," he said.

Todd turned to Emily. He was lost for words.

But before he could think of anything to say, Dave said calmly, "Todd, you have nothing to worry about. Emily has explained everything. You can trust me. I have no intention of saying anything to anyone."

Todd studied the ground for a long time. A part of him felt relieved they finally could speak to someone about everything, and especially that it was Dave. Todd had a lot of time for him.

When they had originally arrived in 2024, Todd had grown fond of Dave, and he'd liked it when Dave and his mother started dating.

"I think you need to tell Todd the other thing," Emily said.

The two men stared at each other for a few moments before Dave inhaled and said, "Your father contacted me today and lied to me about your brother, Jason."

Todd's eyes went wide. He wasn't angry with her for sharing his secrets, just surprised at what he was hearing.

"Dad—contacted you?" Todd said incredulously.

"I'm afraid so," Dave said, disappointment clear on his face.

The three of them sat in silence.

"I just don't get it," Todd said. "Why does he have such an issue with it?"

Dave shook his head before resting his elbows on his knees. "Jason is a smear on his much-revered public persona. If you have regular contact with him, your father is without doubt paranoid it will come out. He'd be worried it'll knock him off his perch."

Emily put her hand on Todd's shoulder and rubbed it gently.

"I'm starting to get really worried about all this, honey," she said before leaning her head on his shoulder.

"He's an okay kid, Dave. He just needs a break. We've gotten to know each other a little. I think he trusts me to a point. He knows I'm just trying to get to know him and be a sort of older brother to him, that's all."

"Does your mother know about him?" Dave asked.

"She admitted it to me before we got back on the plane

in 2024. She knew…" Todd stopped mid-sentence. "Oh, shit," he said.

He rose to his feet, walked into the middle of the room, and muttered the four-letter profanity again a couple of times under his breath. When he was about to speak, the penny dropped for her. She stood up and said, "Oh, my God."

"What is it?" said Dave.

"Mom told me she found out about Jason only when he was tried for Dad's murder."

Now it was Dave's turn to rise to his feet.

Todd finally broke the silence. "But Jason didn't kill Dad. When we came back to 2021, somehow we stopped it from happening."

Now, it all made sense. Andrew Roberts' behavior.

He wasn't trying to save his career from being blemished.

He was trying to save his reputation as a lifelong faithful husband.

In 2021, Todd's mother didn't know her husband's dirty little secret.

✈   ✈   ✈

Tammy realized she'd fallen asleep on the couch again. She was struggling to get a good night's sleep these days. The stress of everything going on in her life in St. Louis weighed heavily on her. It was just after 6pm, and the notion of making dinner was a depressing one.

Lee was out tonight. She'd decided to swipe right a week ago, and to her surprise, the guy she met on Tinder actually looked like his profile picture. Tonight was their second date.

Tammy decided to go and lie on her bed for a little while.

She stared out of her bedroom window in the darkness.

The conversation with Tony tonight had been as good as always; he was chatty and could always lift her from a somber mood. He was out with some guys from the airline, and she could tell he'd had a few to drink.

Tammy had become obsessed with her plans to extract her children from the Show Me State of Missouri. It was about the only thing she thought about now.

Her thoughts centered around getting them back to California, then contacting a lawyer and making an immediate application for custody of Beth and Noah.

She believed it all sounded pretty straightforward. She was confident she would win any battle in court with her sister and Brandon. She'd argue Annie was unfit to have custody of her two children, and had plenty of examples of why.

Tony had always been really cautious about all this, much to her frustration. But this was one of the reasons why she loved him. He was slow and careful about everything, which was a perfect counterpoint to her often spur-of-the-moment decision-making.

When she had told Tony tonight that she felt she had to make the move in the next week or so, he wondered if the idea as a whole was a good one.

By the end of the weekend, Ross and Melanie would be no longer be living at the Beverly Hills Hotel.

Tony would stay at the bungalow for a couple more weeks. He wanted to give Ross and Melanie a little time when they first moved into their new home. They had insisted he come, but he declined.

Tammy agreed with Tony; it was a good idea. In their last conversation, Tony had made her feel truly blessed. He'd told her when she brought Beth and Noah to California, he'd be ready for them. A part of him was looking forward to getting to know her children.

She decided to take a bath; she hadn't had one in God knew how long. As she got into the water ten minutes later, she told herself it was a great idea. After lying there for some time, she realized she'd left her phone in her room. She could have sworn she'd heard it ringing every few moments, but wasn't sure.

When she returned to her room, she lay back on her bed, and picked up her phone to check if she'd been hearing things or not.

"What the hell?" she said aloud.

There were six missed calls from Melanie, and ten from Tony.

She didn't know who to call first.

As she was about to dial Tony, her phone started ringing.

Tony.

"Babe?" she said.

There was a pause, as though the line had gone dead, but she could hear some background noise, and then some unusual, stifled sounds.

"Hon—ey." Tony sounded distraught. Tammy sat up and threw her feet to the floor.

"Tony? Are you there? Tony?" she said, panicked.

For a second, she thought all she could hear was his breathing.

"Tony. What's wrong? Are you there, babe?" she said.

There were another ten seconds of muffled sounds before Tony finally said something.

"Tam, have you heard from Mel—anie?"

Tammy could feel her breaths grow short.

"No, but she just called when you called me. I was in the bath; I missed her call."

Tony sounded like he was crying.

"Tony, what's happened?"

She could hear him breathing hard, and couldn't understand what he was saying.

She had to ask him to repeat what he'd just said.

This time his words came through clearer.

"Ross. He was killed tonight in a car accident."

CHAPTER THIRTY-NINE

The death of Ross Moore made front-page news across the globe.

Anything associated with Flight 19, including the lives of the people on-board, was still of interest to many.

That it was the pilot of the ill-fated flight who had died suddenly made it all the more newsworthy.

A private service attended only by close friends and family was held at White Diamond Funeral Services in Beverly Hills one week after the tragic accident.

It was followed in the early afternoon by a public memorial at Will Rogers Memorial Park. The chosen location was no accident; it was directly across the road from the Beverly Hills Hotel. Darcy and the hotel owners were behind this.

Melanie was inconsolable for the few days leading up to her fiancé's funeral.

Tammy had flown in from St. Louis the day after Ross's death.

She'd been by her friend's side since.

The public memorial was attended by close to three hundred people.

Melanie opted out of attending the public service at the

last minute. The emotions of the private service were enough for her.

Nearly all of the passengers who had come back with the A380 into 2021 traveled from near and far to attend.

Darcy spoke to most of them during the memorial, and invited many to a private wake held at the hotel straight afterward.

Tim and Sandra Erwin were two faces he knew well, and he spent some time catching up with them back at the Beverly Hills Hotel.

When Sandra ventured off to the toilet, Tim spoke in hushed tones.

"Such a tragedy, Michael. What a terrible accident."

Darcy nodded. He knew most of the details, including some the public didn't know.

"Witnesses claim Ross was speeding, but Melanie told me the guy was a very careful driver," Darcy said. "So it doesn't make any sense. Ross just ignoring the stop sign and barreling through the intersection? Melanie had only bought him the SUV the day before."

Darcy wiped his eyes.

"What I'd give to make that plane go back in time again, Tim." He stared into the old man's eyes. "I'd do anything to save the guy's life."

Tim couldn't help but look at Darcy with guilt. He wondered what Darcy's reaction would be if he knew Tim could possibly make that happen.

But he was only home in Alameda for another couple of days. Then he was due back at Homey for stage two of Ben's plan.

Steve King had eventually agreed to Ben's request: Vernon would go to Homey.

The logistics of organizing Vernon's transfer from Joe to the shop were going to be an enormous challenge that would take days to put together. Tim would be of no use sitting around and getting in Ben's way. So Ben sent him home.

"It's sad, Tim." Darcy said. "He had so much to look forward to. He and Melanie had just bought a home up at Monterey. We were all due to take our first space flight with Albert Sargeant in a few days' time."

This piqued Tim's interest. He was always keen on anything related to space travel. He knew all about Berty Sargeant. Tim thought the guy was a living legend.

"Wow, you're going up on his space flight this weekend? It's his third, right? They sound like they have it all working perfectly. Are they flying out of Mojave?"

Suddenly, his wife appeared by his side, smiling at them both.

"Yes, I think Mojave Space Port," Darcy said.

The billionaire waved to a couple of people nearby. As he was about to walk off to see them, he said to Tim, "Melanie's already told me she is not up for the space flight. Why don't you come in her place? As long as it's alright with your lovely wife, of course."

Tim thought it would be a dream come true. But he had other commitments with his son. He wouldn't be able to make it.

Before he could thank Darcy for the offer and decline the invitation, the billionaire had already slipped away and was greeting others nearby.

Sandra patted Tim on the arm, "Look at you. You're a popular man, my love. Just think…" She reached down and placed her hands in his. "If you weren't busy with all this consulting stuff, you could have gone into space this weekend."

Tim gave her a peck on the cheek.

"That's true, honey," he said.

Seven days later.

Melanie spent her first night in the home she'd hoped to grow old in with Ross. To call it bittersweet was a understatement. She wondered if there was any point staying in Monterey now.

But at least she wouldn't be home alone. Tony and Tammy were going to stay for a couple of nights.

Tammy had spoken to Brandon and her parents, who were remarkably supportive of her need to be in California. She told them she'd come home in the next few days, and this seemed to be fine with them all. It boosted Tammy's confidence. She thought they might even end up supporting her wish to take Beth and Noah on a trip to California.

Of course, this was a pipe dream, but it didn't matter.

Tony knew Tammy's suggestion to stay with Melanie for a few nights in Monterey was a good idea.

"Thank you," Melanie said as she came out from her bedroom and realized Tony and Tammy had prepared a fully cooked breakfast for her.

"But when I went to bed, the fridge wasn't even on," she added.

Tammy winked to Melanie and flicked her head in Tony's direction.

"The guy is a freak. He was up at 5.30 this morning, and back from the supermarket by 6.30."

Melanie sat on the first barstool, alongside Tammy, with Tony standing on the other side of the kitchen bench.

He poured them coffee before filling his own cup and looking down to his plate full of bacon, eggs, hash browns, and tomatoes. The guy was obviously hungry.

They ate in relative silence as the conversation hovered

above anything that could turn serious or even thought-provoking.

Melanie thanked them both for breakfast, though she hardly ate anything. She rose from her seat and headed off to the deck outside. She opened the doors and walked out onto the balcony.

Staring at the sea, she looked up at the sky and said, "I miss you."

A little while later, Tammy came out and found her sitting on the swing chair.

"You okay?" she said.

Melanie was staring off into the distance before she said, "I'm fine. Can you go and ask Tony to come out here? I have something to show you both."

Melanie asked Tony and Tammy to follow her, and when she reached the bottom of the driveway, she walked a few meters further down the sidewalk before coming to a stop in front of the house next door.

When Tony and Tammy stood alongside her, Melanie said, "When Ross and I bought our home, this one here was for sale as well."

Tony and Tammy shared a glance before turning back to Melanie.

She was tearing up, but pushed on.

"So we decided…" Melanie could feel the emotions over-coming her. "We'd like to have you both as close as we could."

Tammy stared at the house before the realization of what Melanie had just said dawned on her.

"You guys—you bought us this house?" Tony said.

"It was our way of thanking you both. For being the best friends you could ever ask for," Melanie said.

Tammy started to cry, and as she and Melanie embraced, Tony put his arms around both women.

He eventually turned his gaze up to the bright sky and said, "Thank you, Roscoe."

CHAPTER FORTY

THE TRIP BACK TO HOMEY WAS, ANNOYINGLY, HOODED. Tim wondered why the hell they bothered sticking the thing over his head, for God's sake. He knew how to get there in a car, or even on foot. Did it have to go on when he boarded the chopper at Oakland?

Anyway, at the end of the day, protocols are just that. Protocols.

Tim sat back and let the subtle sways and bumps of the fast-moving chopper send him into a dreamlike state. With his eyes closed, there wasn't much else to do.

Ben greeted him when the chopper landed, and took him on the usual route to where they were heading. He chatted about vanilla things, never straying from vagueness. Tim knew how it worked in these circles. At least Ben was talking. Silence would be more awkward.

When they eventually arrived deep underneath the softball pitch, Ben did the honors of removing his father's hood.

"You're looking good, old man," Ben said as he and Tim laid eyes on each other.

"I've been working out, that's why," Tim mused, winking at his son.

"Wow, really?" Ben had forgotten his dad's need to dish out a little sarcasm from time to time.

"Not really," Tim said, flexing his left arm at his son.

Todd got a message on his mobile from an unknown sender.

They popped up from time to time, so he just opened it, curiosity getting the better of him.

A second later, he realized it wasn't spam.

It was from Michelle Lowne, his friend from the San Bernardino PD.

And the message itself made his blood run cold.

"Get yourself a burner and call me ASAP. Don't reply to this message, either. Just call me on the burner."

Todd read it a couple of times.

This was not good.

If Michelle was contacting him from a burner, it probably meant the shit and the fan were on a collision course.

He reached for his car keys and wallet.

Tony was cleaning up the dishes after Tammy had made them both dinner. Melanie had opted to pass, a habit she'd repeat for some time to come, choosing instead to go to her room and lie down.

Tony couldn't stop thinking about the house next door. He still couldn't believe it.

Tammy's phone rang, snapping Tony straight out of his thoughts. Tammy met his eyes before peering down at the screen of her phone.

Lee.

"It's Lee," Tammy said, before scooping up her phone and answering it.

"Is that my favorite person from the Show Me State?" Tammy said joyfully.

"That's me. Are you all ready for your flight into space?"

"It's going to be pretty cool, I think. How's it all going there, babe?" Tammy said, before slipping out and onto the balcony.

Tony saluted her, rubber glove and all, and returned his attention to the sink full of dishes.

Lee began to answer, and by the time Tammy had reached the swinging chair on the balcony, the joy she'd felt a few moments ago was over.

"Seriously?" she repeated as she sat down on the chair.

"I wish I were, Tam. Brandon was here when I got home just a couple of hours ago. Like the last time, he was waiting for me in the foyer of my building."

Tammy shook her head and said, "But he said what? Just run it past me again; I think the line was a bit fuzzy a moment ago."

Lee took another long drink from her white wine.

"He told me he wants to give you full custody of Beth and Noah, for real."

Tammy knew there was more to it. There had to be.

"Surely there has to be a catch. Is there?"

Lee waited for a moment before she said, "We both know there is, Tam. Let's just say it's a 150-pound catch."

Tammy was about to scratch her head, trying to figure out what Lee meant.

But Lee came straight out and said it.

"I think the guy has lost his marbles, Tam. Annie must have smacked him over the head again. The catch is—him."

Tammy now was shaking her head.

"You've got to be kidding me. He'll give me the children, but I have to take him too?"

"That's the deal, Tam," Lee said. "You can have the kids, but he wants to come. Oh, and he thinks you should all move to California. Wow—how nice is that? You could move next door to the Brady Bunch. Or Charlie from *Two and a Half Men*."

Tammy broke into a fit of laughter. Lee had a way with words, and she'd been making Tammy laugh for decades.

But as her chuckles subsided, she realized Lee had gone silent. For a moment, she thought the line had dropped out.

"Are you there?" Tammy asked.

"I'm still here."

"What's wrong?" Tammy said.

After a pause of a few seconds, Lee said, "There's something else I need to tell you."

Tammy felt sick.

"What happened?"

Lee stared out her apartment window.

"Annie," she said.

Tammy walked to the railing of the balcony and looked out toward the ocean.

"What about her?"

Tammy didn't know at the time, but Lee was now at her kitchen bench pouring another glass of wine, trying to numb the pain.

"When Brandon left, I walked him out of the building," Lee said. "I wanted to make sure he was gone, that's all. So when he walked away, I stood there and watched him walk down the street."

Tammy wondered what the big deal with this was, but had a feeling there was more to come.

"When he disappeared from view, I suddenly had the weird feeling of being watched."

Tammy felt her throat go dry.

"When I looked across the road…" Lee hesitated for a second; she could feel the wine churning in her stomach. "I saw Annie standing there—looking directly at me."

"Shit, Lee, what the hell?" Tammy wished she were there to console her.

A moment later, she could hear what she thought was Lee starting to cry a little.

"Baby, what is it? Did she scare you?" Tammy said.

"She stared at me for such a long time. When I was about to turn around and come upstairs…" Lee's speech slowed. "She held up her index finger to me…" A long pause. "And then, while still just looking straight at me, she slowly ran her index finger across her throat."

"Dad, when we arrive in the cordoned-off area, there is going to be someone there you haven't seen for a while," Ben said as he continued to walk through the facility, looking at his dad. "Just don't freak out, okay. Be cool."

"If you're worried I'm going to freak out about Vernon and his toupee," Tim said, "you don't need to."

Ben's phone bleeped, and he reached into his pocket and pulled it out.

As he continued to walk at a steady pace, he ignored what his old man had said and focused all his attention on his phone.

"Steve is on his way," Ben said, more to himself than to Tim.

The two security guards looked as serious as they had last time. They reminded Tim of the Queen's Guard at Buckingham Palace. Those guys stood ramrod straight like robots, and these guys were exactly the same.

One stepped forward and pulled out a device to scan Ben and Tim's passes.

After he did Tim's pass, he stepped back and reached over to the curtain, which he pulled back enough for the two Erwins to enter.

As Tim made it through and the access door closed, he focused on the replica craft. It still impressed him.

Only after he heard Ben say something did he turn his focus to his son.

"S-h-i-t," Tim whispered.

Someone was standing next to Ben.

The mother of his grandchildren.

Ben's wife.

CHAPTER FORTY-ONE

TODD HIGHTAILED IT DOWN TO THE NEAREST 7-ELEVEN. After picking up the burner, he drove for a few minutes before pulling up in a quiet side street.

His heart was pumping hard.

Todd ripped the package open and pulled the mobile phone out of the small box.

He'd bought a car charger for the burner as well—a smart move, since the phone was dead flat.

When he got it all plugged in and powered up, he brought up Michelle's number on his own phone before pulling the sim out and turning it off.

He dialed the number, and as it rang, his breath grew short and shallow.

For a moment, Todd thought it was a blowout, and Michelle wasn't going to answer. But after about the tenth ring, she did.

Her voice sounded different.

"Who is this?" she said calmly.

Todd knew it was her, and that she was making sure it was him.

"It's me—the blue-eyed ginger."

It was what Michelle had called him throughout their time at the police academy.

"Prove it. Tell me something only you and I know."

Todd had to think quick. A few seconds later, he said, "We shared a joint down at Venice Beach one night. It was after six hours at the Whaler. I've never seen anyone throw back that many Aperol Spritzes in my life."

Michelle felt a wave of relief come over her.

No one in the world knew that she and Todd had shared a joint a week after graduating from the police academy. They'd sworn to each other it would remain their secret forever.

"Talk to me, Shell," Todd whispered.

"Andrew got to the boss," she said, "and I'm either going to be transferred to God knows where, or do what he's demanding and tell him everything I know about you and Jason."

"Damn it," Todd said. "This is now completely off the charts. What the hell are we going to do?"

Michelle was silent for a few moments, before she said, "Todd, I can't get transferred. I just bought an apartment less than ten minutes' drive from here. The asshole must have told Andrew that. But you've been my friend for a long time." Her voice held a hint of regret. "I don't ever betray my close friends."

Todd slammed the dashboard of the car with his fist. "That bastard. I've had enough of this."

Michelle started to cry, and as Todd heard her, he said, "Just tell me one thing before I confront this son of a bitch who is supposed to be my father."

"Fire away."

Todd stared out through the windscreen of his car and said, "Johnny the Mac. Do you think he'd back my father all the way? Is there a chance he was blackmailed?"

Michelle wiped her eyes. "Between you and me," she said, "I think the Mac is a good guy. He just fucked up one night, and your dad has used it against him. My gut feel is he doesn't want to have any part in this. If you think the guy likes you, it's probably true."

Todd thought about it for a moment, and made a decision.

"This ends tomorrow night, Shell," he said

"Why not tonight?" she said.

Todd shook his head. It was a fair call, though.

"Mom and Dad are away for the weekend. They come home tomorrow night. As soon as they walk through their front door, Dad is going to get a rude awakening."

"What on God's earth are you going to do, Todd?" Michelle said.

Todd smiled to himself in the rearview mirror. The idea was beyond stupid, but it would end this for good.

"Dad's going to be reunited with someone he created but never met."

"Are you out of your mind? You can't do that; it's crazy."

The words she heard a second later reminded her of the saying, "The apple doesn't fall far from the tree."

It was more about the tone than anything else.

"Watch me," Todd said, and rang off.

"Jenny," Tim said as she walked up to him.

He offered no greeting, not even his hand. All he could see was Sandra at Jenny's memorial service, struggling to stop the torrent of tears over their daughter-in-law's apparent disappearance and death.

But he found himself coming to his senses a few seconds

later. If what Ben said was true, she was here to help Ben get Vernon out. That had to count for something.

"I know what you're thinking, Tim," Jenny said.

"I don't think you and Ben will ever understand how hard it was for us when you did your little disappearing act," Tim said.

Jenny, like Ben, had made the decision a long time ago. It was the career path they'd longed for.

Tim wanted to ask her why they'd had children, but thought the better of it.

It didn't matter. It wouldn't change anything. In these circles, nothing made sense.

A moment later, they both looked up at the sound of a distant but audible alarm.

"That's the signal," Jenny said. "Homey is now in category six lockdown," she explained before Tim could ask her what he was talking about.

"Cat six is very rare. Only a handful of people actually know what a cat-six shutdown means," she said.

Jenny stared at him for an extended period while he worked it out.

"When an out-of-towner comes to visit," Tim said.

"As far as I know, there have only ever been three cat sixes in Homey's history. All personnel on the base, unless you are with Majestic VA6, have to leave. No exceptions. But most people have already left. The first notification was 24 hours ago. That alarm was the final warning. If you're found on base after this final alarm…" She turned to Tim with a serious look. "Let's just say no one has ever been found on base after a final cat-six alarm."

Ben and Jenny tinkered with their replica craft for some time as Tim sat on a stool nearby and watched. They talked quietly to each other in hushed tones, never raising their voices.

At one point, they both entered the craft, and before Ben shut the access door, he said to Tim, "Put on those earmuffs, Dad. This may get a little loud for a few moments."

Tim put on the earmuffs.

After a couple of minutes, he could hear the strangest of sounds emanating from the craft.

It came and went in pulses, and as the minutes went on, Tim could feel the ground vibrating enough for him to take notice.

Just as he was starting to get used to the sound, the craft let out the most bizarre and extremely loud squawk. Tim nearly jumped, and instinctively closed his eyes. The sound felt as if it were moving through every muscle of his body. He stared up at the ceiling and realized the whole place appeared to be shaking.

But when he turned to the craft, he caught his breath. Tim couldn't believe what he was seeing.

The craft almost appeared translucent. It was if it had nearly disappeared from Tim's sight, but was still there.

As Tim shook his head, and closed his eyes then opened them again to ensure he wasn't seeing things, the sound began to fade. The vibration eased and the craft came back into full view.

About a minute later, after the whole area was completely silent, the access door to the craft silently moved aside, and Ben, then Jenny, exited the craft. They both looked satisfied with how things had gone.

"We're good to go, old…" Ben's words were cut short by a sound from his phone.

"You've got to be shitting me," Ben said, before looking to Jenny with an annoyed expression.

"What is it?" she said.

Ben gave her his handset.

"Damn it," she said, handing the phone back.

"What's going on?" Tim asked.

Ben shook his head. "Vernon's arrival has been delayed. Issues with entry into the States. Steve said they won't arrive until tomorrow night. Damn it."

CHAPTER FORTY-TWO

MELANIE UNDERSTOOD WHY TAMMY FELT THE NEED TO go back to St. Louis and talk to Brandon and her parents about Annie's behavior. But Melanie also agreed with Tony that he should go with her, for her own safety. Tammy wondered if Tony being there would only make things more awkward, though at the end of the day Tony had put his foot down. He was coming whether she wanted him to or not. The three of them knew what happened last time Annie was left to her own devices: she nearly killed Tammy, and Tony could have been killed too.

Melanie felt a pang of loneliness as she waved them into the cab that morning, but knew they needed to sort things out in St. Louis once and for all. She just wanted them both back in one piece, the sooner the better.

To his credit, Darcy was not overly upset when Melanie called him to explain what was going on with the two *T*'s.

Melanie told him they felt awful about pulling out of the space flight scheduled for that night, and that they'd offered to pay him back for the cost of the tickets.

Darcy told Melanie that was the least of his concerns. He was more worried about them.

Todd had contacted Jason the night before, and in an exchange of text messages, Jason had agreed to meet him for lunch. Todd told him that afterwards, he'd take him somewhere to buy him some new clothes. Jason felt he didn't need to do this, but Todd insisted. In the end, Jason agreed—there was no point arguing with Todd. So far, his older half-brother had been very good to him.

Todd had decided to do this as a way to butter him up before talking him into going to his parents' house to confront Andrew.

And for the first time in his life, Jason felt like someone out there actually cared about him.

Todd would later realize that by making contact with his half-brother, he'd helped Jason out of a horrible life on the streets, where drugs and crime were his only friends. Jason knew plenty of people on the streets, but they were not friends. They'd betray him in a heartbeat for a hit or something of value.

"I have a really bad feeling about this," Emily told him as they said their goodbyes just after midday, at her home in Redondo Beach.

"You worry way too much, my darling." Todd gave her another kiss, hoping it would make her feel better.

"You can kiss me like that twenty-four hours a day, seven days a week, honey, but it isn't going to make me any less worried," Emily said.

"I'm a big boy, and I promise you I'll take care of myself. I'll be back here tonight when it's all done."

As Emily watched him reverse out of her driveway and he waved one more time, she prayed to God his assurance he'd be back tonight would hold true.

Tim ate his breakfast after a surprisingly good night's sleep. Jenny and Ben were engrossed in their phones while they ate.

What seemed a little odd to Tim was that they kept swapping their handsets every few moments. Both of them were tapping away feverishly on the screens.

Back and forth, back and forth they went. After Tim finished his coffee, he was about to say something, but Ben and Jenny suddenly looked at each other and then over to Tim.

"Glasses," Ben said to his father, who then realized what Ben meant was—put your reading glasses on.

Tim did what Ben had told him as Ben tapped on his screen some more, then handed his phone over.

When Tim took the handset from Ben, his son indicated he should look at the screen.

As Tim read the words, it dawned on him what Ben and Jenny had been doing.

This facility has more bugs than a Florida swamp, Pop. This is the only way we can communicate without them knowing what we're saying. Obviously, we can't send the messages to each other. They're recorded. We type, read, then delete.

Tim handed the handset back, to his credit keeping his mouth tightly shut.

Jenny studied her father-in-law. She had always been fond of Ben's father. The guy was made of the right stuff.

Ben turned to Jenny and then back to Tim.

He typed away madly on his handset and then handed it to Tim.

Jenny and I are just running through the final plans
for what is going to go down today. Sorry, we don't
mean to make you feel left out.

Tim read the message and decided to type one back
to Ben.

I hope you both know what you are doing. I hope
you know they may try and kill you if they work out
you are letting him escape.

Ben read the message before handing his phone to Jenny.
After she read it, she deleted it from the screen.

She reached over and placed her hand over her husband's.
"Today is going to be a very exciting day," she said aloud,
smiling at them both. "It's going to be a day to remember."

Tim met her smile with his own. "I hope today goes as
well as you both hope it will," he said.

The Erwins—Tim, Ben, and Jenny—being twenty-five
stories under the softball pitch at Homey, did not witness the
spectacular arrival of Vernon to the secret base.

He was transported from the other facility in a special
pod that shielded him from the outside world. It was
climate-controlled and very comfortable, and he spent most
of the trip dozing in and out of his version of sleep and
contemplating the feeling of returning home after all this
time. The pod was placed inside another contraption, which
meant no one except a few knew what they were actually
transporting.

Steve King, along with two specially trained guards from
the main facility, accompanied the pod every step of the way.

A specially built Northrop Grumman B-2 Spirit, known more commonly as a Stealth Bomber, converted for the transport of very special and sensitive payloads, carried them for almost three-quarters of the trip. At a cruising altitude of over fifty thousand feet, it made the trip from São Paulo, Brazil, to Homey Airport, Nevada, in under nine hours.

When the B-2 Spirit entered US airspace, it was escorted all the way to Homey Airport by no less than eight fighter jets. All eight were then replaced with a rolling patrol of fighter jets from Edwards Air Force Base, until they were instructed to return for the night.

When Vernon eventually made it down to the Majestic VA6 facility, he was led slowly through the base until he arrived at the cordoned-off area.

When he and Steve came through the access doors, Ben, Jenny, and Tim were there to meet him.

He greeted them all in his own unique way, smiling mildly at them all and saying "hello" in a calm voice. He studied the replica craft, and Tim could have sworn he appeared to nod. Vernon then turned to Ben and Jenny, and said, "You have made a true copy of my ship. Well done."

"Steve," he said. "I will go and have a look inside. You would be okay with that, yes?"

Steve could feel the tension in his throat. He wanted to say no, but knew this would not sit well with his guest. Vernon had agreed to show them how to operate the craft to fly beyond light speed, after all, so he needed to show him trust in return.

"Please," Steve said, struggling not to grit his teeth.

Vernon looked over to the others in the room, and Tim was sure he spotted a tiny smile appearing on his small mouth.

Tim smiled faintly back. That toupee was just hilarious.

Vernon walked over to the craft as if he were a Teletubby.

Small, slow steps. When he reached the door, it opened silently. He stepped in and disappeared from view.

Steve felt the urge to dive head first for the open door. Something didn't feel right.

Suddenly, everyone standing in front of the craft went silent.

The door closed.

CHAPTER FORTY-THREE

Tammy had called ahead, so Lee knew she was coming. She told her Tony would be with her. Lee, to Tammy's surprise, said she would happily take them straight to her parents' house. Tammy thought she would opt out for fear of Annie and her apparent death threat only the day before. Lee said she wouldn't come in, but would just be on standby nearby when they needed to be picked up. She was sure she would be okay.

Tammy had called her father, too, and told him they wanted to talk to him and her mom about Annie.

Tammy knew the risks, but she had to try. She prayed her parents wouldn't tell Annie she was coming.

To her complete amazement, her father had agreed.

When Lee's car pulled up out the front of the Sanders home, Tammy reached over and gave her a kiss on the cheek. "You have no idea what it means to have a reliable friend like you," she said.

"You just take care of yourself, both of you," Lee said.

And as Lee reached the end of the Sanders' street, she didn't even notice the person who'd dipped her head below the window line of her car, parked nearby.

When Tammy had called her father, he'd thought their conversation was private. As he'd told her, he was in his shed when she called. But what he didn't know was that his wife was standing right outside the door. She called Annie thirty seconds later.

She'd later realize it was a fatal mistake.

"Here he is." Todd's usual greeting to Jason always brought a little smirk to the young guy's face.

"Hey, Todd." Jason seemed upbeat and positive today.

"You hungry, dude?" Todd found himself always wanting to use the word *dude* in these parts of Central LA. He had no idea why; it just seemed come to him the minute he crossed over into the inner city.

Todd had a phone in each back pocket of his jeans. He still had the burner, and had put credit on it just in case Michelle needed to call him. He'd decided the little stunt of pulling out his sim and turning off his phone the other day had been a little paranoid. The way he was feeling today, if his old man wanted to track him, he could goddamn track him.

Andrew was tracking him.

But not from his phone.

Todd had swept his car for tracking devices a couple of times, but there was an inherent issue with automobiles. With the onset of technology, tracking devices were as small as a quarter. This meant there were almost more places to hide a tracking device than one could look.

Johnny the Mac had felt sick when Andrew ordered him to hide a tracking device in Todd's car, and told him that if Todd found it, it would be on the Mac.

And today, under Andrew's instructions, Johnny was

346

spending his day off doing the last thing on earth he wanted to do—following Todd and his half-brother.

He wondered what the endgame was for Andrew. He wondered if he wanted the kid dead, or otherwise. Following them around seemed like a complete waste of time.

Two and a half hours after watching them eat lunch, then watching them from afar shopping for what appeared to be clothes for the punk, the Mac started to wonder if losing his job would have been a better option than ending up like this. But he turned to his phone and touched the power button. The screen lit up with a stunning photo of his Portuguese wife, her belly full of his first child. And it brought him crashing back to reality. If he lost his job under these circumstances, he'd lose her and his first kid. He'd become just another deadbeat ex-cop, single and spending every second weekend seeing his kid, who would end up hating him for what he did to his mother. Glory days.

He parked his car close enough to Todd's to watch him, but far enough away not to be noticed.

"No fucking way, Todd. I can't do it."

Todd stared out through his windscreen and felt his patience waning. It was overcast in Los Angeles, and it looked as if the clouds wanted to take a big leak over the city.

Jason looked out through the passenger-side window of Todd's car and said, "That's why you bought me all the clothes, right? So you could bribe me into going to your house and helping you get back at Dad for how he's been treating you."

Todd shook his head. "He wiped you, Jason. He needs to be held accountable for that. Come on, let's do that together."

Jason was clearly upset. But Todd misread how he was feeling.

The kid was angry.

347

He felt as if Todd had taken him for a ride, to use him as some sort of weapon against his old man.

For all of Jason's shortcomings, there was one thing about that thought.

He was right.

"Fuck you. I'm done with you and all this shit." Jason's anger exploded out of nowhere.

He unclipped his seatbelt and a moment later flung open the passenger-side door, nearly taking out a guy riding past on a bike.

"Watch it, moron!" the guy said, swerving just in time to avoid hitting the door straight on.

"Fuck off," Jason snarled.

He darted across the busy street.

Todd was already out of the car and shouting out to him. "Jason, wait! Can we just talk about this? Jason!"

From his vantage point, the Mac saw Jason shouting to the rider and then waltzing across the road. "What the hell?" he said to himself.

And then he cursed. "Damn it, I'm done with recon on foot."

As he pulled the key out of the ignition, he watched Todd close the passenger-side door and run across the road in the direction of where Jason was going.

"Shit, the Skid," the Mac swore as he slipped his handgun underneath his jacket and waited for a couple of cars to pass him before he followed.

Skid Row wasn't the sort of place he liked spending any time in.

⌐   ⌐   ⌐

Annie watched Lee's car turn the corner of her parents' street and disappear from view. She'd deal with her later. It wouldn't end well for Lee, Annie decided. She'd make her pay for her involvement in this little drama.

Annie had figured out how to slip in and out of her parents' home by her early teens. She could get in and out without having to go near the front or back door. The spare-room window lock had been broken for as long as she could remember. Her father probably to this day still had no idea it was broken. Stupid man, Annie thought. The guy was a dumb as a piece of wood, and had spent nearly half his life in that stupid shed of his. Although she hadn't been in there for a long time, she assumed there'd be one of the world's biggest porn collections hidden in there somewhere.

She was half right.

There *was* a huge collection of magazines hidden there, but not of people doing the business. We'll park that for now.

By the time Annie slipped into the spare-room window, the conversation was well underway in the living room.

"Brandon, I'd like you to meet Tony." Tammy had recovered from the shock of Brandon sitting silently in her parents' living room when they entered. She had no idea he was going to be there. But in the end, she realized it was not a bad thing. She needed to convince him too.

"Brandon," Tony said, shaking his girlfriend's ex-husband's hand, "it's good to meet you."

The two men stared at each other awkwardly for a moment before Brandon retreated to where he'd been sitting when the two *T*'s had entered the room.

Tammy's mother seemed palpably out of sorts, as if she was done with it all.

"So, let's get down to business here," Patricia said a moment later.

Tony and Tammy went over to the nearby couch and sat down.

"Where's Dad?" Tammy said. She turned to her mother and then toward the hallway.

"Here I am," Bart said as he walked in and over to Tony. "Hello, I am Bartholomew Sanders, Tammy's father," he said. Before he could ask Tony who he was, Tony introduced himself, reached up, and shook his hand.

"Hello, Tammy," her father said, bending down and giving her a kiss on the forehead. Only Brandon would notice that he'd bent in a strange way, as if he'd put his back out.

Bart sat on the sofa next to Brandon.

Tammy took a deep breath and came straight out with it.

"I want to take the children to California, to live. With me."

As Brandon nearly fell off the sofa, Tammy decided the time of keeping secrets was over.

"I am with Tony, and we are in love," she said seriously.

Her parents looked at each other and her mother said, "But you only just met a few months ago. Isn't it a bit soon to be talking about love?"

Tammy shook her head, looking quite offended.

"You and Dad were engaged within three months. Mom, wasn't that a bit soon?" she said.

Patricia scoffed and barked, "When it's in the eyes of the Lord, no—it wasn't too soon."

Tammy rolled her eyes and turned to Brandon, still reeling from the shock of seeing his dream shot to flames.

She stared at her father and wanted to bitch-slap him. Why he ever agreed to marry her mother, she would never understand.

"Well, I've been chatting to JC," Tammy said sarcastically, "and he said me taking Beth and Noah back to California is okay with him."

Her Mother sprang to her feet and pointed at Tammy as

if she *had* slapped her in the face. "Don't you ever speak of the Lord's son like that again, or you will never set foot in this house again."

Tammy shot to her feet. Her frustration with all her mother's years of Bible-bashing bullshit was about to come to a head.

"You and I know Annie is not right in the head, Mom. Look what she did to Brandon." Brandon looked like he wanted to crawl up into the nearest corner.

"Stop it!" Tammy's mom barked. "It was an accident."

"Oh shit," Tony gasped.

"Darling, no!" Patricia Sanders screamed.

"What the he…" Tammy realized what Tony and her mother were referring to.

Her sister was standing at the entrance to the living room.

Tammy had never seen an angrier look on her sister's face.

And the pistol in Annie's right hand was pointing directly at her.

"Jason, just stop." Todd was now nearly running at full tilt.

His half-brother was running right through the heart of Skid Row. Homeless people looked up for a moment and wondered what all the commotion was. A moment later, they went back to whatever they were doing.

One man chasing another down the street was just another day in the row.

"Leave me alone!" Jason barked, seeming to pick up his pace as he ran around a corner and down an alleyway.

He had some idea of where he was going. He knew these

parts of Skid Row like the back of his hand. There were plenty of places to hide.

The Mac was struggling to keep up with Todd without getting busted following him. The Mac was fit, so he had no problem with stamina, just stealth.

He saw Todd disappear around the corner, and his heart sank when he realized how long it would take for him to get there.

Jason then came around another corner, and realized the warehouse on the right side of the alleyway had been abandoned for as long as he'd been in the row.

He'd decided he had nothing to lose when he ran to the heavy metal door and grabbed hold of the handle.

It was open.

He flew through it and pulled it shut. He closed it quietly and held onto it after the door closed, in case Todd decided to check to see if it was open.

But after a few seconds and what he thought was the sounds of footsteps running past, he dropped his hand from the door handle and let out a long sigh of welcome relief.

He regained his breath and sat down against the wall for a moment.

To his horror, the door flew open and someone walked in, closing the door with a slam behind them.

"What the fuck?" the rough-looking guy spat when he spotted Jason.

"Jesus Christ," Jason exclaimed, springing to his feet, "you gave me a fucking heart attack, bro." He stepped over to the guy and gave him a slap on the shoulder.

"Whatta you doin' here, man?" the guy said to Jason. "They are the cleanest-lookin' threads I ever saw you in."

Jason shook his head. "A long story, Taz. It's been a fucked-up day. What you doin'? You guys shacking up in here?"

Taz shook his head. "Na, man, we're just feedin' the pet we've put in here."

Jason looked around the near pitch-black warehouse. It was full of garbage, but there was another section on the other side of a big wall nearby. "Funny place to keep a pet, bro," he said.

Taz broke into laughter, exposing his rotten teeth. Jason hoped one day he got to see a dentist.

"More like an avest-ment. We're gonna sell the pet soon; it's gotta be worth a lot to some," he said with a grin.

Jason looked him up and down, and then to his dirty shopping bag. It appeared to be full of food.

"I don't think dogs dig bread, doh," Jason said.

Taz reached up and put his hand around Jason's neck, pulling him close before giving him a friendly head-butt.

"You one of the funniest white boys in the row, that's why we like you all," he said, stepping back. "You want to see our pet, huh?"

Jason thought he had all the time in the world now. He didn't want to bump into Todd anytime soon.

"Sure, Taz." Jason shook his head. "Show me this pet, then."

Jason followed Taz through the dark, rank warehouse. The smell of sewage and rotting garbage was overpowering. It was worse inside these abandoned places than on the streets of Skid Row. At least outside there was the wind.

A minute later, after traversing the rubble, a couple more doorways, and some long, dark corridors, Jason could see the distant flicker of a fire.

There were a few people milling around there, throwing off large shadows on the walls in every direction.

"Look who I found, bruhs," Taz said to the three men standing around the fire.

They all knew Jason. He'd sold them drugs, and they'd helped him out with other punks giving him a hard time.

"Hey white boy," one of them said as the other two greeted him in silence.

"I'm going to show Jason our pet," Taz told the others.

They all studied each other before one of them turned to Taz, looking nonplussed by the idea.

"You trust him, you show him. But he tells anyone, he doesn't see daylight again, huh."

Taz nodded, and indicated Jason should follow him into a small room nearby.

By now, Jason was thinking they must have had a Bengal tiger tied up in there.

When he arrived in the open doorway, Taz picked up a torch sitting on the ground.

A powerful beam lit up the small and dirty room, casting shadows from one side to the other.

On one side of the room was a dirty and rank-smelling single mattress.

Lying on it, bound and gagged, was the gang's pet.

Jason stared at it for a couple of seconds. He went to say something, but stopped himself. The words might have resulted in him never seeing the light of day again.

CHAPTER FORTY-FOUR

STEVE FELT LIKE HE WAS GOING TO BE SICK. HE WAS literally about to run for the craft and start bashing on the front. He'd trusted Vernon, and now wondered if that had been a mistake.

But a moment later, the access door to the craft quickly slid back open.

A small, well-dressed leg followed, and a moment later, Vernon was out and looking over to Ben and Jenny.

"Impressive work, you two." Vernon turned to Steve and then back to the couple. "It is almost identical to my ship."

Steve took a deep breath and could feel the relief calming him down.

Vernon walked closer to Ben and said, "Before I do the demonstration, can I see my ship, please?"

Tim stood watching the little guy. He was still surprised at how well he spoke. Tim would never know that Vernon could speak in hundreds of languages.

Ben studied Steve. He was the boss, and Ben wanted to make sure he didn't suspect anything. He wanted to make sure he felt like the boss.

"Can we show Vern his ship, Steve?" Ben said.

Vernon by now was staring at Steve with those big eyes. Steve, for the first time in a long time, took note of the toupee. He had never mentioned it to Ben, Jenny, or anyone at the facility.

He thought it looked—fucking ridiculous.

Steve returned his attention to Vernon's eyes. He then turned to Ben.

"Show him," he said.

As the false wall slid backwards, the smell coming from the smaller room drifted out and into their nostrils.

None of them said anything. One of the security guards sniffed heavily before Steve tapped him hard on the chest. He shut up immediately.

Vernon walked to his heavily damaged ship.

He remembered the day it happened like it was yesterday.

He thought of his colleagues. He had known them all a long time. They were friends, and they had all died within a few hours of the crash.

He walked around the ship and then, without saying a word, stepped inside. Sitting in his pilot's seat, he could feel homesickness wash over him.

He stared out through the broken window and saw Ben, Tim, Jenny, and Steve standing there looking at him.

The Erwins all seemed sad for him, but Steve was beginning to look impatient. If Vernon had sat in there longer than the one more minute he did, Steve would have said something.

When Vernon exited his ship, he looked over to the humans and for the first time since being on this planet, could understand the true meaning of satisfaction.

When he was in his craft, and without any of them seeing what he was doing, he had activated an emergency signal from a panel that, even after ninety-plus years, no human had ever found.

It was activated by something similar to our retina-scanning technology. So unless you had eyes like those of Vernon's species, you wouldn't have been able to activate it, even if you'd known the device was there on the ship.

Vernon had told only Ben about it. It was the sole reason they had concocted the story about bringing Vernon to Homey. It would be the only way he could get home. Ben's replica craft could get them into space, but Vernon had no plans to take the Erwins home with him. They would return to earth, and Vernon would be transferred to another ship for his journey home.

"Are we ready?" Steve turned to Vernon with his best attempt at a smile.

Vernon looked up at him and hoped the next few moments would be the last time he ever saw this human. The Erwins were another story, but this guy, he had never liked.

"I think we are ready," Vernon said. "You will be pleased."

Ben and Steve stared at each other before walking over to the wall. They went through an authentication process in front of the glass wall, as Ben had done previously.

But this time, it was the actual wall they were standing in front of that moved.

It revealed yet another secret room of the facility.

A bank of lights built into the floor came on.

Ben turned to Tim and said, "Give me a hand."

The two men pushed the craft over into the new room.

When Ben stopped pushing, Tim could feel a draft down the back of his neck. He looked up to see where it had come from.

"Oh, my God," he said to himself.

They weren't standing in a room.

They were standing in one hell of a lift.

"Now you know why they built a softball pitch here at Homey," Ben said.

"Mother of God," Tim said. "To hide in plain view the entry and exit point for anything built at Majestic."

Ben nodded.

The lift started to move upwards.

As they reached the halfway point, the roof above the lift started to move downwards, then stopped and began to move sideways. As it did, Tim could see the night sky coming into view.

Five minutes later, the lift came to a stop. Tim couldn't believe it. It was an eerie sight. The entire base was in darkness.

Vernon walked over to Steve. "Can I take you on a little ride?" he said.

Steve turned to Vernon, struggling to contain his excitement.

"I would, but I need to bring the guards. They come wherever I go. Is that a problem?"

"That's fine. Let me get you all strapped in," Vernon said.

The door to the craft closed.

"Dad, over here," Ben said as he and Jenny made their way to the corner of the platform. Ben had opened an access panel on the floor, and pulled out three pairs of earmuffs.

"Put these on," Ben said.

Vernon's ship began to power up.

A light began to pulse from the bottom. Ben tapped Tim on the arm and shouted, "Get down!"

The sound coming from the ship became incredibly loud.

As Tim watched, the craft became translucent, but this time, rose steadily in the air.

When it reached about twenty feet, it then shot straight

up at an amazing speed, and disappeared from view in a flash.

Tim turned to Ben and said, "I'm lost. Why did he take Steve and his men with him? I thought he was going to escape?"

Ben said, "All part of the plan. Let's just hope our little friend knows what he is doing."

"Annie, no!" Brandon shouted.

A part of him had forgotten he was no longer married to Tammy. He needed to protect her.

"You can all go to hell!" Annie barked, pointing the gun directly at her sister.

Tony cursed to himself. They shouldn't have come to St. Louis. His greatest fear was coming true.

"I hate you all! Especially you, Tammy," Annie screamed. "And you two," she snarled at her parents. "You pieces of shit never gave me a chance. What hope did I have when my own mother mistreated me?"

Patricia Sanders started to sob before Annie barked, "I hope those tears are for me, bitch." She pointed the gun at her.

Tony knew anyone who lunged at Annie would be the first to die.

When he turned to Tammy's father, he found him remarkably calm. He just stood there, hands behind his back, studying his daughter brandishing a handgun.

It was almost as if he was fascinated by the scene.

"Well, before I kill you all," Annie said, stepping a foot closer, "I will be happy to inform you that Beth and Noah will be at the Pearly Gates waiting for you. They are gone."

Tammy screamed, "No!" as she turned to Brandon and said, "You left them with her? And now they are dead!"

Brandon just stared at Annie, and as he did so, the color of his cheeks switched from pale to red.

As Patricia Sanders continued to sob, Brandon said the words that would haunt Tammy for years to come.

"Forgive me," he said.

A split second later, he was on his feet.

It all happened so quickly.

So did the two gunshots—in rapid succession.

"I guess at some point you're going to tell me the score here," Tim said to Ben.

Ben made eye contact with Jenny before staring back up at the night sky.

"Vernon's plan was quite straightforward," Ben said, turning to his father.

"With my help, he learned how to control the disks within earth's atmosphere, enabling him to time travel."

Ben stared up into the night sky for a second before going on.

"Vernon pre-set coordinates to take them to the middle of the Sahara Desert—one of the most remote parts of planet earth. There, he's going to come up with a story to get them out of the craft before he closes the door and takes off."

Tim then thought of something. "So where does the time-travel part fit in?"

"Well, let's just say that when they put their feet on the sand, it will be in 2071," Ben told Jenny.

Tim shook his head. "Wow. Now that is an audacious plan," he said. "They'll be so far in the future they won't be able to do anything to stop Vernon from going home."

A moment later, they all heard a distant sound getting louder by the second. It could only be one thing.

"Earmuffs, now," Ben said.

The sound of the craft grew louder.

As the light on the underside of the craft began to pulse, the craft slowed and a moment later touched down on the platform.

Ben's nerves tightened. His best-laid plans were about to be confirmed or thrown out the door.

The craft powered down before the three of them rose to their feet and waited.

A minute later, the access door to the craft slid open.

Two legs appeared in the open doorway.

Ben held his breath.

Jenny stood frozen like a statue.

Tim saw the toupee and grinned.

Vernon walked toward them, not giving anything away.

When he reached the three Erwins, he said, "I think it is time to go home."

Tim sat down in the seat and did his best to get comfortable.

There was a strange sort of seat belt sitting across him, which felt like a snake, but he just went with the flow.

Ben and Jenny had ensured all the disks were in the correct positions. Vernon had run checks on everything, and a few moments later he sat in the one seat in front. He ran his hands across screens, and as the access door closed, said, "Are you all ready to go?"

"We're all good to go, Vern," Ben said.

When the ship began to lift off the ground, it was as if they were sitting on a feather drifting in the air.

A few seconds later, they felt the most incredible whoosh,

and before they knew it, they were hurtling up into the air at incredible speed.

They continued to climb. Tim could just make out the night sky through the front window. The stars seemed to be moving in all directions.

Twenty seconds later, Vernon said something to himself, though none of them knew what it meant.

A few moments later, Ben realized they were going downwards.

"Everything okay, Vernon?" Ben said.

"I will explain when we land," he said.

When the ship touched down, the Erwins realized they were not back at Homey. Vernon had landed the ship at the very place his had crash-landed nearly one hundred years ago.

Ben wasted no time getting on with it. "Is something wrong with the ship?" he asked.

Vernon looked up to Ben.

"Something does not add up," he said, though no concern was evident on his face. "The ship cannot seem to break free of the magnetic pull of the earth. I don't know why. Everything seemed to work, though for some reason it will not get us into space. I'm sorry, Ben. It may take some time to figure out."

Ben turned to Vernon and said, "I should be the one apologizing to you. I've let you down."

Vernon raised his hand and patted Ben lightly on the arm.

"You and Jenny, William, and Tim," he said, "are the only humans who ever made me feel welcome. You have not let me down."

Ben looked to his father and then his wife, and said, "But

now that Steve is gone, this is not going to go down well. We simply cannot return to life as we know it. We need to get you off this planet."

Ben studied the distant mountains and wondered how the hell he was going to pull off the impossible.

"There has to be a way we can make the necessary adjustments to the replica," he said to Vernon. "Surely we can figure it out."

"It could take some time," Vernon said. "Maybe weeks. Maybe months. We would need to go back to my craft and pull it apart."

Jenny shook her head. "Getting back to your craft may be near impossible now. They may never let us near it again."

Ben kicked the dirt in frustration. "Damn it," he cursed. "Where's a spaceship when you need one?"

As Tim stared up at the stars, an incredible idea came to him.

"Jesus," he said aloud as the thought gained traction.

"What is it, Dad?" Ben said with a slight air of frustration.

Tim stepped closer to him. "Darcy is taking Albert Sargeant's space flight tonight. They're taking off from the Mojave Desert Space Port. Why don't we ask him for a lift?"

Ben was about to burst into laughter, but Jenny stepped over to him and grabbed his arm.

"What do we have to lose? It's worth a try."

Ben turned to Vernon.

"I will take all the disks with me. It's the safest way. We can end all this tonight," Vernon said.

Ben locked eyes with his wife. He could tell she supported the idea. Tim knew there was no other way.

Ben turned back to Vernon and said, "Let's go. I will direct you to Mojave when we are airborne."

Michael E. Darcy and Albert Sargeant had known each other for decades. Many billionaires, funnily enough, were good friends with other billionaires.

It was just how the world spun.

When Darcy had arrived at the Mojave Space Port in his company helicopter, Berty was on the landing pad waiting to greet him.

"Hello, hello." Albert put on his British accent so thick you could lay bricks with it.

Darcy laughed loudly. When Berty did his cockney accent, it always made his sides split. "G'day, cobber," Darcy responded in a just-as-thick Australian accent.

"How's it going, mate," Darcy added just for the fun of it.

"I'm ready to see space tonight," Berty said as the two men embraced.

"I'm scared shitless tonight." Darcy laughed as Albert led him off and into the main building.

"Where is your posse?" Albert said as they walked through the doors to the main operations area of the airport.

"A very long story, my friend. I'll get to that later," Darcy said.

"Alright, then. Follow me; we will get you all suited up," Berty said.

CHAPTER FORTY-FIVE

An hour later, Darcy was staring out the window of the space port, thinking about many things. Ross, Melanie, Tony, and Tammy were now his family, but with Ross gone, he wondered if the other three would stay together. He hoped so; they were good people and he wanted them in his life for a long time to come.

When he heard the door open, he assumed it was Albert, coming to tell him they were ready to start making their way to the ship for boarding.

But he got the surprise of his life.

"You changed your mind!" Darcy said.

"You could say that, Michael," Tim said.

When he walked up and shook Darcy's hand, Tim ensured they were alone.

"I need to quickly run something by you," Tim told him with serious eyes.

Darcy smiled at Tim. "Come on then," he said. "Tell me what's on your mind."

Tim repeated the story he'd told Darcy, but now to Albert. Tim was relieved. Albert was even more open-minded than Tim had hoped. The billionaire had always believed in the existence of extraterrestrials. He just hadn't made these sorts of feelings public. It would brand him as a fruit-loop, which he wasn't.

After a further thirty minutes of discussion, Berty told Tim he would take Vernon into space, but on one condition.

Tim wondered what it would be.

Berty smiled and said, "Selfie."

Tim stared at him curiously, and as the seconds ticked on, Albert shook his head with laughter and put his hand on Tim's shoulder. "I want to get a photo with him!"

Tim liked this guy. He had a sense of humor, and came across as someone who knew what he was doing. No wonder he was revered the world over as a visionary business owner.

Just before they were to leave the room, Tim said to him, "Before or after the selfie, I'm sure Vernon would be more than happy to have a conversation with you."

Albert made the final arrangements to get his new guests on-board his spaceplane. All but Vernon and Ben were led onto the craft under the lights of the hangar. When they were all on-board, Albert instructed the dozen or so personnel to leave the hangar for five minutes, as he wanted to do some-thing privately with Darcy as a tribute to his late friend, the pilot Ross Moore.

A moment later, the airport sedan drove into the hangar and pulled up right next to the stairs leading up to the plane.

They ushered Vernon up into the plane, successfully shielding him from view of anyone outside the hangar.

When the doors closed, Tim formally introduced Vernon to Darcy and Berty.

The two men were lost for words.

Berty asked if Vernon would like to sit next to him.

As the plane started to taxi toward the runway, Jenny grabbed Ben's hand and squeezed it tight. "How are you feeling, my man?" she said.

"Like I could sleep for a week," he said, smiling.

Tim thought Darcy was nervous. But it wasn't nerves; it was something else.

"So he leaves earth tonight with all the things that made our plane disappear, reappear, and then disappear and reappear two and a half years earlier."

Tim read between the lines.

"It all ends tonight, Michael. These objects are just not meant to remain on earth." He looked him in the eye. "They've caused so much heartache."

Darcy said, "But couldn't we work out how to use them, and we could go back to the start and none of this would have happened?"

Tim patted Darcy on the hand. "And where does it end, Michael? If Majestic figures out how to harness the technology to do that, what will become of our lives?"

Tim stared at Vernon, who was in deep conversation with Albert. "It will ruin everything. Imagine—a society without history? A world where time basically has no meaning whatsoever?"

Darcy took a deep breath. Part of him still wondered why they couldn't just go back in time and fix it all.

"We are ten seconds and counting, people," the pilot announced from the cockpit, over the speaker.

Berty was good friends with the pilot. The billionaire had made him an offer he couldn't refuse. Five million dollars to keep his mouth shut about who was on the passenger list.

He would take the secret to his grave.

As the plane began to shoot down the runway, Ben and Vernon met each other's eyes. Ben had never seen such a look of pure joy on his face.

🛩   🛩   🛩

As the spaceplane made it through the earth's atmosphere, everyone took a sharp breath.

Tim peered through the windows and marveled at the view. It was the most beautiful thing he'd ever seen. The curvature and colors of the earth below were mesmerizing, especially with the contrast of black space directly above.

All attention went to Vernon.

He rose from his seat, and although there was no gravity to hold him down, did well to maneuver his away around the cabin.

Everyone knew what he was preparing to do—say goodbye.

He reached out and held Jenny's hand.

"Thank you, Jenny," he said, as the tears formed in her eyes. "Take care of him for me, won't you?"

"I promise. I hope you make it home safely," Jenny said.

Vernon then said goodbye to Darcy before stepping over to Tim.

"Tim, it was a pleasure meeting you. I wish I could have got to know you better. But the time has come for me to go home."

Tim took his hand. He shook it gently.

When Vernon reached Ben, he could see his eyes were misty. Ben pulled out a medium-sized pouch from under his seat. In it was every single disk they had from his craft. He handed it to Vernon and said sadly, "I'm going to miss you, Vern."

Vernon stepped closer, and for the first time since Ben had met him, in zero gravity, made his best attempt at a hug. It took Ben by surprise.

"Before I leave, can I just ask you one last thing?" Vernon said.

"Anything, Vernon. What is it?" Ben said.

Vernon stared long into his eyes and said, "Please look after William for me. See to it that he is taken care of."

"I will make sure of that, I promise," Ben said.

Vernon then worked his way back to where he had been sitting with Albert.

Vernon pulled open the top of the satchel.

And to everyone's surprise, he handed it to straight to Albert.

He told Albert what to do with them.

Albert said, calm as day, "Vernon has invited me to go home with him."

He met each person's eyes, and then looked back to Vernon. "And who am I to refuse such a kind offer?"

"Make sure you send us a postcard, Albert," Ben said.

Albert said, "Some dreams do come true. Until we meet again!"

Vernon stared out through the windows, and was the first to see the craft that had come from millions of miles away to collect him. When the others finally saw it, they let out a collective gasp.

It looked almost identical to Vernon's craft, but at least five times bigger, and it moved in complete silence.

Vernon looked at all his human friends for the final time, his gaze coming to rest on Ben.

As Albert put one of the disks underneath himself, he held the other directly over his head as Vernon had instructed him.

Vernon then did the same, and with his free hand pulled one more disk from the pouch.

Ben knew this was the controller disk.

Within ten seconds, Ben started to see how Vernon and Berty were being transferred to his ship.

They were slowly disappearing, becoming more translucent as the seconds ticked by.

Albert had his eyes completely shut, and was sitting as still as he could.

Vernon sat there and, strangely, just kept looking at Ben.

Twenty seconds later, they were gone.

Ben reached for Jenny's hand. "Whoa, that was incredible," he said.

Darcy shook his head and said, "Albert is going to go where no man has ever gone before. Lucky bastard."

Tim stared out through the windows. "Check it out, guys," he said.

The ship began to shift sideways but stopped for a moment, and made the strangest sound.

They would all talk about it later, and agree that unless they'd lost their minds on the flight, they could all swear it sounded like the most bizarre thing: a car horn making a "toot toot" sound as if saying goodbye before flying away.

Albert Sargeant was behind it.

His sense of humor had always been galactic.

THE END

EPILOGUE

"I'm dying for one of you to tell me," Tim said, looking over to Ben and Jenny. "Where in God's name was the facility you guys called 'Joe'?"

"It's in the most remote group of islands on the planet," she said. "Their name is Tristan da Cunha."

Ben nodded but didn't turn around. He was busy checking the controls before their flight back to Homey.

Ben had never flown the craft before on his own, but Vernon had taken some time to show him how. Suffice to say he was making sure he knew what he was doing before they left the ground.

"One is called Gough Island," said Jenny. "It's about three hundred miles from the main island, and is the most remote."

Tim got it. Now he understood why it had taken so long to get there. "What's with the nickname, 'Joe'?"

"Gough Island. *G—I*," she said. "Did anyone explain to you the other reason it was built there?"

Tim shook his head. "No. I'm just the old mushroom in the corner."

Jenny could see Ben grinning at his old man's wisecrack, but she pushed on.

"Vernon and his craft. It was all about the magnetic field. It's why they can travel vast distances in such a short time. He told the early Majestic people he needed to be somewhere the magnetic force was weak. Gough Island, and the islands, are located within the South Atlantic Anomaly. It's where the earth's magnetic field is at its weakest."

"We're ready to go," Ben said. "You guys better strap in. We need to get back to Homey, and Dad, you need to get your ass home to Mom."

Tim stared down to his lap and thought how happy he would be to see his wife. He was looking forward to being home with her.

He had a lot of explaining to do.

"There's something I never worked out," Tim said. "I wish I'd asked a long time ago. What happened to Alvin, William's co-pilot from the Dallas Spirit?"

Jenny and Ben both went silent and instinctively looked away from Tim. His heart sank, but he hoped one of them would give him an answer.

"Dad, when we told Alvin what had happened, he didn't take it well. A week after we settled them both at Joe, Alvin was found dead in his quarters."

Ben took a deep breath and said, "They told us it was a heart attack. We all knew he couldn't handle the fact that all his friends and loved ones were gone."

Tim looked down to his shoes and felt the sadness of the situation weigh heavily on him. It would be a hard thing to come to terms with.

"What about William? What happens to him now?"

Jenny patted Tim on the shoulder. "He's an interesting cat. He seemed to be upset about it at the start, but as the weeks rolled on, he seemed to come to terms with it. He's going to stay at Joe, and has offered to work there. They haven't figured out what the job will be, but I'm sure he'll be okay."

Ben and Jenny Erwin explained to the hierarchy of the Majestic VA6 program that Vernon and Steve had colluded and planned the escape of the only captive alien on planet earth. They were perplexed someone like Steve King could do such a thing after being so loyal to the program for so long, but they bought it.

Ben and Jenny added that Steve had overseen the top-secret construction of another craft, which even Ben had known nothing of until they escaped from Homey.

The Majestic VA6 facilities of Homey Airport—more commonly known as Area 51 or Groom Lake, Nevada—and Gough Island would continue to operate for years to come. Although Joe had lost its number one guest, with a construction cost of nearly ten billion dollars, it had too high a price tag to be left dormant.

Ben and Jenny negotiated a leave of absence from the MVA6 program. They asked to have a few years off, but at some point wanted to return.

This was agreed to with the proviso they underwent extensive identity resetting, as it was known in those circles, where their identities would be changed.

The other stipulation was that they were not allowed to move back to their hometown of San Francisco.

Wherever they chose to go had to be pre-approved by the Majestic hierarchy.

In the end, the approval was rubber-stamped. It was a place they'd both fallen in love with after staying there just once.

Wanaka, on the South Island of New Zealand.

Tim Erwin would explain most of the story to Sandra, focusing on Ben and Jenny. He left many parts out, especially the one that involved her dying of a heart attack in 2024.

To her credit, she eventually came to terms with why Ben and Jenny had disappeared, but deep down, she still felt upset it had come to that.

After Ben and Jenny settled in Wanaka, they planned to fly Tim and Sandra to visit them and their children. The kids had loved living at Joe, but Lake Wanaka and the mountains that surrounded it also had them hooked in no time.

Albert Sargeant quashed the rumors of his alleged death three months after going home with Vernon.

Back at his own home now, he made an announcement on social media that he had contracted a mysterious illness on his last flight into space, which he'd dealt with in private on Decker Island, his tropical home.

Albert told only his wife of his true whereabouts during his absence. She was skeptical, to say the least, until the day she met the little guy with the toupee. Vernon had dropped in to say hello under the cover of darkness.

Rumored sightings of Albert Sargeant in Wanaka, New Zealand, were laughed off as cases of mistaken identity. But after his third visit, Ben and Jenny told him it was getting a bit risky.

They were always happy to see Vernon, who accompanied Albert when he visited the Erwins. Albert and Vernon had become close friends, and would remain so until Albert's passing fifteen years later.

"You have no idea how happy I am to see you," Melanie said.

Melanie embraced Tony a moment later before she said to them both, "I'm really sorry for what happened."

The two *T*'s followed Melanie into her living room, where they all sat down.

"When are you due back in St. Louis?" Melanie said.

"The funeral is next Saturday," Tammy said.

"Brandon died saving Tammy's life," said Tony. "He probably saved mine too."

Melanie could see the tears in Tammy's eyes.

"He just jumped up out of his chair and a second later, Annie fired. A part of me believes he blamed himself for all this. That bullet was probably meant for me."

Tony took Tammy's hand. "I think she would've killed us all," he said.

The three of them sat in silence for a few moments.

Tammy eventually shook her head and let out what sounded like a stifled laugh.

"Who'd have thought. My father, a gun fanatic," she said.

Tony now followed suit, shaking his head. "And all those years you guys thought he was in his shed with his dirty magazines."

"Well, to Mom they would have been dirty," Tammy said. "I don't know if she'd have been any less angry if the magazines had been full of naked women doing naughty things."

Melanie couldn't believe it when Tammy first told her. Her father was a closet gun fanatic, but had kept it a secret from everyone who knew him.

"When he came into the living room, thankfully he had one of his favorite handguns hidden under his shirt," Tammy said.

"We should all be thankful he spotted Annie coming through the backyard from his shed. He must have known the shit was going to hit the fan. If it weren't for him, God knows who else Annie may have killed."

Beth and Noah were found alive and well shortly after

their grandfather shot their stepmother dead. When the police broke down Annie and Brandon's front door shortly after the mayhem that took place in the Sanders living room, they found the children playing a video game in front of the television. The children wondered what all the fuss was about. Annie had lied to Tammy about their deaths, just to upset her sister, as she'd always done.

Police investigated Bartholomew Sanders' shooting of Annie, but decided not to prosecute. The evidence of it being self-defense was overwhelming, since Annie had drawn first and killed Brandon.

Patricia Sanders would never recover from the death of her daughter. She was eventually committed to an asylum after having a mental breakdown. Her marriage to Bart evaporated six months later, and within twelve, Bart met a woman who loved guns as much as he did.

Tammy stayed in touch with him, but as one year became two, and then five, the annual trips to see him eventually ceased.

Six years after killing his daughter, Bartholomew Sanders would be killed at a firing range by a stray bullet. In the end, he died doing what brought him joy: shooting guns.

"Dad!" Emily shouted from the lounge-room.

"Yes?" Dave responded, from somewhere in the rear of his home.

When Emily did not respond, he gritted his teeth, stopped what he was doing, and grumbled his way to the front.

"You could always just come to where I am, you know," Dave said as he stood and stared at Emily.

When she gazed up from her phone, reading the text

message she'd just gotten from Todd, she took a long, deep intake of air.

"Shit," she said. "She's already here." Looking out through the windows, she saw the figure of a person walking up the driveway.

She jumped to her feet and said to Dave. "Todd just texted me. He told me his mother, Kylie, wanted to…"

The knock on the door was measured and evenly spaced.

Knock. Knock. Knock.

"What is going on?" Dave said, looking down to his jeans and realizing he was quite underdressed for visitors.

Emily muttered profanities under her breath as she walked to the front door.

She opened it a moment later.

"Kylie, hi," Emily said, looking at Todd's mother with the best smile she could manage.

"Hi, Emily. Can I come in?" Kylie said, her tone low-key and pleasant.

"You bet. Come on in. Oh, you can meet my dad too."

When Kylie walked into the living room, Dave stood up from his chair. "Hi, I'm Dave, Emily's father," he said.

Kylie walked up and offered her hand.

"It's nice to meet you, Dave," Kylie said.

She turned to Emily. "Is there somewhere we can talk privately for a moment?"

Emily looked over to her dad, and before she could answer, Dave said, "Why don't I go back to what I was doing and leave you two be for a minute?"

Emily shook her head vigorously, and Dave could tell by the look on her face that she didn't want him to go too far away.

"It was a pleasure meeting you, Kylie," Dave said before disappearing down the hallway.

The two women sat silently on the sofa for a moment.

"I know Todd wanted to meet me here," Kylie said, "But just before I arrived, he sent me a text telling me he couldn't make it. He said something urgent had come up."

Kylie stared across the living room, seeming to gather her thoughts.

"I need you to do something for me, Em." She spoke in a whisper.

"Anything," Emily said.

Kylie stared into space.

"Does my husband have an illegitimate son?"

The question struck Emily hard. But she knew she'd struggle to avoid telling Kylie the truth.

"Yes," Emily whispered, before closing her own eyes to hold back a tear.

Kylie patted her on the shoulder.

"It's not your fault, Em. It's okay."

Emily opened her eyes.

"Todd has been looking for him, right?"

Emily nodded faintly.

Kylie sat back and cursed.

"That cheating son of a bitch. How old is this guy?"

Emily took a deep breath and said, "I think he's around fifteen."

Kylie shook her head. Emily could see she was upset.

"About that long ago, I suspected Andrew had an affair. I think it was a barmaid. She flirted with him even when I was there with him. When I confronted him, he denied anything had ever gone on."

Emily shook her head and wondered what else she could say. She knew there was nothing that would make this moment any easier.

"I overheard Andrew on his phone one morning. He didn't know I was listening. He said to some guy on the phone, 'If Todd brings my bastard son home, your neck will be on the chopping block'."

Kylie started to cry. Emily tried to console her.

When the tears stopped, Kylie sat back and wiped them from her eyes.

The look on her face had changed slightly. Now she'd started to look angry.

Kylie stared out the living-room window before turning back to Emily.

"My marriage to Andrew is over," she said.

Kylie held true to her word. When she left Andrew the next day, it was the beginning of the end for the mighty Andrew Roberts.

With his marriage over, the guy started to unravel. The first restraining order she put on him did not bode well for Andrew at work.

As his reputation began to disintegrate, people within the force started coming forward to tell stories that Andrew believed were safely buried by bribes and intimidation.

Some of those names are familiar to us.

Michelle Lowne successfully stopped her transfer to a police station on the other side of greater Los Angeles. When she went over her boss's head, it took only a few days before it became part of the web of lies revealing itself around the not-so-honest cop Andrew Roberts.

Johnny Kelseanno, better known as Johnny the Mac, took a leap of faith and put all his cards on the table.

After a month's suspension, he returned to work with a new lease on life.

The Mac and Todd became good friends outside work, as, eventually, did their partners. The four became inseparable. Two years later, with Emily by his side, Todd had asked the Mac if he could put down those Big Macs and instead hold onto two wedding rings for a moment.

Andrew Roberts was eventually fired from the California Highway Patrol.

He would leave the state of California in shame, unable to handle his fall from grace. He'd end up on his cousin's farm in rural Texas, working as a farmhand before an untimely accident, involving a tractor, a bottle of whiskey, and a sad and lonely old man, ended his life ten years later.

Kylie Roberts remained a much-sought-after single woman for quite some time after her divorce was finalized twelve months to the day after that awkward conversation with Emily.

She had no desire to jump back into a relationship, and wondered if she would ever get married a second time.

But at Todd and Emily's beautiful late-afternoon wedding, held on the breathtaking roof terrace of the Hotel Casa del Mar in Santa Monica, something really unusual happened.

Kylie had a strange sensation while chatting to one of the guests among the eighty people invited to her son's wedding. She felt as if she'd been in this very spot at another time, talking with this very person.

She and Dave Collins had been speaking about all manner of things. He seemed like a decent guy, and was dressed very nicely. Out of the blue, he asked her if taking her out for dinner would be too unusual for her.

Kylie smiled back to him and said, "Not at all."

Three years later, Todd and Emily Roberts would return to the roof terrace of the Casa del Mar.

This time around, Todd would be the best man, and Emily would be the maid of honor.

For their parents.

EPILOGUE—PART TWO

"But this was your idea," Melanie said to Darcy over the phone.

"I know," he said, with a grin she couldn't see, "but I just had a craving for an almond berry chicken salad sandwich."

"Where are you?" Melanie shook her head and could feel the smile creeping across her face. "My God—you went all that way for a sandwich? I don't think so, Michael Edward Darcy." Melanie could hear his snicker, and it brought joy to her heart. "Well, I guess we'll just have to have this get-together without you. Enjoy the sandwich and get back here as soon as you can. I miss you."

As Michael rang off, those last words of Melanie's would stay with him forever. He couldn't remember the last time anyone had said those three words to him.

Now's not the time to think of that, Michael. You're trying to impress someone.

"There's a familiar face," said Janice Webb, the café's owner, as she saw Darcy sitting at her counter.

She walked up to him. "It's nice to see your friendly face again. How long are you in town for?"

Darcy felt like a teenager all over again. His heart fluttered and his hands went a little clammy.

"Long enough to ask you out for dinner," he said.

Janice shook her head and laughed. She couldn't think of anything she'd like to do more.

"Well, you'd be staying in town tonight, then," she said.

Darcy wondered if he'd ever want to leave Piedmont.

But he would.

Don't worry, it was all for a good reason.

After the sale of Darcon went through six months later, Darcy was a billionaire three times over. He could be anywhere on the planet he wanted to be.

When he bought the luxurious beachside home in Carmel by the Sea, Monterey, it was because he wanted to be close to the people he now treated like family.

Janice Webb eventually moved there from Piedmont, and along with her own daughter they became part of the clan. Although Michael insisted she needn't work, she bought a quaint little cafe on Ocean Avenue, which she ran for a few years before retiring.

Michael, flush with cash, did something else quite commendable.

He saved Pacific International Airlines from bankruptcy.

The year after the A380 reappeared in 2021, the company went to the wall in a matter of months.

No one would dare get on one of their planes. It took years for the trust to return and the patronage to pay the bills.

But Darcy's $680 million injection turned the company around in under three years, and saved the 8,000 employees from losing their jobs. Darcy continued to remain a significant shareholder for many years to come, and also ended up giving away close to two billion dollars of his money to a vast array of charities and organizations. Those generous donations brought relief and happiness to many people around the world.

Melanie rang off from her call with Darcy and shook her head. She was happy for him. He'd flown all that way just to buy a sandwich from a lady he had a crush on. Melanie thought it was the most romantic thing she'd ever heard of.

Darcy was the one who'd organized the barbecue at Melanie's home, part of him doing his best to help her get back into the social rhythm again. He'd teed it up with Tony and Tammy, who would take care of everything on the day. Darcy had planned on being there, of course, but the night before, he decided he couldn't wait any longer. He needed to go to Piedmont the very next day.

🛩 🛩 🛩

The get-together was now humming along. It was mid-afternoon in one of coastal California's prettiest seaside villages. The sun was shining, the breeze coming off the Pacific Ocean was pleasant, and the conversation and drinks were flowing. Tony tended to the barbecue while Tammy took care of the salads and other dishes.

Lee Lather would become a regular face in Carmel by the Sea, and found the idea of living in St. Louis, away from Tammy, less attractive as the weeks and months rolled on. She happily helped Tammy tend to the food. She'd brought her new man to Monterey for the weekend, too.

Tammy couldn't help but giggle like a teenager when Lee eventually told her what his full name was: Quentin Tinderson.

Lee made her promise she wouldn't laugh in his face when he was first introduced. Unfortunately, she failed.

What were the odds of meeting someone on Tinder whose last name was Tinderson?

Darcy had surprised Melanie with a little gift he'd bought her the day before the barbecue—a miniature poodle.

The dog was a tiny ball of black fluff, and so small he fit almost snugly into both of Melanie's hands. She fell in love with him at first sight. At first, she wanted to call him Roscoe, but thought a few minutes later that this felt a bit weird.

So she decided to call him Buster. Being a male, she didn't want him to sound like a sissy, as a miniature poodle and all.

After lunch came and went, and the last song of an album ended, Melanie looked down and realized Buster wasn't sitting there looking up at her.

"I think I'd better find the ball of fluff," she said as she rose to her feet. As she got to her doorway, Tammy shouted, "Please—pretty please, put on my favorite CD. It's on the top of the pile."

Melanie agreed, not sure which disk Tammy was referring to, and went straight for the music system inside before searching for Buster.

"Oh, sweet Jesus," Melanie said to herself, smiling, as she studied the CD on the top of the pile. Hall & Oates—the guys from the seventies with awesome hair and one mustache. The CD was their greatest hits.

Who was she to get in the way of her friend's love of some seventies music?

She put the CD in.

"Thank you, baby," Tammy shouted from outside a few moments later.

Melanie walked into the kitchen and found the ball of fluff in no time. He was chewing on something from the barbecue. It was nearly as big as he was.

Just as she knelt down to pick up Buster, Tammy screamed at the top of her lungs, startling Melanie.

She heard a glass drop and smash all over the balcony.

Melanie put Buster down and, as she rose to her feet, could hear unfamiliar voices coming from the direction of the balcony.

She could hear Tammy crying and Tony saying things she couldn't understand.

Melanie ran from the kitchen and through the balcony doors in a second. When she got there, everyone stared straight at her. Tammy and Tony were in tears and breathing heavily.

Melanie wondered what the hell was going on.

She realized there were four other people standing on the balcony.

Two of the four men were holding up another, who clearly looked like he'd been in the wars.

Jesus, Melanie thought, the guy looks like shit.

As he asked the two men to let him stand on his own, she realized.

It was Ross.

Melanie fainted right there and then, and for real this time.

She woke a few minutes later, lying on the couch. Tammy was by her side.

"I just had the weirdest dream. Ross was alive and standing on the balcony."

Tammy shook her head, and between sobs, said, "I'm glad you're lying down."

As she stepped away, Melanie looked up. Ross was standing there looking down at her.

He dropped to his knees, reached out for Melanie, and said, "I have one hell of a story to tell you, baby."

In the background, the Hall and Oates CD kept going.

Only later would Ross and Melanie remember the actual song that was playing the moment they embraced. It would be their favorite song forever, and the one they chose for their bridal waltz some months later: "How Does It Feel to Be Back."

EPILOGUE—PART THREE

"I want you to meet some people," Ross said as he rose to his feet and began to hobble toward the balcony.

When they arrived outside, Ross told the guys who'd brought him home, "You three, I want you to meet my fiancée, Melanie." They approached her, and Melanie could've hugged all three of them for hours.

"This one here—his name is Todd. Todd Roberts." Melanie gave him a hug and said, "You were on the plane, right?"

Todd said, "It's good to see you, Melanie."

Ross then tapped her on the shoulder and ushered her to meet the next one. "This one here—they call him 'the Mac,' but he tells me his name is Johnny."

Melanie went to shake his hand, but dispensed with the formality and hugged him as well.

"Thank you for bringing my man home to me," she said as she kept her arms around him for a moment.

When Melanie finally backed away, there was only one left.

Ross stepped up to the guy and put his arm around him.

"This one here is special." Ross smirked as the guy

blushed. "If it weren't for him, I may have never made it back here." Ross struggled to keep his emotions under control.

Todd put his hand on the guy's shoulder.

"You've done good, little brother," he said. The boy would never forget those words.

Melanie stepped closer to him and said, "I'll never be able to thank you enough." She put her arms around him and hugged him firmly.

He would tell Melanie later it was the first time he could ever remember a woman hugging him with affection.

It would be one of the turning points in his life.

"His name is Jason," Ross eventually said, when Melanie backed away from him. "I owe him my life. He is one brave guy, I can tell you."

Ross, Melanie, and everyone else on the balcony ventured into the living room.

Ross wiped his face with his hand. He hadn't had a beard in over ten years, and was looking forward to shaving it off.

He sat on the couch with Melanie by his side.

"I was carjacked when I left the charity event at the Arts District." He studied his hands and could recall the moment as if it had just happened.

"There were six of them. I'd just sat in my car, and didn't even have a chance to turn the key. My door flung open and they dragged me out by my throat."

Everyone in the room hung on his every word, but he stared at Melanie.

"All I remember is the commotion, the shouting, the fists. I think one of them head-butted me, and next thing, I'd blacked out. I woke up in this darkened room, my head throbbing, feeling like I'd been run over."

Ross turned to Todd, Johnny, and then Jason. He would never forget them as long as he lived.

"We think they bundled me into their car and one of them took the Jag. It just so happens that the one who took my car also took everything I had on me."

Ross rubbed his wrists. They ached.

"The asshole took my watch, ring, the lot." His face became angry. "But as karma would have it, he was the one who died when the SUV collided with the petrol tanker."

Ross looked over to Todd, then back to Melanie. "Todd confirmed that his body was so badly burned, they couldn't identify it even with dental records. I sort of wish the police had chosen to tell you this."

Melanie shook her head, and placed her hands on his.

She wouldn't let them go for a long time to come.

"The gang must have realized who I was. I remember overhearing a few of them referring to me as 'the pilot from the missing plane.' A couple decided they were going to try and hold me for ransom. They thought I could fetch them a shitload of cash."

"Ross, take a break." Todd stood up. "I'll take it from here."

Ross was quite happy for Todd to continue the story.

"Jason and I had a disagreement about something." Todd stared over to his little brother. "He ran off, but I lost him. About half an hour later, when I'd given up and was walking back to my car, he came running around the corner, nearly knocking me clean off my feet.

"He explained that when he'd tried to lose me, he'd gone into an abandoned warehouse, where this gang was holding Ross. One of them showed Jason what they called 'their pet,' bound and gagged in a filthy room deep inside. Jason told me he recognized Ross from TV, that they were holding him, and that he believed his life was in danger."

Todd turned to his little brother: he was damned proud of him.

"Anyways, when I told Jason to show me where they were holding him, little did I know that at the time, the Mac had been tailing me under orders from my asshole father. So a minute after I stormed the warehouse, we sort of had backup."

Melanie couldn't believe what she was hearing.

"So the short version is, two of the gang members put up a fight, but the other three fled in a panic. It was all over in minutes."

Ross rose to his feet before turning to Jason, walking over to him, and putting his arm around his shoulders.

"You saved my life." Ross could feel his emotions getting the better of him.

Jason felt awkward.

"People have always called me a loser," he said. "I'm not. I just needed a chance to prove I wasn't."

Ross shook his head as he met the eyes of just about everyone in the room.

"You will never be called a loser ever again," he told Jason. "Trust me."

Five years later, Jason became the hundredth cadet to get his wings at Ross and Tony's pilot school.

At the ceremony, Todd and Emily Roberts would be there to congratulate him. So would Dave and Kylie Collins, who had treated Jason as if he were their own son for a long time.

Ross and Melanie and Tammy and Tony were now like aunties and uncles to him. He spent a fair bit of time in Monterey, and was always welcome there. One of Ross and

Melanie's spare rooms wasn't spare at all. They called it Jason's room.

Michael E. Darcy had also become part of his life.

Seven years after saving Ross Moore's life, Jason became Darcy's son-in-law.

Janice Webb's daughter, Carley-Jane, had eventually come into contact with him through the Flight 19 clan of Monterey.

After a whirlwind romance, the two lovebirds had approached Darcy one day and asked if he'd grant them permission to get married. Although Darcy wasn't Carley-Jane's real father, she'd always treated him like one. He told them nothing would bring him more joy, and said yes.

Ten years later, Jason Roberts would become one of Pacific International Airways' most well-known pilots.

And his now quite-sizable family couldn't have been prouder.

Over dinner one night at Ross and Melanie's, he would tell them two amazing things. One, Carley-Jane was twelve weeks pregnant with their first child. And two, on his last flight eighteen hours earlier, while flying over New Zealand, he and his co-pilot could have sworn they saw an unusual object at an altitude of 40,000 feet. It flew alongside them for about thirty seconds before vanishing from sight.

It was the shape of a big kettle.

THE END
(Okay, the real end.)

REVIEW THIS BOOK

You would be helping me greatly as an independent author by taking a few moments to review *Flight 19, Part II* at the place you bought it.

I cannot thank you enough for taking the time to do this.

Grant Finnegan, 2019

KEEP IN TOUCH

Feel free to drop me a line at my website, grantfinnegan.com, or on Facebook at facebook.com/grantfinneganauthorAUS.

DISCLAIMER

The Airbus A380, which forms part of the story of Flight 19, is one of the most technologically and mechanically advanced aircraft ever built.

It is a marvel of modern engineering, and has a pristine record of service since it first took to the skies many years ago.

When you read the entire story of Flight 19, you will know that in no way was the disappearance (and reappearance) of the Airbus A380 connected in any shape or form to the actual aircraft itself.

As with the Dallas Spirit (another plane mentioned in the fictitious story) an alien object was in fact the reason these planes disappeared, and reappeared at a later time.

Although the story surrounding the disappearance of the Dallas Spirit did actually happen back in 1927, the true reason for its unfortunate disappearance remains unknown.

The Airbus A380 is an aircraft the author of *Flight 19* has traveled on, and would not hesitate to travel on in the future.

At no time should anyone who reads *Flight 19* take any part of the fictitious story out of context, to imply that the author is in any way, shape, or form trying to discredit the Airbus A380, or Airbus the company.

ACKNOWLEDGMENTS

I would like to thank the following people for their contribution to *Flight 19, Part II*.

Ben Hourigan, my editor, for everything you do. Your expertise and support is something I could not live without.

Michelle Lowne, Andrew Parsons, and Sandra Finnegan, for reading and being a part of the process of bringing *Flight 19, Part II* to the final result. Your input and help never goes unappreciated. Thank you.

The journey between the release of *Flight 19* and *Flight 19, Part II* has been quite the interesting one.

Suffice to say, there have been some highs and some lows. The release of *Manifest*, a US TV show with a similar premise as my story, less than one month after I released *Flight 19*, came as a shock.

But the highs have been heartwarming, to say the least, and far outweigh the lows.

I have experienced first-hand the kindness of complete strangers who, for no other reason than being good people, showed me the kind of support that kept me believing in the book and in myself as an author.

Many of the characters in *Flight 19, Part II* were named after these people.

In no particular order, thank you—Graeme Joyes, Bob and Judy Philips, Phil Brady, Dianne Scoffield, David and Christine Windebank, Tom Clark, Roberta Wright, Laura Messer, Mila Stibrova, Albert Sargeant, Mandy Clarke, Julia Reichstein, and Ted Frances. Just a quick note to Christine Windebank for the incredible support and personal effort you took on in trying to get me signed on as a published author.

A special mention to all those who sent me messages after reading *Flight 19*, telling me how much they enjoyed the novel and demanding a sequel.

I was fortunate to be able to write a large portion of *Flight 19, Part II* in London. While visiting the newest addition to our family, I wrote the book at the kitchen table, of all places. Between writing and baby-related duties, I kept myself busy around Balham, and the walks down and around Tooting Commons were also a highlight. Those few weeks made me want to spend more time there in the future.

And finally, there is the one we will call Mini-Finney.

You have never wavered from your belief in and support of me as a writer. You will bark at me when it is written terribly and shed a tear when it is written beautifully. You will tell me when a story idea is silly, and high-five me when I nail it. Without you, I don't know where I would be. My wife, Sharon, thank you. I love you.

ABOUT THE AUTHOR

Grant Finnegan is an avid reader of many genres, from action thriller to supernatural mysteries and many others.

Some of his favorite authors and strongest writing influences are familiar names: Stephen King, Clive Cussler, Janet Evanovich, Lee Child, and Douglas Kennedy, to name a few.

Grant lives in the bayside suburbs of Melbourne, Australia. Most days, he can be found walking along the beach with his wife, discussing the world we live in. If he's not there, he's in the kitchen cooking up a storm, at his desk writing, or otherwise staying active.

Grant's other favorite pastimes include snowboarding, windsurfing, and traveling the world. He has a soft spot for London and the United Kingdom, Queenstown, the South Island of New Zealand, and the island of Bali in Indonesia.

facebook.com/grantfinneganauthorAUS

amazon.com/author/grantfinnegan